He shouldn

He'd only made afraid of him. What woman wouldn't be after his caveman tactics? But then he recalled his brother's troubled voice, and his guilt fled. This misunderstanding was her fault. She'd refused to talk inside the bar, leaving him no other choice.

The uncertain light cast by the flickering neon sign revealed her long, slim legs covered by body-hugging, white, denim pants, which cupped her hips. The soft mounds of her breasts swelled against the fabric of her blue blouse.

Sweat beaded his brow. He forced his gaze back to her face.

Her full, red lips parted, and the tip of a pink tongue peeked out as she licked her lips.

He gulped.

"What aren't you telling me?" she asked. "Is Geordie okay?"

Her frantic voice broke through the haze surrounding him. He took a quick breath. "You want to know about Geordie?"

She nodded.

"Well, then, come on." He turned on his heel and started walking across the parking lot, not looking to see if she followed, half hoping she wouldn't.

Kudos for C. B. Clark

MY BROTHER'S SINS
placed first in the
Music City Romance Writers'
Melody of Love
romance writing competition.

My Brother's Sins

by

C. B. Clark

My Brother's Sins

Cover Art by *Debbie Taylor*

The Wild Rose Press, Inc.
PO Box 708
Adams Basin, NY 14410-0708
Visit us at www.thewildrosepress.com

Publishing History
First Crimson Rose Edition, 2016
Print ISBN 978-1-5092-0578-3
Digital ISBN 978-1-5092-0579-0

Published in the United States of America

Dedications

For my husband, Douglas
You are my inspiration and the love of my life.
~*~
To Lin Weich
For your unflagging support
throughout the writing of this book.
~*~
And to my mother, Joan Guldner
You always believed in me.

Chapter 1

Ryan Marshall shoved open the battered door of the Rusty Nail Bar 'n Grill in Antler Springs, Montana, and stepped into a wall of odor reeking of sweat, stale beer and the sweet tang of marijuana. He squinted in the smoke-filled gloom, searching the shadows. Payday on a Saturday night, and a crowd jammed the only bar in the town of 362 residents. Every ranch hand and oil-well roughneck in the county was doing his best to spend his paycheck on booze and losing at pool.

On the far side of the crowded room, a band played off-key country music on a rickety stage. A couple swayed on the tiny dance floor, their bodies welded together. Drunken male admirers, hoping to get lucky, surrounded the few women in the bar like packs of hungry wolves.

He studied the women and sighed. She wasn't one of them.

Well, he'd tried. He'd already spent too much time on this fool's errand. He shook his head and turned to leave, when the crowd shifted. Even if Geordie hadn't described her, he knew she was the one.

She sat alone at a small, round, green plastic laminated table amid the drunken revelers. Her thick fall of golden hair gleamed under the flickering lights, a perfect complement to the creamy paleness of her skin. She perched on the edge of her seat, her body strung tight, her gaze swinging to the door each time someone entered the noisy bar.

His gut tightened, and he blew out a breath. No wonder Geordie was so taken with her.

A burly cowboy swaggered over to her. Staggering, the man leaned close and spoke.

Ryan was too far away to hear what was said, but a reluctant grin of admiration tugged at his mouth when the cowboy's ruddy complexion turned bright red and he scuttled away, a hangdog expression on his blunt features.

The blonde lifted her glass, her full red lips pursing as she drank.

He swallowed, his mouth arid dry.

She turned toward him, and their gazes met. Cool blue eyes assessed him.

He sucked in a gulp of air. *Easy, boy. She's off limits. Man, is she off limits.* The thought acted like a splash of cold water, and he jerked away. She was trouble. He didn't doubt it for a minute, but he'd promised Geordie, and he intended to fulfill his promise no matter what. Taking a deep breath, he shouldered his way through the crowd toward her. "Excuse me, ma'am."

Her mouth tightened. "Get lost, cowboy," she said, her gaze fixed on her drink. "I'm not interested."

"No need to be rude, lady. I only want to talk."

Her blue eyes flashed over him with cool disdain. "Nice, but I don't want to talk to you."

Who the hell did she think she was brushing him off as if he were a pesky mosquito? He'd spent a lot of time looking for her. Too much time. Time he didn't have, not with so much work waiting for him at the ranch; especially now since his foreman had up and quit on him leaving him shorthanded with a thousand acres of land and six hundred head of Black Angus cattle.

He turned away, but he recalled the fear in Geordie's voice as he'd begged him to help her, and he blew out a breath. Who was he kidding? He'd promised. Tonight's adventure was as simple and as complicated as keeping a promise.

Her studied nonchalance didn't fool him for a minute.

Her hand trembled, her drink almost spilling when she lifted her glass. She was afraid. Of what?

He glanced around the crowded room. Countless pairs of hungry, male eyes were fixed on her. With her snug blue blouse, tight white jeans and ripe beauty, she was a prime target for any male with any sense, and especially those without any. As if to prove the truth to his thoughts, a heavy-set, bearded man, who wore a ball cap with the words "Truckers Make the Best Lovers" written across the stained, peaked front, drained his drink, stood and ambled over.

Without thinking what he was doing, Ryan stepped forward and placed his body between the man and his target.

The trucker glared at Ryan through bleary, red-veined eyes and puffed out his already considerable stomach.

Ryan held his ground, fixing him with a steely look. "The lady doesn't want company," he said.

The man cursed, spit a gob of yellow phlegm on the beer-stained floor and slowly retreated to his seat.

Ryan wasn't surprised the burly trucker had backed down. He was a good three inches taller, and the other man's weight was all in his belly. He glanced at the blonde and caught her watching him.

He gulped, his breath caught in his throat as if she'd sucker punched him. If he had any brains, he'd walk, hell, he'd run away. But his father had always told him he hadn't the sense he'd been born with, and so, he turned and strode back to her side.

"All right. Enough games," he said. "We need to talk."

****

Sensing a looming presence, Hallie glanced up, surprised to find the tall, leanly muscled man standing over her again. Her curt brush off usually sent even the most determined, would-be suitor packing. She studied him. He was handsome in a rough, bad-boy sort of way. His curly, coal black hair hung below the collar of his faded, denim work shirt. A bristle of beard shadowed his chiseled cheeks.

Without asking her permission, he pulled out a chair and settled across from her. His vivid blue eyes rimmed by impossibly thick, dark lashes watched her with an unsettling intensity.

A chill settled over her. "What...?" She frowned at the tremor in her voice, coughed and tried again. "What do you want? My boyfriend will be back any minute. He went to get us another drink. He won't appreciate you being here. He's very jealous."

Instead of leaving, he grinned, transforming his rugged features from attractive to all out gorgeous. Matching dimples bracketed his mouth, and even white teeth provided a marked contrast to his darkly tanned skin. "Really? I'll wait for him." His lazy smile set his dimples dancing. "He sounds like a man I'd like to meet."

"He…" She swallowed, faltering under the intensity of his gaze, knowing he'd seen through her lie. "Okay, you found me out. There's no boyfriend. But I am waiting for someone, and I can assure you I don't want any company."

His dark brows rose in unspoken question.

"And no, it's not you, so you can go back to your cave." She held her breath; waiting to see if she'd offended him enough he'd leave. She didn't need this hassle. Not now, not when everything had gone so wrong.

He smiled, showing no sign of moving.

"Look, leave me alone." She sighed, getting right to the point. "I don't want you, I'm not interested in you, I'm not going to have a drink with you, or dance with you, and I'm certainly not going to go to bed with you. So you might as well move on. You're not going to get anywhere with me." He'd go now. No man's ego could handle so much rejection.

His lips quirked, and he grinned.

The effect took her breath away, but this time she was prepared for his smile's devastating impact, and she managed to hang onto her dignity and keep her expression blank, though her heart pounded in her chest.

"Are you always like this?" he drawled.

"Like what?"

He shrugged, and her gaze was drawn to his broad shoulders. The heavy denim of his shirt didn't hide the play of hard muscles in his chest and arms.

"Like a bitch."

For a moment she wasn't sure she'd heard him

correctly. She gasped. Her anger flared, rising above the ever-present fear. "Get the hell away from me," she snapped.

The infuriating grin on his handsome face didn't slip an inch. If anything, his smile widened. "Great idea. We should get out of here." He rose, and in a single motion, gripped her arm, and lifted her out of her chair. "Let's go." He steered her across the crowded room toward the door.

"What do you think you're doing?" She dug in her heels and yanked her arm free.

He grinned again, but this time the smile didn't reach his eyes. "I aim to please, ma'am." The blue irises pinned her with a chilling look. He took her arm again. "I'm doing what you asked me to do."

She frowned. What the hell? Who was this guy? In her confusion, she allowed him to propel her another few feet toward the exit, but as they drew closer and closer to the door and the isolated darkness outside the bar, she jerked to a stop. "What are you talking about? I didn't *ask* you to do anything, but leave."

"Exactly, and leaving is what we're doing."

A frisson of unease edged along her spine. Surely he didn't intend to drag her out of the bar against her will? She saw the determination in his clear, blue eyes. He wasn't drunk. So why was he hauling her out of the bar?

In the next heartbeat, she froze, all her fear roaring back. He was one of *them*! They'd found her. Somehow he'd known she was supposed to meet Geordie here tonight. Her heart raced, pounding so hard in her chest she couldn't think. *He was one of them.* The words ran through her mind in a terrifying refrain.

She struck him, hitting him in his rock-hard stomach.

He didn't budge an inch.

She shoved him again, but her efforts had as little effect as trying to shift a brick wall.

Dragging her along behind him, he ignored her struggles.

The exit loomed nearer. Time was running out. She searched the packed room for help, but the throngs of Saturday night partiers were oblivious to her plight. Where before every male in the place had stared at her, watching her every move, now they avoided looking at her. "Help me," she said, her voice a high-pitched squeak.

The band stopped playing.

"Help me," she shouted. The band stopped playing. "Help me," she cried again in the sudden silence, her voice a high-pitched squeak. "This man is forcing me to leave with him. I don't want to go. I don't know him. Please, help me."

Everyone looked at her and the tall man holding her.

Two, muscle-bound cowboys stepped forward, their faces grim under their matching, faded, black felt cowboy hats.

She sagged with relief and eyed her captor, wanting to witness the defeat in his eyes.

Instead, the blue eyes gleamed, and he grinned.

"Anything wrong, Ryan?" asked one of the men who'd stepped forward.

The man called Ryan chuckled and shook his head. "Nope, nothin's wrong, Jeb. This little lady and I are just steppin' out for a spell," he drawled in good ol' boy tones. "We're hankerin' for some fresh air." He winked. "If you know what I mean."

Her two would-be-rescuers regarded her, and then the man called Ryan, their expressions uncertain.

Jeb asked, "You all right, lady?"

She shook her head. "I don't want to go with him. *Please* stop him."

"She don't look none too happy, Ryan," Jeb said. "Are you sure you have this right, and she wants to leave with you?"

"Oh, yeah, I'm sure," Ryan said. He turned her to face him, his grip strong. "You want to spend some alone time with me outside, don't you, *Hallie*?"

She reeled back a step. He knew her name? Of course, he knew her name. The men who were after her knew who she was, where she lived, where she worked, even her friends. She shook her head. "No—"

He cut her off. "Geordie asked me to meet you here tonight."

"Geordie? Geordie sent you?"

He nodded.

Before she could ask anything more, he draped his arm across her shoulders, drawing her against his hard body. He turned to the people watching and chuckled. "Don't worry, fellas. Hallie and I have some personal business outside. Don't we, sweetheart?"

Jeb chuckled, shaking his head. "You always were a lucky bastard, Ryan." He smiled. "You don't need to worry none, ma'am. Ryan here's one of the good guys. He'll take real good care of you. Now you two kids have fun, you hear?" He turned and walked away, calling to the bartender to bring him another beer.

The band started up again and the twang of electric

guitar filled the room.

In the next breath, Hallie and her abductor were outside.

The cool night air broke her stupor. She shoved against the man's solid bulk, stumbling as he suddenly released his grip on her arm. She faced him, hands on hips, and glared. "How dare you?" Fury strangled her voice. "Where I come from, they call this kidnapping."

"We call it kidnapping here, too," he said, the corners of his mouth twitching.

The yellow glow from the single, street lamp on the far side of the parking lot, cast his face half in shadow and half in light, sharpening the rugged planes. A neon blue open sign flickered and sputtered over the entry to the bar providing enough light to see his eyes and the gleam of teeth as he flashed her another irritating grin.

"You…you said Geordie sent you to meet me. How do I know you're telling the truth?"

"I guess you're going to have to trust me."

She scowled. Trust him? He'd dragged her out of the bar against her will. She fished in her purse for her cell phone, her fingers clumsy. When she finally withdrew her phone, she punched numbers, her gaze fixed on him in case he tried to stop her.

"What are you doing?" he asked.

"What do you think I'm doing? I'm calling the police." Her confidence faded as instead of the fear she expected to see on his face, he smiled.

"Good luck."

She glowered at him, but in the next minute, realized what he meant. The no-service signal on the cell phone jumped out at her like a beacon. Her first instinct was to throw the useless phone at him, but she held back. Antagonizing him further was foolish. She needed every advantage possible to get out of this mess. If he thought she was a quivering mass of fear, so much the better.

They stood in the gravel parking lot surrounded by dust-caked pickup trucks. Rolling prairie stretched endlessly in every direction, broken by the occasional lone pine and the distant ring of jagged, snow-covered mountains. Her small, red, rental car looked out of place amidst the sea of four-by-four trucks.

A dozen steps separated her from the relative safety of her vehicle. She examined the man's long, muscular legs. He'd beat her in a foot race, but she had the element of surprise on her side.

Shifting her handbag out of the stream of light, she reached inside and fumbled for her car keys. Hoping to distract him, she said, "Let's say I believe you when you say Geordie sent you to meet me. Why didn't he come himself?" Her fingers touched cool metal, and she drew the keys out of her purse, keeping them hidden in the palm of her hand.

"I don't know why he couldn't meet you."

"Then why are we out here?" she asked, her mind only half on what she was saying.

"I told you why. I needed to talk to you." He smiled tightly. "You weren't prepared to listen to me inside the bar, so I thought I'd have more luck out here." He glanced at the deserted parking lot. "Fewer distractions."

She shifted her weight to the balls of her feet, summoning her strength, ready to run. "Okay, talk." Her gaze slid toward her car, gauging the distance.

"Geordie wanted me to find you."

"You've already told me he sent you. Why didn't *he* come? Has something happened?"

He didn't answer.

All thoughts of flight vanished, and she grabbed his arm. "Something *has* happened, hasn't it? Is he hurt? Tell me he's not hurt."

Chapter 2

Hallie's face paled, and shadows dimmed her sapphire eyes.

He shouldn't have taken her out of the bar. He'd only made things worse. No wonder she was afraid of him. What woman wouldn't be after his caveman tactics? But then he recalled his brother's troubled voice, and his guilt fled. This misunderstanding was her fault. She'd refused to talk inside the bar, leaving him no other choice.

The uncertain light cast by the flickering neon sign revealed her long, slim legs covered by body-hugging, white, denim pants, which cupped her hips. The soft mounds of her breasts swelled against the fabric of her blue blouse.

Sweat beaded his brow. He forced his gaze back to her face.

Her full, red lips parted, and the tip of a pink tongue peeked out as she licked her lips.

He gulped.

"What aren't you telling me?" she asked. "Is Geordie okay?"

Her frantic voice broke through the haze surrounding him. He took a quick breath. "You want to know about Geordie?"

She nodded.

"Well, then, come on." He turned on his heel and

started walking across the parking lot, not looking to see if she followed, half hoping she wouldn't. He couldn't think with her perfume, something spicy, hinting at sensual delights, wafting on the night air. At least, he couldn't think with his brain. Other body parts were more than willing to do the thinking for him.

"Where are you going?" she called after him.

He rummaged in his pocket for his keys and opened the door of his old, red, four-wheel drive truck. Casting a glance over his shoulder, he saw she still stood where he'd left her. He nodded. He'd figured she was too smart to drive off with a man she didn't know. He couldn't risk another look, but against all reason, he did.

She stood alone, illuminated by the faint light of the distant street lamp, looking frightened and vulnerable.

He rubbed a hand over his face, the stubble rasping in the night air. Sighing, he spoke, knowing he was making a mistake even as the words left his lips. "I thought you cared about Geordie. You said you wanted to know how he is."

A long silence ensued.

The indecision on her ashen face was visible across the distance separating them.

"How do I know this isn't a trick?" she asked. "How do I know you're not one of *them*?" Her voice was barely audible over the dull throb of music escaping the bar.

He climbed inside the truck, closed the door and leaned his head out the open window. "I guess you're going to have to trust me."

She still didn't budge.

He'd done everything short of actually kidnapping her. What more could he do? Sliding the keys into the ignition, he started the truck. As he put the vehicle into gear, the passenger door swung open, and she climbed onto the seat beside him.

Strapping on her seat belt, she said, "Let's go."

"Let's go?"

"Take me to Geordie." She peered through the truck's rear window and sucked in a sharp breath. "Come on. Let's get going. What are you waiting for?"

She sat as close to the passenger door as possible and still be inside the truck. Fear pulsed off her in waves, fear of him. Yet, she'd climbed into his truck willing to drive off into the night.

Again she glanced over her shoulder through the truck's rear window. Her slight body fairly vibrated with tension.

Using his rear view mirror, he scanned the parking lot. He didn't see anything unusual, but something had her spooked. "Are you sure you want to come with me?"

Her gaze was fixed out the rear window. "No, I'm not sure, but let's get the hell out of here. Now."

He shook his head. One minute he'd had to manhandle her out of the bar in order to get her to talk, and the next she was in his truck ordering him to take her away. Unease settled low in his belly. He didn't know how it had happened, but somehow in the past few minutes, he'd lost control of the situation.

"Come on," she said. "Let's move it."

He'd never understand women. Putting the truck in gear, he jammed his foot on the gas and skidded out of the parking lot onto the main road, spraying gravel and dust in his wake.

****

Hallie breathed a sigh of relief. Under normal circumstances she'd never go anywhere with a stranger she'd met in a bar, especially now when the situation was anything but normal. But as she'd stood alone in the parking lot watching Ryan start his truck, the squeak of a car door opening had startled her.

Two burly men climbed out of a black SUV, their menace unmistakable.

Her blood had turned to ice. She recognized them. She'd turned to run back to the questionable safety of the bar, but the men darted toward her, trying to cut her off. They'd have had her before she made it back inside. With visions of what the men pursuing her would do to her if they caught her, she raced toward Ryan's idling truck. As she hauled herself up onto the seat, she prayed she hadn't left one danger for another.

"Where…where are we going?" She winced at the waver in her voice. The past months had been tough. Days and days of looking over her shoulder, jumping at every shadow, and trusting no one had drained her. She hadn't heard from Geordie, and her worry grew each hour she waited in hiding.

For him not to show up at the Rusty Nail Bar 'n Grill when he promised he would was the last straw. Where was he? Something must have happened to him. And who was this man sitting beside her driving her God knows where? He'd said Geordie had sent him, but he could be lying as a ruse to get her to trust him. Was he with the men Geordie had warned her about? She didn't think so, but she couldn't be certain.

The truck jerked and swayed as the big tires sank

into a pothole in the gravel road.

She had to focus. She couldn't let her guard down. Not now. Not when so much was at stake. She turned to the man beside her. "How do you know Geordie?"

He didn't respond.

"Look, Ryan…it is Ryan, isn't it? I mean the man in the bar called you Ryan." Her voice faltered in the face of his continued silence, but she forged on, determined to break through his icy reserve and find some answers. "You seem…you seem like a decent guy." She nearly choked on the lie. He was anything but decent. He'd ignored her protests and dragged her out of the bar, winking and grinning, and bald-faced lying to the drunken cowboys. She didn't trust him. Not for a heartbeat, but at the moment, he was all she had.

Inhaling a big breath, she said, "I have a right to know where you're taking me."

He jammed on the brakes, and the truck skidded to a halt.

Her body flew forward, the seatbelt tightened across her chest, and then her head smacked the back of the seat. "What the hell?" She rubbed the back of her neck. "Are you trying to give me whiplash?"

"Look, calm down. I'm taking you somewhere safe. If you want out, you're free to go." He leaned across her and opened her door. "No one's keeping you against your will."

She stared through the windshield at the darkness, unbroken by a single light or sign of human habitation. Towering trees loomed over the narrow road, ghostly and menacing in the truck's headlights. Her car was at the Rusty Nail Bar 'n Grill. Even if she managed to walk all the way back to the bar, the men she'd seen earlier would be waiting. Shivering, she sank back against the seat. She didn't have a choice. She had to trust him, at least until he gave her reason not to.

Her hand shook as she closed the door, wincing at the heavy clunk of metal.

The dim lights from the dashboard played across the stark planes of his face, casting his prominent cheekbones in shadow.

"Tell me where we're going." She swallowed. "Please?"

He sighed. "Look, I'm not going to hurt you. I promise. Sit back and be quiet. We're almost there. I'll explain everything then."

She stared into his eyes searching for deception.

The light in the cab of the truck was dim and filled with shadows, but almost hidden in the cobalt blue of his eyes, soft lights flickered.

She blew out a breath she hadn't been aware she was holding. He wasn't as hard assed as he acted, but that didn't mean she trusted him. He was up to something, but if there was the slightest chance he could take her to Geordie, sticking with him was worth the risk.

A short time later, the truck lurched up a steep incline more goat track than road and slowed to a stop. He slammed the gearshift into Park, and then turned off the truck's engine.

"Why are we stopping?" she asked, peering through the dusty windshield at the dark night. The headlights revealed an endless sea of tall, blowing grass.

"We're on my land. Over there is a line shack my men use when they round up the cattle in the fall. The accommodation's not much, but this place will serve its purpose for now."

She peered where he pointed and saw the squat shape of a small, wooden building. The pungent aroma of cow manure, ripening hay and road dust floated in through the open window. She shuddered, new fears arising. What was she doing? Geordie had warned her to be careful, and at the first opportunity, she drove off with a complete stranger. She was in the middle of nowhere. Help was a long way away, and she was alone with a man she didn't know, a man who hadn't answered her questions.

How could she have been so stupid? No way was she getting out of this truck until he told her what he knew. "Look," she said, pinning him with a hard stare, "I'm getting tired of this whole tight-lipped cowboy thing you've got going on. Tell me what we're doing here, or take me back to the bar."

His eyes narrowed and his jaw tightened, but then he nodded. "Okay, but let's get you inside first."

"I'm not going anywhere until you answer my questions. Where's Geordie?"

He sighed and ran long fingers through his dark curls. "I already told you. I don't know."

"What? But you said he sent you to the bar to meet me."

"He did."

"Well, then where is he? You've talked to him, right?"

He nodded.

"And?" Getting answers from him was like convincing a starving dog to give up his bone. "Why did he send you to meet me instead of coming himself?

Where is he?"

A look of chagrin crossed his swarthy face. He shrugged. "I don't know. I don't know anything."

"But you said—"

"I said what I had to, to get you away from the bar. Now, let's go inside."

Dread washed over her. He was working with the men she'd seen in the parking lot at the bar, and like a fool, she'd fallen into his trap. For the past two months she'd been expecting something like this. Her mind flew in a hundred directions as she fought through her rising panic, searching for a means of escape.

"Come on." He opened his door, climbed out of the truck, and headed toward the small building.

She opened her own door, undid her seat belt and stepped out of the vehicle. The second her foot hit the dirt, she ran, flying over the uneven ground, stumbling on unseen rocks and hollows. The desperate need to flee from danger drove her onward.

Twin beams of light pierced the darkness.

Her foot caught on something, and she yelped at the painful twist of her ankle. She hit the earth with a thud, knocking the breath out of her. The sound of heavy footsteps turned her blood to ice. She pressed her face into the dusty grass, giving into the primitive urge to burrow into the ground. After all this time, after everything she'd been through these past months, her life had come to this point.

"What the hell do you think you're doing?" he asked. "You could get yourself killed running around in the dark. Gopher holes are everywhere." His harsh voice gentled. "Are you all right? Did you hurt yourself?"

Too frozen by fear to breathe, she waited for his touch.

He grasped her arm and pulled her to her feet.

The second her foot touched the ground, and she put weight on her injured ankle, she moaned and collapsed against him.

"What is it? What's wrong?" he asked.

Gasping at the throbbing pain, she managed to say, "It's my ankle. I think I sprained it."

"Let me have a look." He lowered her to the ground, and with surprising gentleness, removed her high-heeled, black leather boot. "Only a fool would run around out here in boots like these."

Fear and pain in equal measures coursed through her as she followed his every action.

She gasped. In the glare of light cast by the twin beams of the truck's headlights, her ankle was misshapen, and angry purple streaks mottled the pale skin.

Chapter 3

He lifted her in his arms and packed her across the field, past his truck, to the small, wooden hut. Stepping onto the shack's sagging porch, he kicked the door open, and carried her into the dark building. He strode across the room and set her down on a small cot.

A match flared, and the sharp smell of sulphur stung her nostrils. The tiny flame offered a welcome relief to the oppressive dark. He turned up the wick of an old kerosene lantern and lit it. A warm glow suffused the room.

Barely ten feet separated one unpainted, planked, wooden wall from the other. A rickety-looking wooden chair, a white, plastic lawn chair, a battered card table, as well as the narrow bed on which she sat were all jammed into the tiny interior. An old-fashioned metal, wood-burning stove stood against one wall, a cardboard box full of kindling on the floor. The walls were bare, except for an out-of-date calendar sporting a photograph of a surgically enhanced, naked blonde. There was only one window in the room, the cracked pane covered with grime.

She shifted on the cot and a sour, musty smell, mixed with an underlying hint of long-dead creatures swelled around her. She gagged and struggled to rise, but the second her injured foot touched the floor, she blew out a sharp breath and fell back, raising another fetid cloud.

"Cold?"

"This bed is horrible." She grimaced, and pointed at the yellow stains covering the mattress. "Don't you have a blanket or something to cover the mattress?"

The corners of his mouth tightened. "I'm sure these accommodations aren't up to your usual standards, but for now, you'll have to make do." He cast a meaningful glance at her swollen ankle. "It's not like you have a choice, is it?"

Their gazes met.

She blinked at the unexpected compassion in his eyes.

In the next breath, he turned away and she was left to wonder if she'd imagined the glint of kindness.

"I'll light a fire." He crouched before the stove, the faded denim of his jeans tightening around his lean haunches. With deft strokes, he crumpled old newspapers, laid several pieces of kindling in the grate, and used a match to set the pile alight. Within minutes, the wood flamed, and heat flooded the room.

She examined her ankle. The swelling had increased, and her skin was turning blue. Even the slightest movement resulted in a wave of pain. When she'd driven into Antler Springs this afternoon, she hadn't expected this, but then, nothing had gone as planned these past two months.

The last time she'd seen Geordie, they'd both been terrified. He'd told her his life was in danger, and hers as well. He'd convinced her they had to separate for her safety. She needed to hide out somewhere while he fixed the nightmare. He'd promised he'd meet her at the Rusty Nail Bar 'n Grill in Antler Springs, Montana, in two months. By then, he'd assured her, the trouble with the drug gang would be over. They'd be safe.

At least, he'd said they'd be safe.

After two long, lonely months, she'd come out of hiding, rented a car, and driven halfway across the country to meet him, but he hadn't shown up. Instead, the infuriating man standing before her had appeared, refusing to answer her questions and taking her God knows where.

Glancing at the man in question, she noted his sharp profile and rigid jaw and shivered. He frightened her all right, but not as much as the two thugs she'd spied hurrying toward her in the parking lot. No question, those two men would hurt her. Ryan was an unknown. At the time, she'd hoped he was the safer option. Now, she wasn't so sure.

A ripping sound startled her from her dark thoughts. She glanced up to see him tearing a dirty, white, cotton rag into narrow strips.

"What are you doing?" she asked. "Why are you ripping that cloth?

"It's for your ankle. The binding will keep the swelling down."

"You're not wrapping a dirty rag around *my* ankle."

His mouth tightened. "Look, princess, here's the deal. You're not in a hospital emergency room. You're in a line shack on a ranch. I can either wrap your ankle and give you some relief from your pain, or not." His eyes drilled into hers. "Your choice."

She bit her bottom lip. The only thing stopping her from telling him what she thought of his arrogance was the knowledge he was right. Wrapping her ankle would

C. B. Clark

reduce the swelling and give her support. Hating to have to concede, she nodded.

The corners of his mouth twitched as he knelt beside her.

She flinched at the touch of his hand on her foot as he traced the swollen ridge of her damaged ankle. His long, tanned fingers wrapped the strips around the distended area, surprising her with his skill and gentleness. She inhaled a shaky breath. "Thank you, but now it's time you told me where Geordie is."

His fingers stilled, and he regarded her, his startling blue eyes assessing. "I'd hoped you could tell me."

"But you said—"

"Yeah, I know. I told you I'd take you to Geordie. I can't."

"What…?" Her throat closed. She swallowed and tried again. "What…what do you want with me? Why did you bring me here?"

****

Guilt hit him like a hammer as fear dulled her eyes. He'd promised he'd keep her safe, but he sure as hell was doing a rotten job. This was Geordie's fault. He'd asked, hell, he'd begged Ryan to help her. He hadn't wanted to take the time. Too much work needed to be done at the ranch. He couldn't afford to stop feeding cattle and run off on one of Geordie's wild goose chases. Besides, every time he helped his kid brother, trouble followed.

He studied the drop-dead, gorgeous blonde sitting on the old cot, her ankle wrapped in strips of dirty cloth. His fingers tingled where he'd touched her velvety-soft skin. He rubbed his hands on his jeans, gritting his teeth until they ached. Rising from the floor, he backed away, putting much needed distance between them. "Your ankle's not broken," he said. "Looks like you rolled it and stretched the ligaments. A few aspirin for the pain should help." He swiped his hand through his hair. "Sorry, I don't have any ice. I'll bring some over later when I come to check on you."

"Wha…what do you want with me?" Her voice trembled as she asked the question again.

What was her problem? He'd told her he wasn't going to hurt her, but she looked at him as if he were an axe murderer. Some perverse devil made him snap, "What does any man want with an attractive woman?" He regretted his words the instant he uttered them. He lamented them more when her face drained of what little color it had.

Her hand shook when she brushed a lock of hair off her forehead, adding to his self-loathing. *Way to go, buddy. What are you going to do for an encore? Threaten to close down the orphanage?* "Look, I'm sorry if I scared you. I didn't mean to. I simply want you to tell me where Geordie is, and what he's got himself into this time."

"I haven't seen him in months, but even if I did know where he was, I wouldn't tell you." She squared her shoulders and met his gaze, daring him to challenge her.

She had guts; he'd give her that. He had a good six inches on her and outweighed her by at least sixty pounds, but she stood up to him. Grabbing a battered chair, he turned it and sat, leaning his arms across the back.

Her eyes skittered around the room as if she were

seeking an escape route.

He'd better do something quick before she ran off on him again. He took a deep breath. "I said I wasn't going to hurt you, and I meant it. You're safe here. You can trust me." He kept his voice low and soothing as if talking to a skittish calf.

Instead of calming her, his words fueled her anger. Her blue eyes blazed. "Trust you? I don't even know you. I haven't survived these past two months so some low life can get his hands on me."

He scrubbed his hands over his face, silently cursing his brother for getting him into this mess. As far back as he remembered he'd helped Geordie out of one jam after another. Somehow getting involved in his brother's life always backfired. More often than not, he ended up looking like the bad guy, while Geordie smiled his all too charming grin and waltzed unfazed onto his next disaster. When would he learn? He sighed, knowing he had to finish this. "It's time we got a few things straight."

Her luminous, blue eyes probed his, her eyebrows rising in question.

"Like I told you before, Geordie asked me to meet you tonight at the Rusty Nail."

"How is he? Is he all right?"

For some reason he didn't want to analyze, her concern for his brother irritated him. "Why don't you tell me? I haven't seen him in almost two years."

"But you said—"

"I know what I said. He called me last week and asked me to meet you at the bar. He said you were in trouble and needed my help."

She lit up like a beacon, and again her beauty

struck him low in the gut. For a moment, he forgot to breathe.

"You talked to him, though." Her voice rose in her excitement. "Is he all right? Where is he? Please, you have to tell me. I've been so worried."

By the time he remembered to inhale, she fairly bounced on the small cot, her fondness for Geordie written across her expressive face. He hardened his gaze. "You tell me. All I know is my kid brother's in trouble, and you're involved in this shit up to your pretty neck."

****

He was Geordie's brother? A vision of Geordie rose in her mind's eye. His short stature and soft body, combined with his dark-blond hair and gentle, brown eyes were the exact opposite of the man glowering from across the room. The differences weren't only physical. Geordie was kind, but he was also fun and quick with a joke. He rarely took anything seriously. At least, he hadn't until Mexico.

Ryan's smiles hinted of dark secrets and an inner, steely strength. His face was set in rigid lines, his dark brows lowered over his piercing blue eyes. She shivered. "Geordie never mentioned he had a brother."

He shrugged. "We haven't been close for years."

"Why did he ask you to meet me tonight?" she asked. "Why didn't he come himself?"

Again he shrugged.

"He's all right, isn't he? I mean, nothing's happened to him?"

Ryan's mouth thinned to a hard line, and her heart skipped a beat. "What is it? I knew something was wrong when he wasn't at the bar. I should have made him call the police when this whole thing started. I'll never forgive myself if something's happened." She sat up, wincing at the jarring motion setting her injured ankle on fire. "You have to take me to him. Please?"

His expression hardened, his cheekbones looking as if they'd been carved from granite. "Look, lady, get this through your head. I didn't drive you all the way out here to tell you where Geordie is, or to take you to him."

Silence hung like a weight in the small room.

Anger heated her blood. She was tired of his games. He didn't understand how serious the situation was. He didn't know what she and Geordie had been through these past horrible months, but she bit her lip and held her tongue. She wanted to find Geordie. No matter how much he denied he knew Geordie's whereabouts, Ryan was Geordie's brother. He could find him for her. Taking a calming breath, she asked, "Why didn't you tell me you didn't know anything at the bar? Why drag me all the way out here?"

He ran his fingers through his dark hair, rumpling the glossy curls. "Geordie thinks you need protection. From what or whom, I don't know. We were cut off before he could tell me, but I promised him I'd keep you out of trouble."

"You think I need *you* to protect me?" She pointed at her injured ankle. "A fat lot of good you've done. Before you dragged me out of the bar, I was doing fine. Now, look at me. I don't need your help or anyone else's." She paused for breath, her chest heaving. "Take me back to town."

"You're smarter than that, Hallie. I don't know what's going on with you and my brother, but I know you need help. I saw how frightened you were back at the Rusty Nail."

She opened her mouth to protest, but instead sank back on the fetid mattress. As much as she hated to admit it, Ryan was right. The men waiting in the bar's dimly lit parking lot had frightened her. A sudden weariness overcame her. She was tired. Tired of running, tired of hiding, and most of all, tired of being alone. She regarded Ryan's strong, muscular body and determined face. A sudden yearning filled her, a desire to lean on him, to know she wasn't alone, and someone else was with her on this frightening journey.

"Look," he said and glanced at his wristwatch. "It's getting late. Make up your mind. Do you want my help or not?"

The strain of the past hours propelled her over the edge, and finally set her anger free. "Excuse me for keeping you from your very important work. Feel free to walk out the door anytime you want."

His eyes blazed, and a pulse beat in his jaw. "Enough of this bullshit," he exploded, jumping to his feet. "I promised my brother I'd look after you, and damn it, I'm a man of my word. I won't break my promise."

"Why is it so important you do what Geordie asked?" She met his gaze. "From what you've told me, the two of you are anything but close."

He pressed his lips together. "My relationship with my brother is none of your damn business."

She fought against a fresh onslaught of anger ignited by his harsh words, but he'd pushed her too far. "You're nothing like Geordie. Nothing at all." She ignored the menacing gleam in his eyes. "Look at you.

You live in this backwater, little, no-nothing town and do what? Listen to the crickets chirp?" Even as the words spewed out, she recognized their unfairness, but she couldn't stop. "Geordie may have made mistakes, but at least he left and made something of himself, unlike you. You know why you're so bitter? You're jealous of your brother." She stiffened, stunned at what she'd said, knowing she'd gone too far.

She opened her mouth to apologize, but his eyes shocked her into silence.

The blue irises had darkened to pools of bleak emptiness.

Something metallic clattered on the floor beside the bed, and she jumped. Glancing down, she saw the truck keys.

"Take them, and get the hell out of here." His voice was low and clipped. "Leave the truck at the Rusty Nail. I'll pick it up tomorrow. Put the keys under the mat."

She struggled to think of something to say to ease the harshness of her words, but she'd already said too much, so she remained silent. She picked up the keys and her boot and hobbled to the door. Holding it open, she paused and glanced back.

The dark hollows of his eyes watched her in the flickering shadows of the room. An aura of desolation surrounded him.

She blinked back the unexpected sting of tears, stepped onto the porch, and closed the door behind her, feeling as if she'd made the biggest mistake of her life.

Chapter 4

The harsh glare of the headlights outlined a deer, its eyes glowing, frozen in fear, on the road ahead. Hallie gripped the steering wheel and jammed on the brakes. The truck's rear wheels skidded on the loose gravel, the heavy vehicle fishtailing across the road's uneven surface. Her ankle bounced against the floorboard, and she groaned at the sharp stab of pain.

The deer bolted, its panicked flight placing the animal directly in her path. She wrenched the wheel to the left and gunned the motor. The truck's bumper missed the fleeing animal by inches as the deer vanished into the darkness, the white flag of its tail flashing.

Relief washed over her, but in the next breath, she yelped as the truck slammed into the edge of the ditch, bounced back onto the road, and spun. Her fingers dug into the hard, plastic steering wheel. The vehicle hit the bank again, smashing through a pile of loose rocks and landing in the ditch with a reverberating wrench of metal. The engine sputtered and died.

Hallie released the gulp of air she'd been holding and pried her fingers loose from their grip on the steering wheel. Wiping her damp palms on her jeans, she peered through the windshield.

The truck rested at an odd angle, the front end lower than the back end.

She opened the door and leaned out. A deep, water-filled ditch shone in the reflected light from the headlights, the truck's left front tire submerged almost to the top.

She eyed the glowing dash. The lights still worked, so she had power. With a little luck, she could restart the engine, put the truck into four-wheel drive, and maneuver out of the ditch. Muttering a prayer, she turned the keys in the ignition. The powerful motor rumbled to life. She engaged the four-wheel drive system, and pressed down on the gas pedal. The truck lurched forward. Yes!

The big tires spun, the motor roared and then the truck stopped. She shifted into reverse and pressed the gas pedal. With each revolution, the wheels sank deeper into the muck. "Come on," she urged. Something must be stuck beneath the truck's undercarriage. *Damn.* Slamming her fist on the dashboard, she set the brake.

Biting back a groan, she tugged on her boot, easing it over the cloth bandage and her swollen ankle. Sweat dampened her brow by the time the boot was on, but at least she wouldn't have to walk barefoot in the muck. Careful not to bump her ankle, she climbed out of the truck and stepped into cold water, sinking up to her knees. So much for her white jeans. She hobbled around to the rear of the vehicle and squinted into the darkness. A huge rock buried in the muck was lodged under the rear wheel's axle.

She shoved the massive boulder, straining with the effort, but the rock didn't budge. Panting, her arms trembling, she stood up. Nothing short of a backhoe would shift the rock, and with it jammed under the wheel axle, the truck wasn't going anywhere.

A dull ache throbbed behind her eyes, and she rubbed her temples. What a day. Her life had gone downhill from the first moment she'd arrived in this damn town. When she'd thought her circumstances couldn't get any worse, this happened.

She leaned against the truck, her shoulders drooping, icy moisture seeping through her boots to her bare skin. The truck was stuck. Her ankle throbbed with every heartbeat. She was in the middle of nowhere, and no one was likely to come along and help her. What the hell was she going to do?

An eerie howling filled the night.

The hairs along her arms rose. Coyotes? Or wolves? She searched the surrounding darkness for a pack of starving beasts. An owl hooted, its lonely call echoing across the prairie. Crickets chirped in the long grass growing in tufts along the road. A prairie dog barked a warning. She shuddered. The night was suddenly alive with the furtive scurrying of wild animals.

Her heart pounding, she slogged through the muck to the driver's door and jumped into the cab. She slammed the door behind her, secured the lock, and peered through the mud-spattered windshield. No other lights were visible, no buildings, no signs of civilization. How far had she driven from the line shack? How much further to Antler Springs?

The night closed around her, and tears stung her eyes. These past two months she'd been through hell. From the moment she and Geordie had encountered those two thugs on a moonlit Mexican beach, events had gone from bad to worse.

When her boss had announced she and Geordie

were going to attend the import/export company's annual sales convention in Acapulco, she'd been so excited. If she'd known what she was getting herself into, she'd have run away as fast as she could. But she hadn't, and she'd paid for her misjudgment, had been paying every day these past two months.

When she leaned her forehead against the steering wheel, the cool plastic soothed her hot face. Where was Geordie? Why hadn't he met her at the bar as he'd promised? Why had he sent his brother instead of coming himself? He was in trouble. Nothing else would keep him from meeting her. She had to find him. If he wasn't in Antler Springs, where was he?

Shivers wracked her body as she huddled in the seat, wishing she'd worn a jacket. Even in July, Montana nights were chilly. The air was cold and getting colder by the hour. The best course of action was to stay in the truck and wait for help. Someone would eventually come along. If not, when Ryan didn't find his truck parked at the Rusty Nail, he'd come looking for it. Her heart sank. And when he found his truck, he'd find her.

She shuddered as she recalled the insults she'd spat at him and the desolation, which had darkened his handsome features. He'd provoked her with his snide comments and overbearing manner, but his rudeness was no excuse for her hurtful words.

Like her recently deceased beloved Grandpa Joe who'd raised her had often told her, it was time to fish or cut bait. She had two choices: walk to Antler Springs, or wait for Ryan to find her. The prospect of walking on her sore ankle made her cringe, and the trip would probably take her the rest of the night. She pictured Ryan's rugged face and piercing blue eyes; his mouth curled in a sneer at what she'd done to his truck, and shuddered. No contest. Option one it was.

These past months had made her realize her inner strength. Must have inherited it from her anonymous, sperm-donor daddy, since Mother never had any. Leastwise, none she'd ever revealed the few times in Hallie's life she'd been sober. Hallie didn't need anyone's protection, least of all Geordie's infuriating brother. Finding Geordie was her priority. Ryan couldn't, or wouldn't, help her. He'd told her he hadn't seen his brother in years, and he had no idea where Geordie was now. If she was going to locate Geordie, she had to find him on her own.

Searching for something she could use to help her on her journey to the Rusty Nail, she examined the truck cab. A grin spread across her face when she opened the glove box. A flashlight. She wouldn't have to make the long trip back to the bar in the dark.

Once again, she opened the door and eased out of the truck, steeling herself for the inevitable submersion in cold, muddy water. Sloshing to the back of the truck, she shone the flashlight into the truck box. A wooden ice hockey stick lay among a pile of old, stained boards, a small, square bale of hay, and a spool of fencing wire. Why Ryan had a hockey stick in the back of his truck when the nearest ice surface had to be hundreds of miles distant wasn't relevant. The sturdy stick made a perfect crutch.

Opening the tailgate, she heaved herself up onto the truck bed and grabbed the stick. Her foot banged against the side of the truck, and she yelped and lay there panting until the wave of pain passed.

A coyote's howl rent the air, answered by a matching call from across the valley.

She hefted the sturdy stick with the curved blade. It would make a serviceable weapon should the need arise. In spite of her rising nervousness, she smiled at the foolishness of battling hungry coyotes with a hockey stick.

Climbing out of the truck bed, she gripped the stick with one hand and the flashlight with the other. She took a first cautious step, followed by a second step, and then another. Pain radiated up and down her leg. The flashlight's faint beam of light outlined the ruts in the road.

Taking one halting footstep at a time, she'd covered only twenty feet when she stopped. A hushed silence surrounded her. Even the crickets were still. The night was quiet. Too quiet. Several minutes passed. *Relax,* she told herself. *This isn't the inner city.* The enemies here were of the four-legged variety, and the local animals were probably more afraid of her than she was of them.

In spite of her reassurances, her unease grew with each step. The hairs on the back of her neck tingled at the unsettling sensation of being watched.

Gravel crunched.

She froze. "Who's there?"

The night closed around her, all the more ominous for the lack of sound. She recalled the coyotes' eerie howling, and her heart beat a rapid tattoo. Would coyotes attack a human? The thought no longer held any humor.

Another shifting of pebbles on the road ahead.

She shone the flashlight, sweeping the beam in a

wide arc across the road. The feeble light penetrated only a few feet. Her palms dampened. This was no wild animal closing in for an attack. She struggled to speak through her frozen throat. "Ryan...Ryan, is that you?"

Two large shapes loomed out of the darkness.

She choked back a scream.

The men she'd seen at the parking lot at the Rusty Nail grinned at her. They must have followed her to the line shack and waited until she was alone.

Reacting to the terror filling her, she planted her feet. Ignoring the stab of pain as her injured ankle took her weight, she shone the flashlight in the men's eyes. "Wha...what do you want?" She prayed they didn't hear the fear behind her challenge.

The men stepped closer with cruel, menacing expressions on their blunt faces.

A frisson of icy fear ran along her spine. "Stop where you are," she said. "I'm not afraid to use this." She brandished the hockey stick.

"*Hola, chica.* Nice to see you again." The bigger of the two men snickered. "You have been a bad girl. *Muy mala*, and bad girls must be punished."

The smaller man grinned, exposing yellow, uneven teeth. "*Sí*, bad, very bad." They stepped toward her.

And closer still.

Her breath heaved in her chest. She urged her legs to act, to run, but her muscles refused to obey. Alone and terrified, she waited for the men's attack.

Even though she'd encountered them before, their appearance sent shivers up her spine. Their faces wore matching looks of malice, but the similarity ended there. One man was a giant. His massive shoulders strained his white, sleeveless T-shirt. Lurid tattoos of grinning skulls and daggers dripping blood decorated his thick forearms. His face was a nightmare. A livid scar cut across one cheek and over the bridge of his crooked nose, dragging the edge of one eye down in a grotesque manner.

The second man was shorter, though what he lacked in height he made up for in girth. A sagging belly strained his shirt giving him the look of a circus clown. The cruel glint in his beady eyes quickly refuted her notion. He was bald, his bare head gleaming under the flashlight's beam.

Her hands trembled, her palms slick with sweat. For the past two months, these men had featured in her nightmares. She recalled Geordie's bruised and bloodied face and whimpered. Terror immobilized her.

A loud noise rent the night.

She blinked, surprised the panicked cry had come out of her mouth. She screamed again. The primal sound cut through her lethargy and freed her from her frozen fear. Dropping the flashlight, she gripped the hockey stick with both hands and thrust the blade in a sweeping arc before her.

The men paused, their gazes fixed on the moving stick.

Determination soared through her. She could do this. She jabbed the hockey stick at the shorter of the two men.

He easily dodged her wild thrust. "Come on, *chica*. Come and get me." His laughter filled the air.

She lunged toward him. The blade of the stick narrowly missed his smirking face.

He laughed harder, dodging left and right, avoiding her thrusts and swings.

Adrenaline fueled her, and she charged, grunting at the impact of the stick's blade striking flesh.

The man yelped and grabbed his bulging belly.

Teetering on her sore ankle, she spun toward the second man. Her blood chilled.

He was close, too close.

While she'd focused on the smaller man, this brute had slunk around until he stood mere inches from her.

He grinned. The scar tugged at the corner of his eye, and his eye drooped ghoulishly. "You have much spirit, *puta*." His dark, cruel eyes bore into hers, and then his gaze slid over her body. He leered at her heaving chest and ran his tongue over his thick lips. "I am sorry we must do this. Such a waste of a young woman." He licked his lips again. "If you play nice, we promise to go easy on you."

She reeled from the lurid intent in his gaze.

Thick, meaty arms grabbed her around the waist, dragging her against a massive chest. Screaming as his rank body odor overwhelmed her, she dropped the hockey stick and clawed at his hands. His arms tightened, squeezing the air from her lungs.

Her fingernails dug deep, leaving angry streaks of blood on his forearms. She stomped the heel of her high-heeled boot on his foot and kicked back against his knee.

The pressure of his arms around her, vanished. She was free! Ignoring the pain of her ankle, she hobbled as fast as she could toward the edge of the road and the concealing darkness beyond.

Cruel fingers grabbed her hair, stopping her flight.

Tears stung her eyes. She moaned as her captor twisted a thick hank of her hair in his fist and yanked, forcing her to her knees. Gravel bit through the thin fabric of her white jeans and gouged her skin. Her ankle smashed against the ground. Breath whooshed out as a haze of pain rocketed through her. Gasping, fighting back the waves of agony, she collapsed.

"You are *mucho* fun, *chica*, but we have wasted enough time. Let us get down to business. Our *capo* has ordered we finish this now."

"She is *estas buena, mucho caliente*, so, so hot." The other man snickered. "Can we have fun with her first, *amigo*?"

Hallie peered through tangled strands of hair at the men towering over her and shuddered at the coldness of their voices as they discussed her imminent death. "Why…why are you doing this?" Even though she knew the answer, she wanted to hear them say the words. If only to prove to herself everything she'd gone through these past months, everything Geordie had told her, was real.

The bald man chuckled, sending a fresh frisson of fear rippling along her spine.

"You know the answer, *chica*. Your boyfriend pissed off our *capo*. He does not like to be treated with such disrespect. Someone must pay the price." His grin widened. "Looks like you are the lucky one."

She swallowed over a thick lump. "Is Geordie okay? You haven't…?" She couldn't finish the sentence.

He smirked. "He is not *muerto*…yet."

Relief washed over her. Geordie was still alive.

In the next second, the taller man grabbed her arm and jerked her to her feet.

Her weight landed on her ankle, and a fresh wave

of agony washed over her.

The fat thug dug into his pants pocket and metal glinted in his beefy hand.

She shuddered at the menace in his dark eyes as he waved a long, razor-sharp dagger in front of her.

"*Sí*, Manuel," he said, licking his thick lips, "It would be a shame to miss out on this tasty treat. A few minutes either way will not make a difference."

Her other captor assessed her as if she were a piece of meat for sale at the market. He shrugged. "Why not?"

Bile rose in her throat.

"You are so sweet, *chica*. Me and my *amigo* want a little taste." He grabbed his crotch and thrust his hips.

"Cooperate, and maybe we let you go," the man called Manuel said. "But you have to be a good *chica*, and do everything we want. *Everything*."

A spurt of hope flared, but then she looked into his eyes.

Cruelty lurked in the dark depths.

A chill settled over her as the bitter truth sank in. These men had no intention of letting her go. They'd been sent to kill her. They'd rape her and then murder her. Rage filled her. She wasn't dead yet. As long as she breathed, there was hope. If she pretended to go along with them, they might let their guard down, giving her a chance to escape.

The bald man trailed a thick finger along her cheek and across her lips.

She bit back a scream at the rough rasp of his touch, but forced herself to remain still under his foul stroking.

"Let me have her first, Manuel," he husked. He

lowered his hand to her breast and squeezed. "She is full of fire. You know I like my women hot and feisty."

In spite of her determination to play along until she could escape, she couldn't repress a shudder.

The scarred man's forehead furrowed, and he shoved the smaller man out of the way. He grabbed her arms and dragged her against him. "*Bastardo*! I get her first. I do not take seconds." He pawed her breast, pinching and twisting the nipple. His sour breath surrounded her.

Tears of pain filled her eyes. She gagged, acrid bile rising in her throat.

"Manuel, there are many women much like this one. The *capo* wants her dead. I do not wish to fuck with him. He does not like it when we do not follow his orders," said the taller attacker. "The sooner we get this job done, the sooner we can report back to the *capo* she is *muerto*."

A fresh flood of terror engulfed her. She stared at the knife in his hand, unable to look away.

He raised the gleaming blade.

"Please…" she begged, knowing her pleas were useless. She closed her eyes, not wanting her last sight on Earth to be of him. Holding her breath, she awaited the blade's impact.

Chapter 5

The red taillights disappeared in the darkness. Ryan rubbed his hands over his face, the rasp of stubble loud in the night air. Hallie's image was seared into his brain. Every time he closed his eyes, her long, golden curls and lush body tormented him. But then he remembered what she'd said, and all he saw was her wounded blue eyes as they examined him as if he were the lowliest thing on the planet.

You're jealous of your brother.

Her sneering words echoed in his mind, striking deep, all the more painful because of their grain of truth. As much as he hated to admit it, she was right. For the first time ever, he was jealous of Geordie.

He dug into his back pocket and pulled out a crushed pack of cigarettes already anticipating the first puff's sharp tang. Cursing, he tossed the pack on the porch and ground the cigarettes beneath his heel. He hadn't had a smoke in more than two years. The pack was in his coat to prove to himself he could resist the lure of the nicotine hit his body still craved when life got tough.

A coyote howled, its haunting cry drifting across the valley.

Hallie was right. He was jealous of his kid brother, but not in the way she assumed. He wasn't jealous Geordie had left Antler Springs and earned a six-figure salary in a fancy office in the big city. Living in a city had been Geordie's dream, not his. He'd left the valley years ago and had more than his share of excitement working as a Special Agent for the Federal Drug Enforcement Agency. He'd done his time in so-called civilization; now, all he wanted was to be left alone in peace to run the ranch.

He wasn't jealous of his brother's career successes, but he did envy the concern in Hallie's voice when she spoke of Geordie, the worry clouding her eyes at the possibility something had happened to him. He had his share of female friends, any one of who would be more than happy to warm his bed, but none would weep for him if he weren't here. Not one of them considered him the most important person in her world. Certainly, no one would risk her life to save his. Not like Hallie Harkins was prepared to do for Geordie.

He gazed at the stars breaking through the cloud cover. What the hell had he gotten himself into? When Geordie had called him last week, he'd known something was wrong the second he'd heard his voice. His brother was five years younger. As far back as Ryan remembered, he'd been getting Geordie out of one scrape after another.

This time was different.

Rather than asking Ryan to save his own sorry ass, Geordie had begged him to help someone else. He'd refused to tell Ryan where he was or why he was so frightened, but he'd pleaded with him to meet Hallie Harkins at the Rusty Nail in Antler Springs where she was supposed to show the following week. Even now, Ryan recalled the conversation he'd had with his brother word for word.

"What the hell's going on, Geordie? I don't hear from you in two years, and then out of the blue you call and ask me to meet a woman I don't even know at a bar?" he'd asked over the crackling phone line.

"I know how things stand between us, Ryan," Geordie said. "Believe me, I wouldn't call if it wasn't important."

Anger burned a hole in Ryan's gut. There was always something with Geordie. Even after what had happened two years ago, he had the nerve to phone and ask for help. Well, he could shove it. Those days were over. After what Geordie had done, he was lucky Ryan hadn't killed him. Hell, given half the chance, he still might.

Geordie's faint voice broke into Ryan's dark thoughts.

"Something bad's going on and..." Geordie's voice faded.

Ryan strained to hear over the scratchy phone line. "Geordie? Are you still there?"

"I can't talk long," he said. "They're watching me, have been for awhile." Silence sizzled through the line. "Hell, they could have your phone bugged for all I know."

Unease prickled in Ryan's gut at the fear in Geordie's voice, cutting through his anger. "You'd better tell me everything, little brother, and I mean everything."

"I can't. Don't you get it?" Geordie's voice roughened. "This is serious shit, Ryan, real serious."

"It's always serious with you, Geordie. Ever since you were old enough to walk, you've been in trouble for one thing after another." Ryan sighed. Geordie was

twenty-nine going on thirteen. "How much money do you owe?"

A prolonged silence filled the air, and Ryan wondered if his brother had hung up.

"I don't blame you for doubting me." Geordie's heavy sigh echoed through the line. "God knows I've let you down often enough, but you have to believe me when I tell you this is the real deal. No joke, no bullshit. I need your help. I wouldn't ask if this weren't important. I know how angry you are about what happened with…" Static drowned out the rest of what he said.

Ryan's unease morphed into alarm. This didn't sound like his fun-loving brother who never took life seriously. "Where are you, Geordie?"

"I can't tell you."

"You won't tell me where you are or what's going on, but you expect me to do you this favor?"

"Please, Ryan? Do this for me, and I'll never ask anything of you again. I'll stay out of your life forever." A long pause ensued. "Hell, Ryan, I'm sorry, real sorry for what I did, and I'm sorry for what's going on right now. I didn't mean for any of this to happen. I didn't think they'd go this far. You have to believe me."

Ryan grimaced. How many times had his brother told him the same thing? But he said what he always said, what he'd known he'd say from the first moment Geordie made his urgent plea. "Okay, I'll do it. I'll help this damn woman."

His brother's relief was palpable. "I knew I could count on you, bro."

Geordie had gone on to describe Hallie Harkins, and Ryan had quickly figured out Geordie's affection

46

for her. She must really be something if she had his playboy brother talking in such favorable tones. Ryan knew his brother better than anyone. Geordie had a history of using women and leaving them, usually heart-broken, as he progressed to his next conquest.

With an effort, he drove back his anger. This wasn't the time for recriminations. From what Geordie said, this Hallie Harkins was in serious trouble. "When I find her, what do you want me to do with her?" he asked.

"Don't take her to the house. They'll be expecting you to go there. Keep her safe somewhere else. You know the Antler Springs area better than anyone. You'll think of a place."

Ryan's stomach plummeted at the gravity in his brother's voice. He'd never sounded this desperate. "Where are you, Geordie? Who's after you? Tell me. Maybe I can help."

Silence had been the only answer. The line was dead. Geordie had hung up, or been cut off.

Against his better judgment, Ryan had done as his brother had asked. He'd gone to find Hallie Harkins at the Rusty Nail. He hadn't known what to expect, but he sure as hell hadn't been expecting *her*. Geordie's glowing description began to do her justice. Each time Ryan so much as glanced at her, a staggering kick in his gut almost brought him to his knees.

He cursed and pounded his fist on the wooden railing. He was a fool for standing out here in the dark mooning over a woman. He had cattle to tend to and a ranch to run. His part in this fiasco was over. He'd done as Geordie had asked. He'd found Hallie in the Rusty Nail, and he'd offered to help her as best he could.

She'd thrown his offer in his face.

And now, she was gone, leaving an unsettling hollowness behind.

The coyote's call echoed over the valley again, and he grinned sourly at the lonely sound. *I know what you mean, buddy. I know exactly what you mean.* With a rueful shake of his head, he turned and stepped back into the shack.

After extinguishing the fire in the small stove, he switched off the lantern, and walked out onto the porch, closing the door behind him. He crossed to the rear of the shack and headed along the narrow path, cutting across the field to the ranch house. Even in the dark, he found the way. How many times had he and Geordie sneaked out of the house when they were kids and run to the old, line shack to smoke cigarettes and drink the beer they'd pilfered from their parents?

A fresh wave of guilt engulfed him. No matter how he sugarcoated his actions, the truth was he'd let his brother down. He hadn't done what he'd promised. He'd found Hallie Harkins all right, but he'd bungled everything from the moment he set eyes on her.

The situation had gone south from there. Geordie had asked him to keep her safe. And what had he done? He'd dragged her out here, and the first thing she did was sprain her ankle trying to get away from him.

His plan had seemed like a good one. Geordie had warned him to take extra precautions and not take Hallie to the ranch house, but Ryan was a trained Federal agent. He'd have known if he was under surveillance. No one was watching him or the ranch house, but on the off chance Geordie's fears were real, he'd chosen the isolated, rarely-used line shack as a secure location to keep Hallie until Geordie came for her.

Oh, sure, the hut was a little rough and hadn't been cleaned in years, and a few dozen mice might have taken up residence, but the main advantage was the shack was close enough to the ranch house he could stop by every few days and refresh her supply of food and water.

The glitch in his plan, the one element he hadn't counted on, was the inexplicable way she affected him. He couldn't be near her without feeling out of sorts. Every time he opened his mouth, out spewed harsh words. No wonder she'd hurled those accusations at him. He'd practically goaded her into losing her cool.

In the end, he'd known he had to get away from her for his sake, as much as hers, and so he'd let her drive off into the night. Alone. So much for looking after her.

A piercing cry filled the night, and he froze.

Coyote?

The shrieking rose again, higher in pitch, filled with fear. Before he realized what he was doing, he turned and raced along the trail, back to the road, toward the terror-filled scream.

****

A whisk of wind filled the air.

Hallie's attacker grunted in pain.

Her eyes flew open, and she stared, trying to make sense of the scene before her.

The man attacking her dropped his knife and cradled his hand against his bloated body. The hilt of a second knife was embedded in his shoulder, dark blood oozing onto the white cotton of his shirt. His eyes

49

locked with hers in stunned disbelief.

With a hoarse shout, Ryan jumped out of the dark and leaped on him, knocking him to the ground. He was on top of the man, pummeling him in the chest and face. Again. And again. Each blow made a sickening crunch as his fist struck its mark.

Her attacker writhed, his coarse face contorted in pain.

"¡*Ay, caramba!*"

Hallie spun, remembering the second attacker.

He stood, open mouthed, watching the vicious attack on his friend.

Heart pounding, she backed away.

He turned and met her gaze. Anger filled his dark irises, and he bared his teeth in a snarl. He lunged toward her and grabbed her arm, jerking it behind her back.

She screamed as he yanked her arm higher.

A leering grin wreathed his spittle-flecked lips. He enjoyed hurting her.

Furious outrage roared through her, and she lashed back with her free arm, smashing her elbow into his gut. She exulted at his grunt of pain.

His grip loosened.

She spun, driving her knee into his groin.

He sagged, clutching his testicles.

Before he could recover, she grabbed a rock from the edge of the road and smashed it against the side of his head.

He dropped like a felled tree and lay unmoving.

Chest heaving, she wiped the sweat from her brow, drew her foot back and kicked him in the side. "That'll teach you to mess with me, you jerk."

"Lesson learned, lady. Lesson learned."

She turned.

Ryan stood behind her, a grin plastered across his rugged face. His dimples danced. His shirt was torn, his dark hair rumpled, one eye rapidly swelling. Blood leaked from a cut on his lip.

Her heart stuttered. No man had ever looked sexier. She fought back the sudden flare of heat and tore her gaze away and studied the man lying on the ground behind Ryan. Blood seeped onto the gravel from the wound in his shoulder. One arm was bent at an unnatural angle. He wasn't moving.

"Is he…?" Her breath caught in her throat.

Ryan shook his head. "He's not dead, but he'll wish he was." He grinned. "I hit him pretty hard in a few places which are gonna hurt somethin' fierce when he comes to." Bending down, he grabbed the hilt of the knife sticking out of the fat man's shoulder and yanked it out, wiping the bloody blade on his jeans, leaving a red smear.

"How did…?" She swallowed and tried again. "How did you know I was in trouble?"

His smile widened, and he winced as the cut in his lip split open. "You have one hell of a loud scream. I wouldn't be surprised if Oren Phillips didn't hear you all the way over in Antler Springs, and he's deaf as a post."

Instead of smiling back at him, tears filled her eyes, and a sob tore at her throat.

He wrapped his strong arms around her, and pressed her against his hard body.

As the tang of male sweat, leather and something indefinable, but comforting, surrounded her, she gave in to her tears. She'd been alone and afraid for so long. The strong, steady beat of his heart reassured her. He murmured soothing words she couldn't hear, but the deep rumble of his voice melted the cold lump of fear inside her. Her tears slowed as she gave into the security of his embrace and let her mind go blessedly blank.

"Hallie, tell me, why did these scum attack you? Do you know them?"

Reality returned like a dousing of icy water. She backed away from his warmth and brushed the tangle of hair off her face, refusing to meet his probing gaze. Fingers of dread played along her spine, and a deep chill washed over her. If she hadn't truly believed she was in danger before, she did now. Someone wanted her dead. She had a pretty good idea of who and the why. The question was, what she was going to do about her precarious predicament?

"What's going on? Who are these guys?"

"I…" she began, forcing the words over the lump in her throat. "I can't tell you."

"Do these bastards have something to do with Geordie? Is an attack like this what my brother was afraid would happen?"

She didn't answer.

Anger darkened his eyes, and he swore. "Look, I nearly killed a man. Do me the courtesy of telling me why."

She shuddered at his rising ire, but she understood his anger. He'd saved her life, and she owed him the truth. Her glance flickered to the two men lying senseless in the dirt. If Ryan hadn't shown up when he had, she'd be dead. But how was she to explain what was going on and what was at stake? If she told him the truth, she'd be putting his life in danger too. But did she have a choice anymore?

Meeting his blue-eyed gaze, she took a deep breath. "Okay, you're right. You deserve to know what this is about. I'll tell you everything, but not now, not here." She motioned to the two unconscious men. "They're going to wake up soon. We need to be far away from here when they do."

He stared at her as if assessing her response, and then he nodded. "I'll take the truck and grab some rope from the line shack. We'll tie them up until the police get here."

"The truck's stuck."

He raised questioning brows.

"There was a deer. I swerved to miss it, but then I...I hit the ditch." She gulped. "There's...there's a boulder under the rear axle. I tried to shift it, but the rock's too big."

His brow furrowed. He picked up the flashlight from where it lay on the road, turned toward the vehicle and climbed into the ditch. Wading through the knee-high muddy water to the rear of the truck, he bent down and examined the boulder. He cursed and slogged through the muck to the truck's cab, opened the door, and climbed behind the wheel.

The roar of the engine filled the night, followed by the whir of the tires spinning in the quagmire. Gouts of muddy water sprayed in all directions. The truck didn't budge and the rumbling motor stopped.

In the sudden silence, she held her breath as he climbed down from the cab. "Can you get out of there?" she asked.

"Not without help. The damn thing's stuck good."

"Maybe if I drive and you push…" Her voice faded as he shook his head.

"The rock's too big. No one could move a boulder that size without a tractor."

She glanced at the unconscious men; terrified they'd wake up. "Isn't there anything you can do?"

"The truck's not going anywhere any time soon. It looks like you broke the crank shaft when you hit the rock." He wiped his hand over his brow leaving a streak of mud behind. "Jesus, lady, didn't anyone ever tell you to slow down?"

She opened her mouth to protest but stopped at the fire in his eyes. She had been driving too fast. When the deer appeared on the road in front of her, she'd braked, but slowing hadn't made any difference. The truck had skidded on the loose gravel. Now look what she'd done. She'd wrecked his truck, and left them stranded on a deserted road in the middle of nowhere with two would-be murderers for company. No wonder he was furious.

Ryan climbed out of the ditch and picked up the knife her attacker had dropped. He handed it to her. "Here. They probably won't wake up for hours, but in case they do, don't be afraid to use this."

"Where are you going? You…" she began, but her mouth was too dry to get the words out. She swallowed and tried again. "You're not going to leave me here? Alone?"

His gaze softened. "It's okay. You'll be fine. I'll be back with the rope in no time."

"But—"

"Your ankle's too sore for you to walk very far. I'll

be quicker without you." He took hold of her hand. "Look, I know you've been through hell tonight, but you have to be strong for a while longer. I'll be back before you know it."

"Please, don't leave me."

"I have to. The police need to be informed of what happened." He shrugged. "Cell phones don't work in this area. The closest phone's a few miles away at my house."

"No," she blurted. "Don't call the police."

"Why not?" He pinned her with a probing look. "These morons tried to kill you. Even in Antler Springs we call such a vicious attack attempted murder. The police will arrest them and put them away for a good long time."

Fighting to ignore the tingle racing up her arm from the touch of his warm skin on hers, she jerked her hand away and faced him, planting her hands on her hips. "You don't get it. I don't want the police to know what happened. They can't be involved." She enunciated each word clearly as if speaking to a stubborn child. "We need to get away from here. Now."

How could she make him understand the police couldn't be involved? If they knew what Geordie had done, and why these men were after her, they'd put Geordie in jail. He'd messed up big time, but he'd paid for his mistake, was still paying for his lapse in judgment. She blew out a shaky breath as she recalled Geordie's bruised and battered face the last time she'd seen him. Going to jail wouldn't solve his problems.

Ryan's eyes narrowed. "Why don't you want me to call the police?"

She'd like nothing better than to see her two

attackers punished, but retribution would come at a cost. If the police arrested them, she'd have to make a statement. They'd expect her to stay in the area while they investigated what had happened. She'd have to tell them the full story and explain the events leading to this vicious attack. But she couldn't tell them anything. She wouldn't betray Geordie. She'd promised him she'd keep quiet, and she intended to keep her promise.

"Hallie, tell me. I don't understand. Why no police?"

The silence lengthened.

In spite of the chill in the air, beads of perspiration dampened her blouse and trickled down her sides.

A moan shattered the strained silence.

She spun toward the two men lying on the ground.

The larger man's legs twitched, and the muscles in his arm flexed as he fought to rise. He groaned and sagged back onto the road, once again unconscious.

Time was running out. "You have to trust me," she said. "Don't call the police. Things will be better if you don't, better for your brother."

Ryan's blue eyes darkened.

She forced herself to remain still under his penetrating gaze, not knowing what she'd do if he insisted on involving the authorities.

"All right."

She released her breath in a whoosh of air. "Thank you."

The lines between his brows deepened. "Don't thank me. I'm not doing this for you. I'm going along with your decision for Geordie's sake. You seem to think my brother will be better off if the police aren't involved. For the moment, I'm prepared to believe you, but I damn well expect you to tell me what's going on and why you don't trust the authorities." His gaze darkened. "And, lady, your story had better be good."

She flinched at the steel in his voice. "I promise I'll tell you everything. But right now, let's get out of here before these guys wake up." She began hobbling along the road in the direction of the line shack but halted when he didn't follow. "Aren't you coming?"

"I'm trusting you, Hallie. Don't let me down."

She shuddered under the quiet threat. These past months had been difficult. She hadn't had anyone to talk to, no one with whom to share her fears. The road blurred as tears filmed her eyes. She blinked them back. Now wasn't the time for self-pity. She had to be strong. Geordie's life depended on her.

Chapter 6

The corners of Hallie's full mouth tightened with each awkward step as she limped down the road.

Ryan bunched his fists, fighting the urge to take her arm and let her lean on him for support, knowing she wouldn't want his assistance. The lines of strain furrowing her brow reflected her pain all too clearly, but she said nothing of her discomfort. He admired her strength of will.

Not calling the police was a mistake. He'd regretted his decision the second he agreed not to involve them. But when he'd seen the fear dulling her eyes, he'd crumbled. He didn't want to do anything to cause her more pain, even if his choice was the antithesis of everything he believed.

No wonder Geordie had fallen for her. When she turned the full force of her sapphire eyes on a man and fluttered those long lashes, he couldn't put two coherent thoughts together. He wanted to protect her and be her knight in shining armor. He'd taken on two armed men and beaten one to a pulp because they'd threatened her. He'd do a hell of a lot more if doing so meant her smiling at him again.

He scowled into the darkness. What the hell was he thinking? Geordie loved her, and she'd made her feelings for Geordie pretty clear. She cared for him…a lot. He sure as shit better remember she was off limits.

"What are we going to do?"

Her soft voice cut into his thoughts. "There's a short cut behind the line shack. The trail leads to my house."

"And after we get to your house?"

"I don't know. I'll think of something." If she was right, and the men who'd attacked her had followed them from the Rusty Nail, they shouldn't seek refuge at the ranch. But he needed time to think, to plan their next move. Geordie had warned him against taking Hallie there, but Ryan hadn't believed the threat was real. Until now.

He rubbed the tender, swollen lump on his jaw where the big lug had hit him. He'd seen men like them before: hired muscle, who blindly followed orders and thought nothing of raping, maiming and killing. Hallie had indicated they weren't the only goons looking for her and Geordie. If so, she and his brother were in some deep shit.

He gritted his teeth, ignoring the stab of pain from his split lip. He'd promised his brother he'd look after Hallie, and what had he done? Not a damn thing. Since he'd met her, she'd sprained her ankle, driven his truck into a ditch and nearly been killed by the men from whom he was supposed to protect her. Oh, yeah. He was doing a great job.

She stumbled and yelped in pain.

Cursing, he scooped her in his arms. He'd had enough of her stubborn independence.

"What are you doing?" she demanded. "Put me down. I can manage on my own."

"Really? From where I'm standing, you're doing a piss poor job of it." He tightened his hold, keeping her still. "Look, stop fighting me. You're in no condition to walk. Let me help you." He'd promised Geordie he'd look after her. It was time he started.

She stopped squirming. "You're right," she said, her voice almost a whisper. "I was slowing us down. Thank you for helping me."

He blinked at her sudden capitulation. Once again she'd surprised him. From the moment he met her, she'd made clear her stubborn determination to do this on her own and not accept any help, especially from him.

"This whole thing is my fault," she said.

"How do you figure?"

She sighed, the motion pressing a soft breast against his chest.

He sucked in his breath.

"Those men who attacked me know you're helping me now," she said. "They won't forget what you did. I didn't want anyone else involved in my...my problem."

"I was involved the second my brother phoned and asked for my help."

"I ran from you and sprained my ankle, and I drove your truck into a ditch." Her voice thickened. "If you hadn't shown up and stopped those men, I don't even want to think what would have happened back there."

A rush of warmth washed over him. "You'd have done fine without me." She was anything but helpless. He'd never forget the sight of her kneeing the fat brute right in the nuts. The fierce look on her beautiful face was something to behold.

They fell into silence, and he focused on the road, trying not to stumble and jar her ankle. Each step was a strain, but not from the effort of carrying her. He hardly noticed her weight. The constant brush of her breasts and the warmth of her thighs as they pressed against his body drove him crazy. Her scent surrounded him, making him dizzy, and he lurched.

"Are you okay?" she asked. "You can put me down now. I can walk the rest of the way on my own."

Her soft, husky voice added to his troubles. "I'm sure you can," he said, "but it's quicker this way." He hurried his steps and breathed a sigh of relief when the towering outline of the barn and beyond, his house, appeared.

After what had to be the longest two hundred yards of his life, he stepped onto the porch and lowered her into a wicker chair. "Wait here. Let me check and see if everything's okay."

He breathed a sigh of relief as he entered the cool, dark interior. He'd told her only part of the truth. Making certain the house was empty was a priority, but more importantly, he needed distance from her. She struck a nerve deep inside him and made him feel emotions he hadn't experienced in a very long time, things he shouldn't be feeling, especially, not with her. He didn't bother to turn the lights on, needing the cool darkness to settle his senses.

The house was empty. Before he'd left for the Rusty Nail, he'd given the housekeeper the night off, and no one else lived here. His crew of ranch hands stayed in the bunkhouse out back, but he hadn't replaced the two who'd quit, and the remaining three men were gone tonight as well. Moving along the hallway, he entered the dark kitchen and sagged against the wall. He slid to the floor and rubbed his hands over his face.

Hallie Harkins was a complication he didn't want or need right now. He scrubbed harder, the rasp of his beard loud in the quiet kitchen. What in the hell was he going to do? He'd promised his brother he'd help her. He snorted. Helping Geordie always involved trouble. So why was he surprised this time wasn't any different? He was in trouble all right. He was in shit up to his eyeballs.

If he didn't get control of his attraction for Hallie, he was going to do something he'd regret. His brother trusted him to keep her safe. He couldn't, *wouldn't* betray his trust. No matter what Geordie might have done.

"Ryan?" Her hesitant call echoed through the house.

With a resigned sigh, he stood and called, "I'm in the kitchen."

****

Hallie edged toward the sound of his voice, feeling her way in the dim light of the newly risen moon shining through the large windows. She paused at the entrance to what, judging by the lingering aromas of cinnamon and fresh baked bread, had to be the kitchen. She peered into the dark void. "Ryan?"

A light flicked on.

She squinted against the sudden glare.

He was leaning against the wall, his arms crossed over his chest, his expression bleak.

"Is everything all right?" she asked.

He nodded. "Just peachy."

She ignored his sarcasm. She needed his help. It didn't take a genius to know the men who'd attacked her would be after them as soon as they recovered. "Do you have another vehicle?" she asked.

"Why?"

"Those men aren't finished with us. They must know you're Geordie's brother. They'll figure out where we are soon. We need to be long gone before they find us again."

His eyes narrowed, his piercing gaze meeting hers. "Are you going to tell me what this is all about?"

She nodded. "But the story will have to wait until we're somewhere safe."

His brow furrowed, and a pulse ticked a steady beat in his jaw.

"Look, I told you I'd explain everything, but we don't have time now. You have to see we can't be here when those men come looking for us. We might not get away the next time."

"Make the time," he said. "I'm not moving until I know what's going on." He dragged a chair away from the table and sat, stretching out his long legs and leaning back as if they had all the time in the world. "Go ahead, Hallie. I'm waiting."

She bit her lip. "We have to get out of here."

"*I* don't have to go anywhere. No one's after me."

His gaze pierced her and she gulped. "Look, some extremely nasty men are looking for me. You saw them. You saw how determined they are." Tears of frustration stung her eyes. "Don't you get it? I can't stay here."

"You're free to go anytime you want. No one's holding you."

Their eyes met, and she tried not to flinch under the challenge in his blue depths. She opened her mouth to disagree, but one look at the tight line of his mouth and the pulse ticking in his jaw convinced her arguing would be a waste of time.

She sighed. "I'll tell you everything, but if those goons kill me, it'll be all your fault."

Her irritation increased when the corners of his mouth quirked in a smile.

"Lady, if those thugs kill you, I promise I'll take full responsibility. Now spill."

She wanted to slap the smirk off his handsome face, but she wanted to live more than she wanted to teach him a lesson, and since he was her sole means of getting away from this place, she kept her hands by her sides. But she couldn't resist one last dig. "It's amazing how two brothers can be so different. Geordie's always kind and caring, a real gentleman." She left the rest unsaid, her meaning more than clear.

His smirk vanished, and a spurt of satisfaction filled her.

"And I'm what…an arrogant, uneducated, country bumpkin who's jealous of my more successful, younger brother?"

Guilt assailed her as he repeated her earlier insult. "You said it, I didn't." Her face flamed at the childish insult. Two minutes with him and she acted like a spoiled brat. She regarded his closed expression. Did she see a flash of hurt? Even before the awareness of his vulnerability fully formed his face reset into its usual hard lines.

An awkward silence descended, broken by the steady tick tock of the clock on the wall and the electric hum of the large, stainless steel refrigerator.

He stared out the window at the darkness beyond, his shoulders stiff. A pulse in his jaw ticked in time to the beat of the clock.

"Look, I'm sorry," she said.

"It's okay. I get it. You've been more than clear. I'm nothing like Geordie."

He turned and faced her, and she was struck by the forlorn look in his eyes. "Ryan…" she began, wanting to make amends but unsure how to take back the insults she'd spat.

He cut her off. "Forget it."

"But—"

"I said, forget it."

She opened her mouth to try again but changed her mind. The men after them would be here soon. She needed Ryan. No matter how infuriating he was, she needed him. The stubborn set of his jaw made it clear he wouldn't budge until she told him what he wanted to know. Time was running out. "Okay, you win." She sat on a chair and ran her fingers through her tangled hair.

His blue eyes fixed on her with an unnerving intensity belying his careless slouch.

"This whole fiasco began two months ago. Geordie and I were—"

"Get down." He grabbed her arm and dragged her to the floor, throwing his body on top of her.

"Wha…?" she sputtered.

A thunderous roar silenced further words.

In the next second, all hell let loose as the kitchen window shattered, spraying shards of glass like deadly missiles across the room.

Hallie burrowed into the protection of Ryan's large body.

Another bullet struck the table above them, thudding into the wood. A vase on the counter burst into a thousand pieces. The storm of bullets stopped as suddenly as it began.

In the ensuing silence, her breath rasped in and out like a freight train.

Ryan eased off her, prying her fingers from his arm.

"No," she protested, tightening her grip. "No."

He placed two fingers over her mouth silencing her protests. "Shhhh. It's all right. I'm going to turn off the light. We're sitting ducks with it on."

She tightened her hold on him, refusing to let go.

His warm breath fanned her cheek. "It's okay, Hallie. I'll be right back. I promise." He pulled free of her clinging grasp, scrambled to the far wall and flicked off the light switch.

Darkness descended, and with it the balm of sanity returned. She sucked in several lungs full of air and sat up, smoothing the hair off her face.

Ryan was back at her side an instant later, taking her hand and helping her to her feet. She bit back a moan as her foot hit the floor jarring her injured ankle.

"We can't stay here," he said, his voice a hoarse whisper. "Can you walk?"

She winced at the unrelenting ache in her ankle, but nodded.

"Good girl. Come on. Let's get out of here." He led her into the hallway and across to another room.

She stumbled behind him in the darkness, flinching as she bumped against something hard with a soft, springy top. A bed. His bed? An unsettling rush of warmth flooded her before she squelched the images the thought of his bed entailed.

They crept across the room.

A click of a latch and the rush of cool air. He'd opened a door.

They stepped outside onto some sort of patio, the large paving stones uneven beneath her feet.

He halted, dragging her down beside him.

She strained to hear over the thudding of her heart. The night was silent. Where was the gunman? Was there only one? Had he seen them leave the house? Where were they going? A dozen questions raced through her mind, but she knew better than to ask them aloud. Their continued silence meant life.

"Keep low and follow me," he whispered and took off into the darkness.

She hobbled after him, keeping his dark shape in sight.

He ran toward a large building and waited for her to catch up. Motioning for her to follow, he slid along the side of the building to a door, opened it, and stepped inside.

She stayed right behind him as she stumbled through the door. The darkness was too deep to see anything, but the distinctive odors of oil and gasoline stung her nostrils. They were in a garage of some sort. In the next second, she winced and squeezed her eyes shut against a sudden blare of light. When she opened them again, she blinked as her eyes adjusted to the brightness.

They were in a large, high-ceilinged room. Three closed, bay doors were set against one wall. There didn't seem to be any windows in the garage to allow the light to escape and give away their location. A large, shiny, black four-wheel drive SUV towered over her, the bulky outline dominating the entire garage, dwarfing the glistening red, low-slung, sports car parked beside it.

"These are yours?" she asked, struggling to connect these luxury vehicles with the battered four-wheeled drive pickup he'd been driving earlier.

"Are you surprised a simple rancher can afford them?"

A guilty flush heated her face, as he'd read her mind so clearly. She started to apologize, but then she glanced at the gleaming, high-priced vehicles and fear settled like a lump of congealed fat in her gut. "Oh, no!"

"Come on, Hallie. How hard can it be for you to admit you were mistaken? Not all ranchers are struggling. Some of us do quite well for ourselves."

"No...it's not that." She pointed to the SUV's over-sized tires. "Look."

The heavy vehicle rested on its shiny, chrome rims, all four tires flat.

She looked at the sports car and groaned. "*All* the tires are flat. On both vehicles."

Ryan's mouth tightened into a grim line as he examined first one tire and then the others. "Someone slashed them."

Dread coursed through her. These vehicles were their means of escape. "Can you fix the tires?"

He shook his head. "We don't have time. Whoever shot at us made sure we'd be stuck here."

"I don't get it. The men who attacked me on the road didn't have guns. They would have used them if they had."

"These aren't the same men."

"What?"

"Think about it." His gaze met hers. "We beat up those jerks. I know I broke the big one's arm, and the way you kneed the fat one in the nuts made things pretty certain he won't be up and walking around anytime soon." He shook his head. "This is someone else."

"I told you we had to get out of here, but you wouldn't listen." Fear had a hold on her, and she couldn't stop lashing out. "You refused to leave. Now look at the mess we're in. We're going to be shot, and it'll all be your fault."

"Not taking time to explain wouldn't have made a difference. They were already here waiting for us."

She bit her lip tasting blood as the cold weight of his words washed over her. "How could they have known I'd come here? No one knew about Antler Springs. No one knew I was supposed to meet Geordie here."

He met her gaze, his eyes narrowing. "Someone did."

She hadn't told anyone of her plan to meet Geordie at the Rusty Nail. How could she? She couldn't trust anyone. No one knew she'd be in Antler Springs on this date, except…She blew out a breath. "No, you're wrong. I don't believe it. Geordie wouldn't betray me. Never."

"This wouldn't be the first time he stabbed someone in the back to get what he wanted."

She shook her head at the terrible possibility he presented. He was wrong. Geordie was her friend. He wouldn't tell anyone where she was.

"Get in."

Ryan's urgent command broke through her turmoil.

He was sitting in the driver's seat of the SUV.

"What are you doing?" she asked. "The tires are flat. We can't go anywhere."

"Get in, now."

She started to protest, but a flicker out of the corner of her eye drew her attention, and she froze.

A man, clad all in black, stood in the garage, holding a massive gun pointed at her.

She yelped and flew across the few feet to the SUV, launching herself through the open back door.

A bullet smashed into the side of the vehicle.

She screamed, ducking for cover.

"Hang on." Ryan put the SUV in gear. The massive vehicle lurched forward, spinning on its flattened tires, but gaining momentum and plowing across the floor of the garage, its powerful engine roaring.

The closed garage doors loomed in front of them.

She choked on her breath. Ducking, she covered her face as the heavy vehicle smashed into the doors, crashing through in a burst of splintering wood and wrenching metal.

The SUV dug into the driveway's soft ground and surged ahead, sending a spray of gravel into the air behind. The headlights revealed another man dressed in black clothing standing in the vehicle's path.

Ryan accelerated.

The powerful vehicle roared straight for their attacker.

The man remained motionless, his feet planted firmly apart, the gun raised, pointed at them. The deadly intent in his face was clear in the bright headlights.

"Stop," she yelled. "He's going to shoot."

****

Ryan ignored her and kept his foot on the gas pedal.

A flash of light blazed nanoseconds before the windshield spidered into a dozen, fine cracks.

He didn't stop; to do so, meant certain death. Gritting his teeth, he steered the SUV toward the man standing in their path.

The gunman jumped. Too late. The SUV's shiny front fender caught him and tossed him spinning into the night.

Refusing to think of how he'd run down a man in cold blood, Ryan kept his foot pressed to the gas pedal as they careened down the gravel lane.

"Did we…did we hit him?"

He glanced in the rear view mirror.

Hallie was peering over the back of the seat, her face pale, lips trembling.

"No," he lied, "he jumped out of the way at the last minute. We only scared him."

"How far can we drive with four flat tires?"

"Not far. The rims won't hold up long."

As if agreeing with him, the vehicle shuddered, and under the scream of the laboring engine, the grinding of metal on metal pierced the air. "Come on. Just a little further," he urged. He glanced in the rear view mirror but saw no sign of anyone pursuing them.

The faint shape of a large building loomed ahead in the darkness. He breathed a sigh of relief.

The squeal of protesting metal grew louder. In spite of the racing motor, the massive vehicle slowed as the rims collapsed.

He steered the SUV behind a copse of trees,

knowing even as he did so, trying to hide a vehicle this size was a futile gesture. But his actions might buy them time, and time was what they were in desperate need of right now.

Chapter 7

"We're going to do what?" Hallie gaped at the horse towering over her and fought to keep the tremble out of her voice.

"Do you want to stay here?"

"No, but—"

"Do you have a better suggestion?"

"No, but—"

"Okay then, let's go. Mount up." He'd saddled two horses and now held the reins of one, waiting for her to climb onto the saddle.

She stared at the huge horse.

The animal shook its head and snorted, shifting its massive feet.

She flinched; terrified the horse would trample her.

"You do know how to ride, don't you?"

"Of course." She glanced at Ryan and prayed he wouldn't spot her lie. She considered confessing the truth, admitting the one time she'd been on a horse was when she was six years old. Even then, her grandfather had held the reins and led her around the corral in unending circles, until she'd grown queasy from bouncing up and down and thrown up all over the saddle. She gulped at the rigid lines of his face. Any plans of telling him the truth vanished. She wasn't prepared to give him one more reason to resent having to look after her.

Taking a deep breath, she studied the waiting horse. There wasn't a choice. With all of the vehicles on the ranch out of commission, they were left with the horses to make their escape. They had to either ride the horses or drive the harvester, or so Ryan had explained to her. Horses were a lot faster than a tractor. Besides, riding the horses meant they wouldn't have to stick to roads. Traversing cross-country would make their trail more difficult to follow.

"Come on," he urged. "Let's go."

"Okay, okay, give me a second." She took a shaky step closer, wiping her sweaty palms on her pants. Up close, the animal was enormous.

Ryan held the horse steady.

Placing one foot in the stirrup, she heaved herself up into the saddle, landing with a thump.

The horse nickered in protest.

She clutched the saddle horn, terrified the animal would run. When the horse remained motionless, she laughed shakily and sat up, shoving her hair out of her eyes.

"Are you sure you know how to ride?"

She forced a chuckle. "I'm a bit shaky. Who wouldn't be after getting shot at?"

He continued to watch her, his eyes narrowed.

She affected an air of confidence.

He shook his head but handed her the reins. In one fluid motion, he mounted his own horse. "Stay close and follow me. I know the trail." With a last probing look, he turned and spurred his horse out the barn door and across the corral.

She grabbed again for the horn, but the animal kept to an easy walk. After a few minutes, she relaxed. This wasn't so bad. Maybe she'd be okay after all.

Ryan's horse shifted to a canter and then a gallop.

Her horse followed.

Thrown backwards, she lost her grip on the horn. She dug her fingers into the rough hair of the mane and hung on. Her arms ached, and her thighs cramped from gripping the sides of the racing animal. She moaned as her bottom smashed again and again on the saddle's unforgiving hardness. Closing her eyes, she prayed this ordeal would soon end.

An eternity later, her horse slowed.

Her relief transformed to a groan as the horse's gait changed from a relatively smooth gallop to a vigorous up and down trot. The constant bouncing unsettled her stomach. If they kept this up, she was going to throw up. She gulped mouthfuls of fresh air and swallowed back bile. Suddenly, the jarring stopped, and she raised her head and peered around.

No sign of Ryan or his horse.

She'd been so busy hanging on she hadn't seen where he'd gone.

"You lied to me, didn't you?"

Ryan's accusing voice broke through her misery. She blinked past a curtain of tangled hair.

He rode toward her through the trees. His eyes blazed. If he gritted his teeth any harder, they'd crack.

She couldn't for the life of her figure out why he was so angry. Hadn't she done everything he'd asked? She'd climbed on this damned horse and let him take her God knows where. What more did he want from her?

"Aren't you going to say anything?" His voice was icy, a sharp contrast to the blast of heat in his eyes.

"Say what? Do you want me to say you were right?" She sat up in the saddle and frowned. "Okay, I lied. Is that what you want to hear? I don't have a clue how to ride a horse. In fact, they scare the living daylights out of me." She dared him to say something. "Are you happy now?"

"You little fool. Why didn't you tell me? You could have been killed." He dragged his fingers through his hair. "If I'd known, I could have helped you."

She snorted. "Help me? How? We had to ride the horses. We didn't have a choice. Riding was the only way to get away from the men shooting at us. You said so yourself."

He guided his mount beside hers, grabbed her by the waist and slid her off her horse and across to his, setting her on the saddle before him, her back against the firm wall of his chest. His thighs cradled her hips. He tied her horse's reins to his saddle.

"Wha...what do you think you're doing?" she sputtered, not liking the way her heart raced at his all too familiar scent surrounding her. She shoved against him, trying to escape the unnerving warmth of his body.

He placed his hands on her hips, keeping her still and growled in her ear. "You'd be well advised to stop squirming, unless you're offering an invitation."

Heat flooded her face, but she bit back an angry retort and stopped fighting, holding her body stiff and unmoving.

He chuckled.

Her face flamed hotter. She bit her bottom lip, knowing anything she said would only make matters worse.

They rode in strained silence, each mile taking her

further from civilization and the safety of other people. She reflected on all the events from the first moment she'd stepped inside the Rusty Nail Bar 'n Grill in Antler Springs. Was it only a few hours ago? So much had happened since then.

Spraining her ankle had been her fault. She shouldn't have run from Ryan, but at the time she'd been frightened, and fleeing had seemed the sensible thing to do. She knew differently now. He wasn't her enemy. If it weren't for him, she'd be dead. He'd endangered his life to save hers, first on the road against the two, knife-wielding thugs and later at his house when the gunmen had shot at them.

Even now, he risked his life by staying and helping her. He was the most infuriating man she'd ever met, but he had saved her life. "Thank you," she said, breaking the silence.

"For what?"

She sighed. She should have known he wasn't going to make this easy. "You saved my life tonight. Twice."

Once again silence ensued, broken by the steady tread of the horses on the rough ground. An owl hooted in the surrounding trees.

"Don't get any ideas," Ryan finally said. "I'm not your knight in shining armor. I promised my brother I'd look after you. That's all this is. Nothing more."

Her face flamed. "Why you arrogant—" He cut her off before she let loose the string of insults burning the tip of her tongue.

"Easy now, Hallie. Remember what Thumper the Rabbit said, 'If you can't say something nice, don't say nothing at all.'" He chuckled. "I may not be the man you'd like me to be, but you need me. So, you'd better sit back, relax, and let me work on saving your cute little tush." He wrapped his arms around her, pressing her against his chest, the butt in question jammed into the vee of his thighs.

She stiffened and shifted away from his touch, but the tight confines of the saddle left little room for escape. The muscles in his lean thighs cupped her between them. Her breath hitched in her throat. She wanted to strike out, to tell him exactly what she thought of his conceit, but a sudden tiredness overwhelmed her. She didn't have the energy to fight him anymore. Besides, he was right. She did need him. Warmth from his body seeped into hers, and she sank back against him, her body molding to his. She yawned.

The sudden stillness wakened her, and she opened her eyes. The first faint pink streaks of dawn were visible over the distant hills. She stretched and rubbed her face, trying to break free of the thick layer of cotton enfolding her.

She was snuggled against Ryan's body, her head nestled against his chest. His arms enveloped her, one hand resting on her thigh. The heat from his touch burned through the thin denim of her jeans, scorching her skin. She examined his hand, so tanned and broad, so strong. Her breath quickened as she trailed a shaking finger over a thin, jagged scar running across three of his knuckles.

The horse snorted, and the haze surrounding her vanished. Reality intruded, and she snatched her finger away from his hand and lurched up. She shoved his hand off her thigh. A quick glance at Ryan confirmed her worst suspicions.

The corners of his mouth were quirked in a knowing grin.

She slid forward until the saddle's pommel dug into her stomach, but mere inches separated their bodies. Her skin tingled from where his hand had rested as if its imprint were branded there. She rubbed her thigh.

He chuckled, a deep rumble emanating from his chest.

Her face burned. "Where are we?" she asked, wincing at her breathlessness. They'd left the open prairie behind and were in an area of rolling hills and towering pines. "How long was I asleep?" Her breath formed a frosty cloud of vapor with each syllable she uttered. Mountains loomed in the distance, their jagged peaks encrusted with a veil of freshly-fallen snow. She shivered. "Why are we stopping here?"

"The horses need a rest." He slid off the horse and lifted her from the saddle, lowering her to the ground.

She staggered as her legs wobbled, but he held her steady.

"Easy," he said. "We covered a lot of ground last night." His voice was surprisingly gentle. "Your legs will need some time to recover."

Before she could protest, he lifted her as if she weighed nothing and carried her across the small clearing, setting her on the ground beneath a large tree. His carrying her was becoming a habit. She didn't enjoy feeling like a burden, but she needed his help. She doubted she could take a single step on her own.

She sank onto the bed of dry, pine needles, biting back a groan. Who knew riding a horse hurt so much? At least the pain in her legs made her forget her

C. B. Clark

throbbing ankle. "I need a few minutes' rest," she said, "then I'll be fine."

Ryan snorted.

Her face flamed, but she bit her tongue. Let him smirk. When it was time to mount the horse again, she'd be ready. Even if getting on the damn thing killed her.

He led the horses to a nearby stream and allowed them to drink.

"Where are we heading?" she asked.

"A friend of mine owns a place in the mountains. His house is pretty remote. We should be safe there."

"Do you think those men are still after us?"

"I don't know. I can't see how they could follow us, but who knows? I guess it depends how determined they are to find you."

He turned toward her and she gasped. The bright, early morning light revealed the ravages of the past hours. Lines of strain scored his rugged face. One of his eyes was swollen almost shut, and the purple stain of a bruise marred his cheek. The cut on his bottom lip had scabbed over but looked sore. Shadows darkened the skin beneath his eyes. The dark stubble on his cheeks didn't hide his skin's pallor.

She blinked back the sting of tears. His injuries and his exhaustion were her fault. Once again she found herself apologizing. "I'm sorry you're involved in this."

He tied the reins to a tree allowing the horses to graze on the lush green grass and sat beside her, his back resting against the trunk of the tree, his shoulder brushing hers. "Don't you think it's time you told me what's going on?" he asked.

"All right, but I hope I'm not making a mistake.

The last thing I want is for you to get involved any deeper than you already are."

"Don't you think it's a little late? I'm in this up to my neck. I was the second my brother called asking me for help." He patted her knee. "Now come on. I can't help you if I don't know what we're facing."

She swallowed over the lump in her throat, watching the horses graze through a blur of tears. His calm acceptance of the danger they faced lent her strength. She sniffed and wiped her eyes. He deserved to know the truth, but before she could speak, he jumped to his feet and loomed over her, his eyes blazing.

"Look, I'm tired of all this, damned tired," he said. "Either you tell me everything, or I'm out of here."

His unexpected anger silenced her, and she stared, her mouth working like a fish out of water.

He blew out a breath. "Okay, have it your way." He strode across the clearing to his horse and untied the reins.

Panic filled her at the realization he was leaving. "Wait, please." She didn't want to be alone. Not anymore. In spite of his almost constant irritation with her, she trusted him. "I'll tell you everything. I will, I promise."

He slowly retied the reins and walked back to her.

She breathed a sigh of relief.

He stood, arms crossed in front of his chest, towering over her.

She had to crane her head back to meet his gaze.

A pulse twitched in his jaw, and a furrow carved between his brows. Two patches of red stained his rugged cheeks easing his pallor. "Go ahead. I'm listening," he said.

She took a deep breath. "Geordie and I work together. We're friends."

He snorted.

Her irritation flared, but she swallowed it back. She'd tell him everything, no matter if he believed her or not. "As I said, we're friends. We met at work, at Duncan Krantz Associates in Seattle."

His dark brows rose in a silent question, and she hurried to explain.

"Duncan Krantz is an import/export company, specializing in merchandise from Mexico and Central America. Geordie's been with the company for over a year, and already he's been promoted to section manager. The boss thinks a great deal of him. Everyone does. He's always so cheerful and friendly. It's impossible not to like him."

"Trying too hard is part of Geordie's problem," Ryan said. "He's too well-liked, especially by women. His flirting always gets him in trouble."

Before she stopped herself, the damning words blurted out. "You're jealous of him."

"Not likely. I've spent too damn much time getting him out of one bad situation after another. Every time Geordie turns around, he's in trouble." He ran his fingers through his hair, rumpling the glossy locks. "Is that what this is? Is this more woman trouble?"

"Woman trouble?" She rolled her eyes. "What are you, a hundred years old? What sort of *woman trouble* do you think he's in?"

His knowing gaze connected with hers.

She flushed. "You have the wrong idea. Geordie and I..." She paused, uncertain how to explain her and

Geordie's relationship. "Well, we aren't the romantic sort of friends, at least not anymore."

He continued to watch her closely.

Heat rose higher in her face. "We aren't."

"Whatever you say." The ticking in his jaw became more pronounced. "Now cut the crap. Just tell me. What has he done?"

She'd promised him she'd tell him what was going on, and she wouldn't go back on her word, but he wasn't making keeping her promise easy. "Three months ago, Geordie and I were part of a team sent to Acapulco for a sales convention. All the big import/export firms had people attending. On our last night of the conference, Geordie and I strolled along the beach outside our hotel. The night was beautiful. There was a full moon and the stars were so bright. We had the beach to ourselves. It was perfect until two men approached us." She swallowed, her mouth dry. "Those men who attacked me last tonight? They were the same two men."

His eyes narrowed.

"They seemed to know Geordie," she continued. "They called him by name." She paused, staring into the distance as she recalled the shocking confrontation then and the ensuing events. Even now she could hear the crashing waves and smell the salty, humid warmth of the Acapulco night when the two men had approached her and Geordie.

"Hola, amigo. *It has been a long time since we last talked," said one of the men.*

She shuddered at the cold flatness in his dark eyes. Even though his tone was friendly, his mouth curled in a cruel sneer.

A second, taller, more muscular man remained silent, his eyes watching. A scar marred his face, adding to his menace.

"Geordie?" she asked. "What's going on? Do you know these men?"

He ignored her, facing the two men. "What do you want?" *His voice was harsh, betraying his underlying fear.*

"What do you think we want, Señor Marshall?" *The taller of the two men chuckled, the sound harsh over the crashing waves.*

"I told your boss I needed more time."

The man smiled, exposing crooked, yellow teeth. "I guess he thinks you have had plenty of time already."

Warm, garlic-scented breath brushed the back of her neck. The shorter man had circled behind her and now stood so close she smelled his cloying after-shave. She shifted away, but he grabbed her arm, his fingers digging into her flesh. "Get your hands off me." *She tugged her arm.*

His grip tightened, and he drew her closer, his belly brushing against her back, his hips cradling her bottom.

"Geordie?" *His name came out in a high-pitched squeal.*

"Let her go," *Geordie said.* "She's not involved in this."

"She is with you, is she not, amigo?" *The tall man leered at her breasts. He licked his fleshy lips.* "She is fair game then."

She squirmed against the bald man holding her, bile rising in her throat.

He chuckled and ran a callused finger along her

84

cheek, lingering on her mouth. "Que tierna eres. *I bet she tastes sweet too."*

"I said, let her go." Geordie lunged at the man holding her.

In the next instant, the taller man grabbed him, yanking his arms behind his back.

Geordie's face lost what little color it had. "You bastards!"

"There, there. No need to get so upset, amigo. *We are not here to cause trouble. Consider this a friendly warning. If you do not deliver as you promised, this pretty little* chica *is gonna pay the price." The man grinned and winked at her, his eyes cold.*

Hallie's flesh crawled.

The Mexican threw Geordie onto the sand with enough force he grunted in pain at the impact.

The muscle-bound thug holding her released her.

Without another word, both men turned and strode away, disappearing into the darkness.

Silence descended. The only sounds the steady rhythm of the incoming surf and the wind in the palm trees lining the deserted beach.

She sucked in a shuddering breath, fighting back nausea as she searched the darkness, fearing the men's return. The beach was empty. They'd gone. She sank onto the cool, damp sand beside Geordie.

He lay on his side, curled in a ball, as if anticipating a blow, his eyes squeezed shut.

"Geordie? What…" she began but had to take a steadying breath before she could continue. "What did those men want with you? What's going on?"

He scrubbed his hands over his face and through his hair, and lurched to his feet.

"Geordie?"

"Nothing. It was nothing."

"What did they want? Should we call the police?"

The threat of getting the local police involved got his attention.

"We're not calling the police."

"Why not? Those men threatened you. They...they scared me."

He shook his head again, his blond curls tumbling around his boyish features. "We're not calling the police." He turned toward her, his face haggard. "Look, I need you to trust me."

"Wha—"

"I mean it, Hallie. The less you know about this, the better."

She drew in a steadying breath as the memory of the night in Acapulco slowly faded. "He refused to say anything more, though I could tell he was frightened. We walked back to our hotel. The next morning we caught our flight home, and he never mentioned the incident."

"Did those men approach you again?"

She shook her head.

Ryan's face was thoughtful, his brow furrowed. "And you have no idea what they wanted with my brother?"

"Not then, no."

"What do you mean, not then?"

"There's more, a lot more."

His eyes narrowed as they drilled into hers. "You'd better tell me everything."

Chapter 8

The pounding on the door startled her awake. Hallie opened bleary eyes and peered at the clock. It was after midnight. A grainy black and white movie played on the television, the sound muted.

Again the loud hammering sounded on her door.

She stood, dragging a blanket with her, stumbled to the door and peered through the security lens. She gasped. Her fingers fumbled with the dead bolt, and she threw open the door. "Oh, my God. What happened to you?"

Geordie staggered into the room. The light from the front hall struck his face.

"My God. Your face."

His eyes were mere slits, the skin dark and swollen. An ugly looking gash leaking a steady stream of blood ran across one cheek. One side of his mouth was grotesquely swollen. An angry purple bruise marred his chin. Blood dripped from a wound on the back of his hand onto the shiny hardwood floor.

He sagged and would have collapsed if she hadn't grabbed his arm.

"Let's get you to the couch," she said. Taking most of his weight upon her shoulder, she maneuvered him down the hall and into the living room.

He sank onto the couch, groaning as he grabbed his ribs. Sweat beaded his brow. His face was gray.

"What happened to you?" she asked again. "Were you in a car accident?"

He shook his head, wincing at the pain the gesture caused him.

"I'm calling for an ambulance." She picked up the phone and began dialing.

"No!"

The line connected and began ringing.

"You need help," she said.

"No."

"911," the emergency operator said. "What is your emergency?"

Geordie's eyes pleaded, imploring her to hang up.

She hesitated, drawn in by his desperation.

"911. Please state your emergency."

Hallie hung up the phone.

Relief washed over Geordie's battered face. "Thank you."

"I don't know why I hung up." Her voice thickened with imminent tears. "You're hurt. You need medical attention and more help than I can give you."

He sagged against the cushions, his breathing shallow, his skin shiny with sweat and blood. "No ambulance. All I...I...need are some...bandages and maybe...some aspirin."

She shook her head. No simple bandages or over the counter pain medication would be enough to help him. He was in bad shape.

"Please?"

His husky plea cut through her indecision, and she hurried to the bathroom where she grabbed a clean cloth and the first aid kit. When she returned to the living room, her breath caught in her throat.

He lay unmoving on the couch, his skin waxen and pale. The deep purple of countless bruises and oozing red gashes a garish contrast to his ghastly pallor.

Her heart stuttered. "Geordie?"

His eyelids lifted a mere fraction as he peered through swollen slits.

Her relief was short lived. He needed a doctor. The only training she'd had in first aid was a weekend course she'd taken several years ago. Nothing she'd learned prepared her for repairing Geordie's battered face and body.

He grasped her hand, his fingers surprisingly strong as they squeezed hers. "Thanks for helping me." His grip on her hand loosened, and he once again closed his eyes, his body relaxing into the cushions.

She took a deep breath and wiped her damp palms on her pajama bottoms. "Try not to move. This is going to hurt." She grimaced at the understatement. Hurt? Cleaning him up was going to be excruciating for him.

She spent the better part of an hour washing away the blood and cleaning the many wounds on his face and hands.

He remained still and silent, his eyes closed, his breathing ragged.

At one point, she thought he'd passed out until she applied disinfectant to a particularly nasty looking cut, and he stiffened and swore.

His injuries centered on his face, but when he stirred, he groaned and grabbed his side.

He probably had broken ribs, but since he refused to let her call an ambulance, she couldn't help with any broken bones. She covered the worst wounds with gauze and tape, even though some of the cuts needed stitches. When she finished, she sat back. He didn't look much better, but at least the blood was gone, and the worst of the wounds covered.

He opened his eyes. "You got anything to drink?"

"Do you want a cup of tea? Coffee?"

"God, no. Don't you have anything stronger?"

"Are you sure you should drink alcohol? I mean, what if you have a concussion?" She'd read somewhere a person shouldn't drink if he had a head injury.

"If ever I needed a drink, now is the time." He enunciated each word slowly, with great difficulty.

She crossed the room to a cupboard and removed a bottle of rum leftover from last Christmas. Filling a glass, she returned to the couch.

Grimacing, he lurched up and grasped the glass with a shaky hand. He swallowed half the contents in a single gulp. The liquor restored some color to his face.

She waited until he'd drained the glass and then refilled it. "What happened to you?" she asked.

He met her gaze. "Do you remember those two guys we met the last night we were in Mexico? The ones on the beach outside our hotel?"

She nodded. A shiver of apprehension rippled through her.

"They're here, in Seattle. I ran into them again."

She sucked in a breath. "They did this to you?"

He nodded and winced.

"Why? What did they want?"

He took a long pull on his drink. "I took something of theirs. They want it back."

"What did you take?"

He refused to meet her gaze.

"Geordie, what did you take from them?"

"Money."

"Money?" The word reverberated in the silence of her small townhouse.

"This isn't what you think. These people are drug dealers."

Was this some sort of joke? Geordie wasn't involved with drugs. He drank alcohol, but she'd never seen him use any illegal drugs. How could he be involved with drug dealers? The guilty look on his battered face showed her the truth better than words ever could, and her heart sank. "Geordie, no."

"What I did was stupid. I know."

"Why...?"

He shrugged. "I guess I wanted to do something good for a change."

"Good? How could stealing from drug dealers do any good at all?" A new thought occurred, and her heart raced. "Wait a minute. Are you dealing drugs?"

"God, no."

"Then how...?" Her voice trailed off. Her knowledge of drugs and drug dealers was limited to what she read in the newspaper and saw on TV. She'd heard most of the drugs sold in the United States entered the country from Mexico and Central and South America. Big gangs, called drug cartels, controlled most of the drugs. "You expect me to believe you took money from drug dealers? How could you be in a position where you could steal from them? I mean, if you're not involved with drugs, what possible connection could you have with these people?"

His expression turned sheepish. "You know me. I know a lot of people. Some decent, some not so decent."

"But still...drug dealers?"

His eyes pleaded with her. "It's not what it sounds like."

"You stole money. How much worse could this be?"

"These are bad people, Hallie. They break the law every day. In the process, they make millions."

"They also destroy hundreds of lives." She couldn't keep the scorn out of her voice.

"But don't you see? Stealing from drug-dealing scum was the beauty of my plan. I was getting back at them in the one way they could hurt. For the first time in a long time, I was doing something good." His lips flexed in a parody of a smile and revealed a glimpse of his boyish charm. "I wanted to make a difference. If they didn't have money to pay for the drug shipments, they'd be out of business." Dimples flashed in his cheeks, looking incongruous amidst the bruised and battered flesh. "Besides, they couldn't go to the police and tell them they lost money they'd made selling illegal drugs, could they?"

She eyed his swollen and disfigured face. "From the looks of things, they got their revenge."

"I said it was a stupid idea."

Silence descended, broken by the sound of light traffic on the street outside. "So that's what those two men wanted in Acapulco? They wanted their money back?"

He nodded.

"Why didn't you give the money to them? Why let them do this to you?"

"I don't have it. I used the cash to pay off some of my debts, and the rest..." He shrugged.

"*You spent the money,*" *she said. It wasn't a question.*

A sheepish look swept his battered face. "*I told you, my plan was a sure thing. I couldn't lose.*"

"*But you did.*" *She sighed.* "*How did you expect to get away with stealing from them?*"

"*I didn't think they'd know I was the one who took the money.*" *He slouched, sinking further into the soft cushions.* "*Somehow, they found out, and things fell apart from there.*" *He resembled a little boy who'd been caught with his hand in the cookie jar.*

She sorted through what he'd said and realized he wasn't telling her everything. "*I don't believe you.*"

"*Why would I lie? The truth is bad enough.*"

"*Oh, I believe you stole the money, all right. What I don't believe is your explanation of why you did something so stupid.*"

He glanced away.

"*Come on, Geordie, don't you think I deserve the truth?*"

He heaved a sigh and winced, grabbing his side. Beads of sweat broke out on his forehead. "*I told you. I took the money because I wanted to get back at the damn drug cartels. They're everywhere. The police are helpless to stop them. Someone has to do something.*" *He took a breath.* "*I thought if I hit them where it hurt, I'd be doing the world a favor.*"

She examined his face, searching for signs of deception. There were none. His story made a crazy kind of sense, more sense than him being involved with a South American or Mexican drug cartel. She knew him well. He had good intentions, but sometimes he was too impulsive for his own good and acted before he

*thought things through. "And so they did this to you,"
she finally said.*

*He nodded. "I didn't think they'd hurt me, not like
this. I mean, how do they expect to get their money back
if I'm dead?"*

*"They were trying to kill you?" Cold settled in the
pit of her stomach. "They'll try again, won't they?"*

*He didn't say anything, the flash of fear in his soft
brown eyes answer enough.*

*"We have to call the police." She picked up the
phone from where she'd tossed the receiver earlier.
"We have to tell them what happened. They'll protect
you."*

"The police can't help me."

*"What do you mean? Of course, the police can
help. It's what they do."*

*His gaze settled on her. Resignation filled his eyes,
visible even through the puffy slits. "Believe me when I
tell you this. The police can't stop these crooks. I'd be
the one going to jail, not the drug cartel guys."*

*She opened her mouth to protest, but then stopped.
The newspapers were full of headlines describing street
gangs and drug dealers and their executions. Rarely
did she read of any of the culprits being caught and
sent to prison. "What are you going to do?"*

*He swallowed the last dregs of his drink and sat
up, squaring his shoulders, grimacing in pain. "I'm
leaving town."*

"You're what?"

*"I'm leaving. I have to. They're after me." He
pointed at his injured face. "This is only a sample of
what they'll do to me if they catch me again."*

"You're going to run? Leave everything? Your job,

your apartment, your friends?"

"For awhile anyway, until I can get this mess sorted out."

"How are you going to make this right? You told me you don't have their money, and you can't pay them back. What are you going to do to convince them to leave you alone?"

Instead of answering, he grabbed her hands, holding them between his own.

She glanced at his raw and swollen knuckles, evidence he'd fought back against his assailants. She scanned his face, and a lump formed in her throat. This wasn't over. His life was still in danger. If what he said was true, the drug gang wasn't finished with him.

His voice broke through her thoughts. "I came here tonight for a reason other than your excellent first aid skills." He licked his bruised lips. "Those men saw you in Mexico. They know you're my friend. They probably think we're more than friends. They'll use you to get to me."

A chill rippled along her spine. "What are you saying?"

"I want you to leave town, too."

"You want me to go with you?"

"No, There are some things I have to do. I have to make this right." His gaze pierced hers. "I want you to go away for a few months, to hide out until this mess is settled."

She couldn't believe what he said. "You want me to run away?"

He reached into his pants pocket and withdrew an envelope. "Here. It's all I could access at this time of night, but the money should last you a few months."

She studied the bulging envelope. *"You're giving me cash?"*

"This is serious, Hallie. These men mean business. They know who you are. Believe me, they'll hurt you if they can. They'll go to any lengths to get back at me."

"But I haven't done anything. I didn't even know you were involved in this mess until tonight."

"Your ignorance won't matter. They've seen you with me. They'll use you to get to me. I know how these guys work."

She opened her mouth, but no sound emerged. This was like a plot from a bad movie. He wanted her to leave town and disappear. She had a job, a job she liked, and one she was good at. She couldn't leave.

As if reading her mind, he said, "I called Grant tonight. I told him you had a family emergency and would be away for a month or so."

"You called Grant?" Grant Willoughby was the CEO of Duncan Krantz and her boss.

"He was very understanding. He said to take as long as you needed."

"You have this all worked out, don't you? Because you're in trouble, you think I'm going to run away and hide until you decide the situation's safe for me to come back." She tore her hands from his and leaped to her feet. *"Well, you can think again. No two-bit hoodlums are going to drive me from my home. This is your mistake. Not mine."*

"Come on, Hallie, don't be stupid. You're in danger here."

Before an angry retort left her lips, something smashed into the lamp at the end of the couch, tearing into the shade and shattering the bulb. She screamed as the room went dark.

Another loud explosion filled the air, and the screen on the television burst in a flash of lights and sparks. Acrid smoke filled the air.

"Get down," Geordie yelled.

She remained frozen by the couch.

He grabbed her arm and yanked her to the floor.

"What's happening?" she sputtered. "What's going on?"

"Someone's shooting at us."

"What?"

"Now do you see why you have to get out of here?"

Her breath rushed in and out so rapidly she couldn't think. "I...I don't know."

He crawled to her side.

He was a dim form in the dark. "I'll provide a distraction," he said. "You sneak into your bedroom and climb out the window, and then run like hell."

"But, my clothes—"

"Leave them. Leave everything. You can buy new clothes with the money I gave you."

Another explosion rocked the silence.

She shuddered, pressing against the couch for protection. "Where...where will I go?"

"It doesn't matter as long as it's away from here. Don't tell me where you're going. It's better if I don't know."

His words brought home the horrible reality of the nightmare. She fought an overpowering urge to flee, but she couldn't desert him. "What's going to happen to you? I can't leave you. They'll kill you."

"Don't worry about me. I'll be okay."

"But—"

"Hallie, go. Please." *Desperation riddled his voice.*

"How will I know when things are safe, and I can come back?"

He hesitated, but then said, "Look on a map, and find Antler Springs. It's a small town hiding in the shadows of the Beartooth Range of the Rocky Mountains in western Montana. There's a bar in town called the Rusty Nail Bar 'n Grill. I'll meet you there in exactly two months. One way or another, this business should be over by then."

"Geordie?"

"I promise, Hallie. I'll be there, the Rusty Nail in Antler Springs, Montana. Two months from tonight."

His gaze pierced hers.

"Now, go, before they break in here."

Every instinct urged her to run. Still she hesitated. She couldn't leave him. No matter what he'd done, he was her friend.

A bullet whined overhead, imbedding with a thud against a nearby wall.

She screamed.

"Go, now!"

Taking a deep breath, she crawled on her hands and knees across the room. At any moment, she expected the piercing agony of a bullet. She peered back into the gloom. Geordie was one more dark shape in a sea of gray.

With a fervent prayer he'd be safe, she turned, and focused on getting out of the house. She crept down the hall to the back bedroom. The last thing she heard, as she climbed over the window ledge, was the blast of a bullet and splintering wood.

Chapter 9

Ryan examined Hallie's pale, drawn face and clenched his teeth until his jaw ached. Geordie had really done it this time. This current screw-up wasn't a case of an angry husband or a wronged woman. This was bad. Real bad. Not only had Geordie put his own life in danger, but he'd risked Hallie's as well. Her description of those last terror-filled moments in her townhouse fueled his outrage. Someone had shot at them. Someone wanted his kid brother dead, wanted his death bad enough, the piece of scum was willing to risk anything to achieve his goal.

Hallie's explanation of the trouble Geordie had gotten himself into raised more questions than it answered. Why had he done such a stupid thing? How could he possibly have thought stealing money from a drug cartel would help anything? He shook his head. That was just it: Geordie didn't think. He acted, and then ran to his big brother when his actions got him into hot water.

Where had he been hiding these past two months? Why hadn't he shown up at the Rusty Nail as he'd promised Hallie? Ryan recalled the desperate fear in his brother's voice when he'd phoned him and begged him to protect Hallie.

Ever since Geordie was old enough to crawl, he'd been getting into trouble. This latest fiasco was more of the same, but on a vastly different scale. *Drugs.* The word left a bitter taste in his mouth. As far as he knew, his little brother had never been involved in drugs. At least, not the heavy duty ones. Surely, Ryan would have known if he were. He grimaced and rubbed at a painful band of tightness forming in his forehead as a headache bloomed to life.

What was he thinking? Geordie could have been using crack cocaine daily, and Ryan wouldn't have known. He didn't know his brother. Not anymore. He hadn't seen him in almost two years. Two years without any phone calls or communication of any kind. A person can change a lot in two years.

Geordie was capable of deception. He'd made his deviousness clear during his last trip home. Ryan still seethed from the repercussions of his visit. The pounding in his head grew worse. He reached in his jacket pocket for a cigarette but stopped. Damn! He'd crushed his last pack the previous night. He'd kill for a smoke.

"Do you think Geordie's all right? I mean, I know he didn't meet me last night as we'd planned, but he did call you. He's okay, right?"

Hallie's worried voice cut through his turmoil. He blinked back his frustration and studied her pale face. Her lower lip trembled. Tears glistened in her eyes.

A fresh onslaught of outrage fired through him. Geordie was a king-sized ass. He'd put Hallie through a hell of a lot these past months; yet, for some insane reason, she still cared about him. Was she telling the truth? Were they just friends? Was a platonic friendship with a woman even possible for a guy like Geordie?

He regarded her creamy skin, full lips, and vivid

blue eyes rimmed by impossibly long lashes. She was one hell of an attractive woman. He couldn't imagine his brother being *friends* with a woman like her. Geordie would have taken one look at the blonde-haired beauty, turned on his charm, and the rest would be history. Females fell for his brother. All females. All the time. Ryan had seen the same scenario play out again and again. Hallie Harkins was no different.

"Ryan? What is it? What's wrong?" she asked.

He pinned her with a hard gaze. "Are you involved in this mess, too?"

"I already told you. I didn't know anything about the money he took until he informed me the night he showed up at my townhouse."

"You've told me everything you know? You're sure?"

"Why are you questioning me? What more do you want me to tell you? Your brother's in danger. Isn't his safety more important than giving me the third degree?"

"You didn't know Geordie stole money from this gang?"

"Not until he told me." Her eyes narrowed. "Why don't you believe me?"

"You said you and Geordie were friends."

She nodded, her eyes wary.

"I find it hard to believe you wouldn't know what your *friend* was up to. I mean, if you're as good a friend with my brother as you say you are. If he was involved with drugs, it would make sense you were too."

"What are you implying? Do you think I'm a drug addict? Or worse, involved with a Mexican drug cartel?" Her eyes blazed.

He knew his suspicions were baseless. No one

could look as good as she did if she were using drugs. But some perverse devil inside him prodded him, and the next thing he knew, he said, "You said it, not me."

She jumped to her feet, her body bristling. "You're being ridiculous. Geordie and I are friends," she spat. "Do you get it? Friends. I don't know what he did when he wasn't with me. His activities weren't any of my business. When I saw him, he was my friend, charming and kind. He was fun to be around. That's all I cared about."

He snorted.

"What is it with you?" she asked. "Why can't you accept your brother and I are good friends and nothing more?"

A bitter laugh escaped his lips. "Because I know my brother. Geordie never has female friends. With Geordie, women are a game. His sole purpose in *befriending* them is to get them into bed, as soon as possible." He paused, breathing hard. Hallie was just another notch on his brother's bedpost, like all the other women his brother had used and dumped. How could she not see what he was like, especially after everything Geordie had put her through these past two months?

Maybe she's different. The thought slipped through his mind. Maybe Hallie was different from all the other women Geordie had had affairs with. Maybe she meant more than those other women. His brother was sure anxious to ensure her safety. Was it possible Geordie had finally fallen in love?

He rubbed his aching head. Accusing her of using drugs and lying to him wasn't getting them anywhere. The important thing was to find Geordie. His brother was in serious trouble. The men who'd attacked him and Hallie last night were the same men who were after Geordie. They wouldn't quit until either they retrieved their money or—He halted the thought before it fully formed. No matter what his brother had done, he was still his brother. Brothers watched out for each other. They had each other's back. He grimaced. At least, this brother did.

In the meantime, he had his hands full. He took in Hallie's flushed face and tousled, golden hair. She was in as much danger as Geordie. Maybe more, since the men after her had a pretty good idea where she was.

She brushed a lock of hair off her forehead. The movement tightened her shirt, revealing her full, rounded breasts.

He fought to swallow, his mouth arid dry, and tore his gaze from the enticing sight. He'd do his damndest to protect her from the men chasing her, but the real challenge would be protecting her from him and his unbridled attraction for her.

He leaped to his feet. "Let's get out of here before those jerks show up."

"How far is it to your friend's place?" she asked.

He untied the horses' reins and pointed across the valley toward a range of low, rounded hills covered with thick stands of fir trees. "He lives over those hills in the next valley."

She paled. "That…that's a long ways."

"Yep. Should take us most of the day to get there."

"The rest of the day?"

He paused and studied her, noting how her full mouth tightened with even her slightest movement. She must be in agony.

He sighed, resigned, knowing he was going to

regret his next words. "Okay, we'll ride together on my horse again." Riding double cushioned her from the worst of the horse's jolting, but sharing a saddle was a mistake. Her soft curves pressing against him as they rode through the night had kept him on a razor's edge of wanting. He'd vowed he wouldn't put himself through it again. How much more could he take before he did something he'd regret?

****

Hallie returned Ryan's frown, matching it glower for glower. Ride with him? Again? Not on your life. She'd ridden her horse on her own once. She'd do it again. "I'll ride by myself." She regarded the patient horse and winced. The thought of sitting on a hard, unyielding saddle and being bounced around like a yo-yo was enough to make her cry.

Ryan's dark brows rose, and the corners of his mouth twitched. He nodded. "Okay. Have it your way." He held out her horse's reins. "Mount up."

She fumed at the amusement in his eyes. She'd show him. Gritting her teeth, she grabbed the reins and put her foot in the stirrup. Biting back a groan, she threw one leg over the back of the horse and sat gingerly in the saddle.

Her bruised bottom ached, but she forced a tight smile. "What are you waiting for? Let's go." She kicked the horse's side with the heels of her boots and yelped as the beast broke into a trot. Clenching the reins with one hand and the pommel with the other, she clung to the animal, praying she wouldn't fall off.

Ryan's laughter followed her as she trotted into the trees.

After the first hour, her bottom turned numb,

easing her discomfort, and she relaxed. She hadn't fallen off yet. Maybe she was getting the hang of riding. If she held the reins loosely and didn't try to control the horse, the well-trained animal followed Ryan's horse at a steady gait. All she had to do was hold on.

She thought back to her earlier conversation with Ryan. She'd told him the whole story of Geordie and the trouble he was in just like he'd asked, but he hadn't been satisfied. What more did he want? Surely he didn't hold her responsible for what had happened.

She and Geordie were friends. What was so hard to believe? Couldn't a man and woman be friends? They'd gone on a few dates when they'd first met. Geordie was hard to resist. He could be quite persistent when he wanted something, but she'd soon seen beneath his charming exterior and realized a romantic relationship between them wasn't going to happen. But they'd remained friends, and their friendship had grown closer during this past year.

She remembered how beaten and bruised he'd been the last time she'd seen him, and her worry returned. Where was he? He'd promised he'd meet her at the Rusty Nail in Antler Springs. Instead, he'd sent his brother. Why? Was he hurt? The men who'd attacked her last night had said they hadn't killed him. *Not yet.*

She'd wanted to ask Ryan how he planned to find Geordie, but one look at his closed face, and she kept her questions to herself. He was prickly at the best of times, but he fairly snarled anytime she mentioned his brother. What had happened between the two brothers to cause such animosity? Whatever the problems between them, she hoped Ryan could put his anger behind him, and help her find Geordie before the drug

105

cartel got to him.

The sun was sinking behind the top of the distant mountains by the time they rode over yet another rise and across a meadow dotted with bright yellow and purple wildflowers. A barn, the walls painted a deep red, towered over a small lake, the still waters a brilliant, sapphire blue. The scent of newly mown hay wafted in the late afternoon air. A white horse in a wooden corral raised its head at their approach and whinnied.

The single-story, log ranch house sprawled in the distance, a plume of smoke billowing out of a stone chimney. The setting sun's streaks of red and gold reflected off large panes of glass. A covered verandah encircled the house. Rustic wicker chairs in bright, primary colors were arranged in a small grouping on the porch. The weathered front door's once vibrant red paint had faded to a soft rose.

Ryan reined his horse to a halt in front of the barn and leaped from the saddle.

Hallie's horse sidled up to his, its head drooping.

Sympathy for the exhausted animal overcame Hallie. She ran her hand over the horse's warm, sweaty coat.

The animal nickered and ambled ahead several steps.

Hallie yelped, grabbing the saddle horn.

"Easy, Hallie. She's not going anywhere." Ryan tightened his hold on the reins, as he held out his hand and helped her from her horse.

Her feet hit the ground, her legs wobbled, and she staggered and grabbed the horse's neck and hung on.

The horse nickered again but held steady.

She blew out a shaky breath and patted the mane. "Good girl. That's a good girl."

The animal nuzzled its snout into her hand searching for a treat.

"Well, well, well. Looks like you made a friend." Ryan chuckled. "We'll make a horse woman out of you yet." He handed her a handful of oats from a small burlap bag tied to his saddle. "Make sure you keep your hand flat when you give it to her."

"What's her name?" she asked for the first time.

His cheeks flushed red. "Baby Doll."

"Baby Doll?" She raised her brows.

He shrugged. "What can I say? It was a weak moment in my life."

She blinked at the unexpected warmth in his husky voice. Opening her hand, she offered the oats to the horse. "Here you go, Baby Doll."

The animal opened its mouth, exposing big, white teeth.

She gulped but held her hand steady. "Nice, Baby Doll, nice girl."

The horse daintily took the treat with its velvety soft lips.

Hallie laughed in pleasure. "She likes it."

Ryan grinned, the devastating dimples appearing in his lean, battered cheeks.

Their gazes locked, and a frisson of awareness rippled along her spine. She sucked in a gulp of air. Afraid he'd see her flushed cheeks and know how he affected her, she stumbled back and would have fallen if he hadn't grabbed her arm and steadied her. Her skin burned from the heat of his touch, and she yanked her arm free and took another shaky step. Her legs gave out, and she squealed as she landed with a jarring thump on the hard ground.

"Christ, Hallie," he said. "Why do you have to be so damn stubborn?" He crouched, lifted her in his arms and carried her across the clearing to the ranch house and up the steps to the wooden porch.

She hurt too much to protest he was once again carrying her. Tears filmed her eyes at the pain ricocheting through her.

He kicked at the door with a dusty boot.

The haunting, wavering call of a loon echoed from the nearby lake.

The warmth from his body enveloped her, and she squirmed, her heart pounding.

He tightened his grip, holding her against his firm chest. "Stay still," he said.

The door swung open, and yellow light spilled out. A figure stood silhouetted in the doorway. "What the hell?"

"About time you answered the damn door," Ryan said. He shoved past the man standing in the open doorway and strode inside, Hallie still in his arms.

Her eyes adjusted to the dimness, and she studied the spacious room. The light from a single, propane-fuelled lamp revealed heavy dark wooden furniture and three worn burgundy leather chairs and a matching couch. The remains of a fire crackled in a large, river stone fireplace. Several brightly colored scatter rugs covered the battered hardwood floors.

"What have you there, or should I say, who?" demanded a gruff voice.

Hallie turned. A tall man, his body held with a military stiffness hinting at an underlying wiry strength, watched her with a pair of bright eyes. His sunburned, craggy face was wreathed in a sea of deeply etched wrinkles.

"What the hell happened to your face, Ryan?" the man asked. "And who's this?" His sharp gaze swiveled between Ryan and Hallie. Wisps of graying hair sprouted at odd angles out of his freckled scalp. The top button of his shirt was undone, revealing a thick thatch of wiry, gray, chest hair.

"Is the bed in the spare room made up?" Ryan asked.

The man nodded.

Without another word, Ryan strode down a dark hallway and into a room. He deposited her on a bed.

The older man hurried behind them carrying a kerosene lantern, which he set on a dresser. "Sorry, it's so dark in here. The damn generator's quit on me again. I'll be right back," he said and bustled out of the room.

A heavy curtain covered the small bedroom's sole window blocking what little light was left in the day. A soft, wool Navajo blanket covered the narrow bed on which she sat. The blanket's bright red, orange and turquoise intricate geometric pattern added vibrancy to the room.

She leaned against a mound of pillows and inhaled the clean, soothing scent of lavender. A sudden weariness overcame her, and she yawned. She couldn't remember the last time she'd slept. Two days ago? Three? She yawned again and stretched her tired back, barely managing to bite back a moan as the throbbing pain in her legs spiked.

"I know you're hurting," Ryan said. "There's no need to hide your discomfort."

"I'll be all right." A muscle in her thigh cramped, and she bit her lip, tears of pain blurring her vision. Massaging the knot of cramped muscle, she glanced up at him.

His eyes bore into hers, warm, golden lights dancing amidst the cool blue. "You did well today," he said, "but being on a horse for so long when you're not used to riding is pretty painful. I've seen grown men cry after a hard day's ride."

She opened her mouth to protest but sighed instead. "You're right. I hurt everywhere. Muscles I didn't know I had ache."

He chuckled. "I'll bet." The dimples danced in his unshaven cheeks.

She sucked in a breath. How could she have forgotten the power of his smile?

"Here you are." The older man, his arms laden with towels and a washbasin filled with steaming liquid, entered the room. He set everything on the small, rustic, pine table beside the bed. "This should help her."

"Thanks, Buzz," Ryan said. "I'll be out to talk to you soon."

"You're damn right you will." With a last, probing look at Hallie, he turned and left the room.

Hallie yawned again.

"You're tired," Ryan said. "I'm sorry." His voice was a deep rumble.

She blinked. "Sorry? Why?"

"I made you ride too many hours last night and again today."

"It wasn't your fault. We had to get away from those men shooting at us. What other choice did we have?"

He ran long fingers through his hair, tangling the dark curls. "All the same, the riding was too much for you."

A curl fell across his forehead, and she longed to brush it back. She focused on kneading the cramp in her thigh, refusing to look at him, afraid of what she'd do.

"Why don't you lie back and relax? Try and get some rest," he said.

Unwilling to risk facing those vivid blue eyes again, she settled back on the soft bed and closed her eyes. She yawned.

The brush of warm hands on her bare skin startled her. Her eyes flew open.

Ryan leaned over her, his hands tugging at the waistband of her pants.

"What...?" she sputtered.

"Easy," he soothed.

She stared into his eyes, caught again by the unusual glint of gold in their depths. "What...what are you doing?"

The corners of his mouth lifted, and the dimples danced in his cheeks. "Not what you think," he said as he continued removing her jeans.

Cool air wafted over the skin on her thighs, raising goose bumps. She inhaled a shaky breath. Before she could object further, her pants were off, and she lay clad in only her shirt and underwear. "What—"

"Take it easy," he said, cutting off her protest. "I'm trying to help you."

She was fully awake now. "How? By stripping me naked?"

His eyes darkened, the pupils dilating. "Not a bad idea." His gaze settled on her bare legs, lingering on the wisp of pink silk underwear.

Fire stole up her neck onto her cheeks as she followed his gaze. She shoved him away. "Get off me."

He laughed. This time the sound was harsh, and the light didn't reach his eyes. "I see your opinion of me hasn't improved." His mouth thinned, and his gaze raked over her. "Believe me, lady, you haven't got anything I haven't seen before."

She shivered under the force of his glare.

He dipped a washcloth into the basin of steaming water the man called Buzz had set on the bedside table. He wrung out the cloth and gently placed the steaming cloth on her thigh.

She flinched at the first touch but relaxed as soothing warmth seeped into her sore muscles.

He wrung out another cloth and set it on her other thigh. The scent of mint mixed with licorice filled the air.

A flush heated her face. "Ryan..." she began, knowing she'd misjudged him again. "Look—"

"Forget it."

He removed the cloths, rinsed them in the water and replaced them on her aching legs.

As the warmth from the cloths seeped into her body, the vise of pain eased, and her muscles relaxed. "I'm sorry. I shouldn't have..." Her voice trailed off.

A strained silence thickened the air.

"Thank you. It feels good," she said. "What's in the bowl?"

"I don't know, but it works. It's one of Buzz's old family remedies." He didn't meet her gaze as he continued to reapply the warm, wet cloths.

She relaxed under the gentle touch of his hands as

his strong fingers molded the muscles in her calves and thighs. Pain fled, replaced by pleasure.

His touch gentled, his fingers no longer massaging tired muscles, but caressing and sensuous. He slid his hands over her thighs, his long, tanned fingers, their pads callused, raising trills of awareness.

Her breathing quickened.

He stilled, and their eyes locked.

The silence lengthened, broken by the rapid pounding of her heart.

His gaze lingered on her mouth, and he lowered his head and kissed her.

For a heartbeat she froze, her lips unmoving beneath his as the taste of him overwhelmed her. A thousand warning flares flashed through her. Ignoring them, she gave into his touch and his taste and returned his kiss.

He cursed and the intimate connection ended. He sprang to his feet and stood, his hands clenched at his sides. He swore again. "This isn't happening. Not now, not ever."

"What—"

"I promised my brother I'd look after you." He grabbed the wet rags from her legs and tossed the cloths in the basin. Water splashed over the table and onto the floor. "I intend to keep my promise." He stormed out of the room, slamming the door behind him so hard a painting on the wall above the bed shook.

She stared at the closed door and touched her swollen mouth, knowing she'd made a mistake. She needed Ryan, not for sex, but to keep her safe from the men who were after her. More importantly, he could find Geordie.

A relationship with Ryan was just asking for trouble. The sole reason she was here with him was to find Geordie. She wouldn't do anything to jeopardize Geordie's life, not even if every cell in her body hummed from the force of Ryan's kiss and ached for more.

Chapter 10

Ryan's self-disgust drove him into the living room and to the cabinet where Buzz kept his whiskey. He yanked a bottle down, unscrewed the cap and filled a glass with the amber liquid. With a shaking hand, he lifted the glass and drained the contents in one swallow. Tears filmed his eyes as the fiery liquor burned a path down his throat. He refilled the glass and guzzled the contents of his second drink.

"Booze won't solve anything," Buzz said.

Ryan ignored him. Drinking himself into a stupor might not help, but passing out sure as hell would stop him thinking about Hallie and the damned kiss they'd shared. He had to erase the memory of her lips on his, their softness, the tiny gasp of sound she'd made when she'd opened her mouth for him.

He filled the glass once again and swallowed a large gulp. Why in hell had he kissed her? What had he been thinking? He hadn't been. That was the problem. How could he think when he'd touched her silken skin and witnessed the play of muscles in her slim thighs? Hell, it had been all he could do to breathe. With her stretched out on the bed and only a tiny scrap of silk covering her, little was left to the imagination. No wonder he'd lost his mind and kissed her.

The wonder was he'd stopped. At the first taste of her, he was lost. He'd wanted more. He'd wanted it all.

He drained his glass. God, he'd wanted her. Hell, he still did. He gritted his teeth until his jaw ached.

"Who is she?"

Ryan turned and eyed Buzz. "A friend of Geordie's."

Buzz nodded as if the simple statement explained everything. It probably did.

Ryan had known Buzz for years, ever since his days working for the Drug Enforcement Agency. Buzz had been the Special Agent in Charge of Ryan's division at the DEA. They'd been through a lot together, and in all the years since, they'd remained friends. When Buzz retired from the DEA, Ryan had mentioned the place in the neighboring valley to his own ranch was for sale. Buzz had jumped at the opportunity and had been here ever since.

Buzz refilled Ryan's glass and poured whiskey into a glass for himself. "If this is about your brother, I'm going to need a drink." He settled into an easy chair beside the fireplace, raised his glass to his nose, inhaled and then sipped. "Which poor bastard's wife did he screw this time?"

Ryan grimaced. If only the problem were so simple. He took a long drink and met Buzz's steady gaze. "It's bad, Buzz, real bad."

Buzz's expression didn't change. "I figured as much. It's not like you to let someone get the jump on you." His gaze settled on the bruises on Ryan's face. "Your eye looks pretty bad, to say nothing of the welt on your chin. I don't want to think what the other guy looks like."

Ryan ran his fingers through his hair. "Geordie's in big trouble, the kind of trouble that gets you dead."

A log shifted, and the fire in the grate sparked and flared.

Buzz kept his gaze steady as Ryan detailed Geordie's involvement with the drug cartel and how, in his ill-conceived desire to stop the cartel from exploiting people, he'd ripped them off. He described the attacks the previous evening on Hallie and him, and his fear the men were still after them. He didn't mention what had happened in the bedroom. Nor did he tell his friend he couldn't stop thinking of Hallie. He wouldn't share his shameful yearning with anyone, not even his closest friend.

When he'd finished, Buzz's brow furrowed. "You're right. The situation does sound bad. What are you planning to do?"

"Hell if I know."

"But you do plan to do something. I mean, you will find Geordie and save this woman. It's what you do. Isn't it?"

"Do I have a choice?"

Buzz smiled, and his eyes twinkled. "Your brother has always been a challenge. You've helped him out of countless predicaments."

"I hope I can save his sorry ass this time. These men after him don't mess around. They mean business."

"You know what you have to do."

Ryan didn't pretend not to understand what the old man meant. He ran his fingers through his hair again and sighed. "I can't think of another option, and believe me, I've tried."

Again silence descended as the fire crackled and popped.

"What's this woman to you?" asked Buzz.

Startled, Ryan stared. "What?"

"Is she with Geordie, or with you?"

"She's Geordie's *friend*."

"Are you sure?"

Ryan drained his drink, grabbed the half-empty bottle and turned toward the doorway leading to the hall. "I'm going to bed."

"So, I'm to contact Max?"

"What the hell. Why not?" Ryan strode down the hallway to the bedroom he used when he visited Buzz. Storming into the room, he kicked off his boots and flung himself on the bed. He raised the bottle to his lips, not bothering with a glass, wanting oblivion. Wanting it bad.

He woke to loud pounding reverberating through the room. He pried open an eyelid, and then slammed his eyes closed against the bright light driving like a spike into his aching head. Grimacing at the foul taste filling his mouth, he opened his eyelids again and peered around. An empty whiskey bottle lay on the bed beside him. Memories of last night flooded back, and a dull, throbbing ache centered behind his eyes.

He sat up, groaning as the room whirled. His guts roiled, and he swallowed back bile. Sucking in a deep breath, he scrubbed his hands over his face. The pounding increased, growing to a roar, shaking the walls of the room. Staggering to his feet, he stumbled to the window and drew back the curtains. He squinted into the bright sunlight.

A helicopter hovered in the air, coming in for a landing. The rotors stirred up a whirlwind of dust and debris and bent the branches of the nearby trees. An unholy roar filled the air.

The noise beat through the walls and into his head.

The helicopter landed and a lone figure climbed out of the machine.

Damn. His hangover was the least of his problems today. He picked up his shirt where it lay crumpled on the floor, and dragged it over his head. The sharp scent of horse and sweat wafted over him. He wrinkled his nose in disgust. Cleanliness was going to have to wait. Max was here. He knew better than anyone Max didn't like to be kept waiting.

Ignoring the painful ache in his head, he made his way to the living room.

The new arrival was already ensconced in a comfortable chair, sipping a cup of coffee.

Buzz sat in his usual easy chair beside the fire.

The two people were deep in conversation but stopped talking as soon as they spotted him. A strained silence descended over the room. Their sly glances made it clear he'd been the topic of their conversation.

Ryan bit back his irritation. "I see you're up to your usual dramatic entrances, Max," he said.

"Hello, Ryan." Max's full lips quirked in a slow smile. "I see you're as cantankerous as ever."

He ignored her jibe. His head throbbed, and his eyes gritted like sandpaper. He turned to Buzz. "Any more coffee?"

Buzz pointed toward a side table where a stainless steel carafe sat on a tray along with two mugs. "Help yourself. I made it plenty strong. I figured you'd need an extra boost this morning."

Ryan poured a steaming cup and sipped. The hot liquid seared his tongue, and he made a face. Ignoring the pain, he drank again, needing coffee, needing it now. A cigarette would be nice, too, but Buzz wouldn't have any. The old man was against smoking and had been on Ryan's case to quit in the years he'd smoked.

Ryan slumped in a chair across from Buzz and Max, sipped the strong coffee and studied the new arrival.

Maxine Benoit was as stunning as ever. Her long, dark-red hair gleamed in the morning sun. Her green eyes watched him with sultry warmth.

"You came," he said. "I wasn't sure you would."

"Buzz said it was urgent." She leaned back in her chair and crossed one long, shapely leg over the other. "From the looks of things, he wasn't exaggerating. You look like hell."

Ryan ignored her comment. He was reminded of the last time he'd seen the beautiful DEA Special Agent. They'd been assigned to a mission, and their unit had been dropped deep into the mountainous jungles of Mexico where they'd searched for a renegade drug lord. The assignment was grueling amidst steaming humidity, swarms of ravenous mosquitoes, and a desperate, criminal gang willing to stop at nothing to protect their drug network.

The real challenge of the mission had been working with Maxine Benoit. The Mexico project was his last mission. He'd refused to work with a partner he couldn't trust, and when the Agency hadn't seen things his way, and had outright refused to assign him a different partner, he'd resigned.

Relations hadn't always been so tense between them. He remembered a time when he couldn't wait to be alone with Max. He scowled into his coffee cup.

Their relationship and its demise were ancient history. But he couldn't deny the bitter taste her duplicity still left in his mouth.

Max was the last person he would have chosen to ask for help in this situation. But Geordie was in trouble and time was of the essence. Max had access to sources he needed to help him locate Geordie, sources denied him now he no longer worked for the DEA. Her connections with the Mexican Federales were why he'd agreed to let Buzz contact her. His brother was in trouble. He'd meet with the devil himself if it meant they'd find him before the drug cartel did.

"Why is a helicopter here?"

Ryan turned to see Hallie standing in the hall, and his heart skipped a beat. She looked damn good with her hair tousled around her head like a golden cloud and her face softened from sleep. He focused on her mouth as he remembered how sweet her lips had tasted when he'd kissed her. He gulped. What the hell was he doing? He needed a damn drink.

"It's okay," Buzz said. "Max is a friend. She's here to help."

Hallie's pale face brightened.

"There's coffee, if you want," Buzz added.

"Thanks," she said, taking a few tentative steps into the room. "Um, we didn't get a chance to meet last night." She cast a quick glance at Ryan, and her face flamed. "I was…I was…" Her voice trailed off.

Ever the lady's man, Buzz hurried over and poured her a cup of coffee. He handed the steaming mug to her. "It's okay. I completely understand. You were in a great deal of discomfort. Sitting on a horse for such a long time if you're not used to riding is hard on a person's body." He beamed at her. "Did my old remedy help?"

Ryan couldn't help snorting.

Hallie's face flamed, her cheeks turning bright pink. "Yes, thank you. I'm feeling much better today."

"Would someone mind filling me in on what's going on?" Max's sultry voice filled the room. "I went to a great deal of trouble to get here, and I understand time is of the essence."

****

Hallie studied the woman across the room. With her lean, yet shapely body, long, shiny fall of red hair, and perfect, creamy complexion, she resembled a fashion model. Even her clothes were high fashion. The tight, designer jeans fit her curves like a glove, and her silky, green sweater revealed an impressive amount of cleavage.

Next to her, Hallie was decidedly frumpy. She wished she'd combed the tangles from her hair before she made an appearance, but with the unexpected arrival of the helicopter, she'd been too worried to do more than throw back the covers, jump out of bed, and pull on her stained jeans.

The elegant woman's eyes narrowed as she assessed her.

Hallie resisted the urge to smooth her hair or straighten the creases in her blouse.

"And you are?" Max glowered at her.

Buzz jumped in. "Where are my manners this morning? This is Maxine Benoit. Max, this is Ryan's friend."

The auburn-haired beauty's full, red lips curled into a cold smile. "So I see."

Hallie's irritation inched up a notch, but she stepped forward and held out her hand. "Hallie Harkins," she said. Her annoyance soared to the top of the scale when Max ignored her outstretched hand. What was her problem? She met Max's hard-eyed gaze and shuddered. Antagonism filled the sultry, heavily mascaraed eyes.

"Hallie," Buzz said, "Max is here to help."

"She is?" Hallie turned to Ryan, but he sipped his coffee, avoiding her gaze. She glanced at Buzz, and then back at Max.

The other woman's scowl deepened, marring the perfection of her face.

Hallie hid a shiver. The icy chill emanating from Max was enough to lower the room's temperature a good ten degrees.

Max's gaze shifted to Ryan, and her face underwent a transformation. The full mouth softened, the long eyelashes fluttered. "I've missed you, Ryan," she purred. "It's been much too long. I was concerned when you didn't return any of my phone calls or answer my emails."

Ryan's mouth tightened. A pulse in his jaw beat a steady tattoo.

The air thickened with tension.

Hallie glanced from one to the other. Something was going on between them.

A discreet cough broke through the uneasy silence.

Buzz held out the carafe. "More coffee?" he asked.

Hallie shook her head. "No, thanks."

He turned to Max. "Max? Would you like some?"

Max ignored him, her gaze fixed on Ryan. "Ryan, why didn't you respond to my calls? I'd hoped we could talk and straighten things out."

Ryan cursed and turned his back on her.

Her face paled.

"Max?" Buzz asked again.

She glared at him. "What is it?"

"Coffee?" Buzz repeated, seemingly unperturbed by her rudeness.

She blew out a breath and nodded, and he filled her cup.

Max's hand trembled, and coffee slopped on the floor.

Buzz pulled a handkerchief from his jeans' pocket, but before he could clean up, Max grabbed the cloth from him. "I'll do it," she snapped and swiped at the spill. Two red patches stained her high cheekbones.

Ryan's face was rigid, his mouth set in a hard, disapproving line as he watched Max clean the floor.

Hostile undercurrents swirled around the room, impossible to ignore.

Hallie shifted uneasily, her frustration building. Whatever was going on between these two wasn't any of her concern. Buzz had said Max was here to help. She eyed the woman's fashionable, but impractical clothing and the ridiculous, high-heeled sandals. "How can you help me, Miss Benoit?" she asked.

"Call me Max." Max's green eyes met hers.

"Max is a DEA Special Agent," Buzz explained. "She and Ryan used to work together. They were one formidable team, let me tell you." He sighed. "But then Ryan got the idea in his head he wanted to run his family's ranch, and he quit the DEA. A bad day for law enforcement, but a good day for the Antler Springs ranching community."

Ryan had been with the DEA? Hallie turned to Ryan, her mind whirling with this shocking, new revelation.

He stared out the window, the expression on his face hidden, but the pulse in his jaw throbbed.

He'd been a Special Agent with the Federal Drug Enforcement Agency? Wasn't the DEA responsible for enforcing controlled substance laws? Didn't they hunt down international drug dealers? Another piece of the puzzle dropped in place. She'd wondered why Geordie had waited to ask his brother for help until he was desperate and no other option existed. Asking a DEA agent for assistance would be the same as going to the police. Even a retired agent would have no choice but to turn in someone who was involved in the drug trade. Even if the perp was his own brother.

Ryan's federal agent experience also explained his skill at taking down the men who'd attacked her, and his calm reaction when they'd been shot at in his ranch house.

"Ryan and I are *very* good friends, Hallie," said Max. "We met at Quantico at the DEA Training Academy." Her lips curled in a lazy smile. "The two of us have been close ever since. We've always had a *special* relationship, haven't we, Ryan?" Max prodded, her steamy gaze fixed on him.

Ryan's eyes were cold, and a scowl darkened his features. "Cut the bullshit, Max. We've got a situation here. We need access to sources only you can provide." His voice became colder. "Your contacts are why you're here. The *only* reason you're here."

Max's eyes narrowed, and a furrow formed between her perfectly shaped brows. "You're still angry. I would have thought you'd be over your hurt feelings by now."

Ryan's eyes blazed. "Some things can never be forgiven." The air in the room crackled with tension.

"*You're* with the DEA?" Hallie asked Max. She couldn't see this elegant woman fighting vicious, drug gang members, but if she really was with the DEA, Geordie was in trouble. Once she knew the full details of what Geordie had done, Max would insist on involving the police. She was a federal cop and wouldn't willingly break the law. Even though Geordie had stolen money from criminals who dealt in illegal drugs, he'd still committed a crime. His reasons for doing so wouldn't matter to the Feds.

"Why is it so hard to believe I'm a DEA agent?" Max asked.

Hallie ignored the challenge in her voice. Instead she glowered at Ryan. "I thought you agreed not to call the authorities. We were going to handle this ourselves. Remember?"

"Max isn't here on official business," Buzz interjected. "She's doing a favor for friends. Off the record."

Max smiled, her eyes cold as they pinned Hallie. "Old, *dear* friends."

A flash of irritation sparked through Hallie. Was the woman going to continually threaten her? She'd understood the message loud and clear the first time. Ryan was all hers.

"We'd better figure out our next step," Buzz said. "Those men after you two could show up here any minute." He paused and added, "Let's not forget why we're here. Geordie's life is at risk."

"Geordie's involved in this?" Max asked.

Buzz nodded.

"You'd better tell me everything." Her manner was suddenly all business, all trace of her earlier seductiveness gone.

"It's okay, Hallie. Go ahead," Ryan said. "You can tell Max everything. She's here to help."

She searched his eyes, wanting to believe him. He'd saved her life not once, but twice. If she couldn't trust him, whom could she trust? She took a deep breath and proceeded to tell Max everything, starting with the evening on the beach in Acapulco when she and Geordie had run into the two Mexican thugs. She described the night in her house two months ago when Geordie had shown up at her door severely beaten. When she finished, silence hung over the room.

Max sipped from her cup, her smooth brow furrowed. "Geordie's screwed up big time, hasn't he?" Her eyes narrowed. "Are you sure he didn't tell you where he was going or what his plans were?"

Hallie shook her head.

"Are you certain? He didn't say anything?"

Again she shook her head. "He told me he wanted to fix everything, and I was to meet him in two months time at the Rusty Nail Bar 'n Grill in Antler Springs."

"He must have given you some indication of his plans or where he was going."

"Do you think I'd keep any useful information from you if he had? I want to find him as much as any of you."

Max turned to Ryan. "He never said where he was when he called you?"

He shook his head.

"Do you have any idea who he'd turn to if he was in trouble?" she asked.

"You know him better than I do."

The bitterness in Ryan's voice surprised Hallie.

"He's *your* brother," Max said.

Ryan's eyes narrowed, and the pulse in his jaw throbbed. "Aren't I the lucky one?"

Nobody said anything for several long minutes, and then Ryan blew out a loud breath. "I haven't seen Geordie in close to two years." His face hardened. "Other than the phone call last week, I haven't heard from him either. But then you know exactly why he hasn't called, don't you, Max?"

"Come on, you two—" began Buzz, but stopped when the rumble of approaching engines rent the air.

Max pulled a cell phone from her pocket. "What's going on?" she barked into her phone.

The roar of motorized vehicles grew louder.

Max ended the call and leaped to her feet. "My pilot. Four armed men on ATVs are coming this way."

Hallie's breath rushed out of her.

"Let's get out of here. Now," Ryan said. He grabbed Hallie and shoved her ahead of him toward the door. "Come on, Buzz," he called to the older man. "You don't want to be around when they get here. They won't care who they shoot."

Buzz's face was grim. "I'm right behind you."

Max led the way out the door and across the meadow to where the helicopter waited, the wail of the rotors loud as they thundered to life.

Hallie glanced over her shoulder and shuddered as an ATV bounced over the hill and across the field.

Another ATV followed, and then another. Armed

men, dressed in black, their faces covered by black balaclavas, rode on the vehicles. The man in the leading ATV stopped his machine and pointed a long, menacing-looking gun at them.

The gun flashed, but she didn't hear the explosion of the bullet over the rising wail of the helicopter.

"Move," Ryan yelled in her ear. His hand on her arm tightened as he dragged her behind him.

She stumbled on the uneven ground, her injured ankle screaming, but she gritted her teeth against the pain and kept moving.

Roaring filled the air.

She focused on the waiting helicopter, not daring to look behind to see how close the ATVs were.

The pilot had the door open, and the engine screamed, ready to take off the second they boarded.

Max arrived at the helicopter first and jumped inside.

Buzz followed.

Max shouted at Ryan, but her words vanished in the howl of the helicopter and the approaching ATVs.

A boulder in front of Hallie shattered. She screamed.

Another bullet whined past, landing with a thud in the dirt a foot away.

Her heart pounded, blood pumping as her chest heaved, fighting for air. Urging her legs to dig deeper, she ran faster. She stumbled on a rock and yelped as her already injured ankle twisted. Collapsing to her knees, she moaned in agony. Ryan's shout was lost in a haze of pain, but then his arms were around her, and he lifted her and held her tight against his chest.

He was off with her in his arms, running across the

129

ground toward the waiting helicopter.

Max and Buzz, guns in hand, shot round after round at the attackers.

Bullets struck the helicopter, pinging against the metal. Sparks flew.

Hallie held her breath and prayed they'd reach the relative safety of the aircraft before a bullet stopped them.

Ryan grunted and stumbled, almost dropping her.

She screamed, certain he was hit, but he straightened and tightened his arms around her and staggered, lurching toward the helicopter.

The distance between them and safety grew smaller and smaller until only a few steps remained.

Buzz stretched out his arms. "Give her to me."

Hallie reached for him.

He gripped her arms and pulled.

At the same time, Ryan released her, and she landed with a thud inside the helicopter, the wind knocked out of her. She lay dazed, vaguely aware Ryan had jumped in after her.

The helicopter lifted off the ground, the powerful engine roaring as the chopper rose higher and higher.

Sucking in deep breaths, she scrambled to her knees and peered out the window. They were out of range of the guns below.

Six men stood by the ATVs, guns at their sides, watching as the helicopter escaped into the air.

A whoosh of relief soared through her. She grinned and turned toward the others. "We did it." Her smile faded.

Buzz and Max knelt beside Ryan who lay still and unmoving on the floor of the helicopter, his face pale. A pool of blood seeped from a wound in his side.

"Ryan," she shouted and crawled closer, ignoring the pain in her ankle. She grabbed his hand and squeezed. "Ryan."

He didn't respond.

"Ryan," she whispered. "Ryan."

Chapter 11

Hallie limped across the waiting room, her ankle once again bruised and swollen. A doctor had wrapped the injury in a tensor bandage and given her a painkiller so the pain was manageable. She glanced toward the white, double doors leading to the operating room and shivered. Ryan was behind those closed doors. Doctors were operating on him as they fought to repair the damage the bullet had caused in his side. Two interminable hours had passed since they'd wheeled him into surgery.

She bit her bottom lip, recalling his ghostly pale face when he'd lain unconscious on the floor of the helicopter as the chopper arced to safety. Blood had seeped from his wound, forming a dark pool beneath him.

How much blood could a person lose and still live? The doctor had told them the bullet had hit Ryan in the back above his right hip, tearing through skin and muscle before escaping out the front, leaving a vicious-looking exit wound.

In the helicopter on the flight to the hospital, Max hadn't let her near Ryan. When she'd tried to help, Max had scowled at her, hissing, "Haven't you done enough damage?"

Guilt had overwhelmed her, and so Hallie had crawled to the other side of the helicopter and watched as Max applied pressure to Ryan's oozing wound.

When the helicopter landed at the hospital helipad, Max directed the medics to place Ryan's unconscious body on a gurney and followed them as they wheeled Ryan into the hospital. Hallie and Buzz had been left to make their own way to the emergency ward. By the time they found where Ryan had been taken, he'd been whisked into surgery.

The rapid tattoo of high heels on the shiny linoleum waiting-room floor broke through Hallie's worry.

Max bore down on her, a scowl marring her model-perfect face. "Any news?" Max asked.

Hallie shook her head.

"This is your fault, you know."

Hallie opened her mouth to defend herself, but stopped. Max was right. If she'd run faster, if she hadn't stumbled and twisted her ankle again, Ryan wouldn't have had to carry her. He wouldn't have been shot. Tears filled her eyes and slipped down her cheeks.

"Great," said Max. "Just what we need, you turning on the waterworks and playing your 'oh, woe is me' act."

Hallie spluttered. "I—"

"Shut the hell up. You've done enough damage."

Hallie bit her lip. Max's words stung, but she couldn't deny the truth of them. "I know Ryan's wounded because of me."

"You're damn right." Max glared. "You'd better pray he gets through this." She spun on her high heels, stomped across the room and sank onto a hard, plastic chair.

Even as Hallie continued her restless pacing,

Max's reproach weighed on her. She wiped her face with her sleeve and swallowed back her tears. Ryan would be all right. He would survive. The words ran like a refrain through her tortured mind.

Every time the door to the operating room opened and someone came out, she jumped, praying the person was Ryan's doctor. How long did a bullet wound take to repair? Surely, Ryan had been in surgery long enough. Was something wrong? Her blood chilled. Or was he already dead? She shook her head, refusing to think the unthinkable. He'll be okay. He's too stubborn to die.

"Have some coffee," Buzz said, holding two, foam cups, steam rising from them. "You look like you could use some." He offered her one of the cups.

"Thanks." She sipped the hot liquid, hoping the strong brew would give her the strength to survive this ordeal.

"Still no word, I take it," Buzz said.

She shook her head. "They've been in there a long time." Her lips trembled, and she blinked back the ever-present tears.

His eyes softened. "Ryan's tough. It'll take more than a bullet to knock him out of the picture."

"The bullet wouldn't have hit him if I hadn't stumbled and he had to carry me." Tears welled, blurring her vision. "He should have left me behind."

Buzz grasped her arm, forcing her to look at him. "Then you'd be dead. You haven't known Ryan very long, but you must know he would never have left you. He's not made that way."

"He saved my life...again. I owe him."

"I doubt he sees the situation the same way." He

sipped coffee. "Ryan's a man of honor. His innate integrity is why what happened between him and Geordie hit him so hard."

Hallie opened her mouth to ask Buzz to explain, but he spoke before she could say anything.

"This is hard on her." He pointed at Max.

Lines of strain marred Max's perfect features, and dark circles underscored her eyes.

"She has feelings for Ryan," Hallie said, realization hitting like a kick in the gut.

Buzz nodded. "A lot of history exists between those two." He touched her arm again, and his gaze delved into hers. "But their relationship is history, Hallie, ancient history."

Before she could respond, the door to the operating room opened and a doctor emerged, and she forgot everything, except for her need to know how Ryan was.

Max leaped to her feet and hurried to meet the doctor. "Well? How is he?"

Hallie held her breath.

The doctor mopped beads of sweat from his brow with a sodden tissue. "The operation went well. Better than expected. He'll be up and walking in no time." He smiled. "Fortunately, the bullet didn't enter the abdomen or nick an artery."

Breath whooshed out of Hallie. *Ryan was all right.* The words sang through her mind. *He was all right.* "When can we see him?"

"Not for a while. He's still unconscious. He lost a great deal of blood."

"Surely we wouldn't harm him if we peeked in to see how he's doing," Buzz said.

"Please?" Hallie added her own plea.

The doctor looked from one to the other, and his features softened. "Okay, but one at a time and only for a minute."

Hallie smiled her gratitude. "Thank you."

He nodded and turned and retraced his steps through the doors to the operating room.

"Don't even think it," Max said.

"Think what?" Hallie asked.

Max glowered. "I'm going in there first."

"But—"

Max's eyes hardened. "Do you really think he'll want to see the woman responsible for his being wounded and nearly dying?"

Hallie reeled from the venom in her voice.

Max turned and strode through the doors.

Hallie stared after her, her breathing ragged.

"Don't let her get to you," Buzz said. "She's upset."

Hallie blinked back her tears. "Is she right? Will Ryan be angry? If Geordie hadn't asked him to help me, none of this would have happened."

"Ryan knew the consequences when he agreed to help Geordie. He won't blame you."

Buzz's reassuring words acted like a warm balm. "Can Max help us find Geordie?" she asked. "Does she really know what she's doing?"

"Don't let her good looks fool you. Maxine Benoit is one of the best operatives in the DEA. Last year she earned the Administrator's Award of Honor, the highest accolade a DEA agent can achieve. If she can't find Geordie, no one can."

Hallie prayed he was right. The men on the ATVs had meant business. They'd been willing to kill anyone to get to her. They wanted to harm her just because she was Geordie's friend. She could only imagine what they'd do to Geordie if they found him. She had to hope Buzz was right, and Max could help them find Geordie before the bad guys did.

Hallie and Buzz waited outside the door of Ryan's hospital room. Max was still inside.

The door opened, and Max stepped into the corridor.

"How is he?" asked Hallie.

Max ignored her and turned to Buzz. "I have to leave for awhile. Look after him while I'm gone."

"Where are you going?" Hallie couldn't help asking.

Max's gaze swiveled back. Her mouth thinned. "I have to figure out how to get you and Ryan out of this mess you created."

"Me? I didn't start this. Geordie did."

Max snorted and walked away without another word. She was already speaking into her cell phone before she reached the end of the corridor.

Hallie stared after her, tears filming her eyes.

"Ignore her, Hallie, like water off your back," Buzz said. "Remember, we need her."

She studied his kind face and nodded. Buzz was right. Max didn't like her. She'd made her feelings more than clear. Hallie couldn't change the redhead's obvious dislike of her, but if Max could help them find Geordie, she'd put up with her scorn. "Sometime, you're going to tell me why she hates me so much."

The corners of his mouth lifted. "You already know the answer, Hallie. Just think about it."

She frowned at his cryptic response.

137

"Go in and check on Ryan," he said. "I'll wait."

"Are you sure? He's your friend."

Buzz nodded. "Go ahead."

She smiled her gratitude and opened the door. Her smile faded the second she stepped inside the dimly lit room.

Ryan lay, his eyes closed, on the hospital bed, still and unmoving, except for the slight rise and fall of his chest. His rugged face was unnaturally pale. Dark shadows underlined his sunken eyes, and new lines bracketed his mouth.

She swallowed over the lump in her throat. *This is your fault.* Max's words scorched through her mind. Why didn't he wake up?

As if in response to her silent plea, his eyes twitched and then blinked open. "Hey, there," he husked.

"Hey."

Their gazes locked.

A frisson of awareness rippled along her spine. "How…how are you feeling?" She bit her tongue the second the words were out. How did she think he felt? He'd been shot. He was obviously in a great deal of pain.

"I'll be okay." His mouth curved in a smile. "I've been through worse."

"I…I'm sorry you were hurt." She stumbled over her words. "If I hadn't fallen—"

"Stop."

"But—"

"Forget it. It's over." His eyes drilled into hers. "Those men who attacked us mean business. They've shown they'll stop at nothing to get to you. Geordie will

138

be next. We have to find him before they make good on their threats and kill him."

"Max is working on the situation," she said. "She's put out feelers to all her Mexican informants."

"That's good. One of them is bound to crack under the pressure and spill some useful intel on Geordie's location." His lips trembled in a weak smile. "Don't you worry. She'll find him."

His faith in the elegant redhead's abilities stung, but she returned his smile and said, "I hope you're right."

Buzz peeked into the room. "Time's up, Hallie."

She nodded, knowing he was anxious to see his friend. With a last, lingering glance at Ryan, she walked toward the door.

"Hallie," Ryan called after her.

She turned.

Golden lights sparkled in his blue irises.

Her heart skipped a beat.

"I'll see you tomorrow."

Swallowing over a suddenly dry throat, she nodded and left the room, ignoring Buzz's knowing smirk.

Ryan was released from the hospital the day after his surgery. He'd need a few days to recover from his wound before he'd be fit enough to travel, so they'd holed up in a large hotel on the outskirts of Billings, Montana, registered under assumed names.

Max had said the hotel was safe. The DEA used the unremarkable, economy, chain hotel to house witnesses in upcoming court proceedings who needed protection before they testified. Still, Max stressed, they had to be careful. They couldn't afford to be seen in the open, and so they were forced to keep to their rooms.

Over the next three days, Hallie did as she was told. She hadn't seen Ryan since they'd arrived at the hotel, and Max had pushed him in a wheelchair through the lobby and up the elevator to his room.

Buzz was her only visitor. He joined her for every lunch and supper to share a room service meal. While they ate, he filled her in on the events of the past days. Ryan's injury was healing as evidenced by his impatience with his enforced confinement. Actually, impatience was too mild a word for his ill temper. According to Buzz, the man was a veritable terror. He nearly took the head off anyone unfortunate enough to be near him.

He ignored the doctor's orders to rest and spent hours in the dead of night in the hotel's fitness center trying to regain his strength. He refused to use the wheelchair the hospital had provided and instead, shuffled around his room, determined to walk on his own two feet without support.

Hallie's frame of mind wasn't much better. For the most part, she was left alone with nothing to do but worry and while away the time watching mind-numbing television game shows and reruns of old movies. Each minute lasted an hour, each hour, a day. The inactivity was killing her. She was tired of waiting, tired of doing nothing when Geordie's life was in danger.

She hadn't seen Max. Apparently, the DEA agent was using the Federal agency's extensive resources and contacts to try and locate Geordie. So far, she hadn't had any luck.

Hallie yawned and stretched the kink out of her back. The television was tuned to yet another game show, but her mind wasn't on the overweight, middle-aged woman screaming in excitement and smothering the aging game show host with her generous breasts.

All she could think of was Geordie and the men who were after him. At least, she only allowed herself to think of him. She certainly didn't think of Ryan. Well, she didn't think of him during the day. Night, when she lay awake, tossing and turning for hours, was a different story.

A knock on the door startled her, and she tensed, recalling Max's warning. The men after them had plenty of resources. She wasn't to open the door unless she was certain who was on the other side. She climbed off the bed and edged closer to the door.

Another knock, this time followed by a familiar voice. "It's me, Hallie. Open up."

Relief surged through her, and she opened the door. "Buzz."

He stepped inside, closing the door behind him and securing the lock. "How are you doing?"

"How do you think?" she snapped, but instantly regretted her temper. "I'm sorry. All this sitting around doing nothing is driving me crazy."

"I know what you mean."

"How's Ryan? Is he any better?"

"Hard to tell. He's too stubborn to let on if his wound hurts. He's so determined to help Geordie, he'd hobble out of here right now and jump on a plane if I let him."

She sank onto the bed. "How much longer do you think we have to wait here?"

"Not much longer, I hope. At this point, it's either Ryan or me. I can't take much more of his sour mood."

He sat on the room's sole chair and ran his hand over his wisps of gray hair.

"Buzz, what happened between Max and Ryan?"

His eyes turned guarded. "What do you mean?"

She blew out her breath. "Come on. Don't pretend you don't know what I'm talking about. Anyone can see there's something between them. Whatever happened made him hard and bitter. He doesn't trust anyone."

Buzz chewed on his bottom lip.

"Tell me, Buzz, please?"

He sighed and sank deeper in his chair. "You'll probably find out anyway. What happened isn't a secret. Everyone in Antler Springs knows." He met her gaze. "I told you Ryan and Max were both agents in the DEA. They worked together on many of the same missions."

Hallie nodded.

"You can imagine what happened. Two attractive, virile, young people thrown into dangerous situations." He shrugged. "Their attraction was mutual, their relationship inevitable. They grew close, *very* close."

"They were...lovers?" She'd suspected this, but saying the word aloud, making the thought real, staggered her.

He nodded. "For awhile they were inseparable. They couldn't keep their hands off each other. Ryan was happy. Happier than I'd ever seen him." He smiled wistfully. "He was in love, and he was going to ask Max to marry him. He even showed me the ring he'd picked out."

"What happened?"

"Ryan introduced Max to Geordie." Buzz's eyes

clouded. "You're Geordie's friend. You must know what he's like around attractive women."

She froze, as the full meaning of what he'd said sank in. "No," she protested. "Geordie didn't…he wouldn't…" She stopped. Buzz was right. She did know Geordie. They'd been friends for over a year, and she knew exactly what he was like.

When they'd first met, he'd tried his well-practiced maneuvers on her, and they'd worked…for a while. With his boyish, blond good looks and engaging grin, he was difficult to resist. They'd gone on a couple of dates and had fun. Geordie had made sure they had a good time, but she'd soon seen through his boyish charm and realized dating and relationships were all a game to him.

She'd ended things. At first, he'd refused to accept her rejection, and bouquets of expensive flowers and balloons, chocolates and jewelry arrived daily at her home, each gift containing a card attesting to his undying affection. When she returned the items untouched, he'd changed tactics and inundated her with emails, texts and phone calls where he told her how much she meant to him.

His unwanted attentions finally escalated to a point where she'd told him if he continued harassing her, she'd be forced to tell their boss. He'd apologized, and with a wounded look on his handsome face, he'd walked out of her office. The gifts and calls ceased.

For the next month, the only interactions she had with him were work related. Then her grandfather had a massive stroke and ended up in the hospital, half of his body paralyzed, clinging to life. She'd been devastated. After her mother overdosed when Hallie was ten, her

Grandpa Joe had raised her. He was all she had.

Over the next days and weeks, her grandfather had slowly wasted away, his organs shutting down one by one. Not wanting anyone to witness her grief, she'd refused all offers of help from her friends and colleagues.

On the second night of her lonely vigil, Geordie had shown up at the hospital. He'd ignored her attempts to send him away. He'd stayed by her side, silently lending her his support, being there for her, helping ease her pain with his quiet presence. When her grandfather died, Geordie helped her with the funeral arrangements. She'd never forget what he'd done for her, how he'd been there by her side in her darkest days.

A friendship developed between them, one forged by the bond of loss. He too had lost his parents. Searching beneath his handsome, fun-loving exterior, she discovered an unexpected vulnerability. He used humor and jokes to hide his insecurity. The unceasing stream of women who cycled in and out of his life almost weekly was his way of proving his substance to the world.

She'd wondered where Geordie's low self-esteem and self-destructive behavior had originated. Now, she'd met Ryan. Geordie had grown up in the shadow of his big brother. Ryan was a top-ranked DEA agent, a hero fighting the good fight against drug kingpins and other low-life criminals. Hard for anyone to compete with such a paragon, let alone a younger, less-talented brother. Geordie futilely tried to show his brother he was the bigger man by the number of his conquests. Even his latest misstep of stealing from the drug cartel was a result of his desperate need to be better than Ryan. Contrary to what she'd said to Ryan, Geordie was the one who was jealous of his brother.

"Are you okay?"

Buzz's gruff voice broke through her thoughts. "Sorry," she said. "I was just thinking."

"I could tell. I hope I haven't upset you, but you should know the truth."

"I've known Geordie for some time," she said. "He has his flaws, but I can't believe he'd seduce his own brother's fiancée."

"From what I've heard, Geordie will do or say pretty well anything to get what he wants."

She bristled. "You don't know him. You don't know what he's really like."

Buzz's eyes narrowed. "I know enough. Look at what he's done this time. He's dragged you and the rest of us into this snafu he created."

Hallie wanted to defend Geordie, but Buzz was right. Geordie had a lot of growing up to do, but he was also one of the kindest and most caring persons she knew. "I still don't believe you. Geordie would never stoop so low as to steal his brother's fiancée."

Buzz didn't say anything, but his steady regard made his feelings clear.

"You're wrong," she said. "He wouldn't have been able to take Max from Ryan if she hadn't wanted to be with him."

Buzz nodded. "True enough."

Geordie would have flirted with Max. She was exactly the type of woman he liked…all curves and gleaming auburn hair, and big, pouty, red lips. But still, his brother's girlfriend? Having an affair with the woman his brother loved crossed over the line. She sighed. Maybe she didn't know Geordie as well as she thought she did. After all, he'd stolen money from a drug cartel. It didn't take a great stretch of the imagination to believe him capable of stealing his brother's fiancé. "How did Ryan take Geordie's betrayal?"

"How do you think?"

She winced. She hadn't known Ryan long, but she was well aware of how the stubborn, proud man would have reacted. No wonder bad blood existed between the two men, and Geordie hadn't seen his brother in two years. Geordie had screwed up. Again.

Did she really know him? The question had reared itself countless times over the past months. Maybe he'd lied. Maybe he really was involved with drugs. No. Not Geordie; not her happy-go-lucky, joking friend.

Geordie had been there for her when her grandfather died. No matter what he'd done, he was her friend. He was in trouble. She wouldn't desert him when he needed her. He'd do the same for her. She didn't doubt his loyalty for a heartbeat. But she couldn't ignore what he'd done to his older brother. "How…how long were Max and Geordie together?" she asked.

"A month at the most. She realized her mistake pretty quickly."

"And then?"

"She wanted Ryan back. She tried everything to get him to forgive her." He shrugged. "Ryan refused to listen. He wouldn't even answer her phone calls. He's still bitter. You've seen how they are together. Nothing's changed in the past two years."

"So that's why she's helping us."

"She'll do anything for Ryan, especially if she thinks there's a chance she can get him back. She's still in love with him."

Of course she was. Hallie's stomach tightened. The signs couldn't be more obvious. The soft light of yearning in Max's green eyes when she looked at Ryan, her determination to help him find his brother, and her anger after he'd been wounded, all pointed to love. The question was: did Ryan still love her? More importantly, why did the prospect of him loving the gorgeous redhead bother her so much? She jumped at a sudden tapping on the door.

"Are you expecting anyone?" Buzz asked.

She shook her head.

"Stay here." Rising from the chair with surprising ease for one of his years, he crossed to the door. He drew a gun out of his jacket pocket and held it ready.

Hallie's breath caught in her throat. She hadn't known he was armed.

The knocking grew louder.

Buzz motioned for her to back away from the door. "Hide," he mouthed.

She slid off the bed, ran to the closet and slipped inside.

"Who is it?" he demanded.

From her position in the closet, Hallie couldn't hear the muffled response, but she heard him undo the dead bolt and open the door.

"You're back," he said.

"Did you have any doubt?"

Max's familiar, sultry voice sent a chill through Hallie. Before she could open the closet door and leave the small, dark, enclosed space, the door slid open.

Max stood in the doorway looking down on her. "Well, well, well, if it isn't the little mouse."

Chapter 12

Hallie flushed at Max's contempt, but before she could explain why she was hiding in the closet, Max turned back to Buzz leaving Hallie to crawl out of the confined space.

Ryan stood in the room, a grin brightening his rugged features. "Lose something?" he asked.

Her face flamed. "No—"

Buzz cut off her explanation. "What did you find out, Max?"

Hallie tore her gaze from Ryan. "Did you find Geordie?"

Holding up a brown paper bag, Max said, "I'm not saying another word until I have a drink."

Buzz walked into the adjoining bathroom and returned with four plastic glasses. He took the bag from Max and removed a bottle of scotch. He poured a generous portion of liquor into each glass.

Ryan took his glass and limped to a chair. A grimace twisted his handsome features as he struggled to sit.

Handing Hallie a glass, Buzz perched on the edge of the bed beside her.

A fierce scowl on her face, Max paced back and forth across the small room gulping her drink.

Hallie raised her glass and sipped. In the next second, she choked and sputtered as the amber liquid burned a fiery path down her throat.

Max snorted, amusement twisting her full lips.

Her cheeks burning, Hallie took another drink, this time managing to swallow the scotch without making a scene.

"Max, were any of your sources able to pinpoint Geordie's location?" asked Ryan.

Her face transformed as she smiled. "How are you feeling, Ryan? I can see you're still hurting." Max's voice softened. "I'd be willing to help you with your pain, if you want. I'm sure we can figure some way to take your mind off your discomfort."

Ryan's brow furrowed, and his eyes turned cold. "Where's my brother? Did you find him?"

The light went out of her eyes and she sighed. "You're not going to like what I have to tell you."

"Geordie's not...dead, is he?" asked Hallie.

"He might as well be."

"Get to the point, Max," said Ryan.

Max's full mouth tightened. "The cartel Geordie took the money from is connected to Ricardo Montevedi."

Buzz inhaled sharply. "El Lagarto."

A stunned silence settled over the room.

Hallie's gaze flew from Buzz to Ryan, and then to Max. "What is it? Who's Ricardo Montevedi? What's El Lagarto?"

Ryan's expression was stark.

"Ryan? Who is he? Tell me," she repeated.

"Ricardo Montevedi is bad news," Max said. "He runs one of the biggest drug cartels in Mexico."

"He's based in Acapulco, but he has ties to drug syndicates throughout Mexico, the US and Canada. I've heard his network extends into Central and South America," Buzz added.

"What the hell was Geordie thinking?" Ryan burst out.

Max refilled Ryan's and Buzz's empty glasses. "Hell if I know." She swallowed her scotch in one gulp.

"Wait a minute," Hallie said. "Are you saying the money Geordie took belonged to this Montevedi?"

Max nodded.

"And that's why those men accosted us on the beach in Acapulco? They belong to Montevedi's gang?"

The red head nodded again.

"But our business trip to Acapulco was Geordie's first trip to Mexico. He told me he'd never traveled out of the States before."

Max heaved a heavy sigh. "You spell the situation out for her, Buzz. I don't have the patience for amateurs."

Hallie bit down on her bottom lip. She was sick and tired of Max's rudeness, but this wasn't the time or place to say anything. More important concerns faced them than petty slights and bruised egos.

"The drug cartels extend far beyond national borders," Buzz said. "They have people all over the world on their payroll. Geordie could have run into them anywhere in the US."

"Enough," Max said. "What the hell difference does it make where he met these losers? The point is Geordie's in big trouble, and we need to help him."

Ryan turned to Hallie, his eyes fierce. "You and Geordie were lucky you made it out of Mexico. With the money missing and Geordie unable to pay up,

Montevedi would have been plenty pissed."

"He's one mean son of a bitch when you cross him," Buzz said. "He and his gang of goons have butchered and brutalized their way to power. They'll stop at nothing to achieve what they want." He eyed Max and then Ryan. "You two know better than anyone how malicious Montevedi is."

Ryan's scowl deepened. "I have a three inch scar on my shoulder thanks to the slimy bastard."

"Wait a minute," Hallie said. "Are you telling me you and Max know this…this Mexican drug lord?"

"Know him and detest him," Max said.

Hallie gaped at Ryan. "He shot you?"

"And killed two damn good agents." Ryan's voice was a deep growl. He glared at Max whose face flushed red.

Tension crackled in the air.

Buzz coughed and said, "This trip down memory lane isn't getting us anywhere. We need to focus on now and how we're going to find Geordie before Montevedi does."

"You mentioned El Lagarto," Hallie said, trying to make sense of the heated undercurrents seething between the three. "What does it mean?"

"El Lagarto isn't an 'it,'" Max said. "El Lagarto is Montevedi's nickname. It's what the locals call him. Apparently, he likes lizards. Poisonous ones."

Hallie's brow knitted. She still didn't understand.

Max heaved another impatient sigh. "*Lagarto* is Spanish for lizard."

"I see," Hallie said, though she didn't see anything at all, but again she held her temper. "You're sure Geordie's mixed up with him? How would he even know some powerful drug lord who lives in Acapulco? Maybe you're wrong. Maybe he took the money from someone else."

Max glowered. "I don't make mistakes."

Buzz interjected, "This isn't helping anything. We need to work together if we're going to find Geordie. The longer he stays missing, the greater the likelihood he'll end up dead."

****

Ryan listened to the conversation with half an ear. Max's news troubled him. His brother may be stubborn, but he wasn't stupid. He knew better than to have anything to do with a crook like Montevedi.

He downed his drink, barely noticing the burn as the potent liquor coursed his throat. Two years ago, he'd analyzed Montevedi and his cohorts in minute detail when Ryan, Max and their team of DEA agents had been sent to Mexico to take down the vicious drug lord. The mission had been in the works for weeks, and secrecy was high, details of the mission on a need-to-know basis, but somehow Montevedi had discovered they were after him.

The bastard had vanished into the mountains mere hours before their arrival. They'd spent weeks searching, but their pursuit had been futile. Their informants were too frightened to tell them anything worthwhile. What made the situation all the more frustrating was the certainty someone had leaked the details of the raid, someone on his team.

After the DEA squad left Mexico, Montevedi had returned to his mansion on the outskirts of Acapulco and resumed his illegal activities. From what Ryan had heard, he'd become even bolder. In the past year, he was reputedly responsible for ordering the bombing of a police station in the Guerrero province of Mexico, an act resulting in the deaths of ten Mexican Federales.

Montevedi had also ordered the execution of a police commander in Verapaz, Guatemala, who'd dared to confiscate one of his illegal drug shipments. Rumors were rampant of dozens of other executions and countless bodies buried in the Mexican desert. Through the entire debacle, Montevedi sat in his fortified, Acapulco compound reaping in millions through his illegal drug running.

Ryan tasted bitter bile at the thought of his brother's involvement with such a vile group. Geordie had fucked up this time, big time. Lives were at stake, and not only his. Christ, if he had any sense, he'd go back to the ranch and leave Geordie to get himself out of this damn mess. It would serve him right.

Big talk, a voice inside his head sneered. As much as he wished it were otherwise, Geordie was his brother. His only brother. Their father had dropped dead of a heart attack when both boys were children, leaving their mother to run the ranch on her own. Money hadn't been a problem, but the hard work of running a ranch had taken its toll, and within six years, she was dead. The doctors called it cancer, but Ryan knew better. He'd seen how hard she worked, how she never took time for herself, and how gaunt and lined her face grew with each passing year.

Before she died, she'd made Ryan promise he'd look after his younger brother. Ryan was only nineteen, but he'd readily accepted the responsibility, even though fourteen-year-old Geordie was already showing his true colors and getting into one scrape after another.

Ryan had helped Geordie out of plenty of bad situations. How could he stop now? *Easy*, snorted the voice inside him. *You don't owe him a damn thing. Not anymore.* Geordie severed the ties of brotherhood two years ago.

The family get-together was supposed to have been a celebration. Max was the first woman Ryan had loved enough to ask her to marry him, and he'd wanted her to meet the only family he had left. He'd taken her to Seattle and introduced her to Geordie. Instead of the happy party he'd planned, his brother had made a play for Max. Even more unthinkable, she'd returned his interest.

He'd never forget waking up to an empty hotel room and discovering his brother and the woman he loved gone. The note they'd slipped under his hotel room door explained they were sorry; they'd fallen in love and had run off together. Ryan had dived into a bottle. He'd spent the next three weeks in a drunken stupor, barely registering the passing days.

He'd probably be drinking rotgut and living on the streets if Buzz hadn't rescued him. He'd dragged him kicking and screaming out of his self-pity and had forced him to face what he was doing to himself.

The truth hadn't come easy, but over the next weeks and months, he'd managed to put his life back together. He'd completed one last mission with Max as his unwelcome partner, and then he'd resigned from the DEA, and returned to Antler Springs to run the family's ranch.

He never found out what happened between Max and Geordie. They weren't together anymore, so he assumed Geordie had left Max and found another woman's heart to break. Max had tried to contact him several times over the past two years, but he hadn't returned her phone calls or answered her emails. What was the point? Their relationship was over. The same was true with Geordie. Ryan hadn't wanted to see or hear from his brother ever again.

And he hadn't. Until now. Until Geordie had called begging for help.

Now, irony of ironies, he was forced to depend on Max to save the brother who'd betrayed him. No one was better skilled in the field than Maxine Benoit. She had access to the resources they needed to find his brother, but seeing her, being near her again, brought back a slew of unpleasant memories.

"Ryan?" asked Max.

Still caught up in the weight of the past, he grunted in response.

"Are you all right?"

He nodded, though he was lying. He was anything but fine. He cast a glance at Hallie and flinched at the worry in her luminous eyes, worry for Geordie.

"So, we're agreed?" Max asked. "We're flying down to Mexico."

"I haven't agreed to anything," he said. "Why should we risk our lives to save Geordie's sorry ass? He sure as hell wouldn't do the same for us."

"You can't let him be killed," Hallie said, her voice rising.

"Why not?"

"He's your brother. No matter what he's done, he's still your family."

Seeing her love for his brother plastered so clearly across her face cut like a knife. He remembered kissing her, her sweet taste. He studied her full mouth and ached to kiss her again, to drive all thoughts of Geordie out of her.

"Please, Ryan. You have to help him."

Her pleas reminded him of an irrefutable truth. Geordie was his brother. He'd promised his mother he'd look after him. He'd given his word, and one thing he'd learned over the past two years was the value of a man's word. He gritted his teeth until his jaw ached, knowing he didn't have a choice. He'd help his brother this one time, but after this, as far as he was concerned, he no longer had a brother.

He glanced at Hallie's pale face, her eyes clouded with worry. "Okay, let's do it." As soon as the words were out of his mouth, he regretted them. But then, Hallie smiled and suddenly, it was as if the sun appeared from behind the clouds, and he felt ten feet tall. He turned to Max. "Any leads on where Geordie's hiding?" He focused on her, fighting to ignore his growing desire for his brother's girlfriend. He wasn't Geordie. He didn't steal another man's woman, no matter how desperately he wanted her.

"My sources tell me he's in Acapulco," Max said.

"What the hell is he doing down there?" he asked. "Acapulco is right in the heart of Montevedi's territory. Why would Geordie go into the lion's den?"

"Maybe he's trying to fix this," Buzz said.

Ryan snorted. "He doesn't have the money. He told Hallie he spent all the cash. Besides, Montevedi's made his intentions more than clear. He's out for blood. He won't settle for anything less."

"I have everything arranged," Max said. "A plane's waiting. It'll take us to a small, rarely used airfield near

Acapulco." Her eyes narrowed. "We have to act quickly. We don't want to risk one of Montevedi's informants telling him we're coming. Remember what happened last time."

Ryan tightened his mouth, recalling the welcoming party the drug lord had sent to meet them when they'd flown into Acapulco to take him down two years ago. The second the group of DEA agents had stepped out of the aircraft, a hail of bullets had met them. They'd returned fire and had managed to chase the attackers away, but not without consequences. He rubbed the old ache in his shoulder. The bullet had passed cleanly through the muscle, but the wound had left a scar.

"When are we leaving?" Hallie asked.

Max turned to her. "You're not going anywhere."

"But—"

"You're staying here. Buzz will look after you." Her painted lips curled in a sneer. "The last thing we need is a rookie screwing things up."

"I'm coming with you."

"I don't think so."

Before Hallie could protest further, Buzz interjected. "Max is right. This mission is too dangerous, Hallie. Ricardo Montevedi is no joke. He'll kill anyone who gets in his way."

"Look what he's already done," Max said. "Who do you think sent those men to kill you in Antler Springs, and then tried again at Buzz's place in the mountains?"

"I'm going." In spite of her all too obvious fear, Hallie's voice was firm.

Ryan's gut tightened. She was willing to risk her life to save his brother's sorry ass. Well, she was going to be disappointed. No way in hell was he was letting her take part in this undertaking. He agreed with Max and Buzz. This was a dangerous mission. Hallie would be safer in the States with Buzz watching over her.

She grabbed his arm. "Please don't leave me here, Ryan. I want to help."

He tried not to look into her blue eyes, but he couldn't help himself. The second his gaze met hers, his mouth dried. He gulped. "Why are you so damn determined to risk your life for him?" He grimaced at the hoarseness of his voice. "I thought you two were only friends."

"Our friendship is why I want to help. I can't sit here and do nothing. Besides, this involves me too. Those men want to kill me."

He repressed a shudder at the reminder of how close to death she'd been. His resolve strengthened. "The matter's settled. You're staying here." He turned his back on her and spoke to Max. "Let's get ready. We leave in an hour."

Max nodded. "I'll only need thirty minutes." She strode out of the room.

"I'll go and pack my things and meet you back here in fifteen minutes," Buzz said. "I don't think Hallie and I should stay at the hotel. Montevedi's men will be on to us before too long. I don't want to be here when they arrive." His face set in harsh lines. "I know a place where we'll be protected until you and Max return with Geordie."

Ryan trusted Buzz to keep Hallie safe. The ex-DEA commander might be getting on in years, but he hadn't forgotten his old skills. He'd protect Hallie with his life. He prayed the situation wouldn't become so dire. With any luck, he and Max would locate Geordie in Acapulco and take down Montevedi. Destroying Montevedi and his cartel was the only way any of them would be safe.

His gaze lit on Hallie, and he sighed. Until then, she had to be kept safe. He'd promised his brother he'd watch out for her, but more than a brotherly pledge was at stake now. Much more. "Go with Buzz," he said, his voice sharper than he intended. "I don't want you out of his sight until this thing is over."

She opened her mouth to protest, but, to his surprise, she nodded and allowed Buzz to take her arm and lead her toward the door. Before she stepped into the hall, she paused and glanced back. "Ryan?"

"What is it?"

"Take care of yourself." Tears shone like jewels in her sapphire eyes. "Please."

He nodded, unable to speak over the thick lump stuck in his throat.

"And find Geordie."

He scowled. Exactly what he'd feared she'd say.

Without another word, she turned and disappeared into the corridor, leaving him feeling as if he'd been sucker punched.

Chapter 13

"Where's Buzz?"

Hallie stepped aside, allowing Max into Buzz's hotel room. "Isn't he with you?"

The redhead wrinkled her brow. "I haven't seen him. He didn't make the meeting time. I assumed he'd been held up here babysitting you."

Hallie bit back a sharp retort. "He left awhile ago. He said he'd forgotten his glasses in my room. He was going to run down and get them, and then meet you and Ryan to say goodbye. He told me to wait for him here." Max's frown deepened, and Hallie's apprehension grew. "You didn't see him?" she asked.

Max shook her head.

A knock sounded on the door.

Max peered through the spy hole, and then opened the door to let in Ryan.

He'd changed into dark jeans and a tight, black T-shirt, which revealed his well-honed muscles. His dark hair was still damp from his shower, a single, glossy curl falling across his broad forehead.

Hallie gulped, fighting the urge to brush back the stray curl.

Ryan's piercing gaze raked her.

She inhaled sharply, unable to look away.

His eyes shuttered, and he turned to Max. "Any sign of him?"

Max shook her head.

"Where is he?"

"Apparently, he went to Hallie's room to get his glasses. She hasn't seen him in awhile."

Ryan studied Hallie. "How long are we talking?"

She looked at her watch, and a chill coursed through her. "I'm not sure, maybe half an hour."

Max grabbed her cell phone and punched in some numbers.

She spoke too quietly for Hallie to hear what she said, but when she turned back to them, her eyes were bleak.

"No one on our team has seen him. They've checked the lobby, all the stairs, the parking garage, and the restaurant. He's not there."

Dread filling her, Hallie stumbled over to the bed.

The furrow between Ryan's eyebrows deepened. "Has anyone checked Hallie's room?"

Max shook her head.

"I'll go and look."

"Not by yourself, you're not," said Max. "I'm coming with you."

Ryan nodded. He held out his hand to Hallie. "Come on. I'm not leaving you here alone."

The warmth of his touch settled her nerves, and she followed him and Max out of the room. The thick carpeting covered the sound of their footsteps as they hurried along the hall. Her worry increased with each step.

The elevator at the end of the corridor pinged, and the doors slid open. A man and woman, their arms laden with packages, stepped out and walked past them down the corridor.

They waited until the couple unlocked the door to their room and disappeared inside, before they continued along the now deserted hallway.

Hallie stood outside the closed door to her room. The hairs on the back of her neck prickled. In the hushed quiet, her racing heart sounded impossibly loud.

Ryan turned the handle. Locked. "Do you have your key?" he asked.

She shook her head. "I gave my key card to Buzz."

"I have one," said Max. She withdrew a plastic card from her pocket and handed it to Ryan. "I had the manager issue me an extra card for each of our rooms when we checked in."

He inserted the card in the door slot. The light flashed green, and he opened the door a few inches. He turned toward her, his face bleak. Lines of strain bracketed his mouth and furrowed his forehead. "Stay here." He opened the door and stepped inside.

Max sent her a warning glance and followed Ryan.

The door swung closed behind them.

Hallie peered up and down the corridor. She wiped her damp palms on her pants. The seconds ticked by. With each beat of her heart, her tension mounted. Ten seconds. She'd give them ten more seconds, and then she was going in. She was on the last count when the door swung open and Max appeared, her normally wan complexion, even paler.

"Follow me," she said and started walking down the hallway away from the hotel room.

"Wait," Hallie called after her. "What about Buzz? Where is he? Where's Ryan?"

Max kept walking, but she called over her shoulder, "Ryan's checking out some things. He'll be along in a few minutes. You're to come with me."

Hallie hesitated. "No, I'm going in there."

Max frowned, but then she shrugged. "Suit yourself, but don't say I didn't warn you."

Hallie looked at the closed door, and then at Max's retreating back. Inhaling a deep breath, she pushed the partially open door wider and stepped inside.

The room was dark. Someone had closed the curtains, and a light in the adjoining bathroom provided the only illumination.

She shuddered. When she'd left the room, the curtains had been open, the afternoon sunlight streaming in onto the bed. Her heart pounded, her breath frozen in her throat as her eyes slowly adjusted to the dimness.

Ryan kneeled before the open bathroom door, his attention fixed on something on the floor before him.

"Ryan?" she said, her voice cracking.

He stood, swiped at his face and turned toward her.

She swallowed and stumbled back a step.

His eyes blazed with barely controlled anger.

"Wha…what is it?" she sputtered.

His mouth tightened.

"Is it…" She swallowed. "Is it Buzz?"

He nodded, his gaze never leaving hers. "You shouldn't be in here. I told Max to take you back to Buzz's room."

"I…I had to know." She shivered. "Is he going to be all right?"

Ryan shook his head.

Choking back her shock, she craned her head to see into the bathroom.

He shifted his large body, blocking her view. "You

don't want to go in there, Hallie, trust me."

"Is…" She blinked back tears and tried again. "Is he dead?" She swallowed over the lump burning in her throat.

Ryan nodded.

"No," she protested. "No." A sob broke free. "He can't be dead." Ryan was lying. Buzz wasn't dead. This was all a joke. Only a few minutes ago they'd been discussing where they were going to hide out until Max and Ryan found Geordie. How could he be dead? She shoved Ryan's large body, trying to see into the bathroom, to see for herself.

He didn't budge.

She shoved him again, sobs tearing at her throat.

Taking her in his arms, he held her still, her body pressed against his. "He's gone, Hallie. We can't help him," he said, his voice thick with emotion. "Not anymore."

"I don't believe you," she said. "How…how could he be dead? He only came back here to get his glasses. What happened? Did he fall, have a heart attack? What?"

"Someone shot him."

Her breath whooshed out of her. "Who?" As soon as she asked the question, the answer blazed before her. The men who were after her had killed Buzz. Somehow they'd followed them from Buzz's ranch house and discovered where they were staying.

"Montevedi's men caught onto us quicker than we expected," Ryan said and then he cursed. "We shouldn't have underestimated the bastard's resources."

"Why would they kill Buzz? He didn't have anything to do with this. He was helping us."

165

"They weren't after Buzz."

"But they…they murdered him." Even in the gloom of the darkened room, she sensed the weight of his penetrating gaze.

"They weren't after Buzz," he repeated.

She shuddered as his meaning sank in. "Oh, my God." Her legs wobbled, and she sank to the floor. "He went to get his glasses. He'd left them in my room." Her voice was wooden as she struggled with the horror. "He said he'd only be gone a few minutes." Her lower lip trembled. Tears pooled in her eyes. "This is *my* room. They thought…" She hiccupped. "They thought Buzz was me."

Ryan crouched beside her and took her by the arms, shaking her gently. "Don't do this, Hallie. Blaming yourself won't do any good."

She shook him off. "This *is* my fault. If I hadn't involved you in this mess, Buzz would still be alive." Tears streamed down her face.

"Stop it," he ordered. "This is not your fault." He placed a finger under her chin, forcing her to meet his gaze. "Do you hear me? This is not your fault. Buzz knew what the risks were when he agreed to help." His mouth thinned to a grim line. "If anyone's to blame, it's Geordie. He got us into this."

"But—"

He wiped the tears from her cheek with the back of his hand. "This is not your fault, Hallie," he repeated, each word enunciated as if speaking to a child. "Montevedi's men set a trap for you. Buzz walked right into it. If it's any consolation, his knuckles were bleeding. He must have gotten in a few punches before they took him out. He went down fighting. He would

166

have liked fighting till the end."

Her lips trembled. She wanted to believe him, wanted to think she wasn't responsible for an innocent man's death, but deep down, she knew better. She opened her mouth to protest, but Ryan placed a gentle finger over her mouth and stopped her.

He shook his head. "Don't." He released her and stood. "Come on. We'd better get out of here. The men who did this can't be far." He helped her to her feet.

"We…we can't leave him here."

He placed his hand in the small of her back and propelled her toward the door of the hotel room. "He'd want us to find who did this. We can't locate his killers if we have to field questions from the local police. Buzz would understand. He knew how this business worked. The mission is always the priority."

He opened the door and maneuvered in front of her so his body blocked her from any shooter's view, as he peered up and down the corridor. He grabbed her hand and stepped into the hall, pulling her along behind him.

"But—"

"The men who killed Buzz have a job to do. They won't stop until they kill you and anyone who stands in their way. The best thing we can do is find Buzz's killers."

An icy chill settled over her. She wanted to refute his words, but he was right. The men after them had shown they wouldn't stop until they made Geordie pay for taking their money. With a nervous look over her shoulder at the empty corridor stretching behind them, she hurried her steps.

Ryan opened the door to Buzz's room, and she followed him inside.

Max sat on the bed talking on her cell phone.

Hallie caught her breath at her ghostly pallor.

Max ended her conversation. "Everything's ready."

Ryan nodded. "Good. Let's go. Montevedi's hired killers are close. They could be here any minute." He turned on his heel, grabbed his pack and strode toward the door.

"What about Hallie?" asked Max. "What's she going to do?"

Ryan studied Hallie and then nodded. "She's coming with us."

"What?" Max burst out. "No way." She leaped to her feet, her hands on her hips, her eyes flashing. "What the hell are you thinking? She'll just get in our way."

"We can't leave her here," he said. "Montevedi's men know she's in the hotel. How long do you think she'll last without someone looking after her?"

Hallie ignored the fact they were talking about her as if she were a troublesome child. She'd been resigned to staying behind. Even though Max's disdain rankled, the redhead was right. Hallie's inexperience would put the others in danger. But now Ryan wanted to take her with him to Acapulco. Relief washed over her. Mexico would be dangerous, but she didn't want to stay here alone. Not now. Not after what happened to Buzz.

"This is crazy," said Max. She cast Hallie a look of derision. "Buzz is dead because of her and her stupid actions. Who cares what happens to her? She's collateral damage."

Hallie reeled under the verbal assault.

"I care." Ryan's eyes blazed at Max.

"I'm not going if she's going. I refuse to risk my life because some rank greenhorn makes a stupid mistake."

Tension crackled in the room. Ryan's face was cold, devoid of expression. "Okay. You stay here." He motioned to Hallie. "Come on, let's go." He took her hand and led her across the room to the door.

"Ryan, don't be stupid," Max said. "Use your brain, not your penis to think this through. She's just another pretty face. Girls like her are a dime a dozen. What does she know about dangerous operations?"

He ignored her. After checking the corridor was clear, he led Hallie into the hall.

Max stood in the doorway of the hotel room, indecision written across her face. "What the hell," she said and disappeared into the room. In the next second, she reappeared carrying a brown leather bag. She hurried after them. "I must be crazy. We're going to confront one of Mexico's most notorious drug lords with a man who has a bullet hole in his side and an inexperienced rookie. How the hell am I supposed to keep everyone alive?"

Hallie shuddered. Max was right. They were crazy.

Chapter 14

The roar of the small plane drowned out all other noise. Hallie sat in the seat behind the pilot and across from Ryan, her seat belt tight across her lap. Her hands clenched the worn leather armrests as the small, sleek, five-seat, turboprop aircraft lurched and bumped its way south. An air vent above her head blew a steady stream of cold, stale air in her face, making her eyes water.

Three hours ago they'd taken off from the small airfield near the Mexican border. She peered through the scratched acrylic window beside her. The view hadn't changed. A bed of puffy white clouds lay below. Above, clear blue sky and brilliant sunshine.

Shaken by Buzz's death, they'd left the hotel in a rush. One of Max's accomplices had driven them to the airport, but rather than board a flight to Acapulco as Hallie had assumed they would, they'd climbed aboard a private jet and flown to a small, dusty town situated on the Mexican-US border. From there, they'd transferred to the single engine plane.

Max had explained the smaller, propeller-driven aircraft was capable of flying below Mexican radar. Hopefully, their low altitude flight would enable them to arrive in Acapulco without Ricardo Montevedi knowing.

Max's sources had informed her Geordie was holed

up somewhere in the city of Acapulco. They hoped by the time they arrived, his exact location would have been determined. Once they found him, they'd convince him to give up whatever foolishness in which he was involved and return to the United States with them. With any luck, they'd be out of Mexico before Montevedi knew anything.

Once back in the States, they'd contact the American authorities and let them take care of Montevedi. They hoped with Geordie in a safe house and out of Montevedi's reach, and with the US authorities after him, Montevedi would decide chasing them down wasn't worth the risk, and he'd call off his men.

The unknown factor in their plan was Geordie. They didn't know why he'd traveled to Mexico. Was he attempting to convince Montevedi to lay off, or was he doing something even more reckless? Had Geordie joined Montevedi and his fellow gang members as a way to pay off his debt? The thought of Geordie working with the murderous drug lord filled her with revulsion. Geordie hid his true character beneath layers of jovial charm. His actions these past months made him a stranger, a man capable of any number of poor choices.

The plane dipped as they lost elevation.

She squinted at the glare of the brilliant sunlight. The clouds parted, revealing an azure expanse of ocean below. A faint hint of wood smoke, man and leather wafted toward her, and she glanced at Ryan. Tension vibrated off him in waves. Mere inches separated them across the narrow aisle, but the distance might as well have been miles. Immersed in the papers he'd been examining since the plane had taken off, he hadn't glanced at her once. The muscles in his jaw were clenched, his brow furrowed, his mouth a tight line.

She could only imagine his strain. His friend had been murdered, and his brother's life was in danger. And now he'd embarked on a desperate mission to save Geordie.

In spite of his injury, Ryan looked ready for action. He wore a lightweight, black jacket over his dark T-shirt. The coat wasn't for warmth. Before they'd boarded the plane, he'd withdrawn an ominous-looking gun from his backpack and placed the revolver in a leather holster strapped across his broad chest. The jacket concealed the gun's bulge.

Max, long red hair gleaming in the sunlight streaming through the windshield, sat in the copilot seat. Her model-perfect body did nothing to hide the fact she too was armed. She wore a gun strapped to her ankle and another tucked in the waistband of her jeans.

No one had offered Hallie a weapon. She wouldn't have a clue how to use a gun if they had given her one, but knowing she at least had a chance to protect herself would have helped ease her worry. She swallowed over the lump of fear lodged in her throat. They didn't know what they'd be facing when they found Geordie.

She peered out the window. A large bay, rimmed by pristine, white sandy beaches extended below them. A multitude of boats sailed across the brilliant blue water. An endless stretch of hotels and condo developments faced the beach, their white towers gleaming. The resort city of Acapulco was a paradise, making it difficult to believe the horror lurking beneath the peaceful façade.

The engines rumbled as the small plane soared over the water, past the cluster of hotels, and above endless blocks of closely packed, white plaster houses, roofed in red tiles. The buildings thinned out, leaving green fields and acres of mangrove swamp as the plane sailed lower.

A clearing loomed ahead, overrun with a thick tangle of bushes and shrubs, flanked by tall palm trees. The landing strip's rutted surface was littered with rocks and other debris.

The plane circled and flew over the field again.

The pilot banked the aircraft, and Hallie gripped the arms of her seat as the ground outside the window rushed by in a blur. A high-pitched roar filled the air, followed by a jarring impact, which pressed her against the back of the seat. The turboprop raced along the ground, bumping and jolting, the engines screaming. Skidding and swerving, the plane rolled to a stop.

She released her breath and opened her eyes. Unclenching her hands, she wiped their dampness on her jeans and fumbled with the clasp on her seat belt.

Ryan opened the door, and a burst of warm, humid air, redolent of palm trees and rotting vegetation, filled the plane. Sunlight streamed inside.

A sharp ache filled her at the sound of wind rustling through palm trees, and she remembered tropical holidays of the past. If only this trip were a simple holiday with nothing more on her mind than hanging out with her college friends and finding the best swimming beaches with the hottest guys.

The plane's steps unfolded with a loud, whirring screech.

Ryan grabbed the railing and leaped down the

stairs, followed by Max.

Hallie climbed out of her seat and walked on rubbery legs to the open doorway and down the steps. Blinking under the bright noonday sun, she wished she'd brought sunglasses, but they were back in her rental car parked in the parking lot of the Rusty Nail in Antler Springs.

Small trees and shrubs covered the hard-packed, dirt runway. In the distance, palm trees swayed in the warm, tropical breeze. A haze hung in the heavy air. She wiped the beads of perspiration forming on her forehead and the back of her neck under her heavy fall of hair.

Max and Ryan stood at the bottom of the steps.

"See anything?" Max shielded her eyes with her hand and peered into the distance.

Ryan shook his head. "The area looks clear." He donned a pair of dark sunglasses and withdrew a black ball cap from his backpack. He placed the hat on his head, covering his unruly curls and concealing his face in shadows.

Max too had come prepared. She'd drawn her long hair into a ponytail and tucked it under a floppy sun hat, hiding the vibrant red.

"Your first mission?"

Hallie jumped at the sound of the deep, male voice.

The pilot of the small aircraft stood behind her. His blond, brush cut hair, stiff posture and no-nonsense attitude screamed military. He'd been introduced as Vince, but other than a quick nod in her direction, he hadn't spoken until now.

"No," she said. Moisture trickled down her sides. "I mean, yes, it's my first mission, but I'm not..." She paused and nodded at Ryan and Max below. "I'm not like them. I'm just a rookie. I've never done anything like this before."

His eyebrows lifted and the corners of his mouth twitched. "Really? You'd never know it."

A cloud of dust billowed in the distance moving closer, and a chill settled over her. All too well she remembered the men on the ATVs who'd attacked them at Buzz's house in the mountains. "Someone's coming." Her voice quavered.

"That'll be José," Vince said. "He's the guy who's taking Max to meet her contact. Let's hope her contact was able to determine Geordie's exact location. I have a bad feeling about this place. The sooner we take off and get back into US air space, the better."

A rusted, dark green hatchback, belching gouts of black diesel, approached the plane in a swirl of yellow dust. The driver remained in the car, the engine running. He leaned over and flung open the passenger door.

Max removed the gun strapped to her ankle and checked to see if the chamber was loaded. She did the same with the gun tucked into the waistband of her tight pants.

"Are you set?" Ryan asked.

Max nodded and turned to Vince. "I should be back before dark. If not, take off. Don't wait for me."

The pilot nodded.

"We'll wait," Ryan bit off.

Max smiled, her eyes softening. "You always were a stubborn cuss." She grabbed her bag, climbed into the car and slammed the door. With a screech of shifting gears, the ancient vehicle rumbled off.

In the ensuing silence, Hallie asked, "She's going alone?"

Ryan nodded. "Her contact will only meet with her. He'll run like a scared rabbit if anyone else shows up."

"She'll be back soon, won't she?" She met Ryan's probing gaze. "I mean, once she meets her contact and finds out where Geordie is, she'll come back, right?"

"Yeah, she'll be back."

Relief soared through her. Despite the tension between them, she couldn't bear the thought of Max getting hurt because she was helping her. Bad enough Buzz had been killed; another casualty on her conscience would be too much.

"Come on," Ryan said.

"Where are we going?"

"Max won't be back for awhile. Vince says there's a hacienda behind those trees. We'll be more comfortable waiting in a cool building than in the hot sun. In a few hours, the inside of this plane is going to be an oven." He strapped on his backpack, picked up a large plastic bag from inside the plane, and began walking across the field toward the row of towering palm trees.

Vince climbed the plane's steps.

"Aren't you coming with us, Vince?" Hallie asked.

The pilot shook his head. "I'm not leaving the plane." He disappeared inside the small craft making it clear he didn't want company.

She licked her suddenly dry lips and glanced at the sky. The sun had passed its zenith, but dark was hours away, hours in which she'd be alone with Ryan. The sun beat down. Perspiration filmed her brow. Her hair weighed damp and heavy on the nape of her neck. A rivulet of sweat trickled between her breasts.

Ryan was a good hundred feet away, the distance between them increasing with each frantic heartbeat. Her choice was simple: bake out here in the sun, or follow Ryan. The image of a cool, air-conditioned house made up her mind. She hurried after him, stumbling across the uneven ground on her injured ankle. She was out of breath when she caught up with him. He was fast for someone who'd been shot in the back three days ago.

"So you decided to join me," he said. "What changed your mind?"

She flushed, realizing he'd been all too aware of her reluctance to spend time alone with him. "There wasn't much choice. Vince wanted to be by himself, and I didn't want to die of sunstroke."

"Ouch." His mouth quirked.

They crossed the runway and passed through the row of palm trees into a thick snarl of scrub. Stones dug into the soles of her high-heeled boots, and barbed branches tore at her clothes as they fought their way through the bush. In spite of the oppressive heat, she was glad she wasn't wearing shorts. Her white jeans, impossibly stained, in spite of being cleaned by the hotel staff, covered her legs and protected her from the worst of the thorns.

They entered a clearing. A small, dilapidated building, the whitewashed, crumbling walls yellowed with age, stood in the center of a ring of towering palm trees. Weeds climbed the walls, nearly obscuring the shuttered windows. Swirls of dust and dried leaves blew across the hard-packed dirt.

"This is better than waiting in the plane?" she asked.

"Oh, ye of little faith," he said. He removed a key from his pocket and unlocked the sun-bleached, wooden door. Indicating she should wait outside, he entered the house. After a brief moment, he was back, beckoning her to join him.

She stepped over the threshold and sighed as a balm of cool air soothed her hot, damp skin. Bright sunlight streamed through the open doorway behind her, revealing whitewashed, adobe brick walls. Instead of the rat-infested hovel she'd expected, the interior of the hacienda was clean and obviously well cared for. Heavy, dark, wooden furniture and a large, white, leather couch filled the room. The floor was covered with gleaming, white tiles. Thick, woven carpets added splashes of color. The sweet smell of roses wafted in the air, and she spied several small, clay pots containing dried flower petals set about the room.

A grin wreathed Ryan's face, dimples dancing in his lean cheeks.

"What?" she asked, trying to swallow over the sudden dryness in her mouth. His blue eyes twinkled, and he was grinning like a young boy...a very handsome young boy.

His grin widened. "You shouldn't let first impressions fool you. Haven't I told you the same thing before?"

A rush of heat flamed along her cheeks at his teasing tone. He wasn't talking about houses. All too well, she recalled her snide remarks about him being a hardscrabble farmer struggling to make ends meet the night in the line shack. She'd misjudged him, just as she had this hacienda. "Who...who owns this place?"

"A friend of Vince's." He closed the door, and then crossed the now darkened room and threw open the wooden shutters covering one of the windows. Once again, light flooded in. "Are you hungry?" He held up the plastic bag he'd taken from the plane. "I brought us some food."

She hadn't eaten since she'd grabbed a chocolate bar from the vending machine at the tiny airport in Douglas, Arizona. Her mouth watered as he removed three, plastic-wrapped sandwiches, a package of cookies and two apples from the bag. Her eyes widened at the bottle of white wine he produced.

He held up the bottle and grinned. "I saw this in the airport gift shop, and I couldn't resist. The wine's not a great vintage, but you never know. What do you say? This seems as good a time as any to try some." His blue eyes flashed golden sparks.

Reeling under the impact of gold-flecked eyes, even white teeth, and a smile guaranteed to win over even the most-hardened spinster, she limped over to the couch and sank into the soft leather cushions. "I...I guess a sip or two won't hurt."

He handed her a sandwich.

Unwrapping the plastic, she examined the thin, limp, white bread, filled with an unrecognizable mixture of lumpy, gray chunks of processed meat product and gobs of mayonnaise. The sandwich didn't look appetizing, let alone edible. She glanced at Ryan, hoping this was some sort of joke. He watched her with an expectant expression, as if awaiting her approval. She nibbled at the crust, and then took a small bite. Her eyes widened in surprise. The soggy sandwich tasted like the best meal she'd ever eaten.

Ryan removed a small knife from his trouser pocket and used a corkscrew attachment to remove the cork from the bottle of wine. "I don't have any glasses. Do you mind sharing?" He held out the bottle, his gaze settling on her mouth.

She resisted the urge to lick her suddenly dry lips, accepted the bottle and took a tentative sip. As the cool liquid slid down her throat, she regarded him with surprise. "This is good."

He chuckled. "What did you expect?"

She took another swallow and handed him the bottle.

He raised the wine to his lips and drank.

Her heart thudded at the play of light and shadow on the powerful muscles in his throat as he swallowed. She prayed he couldn't hear her heart's frantic pace.

Their gazes locked.

The heat in his eyes drew her in, deeper, and deeper still. She couldn't breathe.

A loud bang echoed through the room.

She stumbled away from him, expelling a whoosh of air, diving for the floor, covering her head with her hands. Someone was shooting at them!

Ryan stood watching her, his face void of any expression. "I guess I forgot to latch the shutters." His voice was a husky rasp. He held out his hand. "Come on, I'll help you up."

Shaken, feeling foolish, she took his hand and allowed him to pull her to her feet. While he secured the shutter, she picked up the wine and drank, desperate for the alcohol's numbing effect.

He took the bottle from her and set it on the table.

"Better take it easy with the wine. Anything can happen today. We don't know what Max is going to find when she meets with her contact."

She looked into his eyes and shivered. Once again he'd undergone a transformation. Gone was the teasing grin and twinkling eyes, replaced by his usual serious demeanor.

He handed her half of another sandwich and sat on a chair by the window eating his own sandwich, his gaze steady on the view outside the window.

She rubbed the back of her neck. He was right. Anything could happen. She feared it already had.

Chapter 15

Hallie sat on the couch, sinking into its softness. Her back throbbed from sitting on the hard, wooden chair by the table; her legs ached from standing and staring out the casa's single window. She'd done plenty of both as they waited for Max to return with news of Geordie.

As the hours passed, Ryan grew tenser, the lines in his face more pronounced. Once again he'd withdrawn into the cold remoteness she found so intimidating. He kept his vigil at the window, his gaze never wavering from the scene outside. Every once in a while he grimaced and shifted his position. His side pained him, but still he kept watch. He hadn't said much of anything in the past four and a half hours, content to stare out the window in silence.

The waiting drove her crazy, and she searched for something to say to ease the tension. "You don't think Montevedi knows we're here, do you?"

He shrugged, his eyes fixed on the scene outside.

"Did he send those men after us at Buzz's house? And again at the hotel?" she asked.

"Probably."

"And they…they killed Buzz."

He turned. His face bleak, his eyes haunted.

"Buzz…" She swallowed. "He was a good friend, wasn't he?"

Ryan's mouth tightened. A pulse ticked in his jaw. "He was the best."

"I liked him a lot," she said, pushing her hair behind her ear.

He didn't respond, his gaze once again riveted out the window.

The seconds ticked by, each one longer than the one before.

Suddenly, he rose and headed toward the door. "I'm going to check around outside."

She stood, thinking to go with him, but stopped.

His broad shoulders were stiff, his muscular body tight, making his feelings clear. He wanted to get away from her, to be alone with his over-riding concern for Max.

With a heavy sigh, she sank into the cushions and closed her eyes. What was she doing here in Mexico, hiding from a Mexican drug lord, running from men determined to kill her and anyone else who was in their way?

Before all this started, the most dangerous thing she'd done was drive alone through East Los Angeles in the middle of the night. She took a deep breath and drew her feet up on the couch, draping the colorful, wool blanket on the back of the sofa over her. In minutes, her body relaxed. Her breathing slowed, as her eyelids grew heavy. She forced them open. She had to stay awake and alert. As Ryan had said, anything could happen. They wouldn't be safe until they were out of Mexico and back in the States.

A flicker across the room caught her attention, and she peered into the deepening shadows. Her breath caught in her throat.

A snake glided across the floor, its body ringed with bands of black, red and yellow, a forked tongue flicking in and out.

She swallowed her fear, and with infinite slowness, sat up, sliding the blanket off her legs, ready to run.

The creature stopped its slithering progress, raised its blunt head and regarded her with cold, yellow eyes. The triangular-shaped head weaved back and forth, the forked, red tongue flicking the air.

She stared transfixed, a scream building in her throat. *Move.* Her body refused to obey, her muscles frozen under the creature's mesmerizing gaze.

The snake lowered its head and once again slithered toward her. Each lateral undulation propelled the venomous reptile closer and closer.

****

Ryan breathed in the humid air and wiped sweat from his brow. He squinted into the lowering sun. Where the hell was Max? She'd had more than enough time to meet her contact, find out where Geordie was hiding, and get back here.

He shook off his worry. Montevedi couldn't possibly know they were in Mexico. They'd been too careful, taken too many precautions. They'd learned their lesson the last time they'd entered Acapulco thinking they were undetected. Montevedi had spies everywhere. Max knew to take extra measures.

Max was doing what Max did best. She was a well-trained, skilled field operative and could take care of herself even in the most difficult situations. Hell, she always took care of herself first. She'd proven her self-serving nature when she'd run off with his brother. He held his breath, waiting for the stab of pain the image of

184

Geordie and Max together always entailed. His scowl deepened. The ache was there deep in his gut, but not the sharp pang he usually had.

He retraced his steps to the front of the hacienda and swiped again at his damp forehead. Hallie. She was all he'd thought of since he'd first set eyes on her. Damn Geordie. Why had he asked *him* to meet her? Why hadn't he asked someone else, someone who wouldn't fall apart every time she looked at him, someone immune to her luminous blue eyes and soft red lips?

A vision of her silky fall of long, blonde hair flashed before him. He rubbed his head in a futile attempt to ease the throbbing and the sense he was spiraling out of control. Why the hell had he suggested they wait for Max in the hacienda? The little casa was more comfortable than the plane, but the waiting in the small house meant being alone with her, alone and tempted.

They hadn't been in the hacienda more than a few minutes before he'd lost all his sense. He'd been desperate to kiss her. Hell, he couldn't stop wondering if her lips tasted as sweet as they had when he'd kissed her in Buzz's ranch house. If the damn shutter hadn't banged and distracted him, he would have kissed her right then. And once he kissed her, he wouldn't have stopped. He wouldn't have stopped for anything, not until he'd drank his fill.

Kicking a pebble, he sent it skidding across the dirt. This damn mission couldn't be over soon enough. Once Geordie was back in the States and they were all safe, he'd never see Hallie again. A hollow ache settled over him. *Stop thinking of her. She loves your brother.*

185

Remember? He emphasized each word clearly in his mind, hoping to ingrain them on his brain.

Muttering a curse, he forced himself to remember why he was here. He scanned his surroundings, searching the thick brush for anything untoward. Nothing but palm trees, scrub brushes, and dust, the same vista he'd stared at for the past five hours.

Hallie's scream echoed in the still air.

He froze for a heartbeat, and then he ran, ignoring the pain in his side, flying over the uneven ground toward the hacienda.

She screamed again.

He flung open the door and ran inside, skidding to a halt and freezing.

Hallie lay on the sofa, a multicolored quilt on the couch at her feet. Her face was white, her mouth open in terror, her eyes wide and staring at the snake coiled on the white tiles below the sofa, its blunt head swaying and bobbing.

His heart thudded. He examined the cylindrical body ringed with bright bands of yellow, red and black. Mexico was home to several species of poisonous snakes. Was this one of them? He didn't know. Couldn't take a chance. "Don't move," he said. He edged toward Hallie, his gaze never straying from the snake.

The snake's head turned, and the yellow eyes observed him, its tongue flicking the air, smelling him.

"Ryan?"

"Don't move." He spoke softly, hoping his voice didn't betray his fear. "I'll get rid of it." As soon as the words were out of his mouth, he wondered how he was going to remove the snake from the casa and prevent the serpent from striking her. He risked a glance at Hallie. The trust in her eyes, her certainty he'd save her filled him with warmth and strengthened his resolve.

With studied movements, he withdrew the gun nestled in the holster at his side. His fingers curled around the grip and he released the safety catch and inched toward the serpent.

The snake swayed back and forth, the body coiled, ready to strike.

The beast was directly in front of Hallie. If he shot at it and missed, the bullet could strike her. Sweat dampened his hand. His finger tightened around the trigger. He hadn't fired a gun in months. He had one chance, and one chance only, to do this right. "Hallie, I'm going to shoot the snake. Whatever you do, stay still. Don't even breathe."

"Okay." Her voice trembled.

She was afraid. Who wouldn't be? But he couldn't think of her now. He had to focus on aiming at the snake. He swallowed. "Stay where you are. Do not move."

She didn't answer, and he slid a glance in her direction.

Her eyes were closed, her lashes dark against her pale face.

He took a deep breath, sighted along the muzzle and squeezed the trigger.

An explosion filled the air, followed by the pungent, chemical smell of gunpowder. The snake's head vaporized.

Ryan grabbed the snake by the tail. In two strides he was out the door and tossed the serpent's still-writhing body into the shrubs. When he walked back inside, Hallie sat on the couch staring at the blood-spattered, shattered tiles.

"Is...is it gone?"

He blew out a puff of air. "Yes, it's gone."

Her eyes were glowing pools of blue in her pale face. She leaped off the couch and into his arms.

He held her close, breathing in her scent. Relief washed over him, making him weak.

"I was so scared," she sobbed.

He smoothed her silken curls. "It's okay. You're safe now."

"Where...where did it come from? How did a snake get in here?"

"I don't know. It must have crawled in through a hole somewhere. This place isn't used very often. Maybe the snake lived here."

Tears glistened on her dark lashes.

Without thinking, he ran his thumb along her cheek, wiping her tears.

"You saved my life. Again."

He was helpless to stop the foolish grin. "I aim to please, ma'am."

Her lips trembled and curved into a soft smile. "Thank you," she whispered. "Thank you." Curling her fingers around the back of his neck, she drew him closer, pressing her lips to his.

He groaned, lost at the first taste of her.

The kiss deepened.

She opened her mouth inviting him in.

He stopped thinking, stopped wondering what the hell he was doing. He needed, and he took. Wanting to taste more of her, he dragged his mouth from hers and kissed the tender skin along her neck.

She arched her neck allowing him better access.

He caressed her shoulders and back, discovering her soft skin, the shape of her body, and the supple play of muscle along her back. Sliding a hand beneath her top, he bit back a groan at the velvety warmth of her skin. His fingers traveled over the slight indentations of her ribs, moving higher until they brushed against the undersides of her breasts. He cupped them, cradling their soft fullness as his thumbs teased her hardening nipples.

She touched him, her hands smoothing the muscles in his back and shoulders, kneading them.

Shivers of awareness rocketed through him. He tore his mouth from hers and grasped her chin, forcing her to meet his gaze.

Her mouth was swollen from his kisses, her eyes heavy lidded.

"Are you okay with this?" he asked. He wanted her. Hell, every cell in his body cried out for her, but he wouldn't go any further without her okay. She had to be willing. She had to want this as much as he did.

She blinked.

"Hallie, is this what you want?"

She drew his head down and met his lips in a passionate kiss leaving no doubt as to her answer.

He'd have cheered if his attention hadn't been caught by the weight of her breasts in his hands and her warm tongue in his mouth. The next minutes were a sensual blur as his blood heated, filling him with a desperate ache only she could appease.

Her hands slid under his shirt, gliding across his skin, teasing the small hairs covering his chest and belly, moving lower and lower still.

189

He drew her closer, pressing his arousal against her softness.

Her breath whooshed out in a moan, and she melted in his arms.

"Well, well, well. What have we here?"

He froze.

"I guess that's one way to pass the time."

Max's cynical voice acted like a pail of icy water. He removed his hands from under Hallie's shirt and turned his body, shielding her, giving her a chance to regain her senses before she faced Max. He took a deep, steadying breath and glared at Max. His anger rose at the censure in her gaze. She didn't have a hold over him. Not anymore. "Where have you been?" he demanded.

She smiled, the light not reaching her eyes. "Is this any way to greet me after everything I've done for you?" Her gaze slid to Hallie. Her eyes narrowed. "But then I can see you were…ah…busy."

"Max," he warned.

"I see now why you were so determined to drag her along with us. You wanted something, or I should say…someone with whom to occupy yourself while you waited for me to do the hard work."

His anger swelled, and he glared. "Leave it alone."

Outrage flashed in her green eyes, but she nodded. "I know where Geordie is."

"Good. Let's get this done before Montevedi finds out we're right in his backyard."

"Are you sure you want to leave now? I mean, if you've got something else to do…"

Ryan's irritation neared the breaking point, but he gritted his teeth, keeping his anger in check. He needed

Max. They all needed her. "We're doing this tonight."

"What about *her*?"

He turned to look at Hallie. Other than a stray lock of hair, which had fallen across her forehead, she was remarkably composed considering what had happened.

What the hell had *happened?* He'd kissed her. Hell, he'd had his hands all over her. If Max hadn't shown up when she did, he knew what would have happened next. Self-loathing filled him. He was no better than his damn brother. He didn't think twice before taking what he wanted, and betraying a trust.

"Ryan? What are we going to do with Hallie?" asked Max. "She can't go with us."

"Hallie will wait in the plane with Vince."

Hallie opened her mouth to protest.

He cut her off. "You'll be safe in the plane. Vince knows what he's doing. He'll look after you."

"But—"

"Be ready to leave the minute we get back. Once we grab Geordie, we'll have to act fast. Montevedi may have Geordie under surveillance. Once we contact Geordie, Montevedi will know we're here."

To his surprise, Hallie didn't offer any further protest.

"Okay," she said.

He turned back to Max. "Okay. We're set then. Let's get this done."

Chapter 16

Hallie peered through the plane's dusty windshield. The moon's white light streaming across the uneven ground of the runway, cast harsh shadows. She glanced at her watch. Ryan and Max had been gone two hours.

Vince had reclined his seat and lay with his long legs stretched before him. His eyes were closed, but he wasn't sleeping. Any change in the steady murmur of night insects had him jumping to his feet and reaching for his gun.

She studied her watch again. Time seemed to have stopped. Where were they? Had they found Geordie? What if he refused to come with them? Even more disturbing, what if Montevedi, or his men, harmed Ryan and Max? She chewed on her bottom lip. Max and Ryan were experts. They'd done this sort of thing many times before. Nothing was going to happen to them.

But where were they? Ryan had said they wouldn't be long. Their plan was simple. They'd follow Max's information, locate Geordie, and convince him to return to the plane with them. With any luck, they'd be back in the States shortly after midnight.

The agony of the interminable wait grew with each passing second.

Vince sat up, his body tense. He cocked his head as if listening to something. Grabbing his gun from the seat beside him, he stood and crossed to the doorway. He peered outside.

"What is it?" she asked. "Are they back?"

"A car's coming." Relief filled his eyes. "It's them."

She exhaled a gust of air and stood beside him, looking out into the dark.

Twin beams of light lit the dark runway, bobbing as the vehicle sped toward them over the rough ground. The sound of the vehicle's laboring engine grew louder.

"You'd better get in your seat and strap in, ready for takeoff. They'll want to leave right away," he said and bounded down the steps. "I'll do a final check of the landing gear."

She hurried to her seat and buckled the seat belt across her lap.

The sound of the approaching car grew louder.

Footsteps pounded up the metal stairs. Vince leaned in the doorway, his face pale. "Something's not right. It isn't their vehicle."

"What? Are you sure it's not them?" Her heart raced.

"Get under cover, and stay here." He disappeared down the steps.

She fumbled with her seat belt. When the clasp finally opened, she stood on quaking legs and edged toward the door. She had to see what was going on.

A shot rang out.

She crouched low, ducking behind a metal storage box. Her breath rasped in and out in rapid pants.

Another shot pierced the night, and then another.

She bit the inside of her mouth, fighting back a scream.

A volley of shots filled the air, followed by an ominous silence. Seconds ticked by. Unfamiliar, male voices shouted orders in Spanish. The metal steps creaked as someone slowly ascended.

She sank lower and held her breath, her gaze fixed on the plane's open doorway.

The long, black barrel of a gun appeared, and then a dark figure stepped into the plane.

She bit back a moan and squeezed her eyes shut.

The tread of stealthy footsteps moved about the plane, and then approached her hiding place.

She bit her bottom lip, tasting blood.

"*Hola, chica.*"

A chill washed over her. She opened her eyes and gasped.

The man who'd accosted her and Geordie on the beach in Acapulco and again in Antler Springs stood over her, holding a large, gleaming pistol pointed at her chest. She'd never forget his bald head or the cruel glint in his ferret-like eyes.

She stared at the deadly gun as a hundred images raced through her mind: her ears ringing from the loud explosion in the casa, the sting of gunpowder, and the blood on the shards of white tiles after Ryan shot the snake. She held her breath and waited for the flash and impact of the bullet. *Would it hurt?*

The man snickered, exposing crooked, yellow teeth. "I see you remember me, *chica. Bueno.* I have not forgotten you." He lifted his stained shirt and exposed his bloated belly. Purple and red bruises mottled the hair-covered skin. "See what you did to me?" His lips curled into a cruel smile. "How lucky for me I found you, and I am able to take my revenge." He waved the gun at her.

She shuddered. "Where's Vince?" she croaked through a mouth made dry by fear. "What have you done to him?"

He grabbed her arm, yanked her from behind the crate, and then dragged her to the door and pointed outside.

Icy terror gripped her heart, and she moaned. "No!"

Half a dozen, heavily armed men stood in a semi-circle around the base of the stairs facing her. Their cruel faces and cold eyes made their menace clear. A dark shape lay on the ground in front of them.

Her breath caught in her throat.

Vince, his arms and legs bound, lay motionless, a pool of dark blood staining the ground beneath him.

"Vince!" She yanked her arm, trying to break free from the thug holding her.

His fingers dug into her skin, and he gripped her tighter.

"Vince," she called again. Tears burned her eyes.

"I do not think he hears you, *chica*." The man grinned, his thin lips stretching obscenely.

The pilot's eyes were closed, his face unnaturally pale and waxen in the moonlight. "Is…is he…?"

The man chuckled, the cruel sound sending shudders through her. "Is he dead?" he said. "No, not yet, but soon, I think." He thrust her down the steps and shoved her toward Vince's body.

She yelped as she stumbled over him and fell. Her shoulder struck a rock, and she grunted in pain.

"Get up."

Swiping her hair off her face, she swallowed the

cold lump in her throat. "Wha…what do you…?" She tried again. "What do you want with me?" Even as she asked the question, she knew the answer. He'd been ordered to kill her. He'd tried once before and failed. The look in his cruel eyes made it clear he wouldn't fail again.

His gaze raked over her, and he licked his lips.

She swallowed fresh fear.

He knelt beside her, his garlic-laced breath warm on her face. "Oh, *bella, chica*, we have unfinished business, you and me." He trailed a callused finger down her cheek and along her neck. Dipping his hand beneath her shirt, he curled his fingers around her breast and squeezed.

Pain shot through her. She screamed and shoved against the intruding hand.

He chuckled, unfazed by her attempts to free herself. His hand continued to fondle her, his nails digging into her tender skin, pinching her nipple. "After all, I owe you." His eyes narrowed in his sallow, acne-scarred face. "You were not very nice the last time we met, *chica*. My *amigo* is still in the hospital from what your friend did to him."

In spite of her fear, a spurt of satisfaction filled her. *Good for Ryan.*

He squeezed her breast.

She thrust his hand away and kicked him hard in the stomach. His grunt of pain lent her strength, and she redoubled her efforts to free herself, kicking, punching, and biting.

He grabbed her arm and wrenched it behind her back.

Tears squeezed from her eyes as he yanked her arm

higher and higher still. The pain was unbearable. Surely he'd break her arm. But then the agonizing pressure stopped, and he released his grip.

Chest heaving, she scrambled to her knees, hands fisted, ready to strike. She wouldn't go down easy. If this brute planned to kill her, he'd have even more bruises with which to remember her.

He stopped fighting with her and stood, hands on his hips, eyes blazing, facing another man.

They shouted at each other in angry, rapid Spanish.

Her attacker pointed at her, and then at the bruises on his belly.

The other man spat in the dirt and withdrew a gun from his waistband. He pointed the long, ominous-looking barrel at the fat man. "¡*Silencio*!"

The man who'd attacked her held his hands in front of him in a placating manner. "*Sí, sí*, Pedro." He turned to her. "Get up," he said, his voice hard.

She shook her head, but then she cast a quick look at the circle of men surrounding her.

Their hard eyes narrowed. Two of them snarled.

"Get up, *puta*." He brandished his gun in her face. "Now."

She rose to her feet. Her legs trembled, and she prayed they'd support her.

He slammed his fist into her face.

She reeled back and would have fallen if the man called Pedro hadn't grabbed her and held her, sagging in his arms. Her head swam. Blinking, trying to focus, she tasted blood.

The man who'd hit her, loomed out of the fog surrounding her. He smirked, taking in her pain, enjoying her agony. "I have more of the same for you, *mucho* more, *chica*, if you do not do as we say."

She glared at him and then spit, hitting the scuffed toe of his shoe.

His mouth tightened, and his eyes narrowed. He raised his meaty fist and drew back his arm.

She held her breath, preparing for the blow, wondering if the second punch would hurt as much as the first one.

"¡*Basta*!"

The brute before her slowly lowered his arm and turned toward Pedro.

"Enough, Juan," said Pedro.

A flurry of angry Spanish ensued. Pedro turned and shouted at the circle of men.

One of them grabbed her arms and dragged her to the waiting car. He shoved her onto the back seat and jumped in beside her. The door slammed shut. Another man climbed in, crowding against her, his foul body odor gagging her. The engine thundered to life, and they were off.

She twisted around to look through the back window. Her heart sank at the sight of Vince's still form, clearly outlined in the moon's cold light. Two of the attackers stood over him, their guns drawn. She prayed Vince was still alive and Ryan would return in time to help him.

Where was Ryan? Had he and Max been captured and forced to tell their attackers where to find the plane? She shook off the thought. Ryan was safe. He'd come looking for her. He'd save her life again. It's what he did. After all, he was her hero. She found the strength to ask, "Where are you taking me?"

Seconds ticked by before Pedro answered. "*Señor*

Montevedi wishes to meet you, *Señorita* Harkins."

His words struck like a blow, and she sagged against the seat. *Montevedi!* All the horror stories she'd heard of the Mexican drug lord ricocheted through her mind. She forced the terrifying thoughts back. She had to be strong. If she was going to survive this ordeal, she had to keep her wits and stay alive long enough for Ryan to save her.

Chapter 17

"Your source was wrong," Ryan said.

Max ran her red-tipped fingers through her long hair. "I don't know what happened. He assured me his information was solid."

Ryan examined the empty apartment, taking in the broken furniture and dust-covered floor. Cobwebs hung from the ceiling. The lone window was cracked and grime-encrusted. He kicked a pile of rubbish and grimaced as a huge cockroach darted out and skittered away.

"This was a wasted trip. Geordie's not here." Max sighed. "Your brother's probably hiding out in the States in some luxury health spa. I bet he was never in Mexico. Even Geordie wouldn't be stupid enough to waltz right into Montevedi's territory."

A jolt of alarm coursed through him. "Come on." He ran for the door, ignoring the pain in his side as he leaped down the steps and raced across the patio to the car.

Max hurried after him.

This was a set up. Why hadn't he figured that out before now? Someone had lured them to Acapulco by leaking the false information Geordie was hiding out down here. Ryan didn't have to ask who had betrayed them. The plan reeked of Montevedi's involvement. The drug kingpin had found someone willing to sell them out for money. At the moment, it didn't matter who their betrayer was; the damage had already been done.

Fear congealed in his belly. He kicked the driver out of the car, ignoring his protests as he drove off, Max in the seat beside him. He didn't trust anyone but himself to reach the plane as fast as possible. The engine screamed as he pressed the gas pedal to the floor, but the little car refused to go any faster. They careened around a corner and onto a straight stretch leading to the deserted airfield.

Hallie.

Her name ran through his mind in a frantic plea. Let her be safe. Let his suspicions be wrong. But deep in his gut, he knew he was right. Montevedi had orchestrated this entire setup to lure them into his territory. The only reason he'd have gone to all the trouble was to get at Hallie. She was his ticket to Geordie. If the drug lord didn't kill her first.

"She'll be all right." Max's voice broke through the tension. "Vince will look after her. He knows what he's doing."

He didn't say anything, focusing on steering the rickety car through the rusted entranceway and onto the rutted runway. Moonlight lent the scene a surreal air, outlining palm trees, rocks and shrubs with a glaring intensity. Peering through the dust-caked windshield, he made out the distant shape of the airplane. He breathed a sigh of relief. The plane was still here.

They skidded to a halt in a cloud of dust beside the aircraft. He turned off the engine, leaped out of the car, and then froze. The hairs on the back of his neck prickled. Everything looked the same as when they'd left mere hours earlier, but something wasn't right.

He reached under his jacket and took out his gun. Glancing to his side, he nodded.

Max held her pistol as well.

He gestured to let her know she was to check the outside perimeter, and then he crept toward the silent plane. His heart thudded in his chest as he mounted the stairs, wincing at the screech of creaking metal. The plane's dark interior loomed before him. He took a deep breath and stepped inside, his gun ready.

As his eyes adjusted to the dim light, he scanned the interior. No one was here. The plane was empty.

Max appeared in the doorway. "I didn't find anyone outside, but there're signs someone's been here."

He nodded. His gaze settled on something. He crossed to the rear of the plane and knelt on the floor by the storage locker. A dark smear marred the shiny, metal surface. A lump of ice formed in his gut. He ran a finger over the dark streak. Blood. Taking a deep breath, he lifted the heavy lid. His breath whooshed out in a gust of air, and he reeled back. A body lay crumpled inside.

"Vince," Max breathed.

It wasn't Hallie.

Relief flooded through Ryan, followed by a stab of guilt.

Max helped him ease Vince out of the cramped container and onto the floor. Vince's arms were tied behind his back. Another rope bound his feet together.

With a quick slice of his knife, Ryan cut the ropes and examined the injured pilot.

"Is he dead?" asked Max.

"He's still breathing."

Dried blood stained Vince's nose and mouth. One eye was bruised and swollen. Fresh blood leaked from a bullet wound on his forehead.

Ryan gently probed the injury and discovered a flesh wound. The bullet had grazed Vince's forehead, resulting in copious amounts of blood, but no serious damage. "Vince," he urged, shaking him gently. "Wake up, man. What happened? Where's Hallie?"

The pilot groaned, but his eyes remained closed.

Ryan bit his lip in frustration. He had to find out what had happened to Hallie. Every second counted.

"Footprints are all over in the dirt outside. At least six or seven assailants were involved in the attack. Tire tracks lead away from here." Max's voice was steady as she relayed the facts, a professional on a mission gone wrong.

"They were outnumbered," he said. "They didn't stand a chance."

"This wasn't your fault, Ryan. You did what you thought was best."

He snorted. "Tell that to Hallie."

"Vince is good. Damn good, but he was only one man against so many attackers. They would have been heavily armed."

Vince moaned, and his eyes flickered open. He blinked and groaned again. "I'm sorry, Ryan," he husked. "I thought the car was you and Max returning. They were on us before I knew what was happening."

Ryan forced his anger away. "You did your best."

Vince struggled to sit up, but Max held him back, cradling his head in her lap. "Take it easy."

"They...they were Montevedi's men." Vince's

breathing was labored. "They assumed I was out cold, but I heard them talking." He closed his eyes, his face drawn and haggard, pale beneath the dried blood.

He was in pain. Just talking was a struggle for the injured man, but Ryan had to know what happened to Hallie. "And?" he urged. "What about Hallie? Where is she?"

Vince opened his eyes. "They...they took her."

Ryan groaned and staggered back as his worst nightmare became a reality. Montevedi had Hallie. He leaped to his feet. He had to find her. And he had to find her soon. This mission had become more than a promise he'd made his brother. Much more. He had to save Hallie. Her life was at stake.

Vince grabbed his leg, stopping him. His eyes blazed into Ryan's. "One of the bastards hit her, Ryan. Hard."

Ryan gritted his teeth as the horror of his words sank in. He closed his eyes, fighting off the terrifying images running through his mind. He swallowed back icy fear.

"I'm sorry, Ryan."

Vince's strained voice cut into his tortured thoughts. He studied the injured man, seeing the lines of pain carved into his youthful face. "It's okay. You did your best." It was true. He didn't blame Vince. He'd done everything any man could have to fight off the attackers.

Ryan blamed himself. He'd left Hallie behind and played right into Montevedi's hand.

Anger boiled through him. He grabbed his pack and rifled through the contents.

"What are you doing?" Max asked.

"I'm going to get her." His mind worked furiously as he ran through a list of supplies he needed. He withdrew a handful of bullet cartridges and shoved them in his pocket. He didn't know what he'd be facing when he found Hallie, but he wouldn't hesitate to shoot and kill anyone who stood in his way. He'd rescue her. Anything less was unthinkable.

"You can't do this alone. You need help."

He narrowed his gaze. "You can call for help. I'm getting Hallie."

She opened her mouth to protest, but then she nodded. "All right. I'll call for backup and wait here with Vince."

He ignored her, intent on packing his gear. He didn't give a damn what Max did. He knew what he had to do.

Without another word, he stepped onto the ramp and jumped to the ground, his mind focused on one objective and one objective only: Hallie.

****

Hallie tried the door handle, twisting and pulling, even though she'd done the same thing a dozen times before. The door was locked. She kicked the wooden frame, venting her frustration. Sinking to the floor, she drew her knees to her chest and leaned against the thick, wooden door.

The swollen welt on her cheek throbbed with each beat of her heart. She licked the corner of her mouth and tasted dried blood. Exhaustion filled her, dulling her fear. She couldn't remember the last time she'd slept. Two days ago? She shook her head. Sleep didn't matter. Nothing mattered, but getting out of here.

Why was she here? Why hadn't Montevedi's men

shot her at the plane like they had Vince? Montevedi had sent his men to kill her before, why not finish the job? Was he toying with her? Did he want to torture her before he killed her? Her headache worsened from all the questions blazing through her mind.

She regarded her prison cell and sneered. *Prison cell.* She was surrounded by luxury. A king-sized bed dominated the large, well-appointed room. The other furniture consisted of an antique mahogany dresser and two matching bedside tables. A burgundy, velvet-covered wingback chair and a small, white, French provincial table flanked a set of expansive French doors offering a stunning view of the beach below and the ocean beyond. An adjoining bathroom with a sunken, jetted bathtub and spacious shower completed the opulent suite.

Once again she studied the glass doors to the outside and winced as she rubbed her hands, bruised from pounding on the thick glass. The panes had to be made of some sort of bulletproof material. The glass hadn't shattered no matter how hard she'd struck the thick panes.

Not yet ready to give up, she climbed to her feet and examined the scene outside the mansion. Under other circumstances, the view from the window would have inspired awe. A white, pristine, sandy beach stretched in either direction as far as the eye could see, fronted by the aquamarine waters of Acapulco Bay. The beach was deserted, though boats of various shapes and sizes, some sporting billowing, multicolored sails, cruised across the smooth waters of the bay.

A movement on the beach below drew her eye. A man, dressed in camouflage-printed army fatigues, and wearing dark, mirrored sunglasses, marched across the sand in front of the mansion and disappeared around the side. He was one of Montevedi's guards. The deadly looking rifle he carried on a strap slung over his shoulder, combined with the pair of revolvers on his hips, was meant to intimidate anyone foolish enough to contemplate sneaking into Montevedi's fortress. A team of similar, heavily armed men patrolled the estate day and night working in regular rotation.

She rubbed her aching eyes, crossed to the bed, and sank onto the pink satin cover, resting her head on the pillow. A yawn overtook her. Her eyes drifted closed. She forced them open and sat up. She couldn't afford to sleep. She had to remain alert. Who knew when an opportunity to escape would present itself? She had to think, to plan a way out of her fortified prison.

But she was so tired. Once again, she lay back on the soft mattress. Her eyes closed. She forced them open, but they weighed too much. They closed again. Her muscles grew heavy as she relaxed into the warm comfort of the bed. She'd rest for just a minute.

Someone was shaking her. She opened her eyes and blinked at the scowling, dark-haired man looming over her.

"Wake up," he said. His fingers dug into her shoulders as he shook her again.

She shoved off his hands and sat up. "Leave me alone, you bastard."

The man's acne-scarred face cracked in a sneer.

She shivered at the cold cruelty in his dark irises.

He muttered something in Spanish she didn't understand and backed away from the bed.

An older woman stood behind him, holding a tray

bearing a plate heaped with steaming food. She set the tray of food on the bedside table and smiled. "*Coma.*"

Even though Hallie understood little Spanish, the woman's meaning was clear. She wanted her to eat. The heady aroma of food filled the room, and her stomach rumbled. She hadn't eaten anything since the sandwiches she'd shared with Ryan in the small house by the airfield while they'd waited for Max's return. A rush of longing to see him again filled her and a desperate desire to escape. She glanced at the man who'd awakened her.

He stood by the door, watching her with narrowed eyes. A large, menacing-looking gun was strapped around his waist in a leather holster.

Her gaze shifted to the woman. The graying hair pinned up in a simple bun and her heavily lined face offset by a pair of soft brown eyes gave her hope. Hallie forced a smile. "*Gracias, señora,*" she said as she took the tray of food and set it on her lap. "Do you speak English?" she added quietly, praying the guard couldn't hear her.

Eyes widening, the woman shook her head and stepped back from the bed.

Hallie grabbed her arm, stopping her. "*Señora, por favor, me puede...*" she began in halting Spanish, but then gave up in frustration. "Help me."

The woman's face paled.

Hallie sighed in frustration. Why hadn't she paid more attention in Spanish language class in school? "Help me, please," she tried again, enunciating each word slowly as if by doing so she could make her understand.

The Mexican woman shook her head again, her

eyes sliding toward the watching guard, fear radiating off her.

"Please."

She yanked her arm free and scurried to the door.

The guard glared at Hallie and ushered the woman ahead of him into the hall. In the next instant, the door slammed, and the lock clicked in place.

She leaned against the pillows. Tears welled in her eyes. The old woman was too frightened to help her. Besides, how could she try anything with the guard in the room watching? She perused the tray of food. One plate was heaped with a mound of fluffy, scrambled eggs, two slices of buttered toast, and three rashers of bacon. The other plate contained a variety of delicious looking, fresh, tropical fruits. At least they weren't planning on starving her to death. Her stomach rumbled as she picked up the fork and ate.

She'd finished the last mouthful when the door burst open, and the same menacing guard stepped into the room.

"Come with me," he ordered in halting English.

She shook her head. She wasn't going anywhere with this monster.

He scowled and marched across the room, tossed the tray of dishes onto the floor and grabbed her arm, dragging her from the bed. "You come!"

Dread filled her. This was zero hour. They'd fed her her last meal. Now they were going to kill her. She wasn't going quietly, that's for damn sure. Swearing at the surly guard, calling him every bad name she could think of, she shoved against him, fighting and kicking for freedom, for life itself. Hitting him was like striking a mountain and as futile.

Seemingly oblivious to her blows, he hauled her across the room.

Stumbling, trying to stay on her feet, exhausted from her efforts, she gave into the inevitable and stopped struggling, and allowed him to lead her from the room. A sob tore at her throat.

They walked along a wide, tiled hallway and down a set of steps into a large room open on two sides, allowing unbroken views of the ocean and the surrounding hills. A warm breeze redolent of salty ocean, lush tropical flowers, and rotting vegetation wafted in through the open windows. A flock of screeching cormorants wheeled over the bay and splashed onto the water.

The guard, his fingers digging cruelly into the tender flesh of her upper arms, steered her toward a heavily carved, wooden door. He knocked. At a muffled command from within, he opened the door, and shoved her into a room.

She stumbled, but managed to right herself before she fell. Smoothing her hair out of her eyes, she took stock of her surroundings. A large, rectangular, glass-enclosed structure dominated the room, taking up most of one wall. Something moved behind the glass. She edged closer.

A large lizard, over two feet in length and weighing close to six pounds, lumbered across the interior of the enclosure. Small, pebble-like bumps covered the reptile's black skin. Yellow stripes ringed its thick tail. The feet ended in sharp, vicious-looking claws. A black tongue flicked in and out of a gaping, red mouth. The lizard turned its head and regarded her with beady, black eyes.

She staggered back a step and shuddered.

"*Hermoso*, no?"

She jumped and turned.

A pleasant looking, middle-aged man sat behind an enormous wooden desk on the far side of the room, a wide smile wreathing his lined face, white teeth flashing.

"Wha...what?" she stammered.

He pointed toward the glass enclosure. "I see you are admiring my little darlings. They are stunning, are they not?"

She glanced back at the terrarium.

A second lizard, equally as large as the first, lumbered its way across the fine gravel on the bottom of the cage.

She shivered. "These are your...pets?"

"*Sí*, they are Mexican beaded lizards." He smiled, his eyes cold. "Quite poisonous, I assure you." Rising from behind the desk, he strode to the glass enclosure. He tapped gently on the glass and smiled when one of the lizards raised its head, the feral eyes watchful. "They are like family to me. This one I call Monstruo."

The two, large lizards crawled across the floor of their cage, tongues flicking.

Hallie shuddered, repulsed, yet unable to look away. As much as she feared lizards of any sort, she had to admit they were beautiful in a reptilian kind of way.

The man's gaze settled on her. "So, *Señorita* Harkins, we finally meet." He took hold of her hand and raised it to his lips, brushing a kiss across her knuckles. "I am Ricardo Montevedi."

"Montevedi," she breathed, tugging her hand free,

wishing she dared wipe her palm on her jeans. "El Lagarto."

He nodded, a small smile playing on his thick lips. "*Sí*, it is true. Many call me El Lagarto." He shrugged. "The name is apt, I suppose."

He was a few inches shorter than she with a rounded belly protruding from beneath his tailored linen slacks and open-necked, floral, tropical shirt. A heavy gold chain hung around his thick neck, the gold gleaming amidst a thick pelt of black chest hair, and a gold, designer watch gleamed on his hairy wrist. An overpowering cloud of expensive men's cologne swirled around him, making her stomach roil. His receding hairline and soft, pudgy face gave him the appearance of an amicable uncle, not the notorious drug lord she knew him to be. But the cold malevolence lurking in the dark depths of his eyes, told the truth. He was a heartless monster.

She shuddered.

His mouth curled in a knowing smile.

Anger filled her. He was responsible for so much carnage. He'd sent men to kill first Geordie, and then her. This man was the reason Buzz and Vince were dead. For all she knew, this scum had murdered Geordie as well. El Lagarto was responsible for so much pain and heartache. Who knew how many lives he'd destroyed?

He chuckled. "I see you have heard of me, *señorita*. That is good. Now we understand each other." He crossed to his desk and removed a cigar from a wooden humidor sitting on the glossy surface. He clipped off the end and proceeded to light the cigar with a silver lighter. Puffs of fragrant smoke billowed around him. "You do realize, of course, you are to blame for this regrettable situation. I do not like to resort to violence, especially with such a beautiful woman, but…" His eyes narrowed and he frowned. "You do not choose your friends wisely, *señorita*."

A shiver rippled along her spine. "Where's Geordie Marshall? What have you done with him?"

He blew a perfect smoke ring, and then another, before he set the smoldering cigar in a large, glass ashtray. "Why are you so certain I have done anything to *Señor* Marshall? I am a simple businessman." He smirked. "Perhaps you should check with your American consulate. They are responsible for locating missing American citizens, are they not?"

"Where is he?" she repeated, hating the way he was toying with her. "If you've harmed him, I'll—" The look in his eyes stopped the rest of what she was going to say.

"You'll what?"

She shivered and rubbed at the goose bumps prickling her arms. What was she doing? She was at this man's mercy. He could do what he wanted with her, and no one would stop him. Making futile threats would get her nowhere, but dead. Taking a deep breath, she tried a different tack. "Tell me if Geordie's okay. Please?"

Montevedi's flat, lizard-like gaze never left her face.

"How did you know where to find me?" she asked. "Who told you? No one knew we flew down here. Where are Ryan Marshall and Maxine Benoit?"

"Tsk, tsk, tsk." The corners of his mouth quirked. "You do seem to have a difficult time holding on to your friends, *señorita*."

Fighting for control, keeping her voice steady, she asked again, "Ryan Marshal and Maxine Benoit? Where are they?"

"I do not know."

She didn't believe him. The only way he could have known she was in the country was if they'd told him. And the only way they'd have told him anything was if his men had captured them. Even then, she couldn't see Ryan saying anything. Unless...unless he'd been tortured. "What have you done to them?" she asked again.

"Mexico can be a dangerous country for tourists, *señorita*. Accidents happen here all the time. These incidents are most unfortunate."

He picked up a pair of thin, black, leather gloves from the desk and put them on. Lifting the lid on the terrarium, he grabbed one of the lizards and removed the squirming creature from the glass enclosure.

The animal's mouth gaped, exposing needle-sharp teeth. Hissing and thrashing, the lizard fought Montevedi's grasp.

Hallie shrank back.

Montevedi held the squirming creature close to his body, the fingers of one hand caressing the pebbled skin. "Do not be afraid of Monstruo, *señorita*. If one knows what one is doing, these sweet creatures can be safely handled."

The lizard hissed again.

Her stomach roiled, and she resisted the urge to run.

"It is said the bite of the Mexican beaded lizard is extremely painful and often fatal. They bite much like a

214

pit bull, chewing and tearing at flesh as they release their venom into their victim's bloodstream. Not a pleasant way to die, I can assure you."

Unable to look away, Hallie stared at the large, squirming, hissing creature in Montevedi's arms.

"Monstruo is only one of the many dangers awaiting the unwary in my country. Countless ways exist to die in Mexico."

She gulped. A flash of Vince's body surrounded by a pool of blood rose before her.

The lizard's mouth gaped, and the black, forked tongue flicked out, testing the air. Its tail twitched, and the legs scrabbled, fighting Montevedi's grip, trying to break free.

"*Sí*, my lovely boy," crooned Montevedi, one gloved hand caressing the beaded skin. "I know you are hungry." He set the lizard back in the glass enclosure.

Hallie breathed a sigh of relief.

Montevedi picked up a wooden box from the shelf below the terrarium. He opened the lid and removed a small, wriggling, white mouse. Holding the animal by the tail, he placed the mouse in the terrarium.

The mouse froze, and then as if sensing the danger, the animal scurried under a piece of driftwood.

Both lizards flicked their forked tongues, prowling the cage searching for their prey. A lizard surged forward with lightning speed and bit down on the hapless mouse. Blood spurted as the mouse, legs squirming, disappeared down the reptile's gullet.

Hallie turned away, gorge rising in her throat.

"As you see, life is harsh. The more powerful always destroy the weak. This is the law of nature, is it not?"

She closed her eyes, fighting the terrifying image of being bitten by one of the frightening creatures and dying an excruciating death. She swallowed. "Why have you sent your men after me? Why do you want to kill me?"

He chuckled. "So much anger in one so attractive, *señorita*. You American women are all the same." He shook his head. "A pity."

"What do you want with me? I've done nothing to you."

He stared at her.

She shuddered at the malice in his beady eyes. Meeting his gaze was like looking into the eyes of the lizard before the animal had struck the mouse.

"An unfortunate mistake," he said. "My men can be overzealous in their actions at times, I am afraid."

She glared at him. Mistake? He'd sent men to kill her three times. Only luck and Ryan's help had saved her. Others hadn't been so fortunate. "You murdered Buzz. Your men killed him."

"What can I say, *señorita*?" He shrugged. "A mistake, nothing more. What do you Americans call it? Collateral damage?" He pursed his lips. "These things happen."

Her fear erupted into outrage. "You bastard. You killed Buzz in cold blood because he was in the wrong place at the wrong time. He'd done nothing to you. He was only helping me."

"*Lo siento*. I am sorry." He picked up his smoldering cigar and blew another smoke ring, his cold, calculating eyes making a farce of his words. "*Con permiso, señorita*. You must excuse my lapse of manners. I am not being a good host." He crossed to a table where bottles of liquor sat on a silver tray. He held up two cut crystal glasses. "What may I get you, *señorita*?"

"Let me go."

All trace of humor vanished. "I am afraid I cannot do as you wish."

"Why not?" She shook her head. "I'm no good to you. I can't help you find Geordie Marshall. I don't know where he is. I haven't seen him in months."

He filled a glass with amber liquid and sipped. "Ah, but there you are mistaken." His gaze bore into hers.

She fought the urge to back away. "I…I told you I don't know where he is."

He smiled. "Señor Geordie is no longer my priority. I know where he is, and I will deal with him when the time is right." His smile widened, exposing unusually sharp canine teeth. The effect was chilling. "But his brother…" He shrugged. "*Sí*, Ryan Marshall is another matter."

"What do you want with Ryan?"

"*Señor* Ryan and I have met before." He puffed on his cigar. His eyes narrowed to slits. "Our encounter was not a pleasant experience."

"What do I have to do with any of this?"

"You do not know?" He snickered. "You are bait, *señorita*, much like the little mouse. Once *Señor* Ryan discovers you are my guest, he will come to me."

I…" She swallowed over the sudden lump in her throat. "I don't understand."

Montevedi's eyes hardened. "No one enters Acapulco without my knowing, no one. Especially one who wishes to interfere with my very profitable business dealings."

"Ryan only wants to find his brother."

Montevedi chuckled again. "I am not foolish enough to believe you, *señorita*. He is a member of the American Drug Enforcement Agency. So is *Señorita* Benoit. This I know."

"Ryan doesn't work for the DEA anymore. He's a rancher now. He raises cows in Montana. Give him back his brother, and he'll leave Mexico. He won't bother you."

"Even if I were to believe you, *Señorita* Harkins, my opinion makes no difference. Once a DEA agent, always a DEA agent. I know this. Everyone knows this."

She opened her mouth to argue, but the phone on the desk rang before she could say anything.

"*Un minuto, por favor.*" He picked up the phone. "*¿Bueno?*" he spoke into the receiver. His brow furrowed, and he responded with a stream of rapid Spanish.

Hallie listened with half an ear as she mulled over everything he'd told her. Nothing she'd said had convinced him Ryan was an innocent civilian trying to save his brother. Montevedi was certain Ryan and Max were in Mexico to destroy him. He was partially right, she admitted, but taking down Montevedi wasn't the main reason they were here.

"*Perdón, señorita.*" Montevedi's mouth pursed, the light in his eyes cold, the phone's receiver still in his hand. "I am sorry, but I must cut our visit short. I have enjoyed our little conversation. We will talk again soon, no?"

Not willing to leave until she'd convinced him

Ryan meant him no harm, she made one more attempt. "Ryan Marshall's only in Mexico to find his brother. As soon he has him, he'll go back to the States. He doesn't want anything to do with you or your damn drug cartel."

He glowered and tapped his foot impatiently. "My sources tell me different. They say he plans to destroy me. I wish to meet this man and see his intentions for myself. This is why I arranged for you to be my house guest."

She blinked at him for several long seconds. "You...you told Max's contact Geordie was in Acapulco."

He smiled. "How else to convince you and your compatriots to come to me?"

The door behind her opened.

She turned to see the burly guard waiting. As he led her from the room, Montevedi resumed his phone conversation, his voice rising with increasing annoyance.

She stumbled after the guard, stunned at the full extent of Montevedi's trickery. The events of the past few days had all been a setup, orchestrated by him. The entire charade had been a plan to get her to come to Acapulco where he could take her hostage, and as a result, lure Ryan to him.

How had they not seen the trap waiting for them? How had they been so easily fooled?

Chapter 18

She'd been Montevedi's prisoner for two long days and even longer nights, locked tight in her luxurious prison. Montevedi's devious plan to use her as bait to lure Ryan into the drug lord's clutches frightened her. Ryan would try to rescue her. She didn't doubt that for a minute. But instead of saving her, he'd walk into Montevedi's trap. And after that...She blinked back tears. She wouldn't think about what Montevedi would do to Ryan. Not now.

Her priority had to be to break out of Montevedi's compound so she could warn Ryan before it was too late. The idea of escape was daunting, especially given Montevedi's tight security, but she was determined.

She peered through the French doors. The sun, a large, orange orb hung low on the horizon. This far in the tropics, sunset was brief and vibrant, followed by sudden darkness. Darkness was what she waited for.

After her meeting with Montevedi, she'd been left alone. Her only visitor was the Mexican woman who brought trays of food three times a day. Hallie always spoke to her, trying to make some sort of connection and enlist her as an ally, but the woman was too frightened, and she ignored Hallie's pleas.

But then, during today's visit to deliver her lunch, the woman met her gaze, and a miracle happened. Hallie swallowed her excitement as she recalled the footsteps in the hall outside her room signaling the arrival of the next meal. The door had opened, and the gray haired woman, bearing a laden tray, entered the room.

As usual, the guard followed closely behind her. After a scowling look around, he stepped back into the hall and closed the door, leaving the two women alone.

Hallie couldn't believe her luck. This was the first time he'd left when the serving woman was in the room. "Buenas noches, señora," *Hallie said, forcing a friendly smile. Her life depended on her ability to convince this woman to help her.*

The woman didn't meet Hallie's gaze, but she nodded, setting the tray on the table beside the bed.

Hallie tried again, keeping her voice low. "Señora, I must escape from here. Please help me. A man's life is at stake."

The woman's eyes met hers for a brief moment, but then slid away.

"Please. I know you understand English. Help me. They'll kill my friend if you don't. I have to warn him he's in danger."

Shaking her head the woman backed toward the door.

Hallie bit her lip in frustration, but she refused to give up. "Señora, I beg of you. Un minuto, por favor."

The woman stopped and turned, her brown eyes pleading. "I cannot help you, señorita." *Her English was stilted and awkward.*

A spurt of hope soared through Hallie. "This is a matter of life and death, señora. Please."

The other woman shook her head. "No one escapes from El Lagarto. Those who attempt to do so, die

221

terrible deaths. I have seen this."

"Do you have access to the key to the door? Could you slip the key to me? I promise no one will ever know of your involvement."

Indecision clouded the maid's eyes.

"Please," Hallie begged, tears welling in her own eyes. "Please."

The serving woman opened her mouth to answer but pressed her lips together when the door opened, and the guard entered the room.

He glared from one woman to the other. "What is taking so long?" he asked. "Vamos."

"Sí, sí." The serving woman bowed her head and followed the guard from the room. Before the door closed, her eyes met Hallie's, and she nodded.

Hallie bit her lip to stifle a cry of joy. She leaped to her feet and punched her fist in the air. Yes!

Now, hours later, she waited, praying the maid would come through for her. She glanced again out the window. The sun had set and night had settled in. Where was she? She was late. She should have brought the supper tray by now. Was something wrong? Seeds of doubt entered her mind. Had the woman told Montevedi Hallie wanted her to help her escape?

She jumped at the sound of a small click and spun to see the door handle turning.

The door swung open, and the maid slipped into the room bearing the dinner tray. A delicious aroma rose from the steaming plate of food.

The ever-present, glowering guard followed. He examined the room, and then with a suspicious look at Hallie, turned and stepped into the hall, closing the door.

Hallie wanted to ask the woman if she had the key but read the warning in her eyes. Instead, she remained on the bed. "*Gracias, señora*," she said in a loud voice, hoping the guard was listening to her trivial conversation. "This food looks delicious. *Muy bien*."

The maid set the tray on the table. Her gaze met Hallie's. Fear dilated her pupils.

Hallie blew out a breath. *She had the key.* "Thank you. Oh, thank you so much for helping me."

"*Madre de Dios*, be quiet, *señorita*." The maid glanced nervously at the door. "He will hear." She dug in the pocket of her dress. "I have the key." She held a small, brass key in her hand.

"*Gracias, señora, gracias.*" This woman risked a great deal by helping her. Montevedi would not take kindly to anyone who dared betray him, and she didn't even know her name. "What is your name?" she asked.

"Maria."

"Thank you, Maria." Hallie hugged her.

Maria tugged free. "There is no time." Her gaze slid to the door.

"This is the key to the door?"

Maria shook her head. "No, *la ventana*. This key unlocks the window."

"But—"

"The guard is in the corridor. Always. He never leaves." Maria shrugged. "The window is the only way."

Hallie's brow furrowed. Her room was on the third floor of Montevedi's mansion. The drop from the window had to be at least thirty feet onto an unforgiving brick patio. A fall from this height would ensure broken bones. *Better than sitting here waiting to die*. She studied the key in Maria's hand, and with a gulp, grabbed the small brass object. She'd risk a fall. Anything to escape and warn Ryan. He'd saved her life countless times. Now, it was her turn to save his. "*Gracias*, Maria."

Maria nodded, picked up the tray of dirty dishes from lunch and carried the tray toward the door. She paused, and turned back to Hallie. "*Vaya con Dios, señorita*. Go with God."

"*Muchas gracias*." Hallie's heart thudded in rising excitement.

The guard let Maria out, and then closed the door, once again setting the lock with a loud snap.

Hallie forced herself to wait to the count of one hundred before she leaped off the bed and ran to the glass doors. She peered through the glass and shuddered.

The distance to the ground was further than she remembered. Could she do this? Did she have a choice?

She tiptoed to the door of her room and pressed her ear to the wood, listening. A wisp of cigarette smoke drifted from under the door. The guard was in the hallway smoking. Good. He was distracted.

On shaky legs, she retraced her steps to the window. Strobe lights lit the lower wall of the mansion and the surrounding beach with a glaring intensity. If...she paused. No, not if, *when* she made her escape down the wall, she'd be an easy target for anyone looking out of the mansion's many windows.

She checked her watch and studied the expanse of beach. Right on time, a heavily armed guard marched across the brightly lit, sandy beach in front of the mansion. She leaned back out of sight, as he crossed below her window and turned the corner of the mansion, disappearing from view. If he held true to his routine, she had fifteen minutes before he returned to patrol along the beachfront. She had to act fast.

Removing the key from her pocket, she slid the tip into the lock. She gripped the handle and turned the key. A soft click sounded, and the door swung open on silent hinges. She let out her breath, and wiped the dampness from her brow.

So far, so good. Now for the next step.

She leaned out the window searching for a way to climb to the ground. The walls of the mansion were smooth with no convenient trellis or fire escape at hand like there always was in the movies. Movies! She almost laughed out loud as an idea occurred to her.

She ran back into the room, yanked the satin cover off the bed and tossed the blanket to the floor. Next, she removed the sheets and tied them together with secure knots. She opened a wardrobe and removed another set of sheets and joined those to the first two. She eyed them. Still too short, but the makeshift rope would have to do.

Wrapping one end of the string of sheets around the bedpost, she tied them to the sturdy, wooden post. She tugged and was almost surprised when the knots held. She couldn't believe she was doing this. As a kid, she'd watched countless movies where the hero escaped by tying bed sheets together and climbing down from great heights. Was such a feat possible in real life?

Her heart thudded in her chest as she regarded the open door. She checked her watch and closed the window, waiting and watching until once again the guard appeared. As he'd done countless times, he crossed below her and rounded the far corner of the building.

The time for escape was now or never.

Wiping her damp palms on her pants, she took a firm grip on the string of sheets, opened the door and stepped over the threshold onto a small balcony. She had less than fifteen minutes to climb down the wall and make her escape across the open sand before the guard returned. She had no idea where she'd go once she was on the ground. Getting out of the room where she'd been held captive these past days was enough for now.

Taking a deep breath, she climbed over the railing and swung free. She bit back a yelp of pain as the sheet jerked, and the silken fabric took her weight. She smashed against the stucco wall with a jarring thud.

Clinging to the sheets, she blinked back tears of pain. She could do this. She *would* do this. Taking a deep breath, she inched down the rope, one handhold at a time.

****

Ryan lay on his belly, pressed against the damp sand. He peered over the small dune at the mansion looming overhead. The moon hadn't yet risen. The night was dark, but a series of spotlights illuminated the building's white walls and surrounding grounds.

Lights were on in several of the rooms in the mansion, but so far he hadn't caught sight of Hallie. He'd examined the schematics of the layout of Montevedi's mansion, and the general consensus of his team was she was being held in one of the front bedrooms on the second or third floor.

He'd been watching the mansion for the past

several hours and still had no fix on her location. At one point, he thought he'd seen her looking out a large, glass door on the third floor, but he wasn't sure.

An armed guard rounded the corner of the building and patrolled along the front of the mansion.

Ryan counted.

The guard marched seventy-four steps across the front of the building before he turned and continued along the side of the mansion to the back.

Ryan checked his watch and nodded. Fifteen minutes. He had fifteen minutes before the guard returned. Montevedi, with all his resources had only one guard patrolling the perimeter of his house. This blatant lack of security showed his arrogance. The powerful drug lord couldn't conceive of anyone foolish enough to attack him in his own home.

He was in for a surprise tonight.

A movement high in the building before him caught his eye. Someone had opened the glass doors on the third floor. He looked through his high-powered binoculars, zeroing in on the walls of the mansion. A pale face appeared, but the figure disappeared inside before he could get a fix on the person's identity. Had he seen a flash of blonde hair? He rubbed his eyes, trying to erase the fatigue brought on by not sleeping these past days.

He sighted again, fighting to steady the binoculars in his shaking hands. The window was closed. Deflated, he ducked his head as the guard crossed the beach in front of him, and headed around the side of the big house, disappearing into the shadows.

Ryan checked the time. Right on schedule. Montevedi was making this too easy.

He waited until the guard turned and followed his standard route to the back of the mansion. Raising his head above the dune, he withdrew his flashlight and signaled across the sand to the bushes on the far side of the clearing. An answering flash told him the other operatives were in place and ready for action.

Even though he'd been determined to tackle this rescue mission on his own, he soon realized he needed help. He'd found out where Montevedi's men had taken Hallie, but breaching the walls of the drug lord's stronghold was impossible without support. And so he'd called on his old DEA friends. After what had happened to Buzz and Vince, they were more than willing to take down Montevedi, even if this rescue mission wasn't an officially sanctioned assignment.

The agents in the Special Operations Division of the DEA held to one tenet: harm one of their members, you harm them all. Within ten hours of his call for help, five heavily armed Special Agents arrived in Acapulco ready to avenge Buzz's death.

They'd reconnoitered the mansion and realized Montevedi had a contingent of well-trained men who looked after his safety. Aside from the lone patrol, Ryan's intel indicated a dozen, heavily armed soldiers were inside the mansion. Security cameras were situated at strategic points around the property, and infra red alarms guarded the perimeter. At first glance, the mansion appeared impregnable, but Ryan was determined to break through Montevedi's tight security and find Hallie.

On his signal, the Special Agents' unit keeping under cover in the swath of shrubs lining the landward side of the property would open fire, providing a distraction. Their firepower would allow Ryan an opportunity to enter the building from the ocean side and hopefully locate Hallie and free her.

He glanced at the green, luminescent dials on his watch and nodded. Almost time. Any second now, his men would open fire, and all hell would break loose. Saving Hallie was up to him. Failure was unacceptable.

Taking several, deep, steadying breaths, he prepared for the imminent attack. He checked his gun, ensuring the safety catch was off and the pistol ready to fire. A switchblade was hidden in a sheath strapped above his ankle, and his combat knife with the six-inch, serrated blade was stashed in a discreet holster on his hip.

He was ready.

A flicker of movement caught his eye, and he squinted at the mansion. A dark shape stood out against the building's exterior, lit by the bright strobe lights. The shape shifted. His breath caught in his throat. Someone hung from an upper story by a rope of some sort.

Not someone.

Hallie.

He rubbed his eyes. Hallie? What the hell did she think she was doing? With the bright lights illuminating the exterior wall, she was a sitting target. If one of the guards saw her, they wouldn't hesitate to open fire.

Forgetting his back-up team, forgetting everything he'd ever learned about rescuing hostages in his years working with the DEA, he jumped to his feet and sprinted across the open sand. He hadn't taken more than ten steps when a loud bang reverberated through the air. The ground shook beneath him.

Another blast followed and then another. In between explosions, rapid gunfire filled the night. The guards inside the house were returning fire. The exterior lights went out.

Grateful for the sudden darkness, he dug his feet into the sand and raced onward, each step taking an eon. The bullet wound in his side ached with the strain. He ignored the pain and kept his eyes on the figure dangling from the side of the building.

His chest heaving, he stood at the base of the wall and looked up.

She hung twenty feet above him, frozen in place.

Explosions at the back of the house rent the air. The men inside the mansion wouldn't take long to figure out the ruse and check the front of the building.

"Hallie," he called up to her. "What the hell are you doing? Get down here."

She didn't budge.

He gritted his teeth. Time was running out. "Hallie," he tried again, forcing calm into his voice. "It's me, Ryan." He couldn't be sure she heard him over the deafening explosions. "Keep going. I'm here. I'll catch you." Why didn't she move? "Hallie, please," he urged.

Her body twitched. She shifted a hand, and then her leg.

His breath whooshed out. "Atta girl. You can do it."

With infinite slowness, she inched down the rope.

He had to fight the urge to holler at her to hurry. The periods between detonations were lengthening. His friends were running low on ammo. They had to get the hell out of here.

Finally, she was within arm's reach.

He grabbed her, and her arms snaked around his neck. Unable to stop himself, he drew her closer, breathing in her familiar scent.

"You came." Her warm breath washed over him.

"Did you have any doubt?"

She shook her head and burrowed deeper into his embrace. "I knew you would."

His breath hitched in his throat. Without thinking, he lifted her face to his and kissed her. The second his mouth touched hers he was lost. Time stood still as if kissing her was life itself. An explosion rocked the ground beneath them, and he stopped, his lips frozen, her breath hot in his mouth. What the hell was he doing?

"Let's go," he said. "Follow me." He grabbed her hand and dragged her behind him across the bare expanse of ground to the beach. He ignored the many hidden cameras and security beams. Stealth made little difference now. Montevedi was well aware of the attack.

They sank up to their ankles in the soft, wet sand, and his lungs burned.

Hallie's labored gasps filled the air as she stumbled beside him.

Still they ran on.

She yelped and fell to her knees.

Cursing, he bent to help her up.

"Wait," she panted. "Where are we going?"

"It's not much further. I have a dinghy down the beach."

She opened her mouth, but he yanked her to her feet and urged her onward before she could speak.

Plenty of time for questions once they were safe.

The night grew quiet behind them. The attack was over. Having used up their ammo, his team would have retreated into the shadows. Their part was over. The rest was up to him.

Montevedi's men would be in turmoil. A quick search of the house would confirm Hallie was missing. They'd start looking outside the mansion. And then they'd find their footprints on the beach.

Only ten more steps to the dinghy.

He dropped to his knees and dug frantically in the sand exposing the dinghy he'd buried earlier. He hit the automatic inflate button. A hum filled the air, breaking the quiet as the small vessel filled with air. Digging deeper in the sand, he unearthed two fiberglass oars.

"You thought of everything," she gasped.

"Hurry. Help me carry this raft to the water," he said. Montevedi's men were on their trail. The sooner they got the hell out of here, the better.

The inflatable raft hit the water, and he helped Hallie into the tippy boat and shoved away from the beach. He leaped in after her, the dinghy swaying and rocking as he settled himself and took up the oars, locking them into position. He was fighting the incoming tide, but with each swing of the oars, he propelled the tiny vessel a few feet further from shore.

Lights flickered on the beach. Distant sounds of shouting carried over the swell of the surf.

Hallie pointed toward the beach. "They see us. Hurry. They have guns."

The terror in her voice impelled him to dig deeper and demand more of his exhausted body. Montevedi's men wouldn't hesitate to shoot, and they'd aim to kill.

Something splashed in the water beside the boat, and Hallie yelped. "They're shooting at us."

Another bullet struck the ocean behind them.

Sweat dripped off his brow stinging his eyes. His shoulders burned with each stroke, and his injured side screamed in agony. "Not long now." A dark shape floated on the water ahead, and he breathed a sigh of relief. A few more pulls on the oars and they were beside the anchored boat.

"A boat?" Hallie said. "You have a boat?"

"What else? Did you think we were going to make our great getaway in this dinghy?"

Chapter 19

Hallie grabbed the railing and held on as the boat sank into yet another swell. Her stomach roiled, and she sucked in a deep breath, willing the nausea away. She focused on the horizon hoping to steady her gaze and settle her stomach.

"Still not feeling great?" Ryan asked.

She groaned. "I'm not much of a sailor."

He grinned, exposing the gleam of even white teeth in his tanned face. "We'll be out of the worst of the storm in a few hours. The wind's pretty strong right now, but according to the maritime weather report, the seas should calm down soon."

Shortly after they'd climbed aboard the boat, the waters had turned rough, as they'd made their escape from Montevedi's beach and out of the protected waters of Acapulco Bay. So far they hadn't seen any sign of Montevedi's men. She'd like to think they'd left them behind on the beach, but she knew better. Montevedi had gone to too much trouble to lure them to Mexico. He wasn't letting them escape.

The powerful engines propelling the sleek craft through the choppy water howled as once again the boat plunged into a watery trough.

Hallie moaned and leaned over the side. Her stomach heaved, and she gagged, emptying its contents into the swirling water. She sagged against the railing and brushed her tangled hair off her damp forehead, taking deep breaths of ocean air. Her hand flew to her mouth as the boat bucked again and bile rose in her throat. She choked, somehow managing to swallow the bitter taste. Too weak to stand, she collapsed on the deck.

She glowered at Ryan, hating him. Hating the way he stood, legs braced, facing into the wind, his hands steady at the wheel, oblivious to the boat's wild rocking and plunging. Dawn's early light lit his face with a red glow and accented his rugged features. A smile played across his lips. He enjoyed the rough ride.

The bastard!

Another bout of nausea rocked her, and her stomach churned. She closed her eyes, gripping the deck, praying this nightmare would end. She must have dozed off because the next thing she heard was Ryan's voice calling to her.

"Wake up, sleepy head."

"Mmmm," she murmured, not wanting to abandon the dream of swaying gently on a hammock stroked by gentle breezes, the sun warm on her face.

Hands gripped her shoulders and shook her.

She moaned in protest but pried open her heavy eyelids.

Ryan crouched over her, looking fresh and rested. A grin wreathed his handsome face. "Here," he said, holding out a mug. "This will make you feel better."

Blinking in the bright sunlight, she sat up, took the mug, and inhaled the welcome aroma of strong coffee. She was surprised to see she was sitting on a padded bench at the rear of the boat. The last thing she remembered was being miserably ill and collapsing on the hard, wooden deck. Somehow, she'd ended up on the far more comfortable bench seat. More surprising, the boat wasn't plunging up and down like a crazed, bucking bronco. The small, sleek craft swayed from side to side in a soothing, gentle motion as the engines cut through the smooth water. "Where are we?" she asked.

Ryan leaned against the rail and scanned the distant horizon. "Just off the coast, near Balsas, if I'm reading the chart right."

"We're still in Mexico?"

"We're following the Mexican coastline, heading north."

She sipped her coffee, and a rush of caffeine coursed through her blood stream clearing her mind, and she asked the question she should have asked last night. "How's Vince? Is he…is he all right? He isn't…?"

"He's not dead." Ryan's eyes turned cold. "No thanks to Montevedi's goons. They caused Vince some serious damage."

"Is he all right now?"

"Max called for help. Once the rescue team arrived, she and Vince flew back to the States with them. The doctors say he'll be fine in a few weeks. Vince is a pretty tough guy. He'd have to face a hell of a lot more to take him out of the game."

Relief washed over her, but then she remembered why they were here, and she sat up and scanned the horizon. "And Montevedi? Is he following us?"

He shook his head, distracting her with his glossy, dark curls. One shiny lock fell over his forehead.

She itched to smooth back the wayward curl,

imagining its silkiness.

"I haven't seen signs of anyone following us," he said. "We made pretty good headway in spite of the headwind we fought all night." He patted the wooden railing. "The *Wind Song* is sleek and fast. I'd be surprised if any of Montevedi's boats could catch her."

"This boat is yours?"

"Surprised a simple rancher from the boonies could afford this?" His dimples deepened.

Her face heated. "No," she stammered, "I'm…" She took a deep breath and tried again. "I'm just surprised you had your boat in Mexico."

"Actually, she's not mine. She belongs to a friend. When Montevedi's men kidnapped you, I explained the situation to him. He's not a fan of Montevedi, and he was more than willing to loan her to me. He keeps her moored in a small marina down here."

"And you know how to sail this boat…on the ocean?"

The corners of his mouth twitched. "I do."

"Well, make sure you thank your friend for me. We'd never have escaped without his boat." She shuddered. If Ryan hadn't been waiting for her outside Montevedi's mansion, and if his boat weren't anchored in the bay, she'd never have escaped. Climbing down thirty feet of knotted, silk sheets was far more difficult than she'd expected. The palms of her hands burned after being rubbed raw from gripping the slippery fabric.

She'd never forget her desperate descent.

Tears stung her eyes as she hung suspended high above the ground, unable to lower herself any further. Her shoulders screamed, and sweat dampened her palms and stung the open wounds. The guard was due back any minute.

She considered letting go. Falling would be better than being shot, or worse, recaptured by Montevedi and bitten by one of his vicious lizards. She had to think of Ryan. His life was in her hands. She had to warn him of Montevedi's plan.

Tears streamed down her face, blinding her as she dangled from her makeshift rope, fully exposed by the blinding strobe lights. Then loud explosions shattered the night, and all hell broke loose. She'd frozen; terrified they were shooting at her. But then she heard Ryan's voice, urging her not to stop. Somehow she found the strength to maneuver down the rigged together sheets until she was in his arms.

The second his mouth touched hers, she forgot everything except the delightful way his lips covered hers and the press of his hard, muscular body against hers.

Another loud blast rent the air, and his lips stopped moving. He released her.

She'd mewed in protest, not wanting him to stop...ever.

She drank the rest of her coffee in silence. Sunshine caressed her shoulders, and a gentle breeze rustled her hair.

A seagull flew overhead, riding on the warm air currents.

She inhaled, savoring the fresh tang of sea air. If not for Ryan and his selfless bravery, she wouldn't be here to enjoy such a beautiful day. She'd be dead. She owed him so much. "Thank you," she said past a lump in her throat.

"For what?"

"For saving my life…again."

His mouth curved in a slow grin, setting the dimples in his rugged cheeks dancing. "You looked like you had the situation pretty much under control by the time I arrived."

"If you call dangling like a fish on a line in full view of everyone taking control, then I suppose I did."

The light of humor in his eyes faded, and his expression turned serious. "Montevedi didn't…" He cleared his throat. "He didn't hurt you, did he?"

She shook her head. "I only met him once, but one meeting was more than enough." A chill settled over her, and even under the hot, tropical sun, she shivered. "He frightens me."

"He frightens a great many people." He ran his fingers through his hair. "I should never have left you at the plane."

"You couldn't have known Montevedi's men would attack. They weren't supposed to know we were in Mexico."

"That's just it. I *should* have known Montevedi would figure out we were in his territory. I'm trained to know such things."

She set her cup down and took his large, bronzed hand between hers. "No one could have known what Montevedi planned. He went to a great deal of effort to lure us to Acapulco." She squeezed his hand. "He was using me as bait. He knew you'd try and rescue me. Montevedi despises you. I saw the hatred in his eyes when he spoke your name." She tightened her grip. "I told him you'd resigned from the DEA and you weren't a DEA Special Agent anymore, but he didn't believe me. He said once a DEA agent, always a DEA agent."

"He's right."

"But you quit the DEA. You're a rancher in Antler Springs now. Taking down Montevedi isn't your fight. Not anymore. The authorities can deal with Montevedi. You don't have to get involved in this."

"I don't have a choice."

"What do you mean? Of course you do." Her voice rose in agitation. Why didn't he understand the danger he was facing? She shuddered to think what Montevedi would do to him if he ever caught him. "Is it Geordie? Is he what this is about? Didn't you and Max find him?" A frisson of fear rippled along her spine. She released his hand and jumped to her feet. "Ryan, what's going on? You did find Geordie, didn't you?"

His eyes turned cold. "It was a setup. Montevedi must have gotten to Max's source. He sent us on a wild goose chase. We were left looking like fools."

"You mean Geordie wasn't hiding out where you'd been told he was?"

He shook his head. "The place was deserted. He'd never been there. No one had, not for a very long time."

"Where is he then? Where's he hiding?"

"Damned if I know." He snorted. "He's probably holed up in a luxury hotel somewhere, screwing some poor fool's wife while we risk our lives down here trying to find him."

Hallie winced at the bitterness in his voice. "Okay, maybe Geordie isn't in Mexico. Maybe we were wrong, but we still have to find him. Montevedi told me he's looking for him. You know what he'll do to Geordie if he finds him."

Ryan shrugged. "My priority is getting you safely

out of Mexico, and then helping the DEA destroy Montevedi and his network. That bastard has done enough damage. He needs to go down. None of us will be safe until he's out of the picture."

"What about Geordie? Aren't you going to help me find him?"

"I told you, he's not in Mexico. He'll turn up safe and sound when this is all over."

"Montevedi still wants to kill him. Geordie needs your help, Ryan. He's your brother."

"Lucky me," he snarled and turned and strode across the deck, disappearing below.

Hallie watched him go, a frown on her face.

****

Squinting against the glare of the midday sun, Hallie pulled her hat lower and wiped the sweat off the back of her neck. They'd been motoring north for two days following the coast of Mexico. The seas continued to be calm, the skies clear. To her surprise, she enjoyed life at sea. They passed schools of dolphins and marlin and were followed by dozens of screeching gulls. They'd spotted a humpback whale breaching in the distance. At night, they anchored in quiet bays where the stars loomed so close she could almost reach out and touch them.

Other than a lone container ship outlined on the distant horizon, they hadn't seen another boat. They were running low on fuel but had enough gas for one more day of travel. They were meeting a DEA friend of Ryan's in a tiny, coastal village called Los Caribuenos the following day. Ryan's contact would take them inland to a deserted airfield where another one of Ryan's friends would meet them with a plane, and they'd fly back to the States.

The back of her neck tingled, and she turned and met Ryan's blue-eyed gaze.

A sizzle of awareness arced between them.

Her breath caught in her throat.

He turned to make an adjustment to the wheel, and the connection was severed.

She fought to steady her racing heart. Each time she met his penetrating gaze her body tingled. She'd lain awake the last two nights, tossing and turning on her narrow bunk thinking of him.

He'd saved her life. Several times. His heroic actions were enough to make any woman swoon. Add in the fact he had an impressive set of well-honed muscles and perfect abs, and no wonder she couldn't keep her eyes off him. She shook her head, tearing her gaze away. The tropical heat and the fact they were alone on a boat in the middle of the Pacific Ocean affected her judgment. He still loved Max. She couldn't let herself forget the power of his love for another woman.

"Well, what do you think? Are you game?" He grinned, sparks of gold flaring in his blue eyes.

"Wha…?"

"Do you want to?"

"Do I want to do what?" Her face heated at the thought of what she wanted to do with him, what she dreamed of doing.

He grinned, his teeth flashing white in his tanned face. "Go for a swim." His grin widened. "What did you think I meant?"

His scent, a mixture of sweat, salt and man surrounded her. She prayed her hat hid the spots of red surely emblazoned on her cheeks. She forced a chuckle. "Swimming, of course. I wondered where we'd swim. I mean we can't jump off the boat in the middle of the ocean. Can we?"

"Why not? The water's shallow enough here for the anchor." He pulled his shirt over his head revealing taut, tanned skin and a definite six-pack. Still grinning, he lowered his jeans over his hips and tossed them to the deck. Wearing nothing but a cheeky grin and a pair of striped boxers, he asked, "Are you joining me?"

Her throat worked but no sound escaped. Her face must be glowing like a torch, but she couldn't stop staring.

His broad shoulders tapered to narrow hips and long, muscular legs. A dusting of dark chest hair covered his well-defined muscles. An intriguing line of hair disappeared beneath the waistband of his underwear.

She forgot to breathe.

He climbed onto the railing, and with a final grin in her direction, dove into the water.

She ran to the side of the boat and peered overboard. A swirl of bubbles in the aquamarine water drew her attention.

He swam toward the surface and burst forth in a whoosh of water. Shaking his head, he sprayed a rainbow of glistening droplets. "Come on in. The water's great." He dove beneath the waves again, slipping through the ocean like a seal.

The sun beat down and beads of perspiration broke out on her forehead.

Ryan splashed and dove through the clear, cool, sapphire water.

She licked her upper lip, tasting the salty moisture. What was she afraid of? This was just swimming; two people swimming in the ocean. What could be more innocuous? They wouldn't be naked. She quickly willed away the torrid image of his hard, naked body pressed against hers.

Ryan cut through the water, each powerful stroke revealing his muscular, sun-bronzed arms gleaming with droplets of water.

She swallowed over the lump in her throat. *What the hell?* Forcing back her trepidation, she tossed her hat to the deck and slid out of her shirt and pants. Clad in her panties and bra, she climbed onto the railing and jumped.

The first shock of cool water stole her breath, but she soon relaxed and relished the silken water sliding over her body. The buoyancy of the salt water allowed her to float on the warm surface. She closed her eyes and gave into the pleasure of the moment.

A hand grabbed her ankle, and she yelped as she was dragged underwater. Sputtering to the surface, she turned on her attacker.

Ryan grinned, daring her to retaliate.

With a whoop, she attacked, scooping handfuls of water and splashing him mercilessly. She dove beneath the waves and swam away from him. She was a strong swimmer and had been a member of her college swim team, but within seconds, he was on her, tugging on her leg, dunking her beneath the waves.

The game was on, and they played like children until they were both exhausted.

Panting, she held up her hands in surrender. "Okay, I give. You win."

"About time." Drops of seawater sparkled on his eyelashes.

She stared, unable to look away.

The teasing glint in his eyes faded, replaced by something hot and intense.

A chill coursed through her, and she shivered.

"You're cold."

She shook her head, shivering again. She was anything but cold.

"Come on." He gripped her hand and led her to the ladder leaning against the boat's hull, holding the aluminum railing steady while she climbed aboard.

Her steps were unsteady under the heat of his gaze. Once on deck, she grabbed a towel and wiped the water off her face, her movements jerky and stiff. She risked a glance at him and stopped breathing.

Heat radiated from his eyes, threatening to burn her with its intensity.

His gaze raked over her.

She resisted the urge to cover herself with the towel. Her heart pounded as their gazes locked.

"You're so beautiful." His voice was rough.

Goosebumps broke out on her flesh.

He walked toward her, one slow, deliberate step, and then another. "So beautiful." He placed his thumb under her chin and lifted, forcing her to meet his gaze. "Tell me you want this as much as I do, Hallie."

She couldn't speak, could barely breathe.

He frowned, and then he released her.

"No," she sputtered, her breath gusting out in a whoosh. "I…I want…" She swallowed. To hell with the consequences. To hell with tomorrow. Right now, right here, she wanted him. She rose on tiptoes and kissed him on the mouth.

He growled deep in his throat and returned her kiss. Cupping the back of her head, he explored her mouth, tasting her as his hands, warm and callused, roamed over her skin, slipping the damp straps of her bra over her shoulders. He released the catch of her bra, freeing her breasts and trailed kisses along her throat, igniting a path of fire, which had her gasping. He lowered his head, and his warm breath teased a sensitive bud.

She arched toward him as the moist heat of his mouth engulfed her. She moaned.

His thumb brushed one nipple while his mouth played havoc with the other.

She ran her hands over his body, exploring the ridges and hollows of hard muscle and bone. Elation soared through her when he shuddered and groaned.

He suckled at her breast until she moaned again.

Her legs wobbled, and she sagged against him.

He held her close as they slid to the deck floor, wrapped in each other's arms, his lips never leaving her. His hand smoothed along her belly, and he tugged at her panties. "Is this okay? Are you sure this is what you want?"

She met his gaze and sucked in a deep breath at the fire in the blue depths. *Was this okay? Oh, man, was it okay.* She couldn't bear him to stop. She lifted her hips in unspoken acceptance.

A grin flashed across his face. He kissed her, his tongue delving deep into her mouth. At the same time, he stroked between her legs, making her whimper.

Desperate to touch him, to drive him as wild as he drove her, she slipped her hands lower and grasped him. Rock hard, yet soft like satin. Her hand caressed his length.

"You probably shouldn't touch me there right now," he wheezed. "Not if you don't want this to end before we even get started." His face was flushed, his breathing ragged. A pulse beat in his jaw, the veins standing out in his neck.

A wave of heat flooded her. She did this to him.

He kissed her again, his tongue swirling with hers as his fingers played between her thighs.

She opened her legs and arched her back, frantic for more, needing him inside her, filling her. Now.

He leaned over her, his hardness poised at her core. With agonizing slowness, he entered her.

Her body welcomed him as her inner muscles tightened, drawing him in, urging him deeper and deeper.

****

Ryan gritted his teeth, fighting for control. She was so wet, so warm and so damn tight. He groaned and forced himself to pull out until once again, he hovered at her entrance. Every fiber of his being demanded he plunge into her again and again and never stop. But he held back. What he was doing, what he wanted to do, was the worst kind of wrong. How could he live with himself if he finished this? How could he live with himself if he didn't?

Her eyes were closed, the long lashes sweeping her flushed cheeks, her mouth swollen from his kisses, her hair a tangle of gold. The rapid rise and fall of her chest as she panted thrust her breasts against him, teasing him with their touch.

"Are you sure you want this?" he gasped, afraid

she'd say no, terrified she'd say yes.

She drew her knees up and arched her hips. "Don't stop," she said. "Don't you dare stop."

He groaned, knowing he was going to Hell and thrust deep and deeper still, closing his eyes as the pleasure nearly overwhelmed him.

She tightened around him, her body straining for release, and then she convulsed around him.

Her sounds of surrender pushed him over the edge, and giving one final push, he exploded in a spasm of pleasure. He collapsed on the deck, wrapping her in his arms. His chest heaved as he gasped for breath, her cries of release echoing in his mind.

But then she tensed, her muscles transforming from relaxed to taut in a heartbeat.

Dread replaced his complacency.

Without seeming to move, she managed to shift so no part of her body touched him. Guilt radiated off her like an icy shield. She sat up and grabbed the discarded towel, covering her nakedness. "This...was wrong. I...we shouldn't have done this." Her gaze didn't meet his. "This was a mistake." Tightening the towel around her, she leaped up and ran across the deck, disappearing below.

He wiped the sweat from his brow. He'd wanted her. Hell, yes. Making love to her was all he'd been thinking of for days. He hadn't slept since they'd left Acapulco. He'd tossed and turned for hours every night, and when he still couldn't sleep, he'd paced the deck trying to make sense of his growing need.

He'd managed to keep his hands off her. At least he had until he'd seen her in her skimpy, wet underwear. One look and it was game over. The lacy, white cotton embroidered with tiny pink flowers did nothing to conceal her curves from his hungry gaze.

Kissing her was like jumping off a cliff. There was no going back. He couldn't have stopped, even if Montevedi himself had boarded the boat. He hadn't cared she loved his brother. He hadn't given a damn Geordie loved her. Nothing mattered but his overriding need to be with her.

Even after the most explosive sex he'd ever had, he still wanted her. He scowled. What the hell was wrong with him? He wasn't like his brother. He didn't steal another man's woman. He didn't live by the same creed. *But you* are *like Geordie,* whispered an insidious voice in his head. *Two peas in a pod.* If Geordie and he were typical Marshall family members, betrayal ran like a poisonous weed through the gene pool. Bile filled the back of his throat as disgust washed over him.

He jumped up, ran to the railing and leaped into the water. The second he surfaced; he started swimming away from the boat. He'd swim until his muscles ached, and he couldn't swim any more, anything to take his mind off what he'd done.

Chapter 20

Hallie leaned against the railing at the bow of the boat watching as the coastline drew closer. A village nestled in the lee of rolling, copper-hued hills. A lopsided, wooden dock jutted into the small bay where several ancient fishing vessels bobbed at anchor in the still waters. A dozen white-washed adobe buildings, their red roofs glinting in the afternoon sun, lined the waterfront. A single church spire rose above.

Los Caribuenos wasn't a bustling hub of industry, but then, she supposed, the village's isolation was the very reason they were here. After all, they were fleeing Montevedi. The smaller and more remote the village, and the fewer people who saw them, the better.

She couldn't get off the *Wind Song* soon enough. The past hours had been unendurable. For the hundredth time, she slid a glance at Ryan.

The scowl had become a permanent fixture on his handsome face.

Ever since they'd made love the day before, the tension between them had grown until the air lay thick and cloying, making breathing a struggle. She'd stayed below deck trying to concentrate on an old paperback book she'd found on the shelf in the galley. A wasted effort. Every creak and groan of the boat reminded her of his presence. Her lips were swollen from his kisses, and her body still tingled from his touch.

He'd stayed on deck and hadn't slept in his bunk.

Even though she was grateful she didn't have to face him and his guilt-ridden face, his determination to keep away from her, stung. She hadn't slept a wink and judging by Ryan's sour mood this morning, she doubted he had either.

The awkward tension between them was her fault. She never should have jumped into the ocean. Swimming with him, wearing next to nothing was the beginning of the end. Once he'd touched her, she'd melted. Everything following was a sensual blur. Her face heated as she recalled how she'd thrown herself at him. She'd wanted him, wanted his touch, his taste. No question. The heat simmering between them had grown with every minute spent together on the boat. It was inevitable they'd give into their desires. Sex between them wasn't a question of if, only a matter of when.

After they'd made love and collapsed, spent in each other's arms, reality had come crashing in like a dousing of icy water. She'd leaped up and ran away, afraid to look back, knowing if she saw his long, lean, muscular body, she'd once again ignore the overpowering guilt and return to him and beg for more.

She risked another glance at him, and her breath hitched in her throat.

He was watching her, his gaze hooded, but as soon as their eyes met, his mouth tightened, and he jerked away.

She brushed a strand of hair off her forehead with a shaking hand. They'd had sex. So what? Sex didn't mean anything. She was a big girl. She swallowed back the sudden sting of tears. If only—she stopped, refusing to complete the thought. What ifs were wastes of time.

He may have had sex with her, but his heart rested with another woman. Hallie was a distraction, a convenient, warm body to satisfy an itch. She was a fool if she thought otherwise. The sooner she accepted he loved Max, the better.

The boat's engines slowed as they neared the wharf, and she studied the approaching village. The sun beat down on the deserted waterfront. A rusted van sat in the middle of the lone street, resting on its rims, the tires missing. A scrawny, short-haired, yellow dog lying in the sun in the middle of a small square raised its head and barked once at them, before lying back down as if getting up and greeting them required too much effort. Other than the dog and a flock of chickens pecking in the dirt among the rustic buildings, the town appeared uninhabited. She glanced at her watch: midday. The villagers must be having their afternoon siesta.

Ryan had said his friend would meet them in the village to take them to a nearby airfield. Once back in the States, she'd go her own way. Ryan and Max could resolve the situation with Montevedi. Hopefully, Geordie would show up, safe and sound. She was done. All she wanted was to return to her old life: a life free of Ryan and Geordie Marshall.

Ryan steered the boat to the dock, leaped out and tied the bow to a rusted cleat affixed to the weathered wood. He repeated the procedure with the stern line. "Ready?" he asked.

Their gazes met.

She turned away, ignoring his offer of help as she climbed over the boat railing and stepped onto the unsteady dock. The sun-bleached, wooden boards rocked and swayed. She stumbled and would have fallen if he hadn't caught her.

He drew her against the firm wall of his chest, and she gave into the pleasure of being in his arms. He placed a hand beneath her chin and turned her to meet his gaze.

She blinked at the golden lights streaking his vivid blue irises.

He lowered his head, and his warm breath washed over her. His mouth claimed hers, and she was lost in a sea of sensation.

The kiss ended. Too soon.

She opened her mouth to protest, but he pressed a finger over her lips, silencing her. "Look, I…" He paused, and his throat worked as he swallowed. "I want you to know I'm not sorry for what happened." His thumb stroked her bottom lip while his gaze traveled over her face as if memorizing her features. "What we did was wrong on so many levels, but I sure as hell will never forget making love to you."

"I—" she began, but froze at the sound of a shout.

"Finally, you decide to show up. I thought you'd never get here."

Ryan's gaze pinned hers for a long second, then he released her and stepped away, turning to face Max as she strode across the unsteady dock toward them.

Hallie blinked. *This* was the friend they were meeting?

Ryan scowled. "What the hell are you doing here, Max? Where's Chet?"

Max laughed, her full, red lips parting to expose impossibly white, even teeth. Her long, auburn hair was perfectly coifed, unaffected by the steady breeze and the humidity. With her skimpy, pink bikini top and cheek-baring, white shorts, she looked like she'd stepped off the front page of a "Hot Babes At the Beach" magazine.

Hallie ran a hand over her own unruly mass of hair and grimaced. Fresh water had been in scant supply on the boat, and she hadn't been able to do more than sponge the sweat off her body in days. Her hair and skin were sticky from swimming in the ocean. She examined her crumpled jeans and stained shirt and scowled again.

"Where's Chet?" Ryan asked again.

Max pursed her full, red lips in a pout. "If I didn't know better, I'd think you weren't happy to see me."

"Where's Chet?" Ryan repeated, his voice hard. "He was supposed to be here."

"Chet was called away on another mission." She shrugged. "I told him I'd take his place. What's wrong? I thought you'd be happy I was here."

Ryan's mouth tightened, but he didn't say anything.

"I arrived last night. I expected you'd already be here," Max said. "Chet told me you were due to arrive yesterday." Her sharp green eyes settled on Hallie. She turned to Ryan, laying her hand on his arm. "I was surprised the trip took you so long, what with the seas being so calm. What was the hold up?" An awkward silence descended as Max's bright-eyed gaze swung between Ryan and Hallie.

The silence lengthened.

Ryan cleared his throat. "We had to fight a head wind coming out of Acapulco Bay."

Max's eyes narrowed.

Hallie shuddered under her suspicious glare.

Turning to Ryan, Max said, "Well, you're here now. That's what counts." She linked her arm with his.

"Is the plane ready?" he asked. "When do we take off?"

"I'm afraid there's been a slight delay." Max caressed Ryan's arm, staking her claim, her every action telling Hallie clearer than words the man was hers. The redhead leaned closer, her full breasts pressing against Ryan's arm, allowing him a good view of her generous cleavage.

"How long a delay?" Ryan asked, removing her hand and stepping away.

"A day, maybe two." She shrugged. "Convincing a pilot to fly out of this backwater town wasn't easy, especially with Montevedi involved." She rubbed against Ryan again like a cat in heat.

A bitter taste rose in Hallie's throat, and she fought to keep her face expressionless. Ryan loved Max. What happened between her and Ryan on the boat would stay on the boat. She wouldn't say anything about their lapse in judgment, and she was pretty sure Ryan wouldn't either. "Are we staying aboard tonight?" she asked.

"You can," Max said. She turned back to Ryan and purred, "I've booked us a room in the hotel. They only had one room left." Her mouth curved in a seductive pout. "But I don't mind sharing. I'm sure you don't either, Ryan. Being alone with you in a quaint little hotel room on a hot night will be just like old times."

"You and Hallie take the room," Ryan said. "I'll stay on the boat. I have a few things to do before I leave the *Wind Song* docked here."

Max ran red-tipped fingers across his chest. "Really? Are you sure? Hallie won't begrudge us some *private time* together." Her gaze switched to Hallie and hardened. "Will you, Hallie?"

Hallie bit her lip to stop the sting of tears. The thought of Ryan and Max kissing and making love, hurt. She forced a smile and lied. "Of course not. You two go ahead. Have fun. I'll be fine on the boat."

Ryan's gaze sharpened, but he turned to Max. "Take Hallie to the hotel. I'm sure she'd welcome a shower." He leaped into the boat. "I'll meet you both at the cantina in a couple of hours." He vanished below deck, leaving Hallie and Max alone.

A heavy silence descended.

"Look, Max, um...nothing...I mean...we didn't..." Hallie faltered under the redhead's cool stare. Her face flamed. "It's not what—"

Max raised her hand, halting her. "Stop. I don't want to hear whatever juvenile confession you're trying to spit out." She turned and strode across the dock toward the little village, calling over her shoulder, "Do you really think I care what schoolgirl games you played with Ryan on the boat?"

Hallie winced, realizing Max was right. What good would it do for her to know she and Ryan made love? It wasn't as if the sex had meant anything. Far better to say nothing and let Max and Ryan work out their relationship. Max loved Ryan; he loved Max. She'd better remember the irrefutable fact, or she was in for a hell of a lot of heartache. With a sigh, she followed Max across the empty square.

The hotel was a surprise. The exterior, whitewashed, brick walls were blinding under the glare of the setting sun, but the second Hallie stepped through the door into the dim interior, she was met with cool shadows and the enticing scent of lemons. White lace curtains covered two large, open windows and fluttered in a welcome breeze. Gleaming, dark, tile floors stretched across the lobby.

"*Hola, señoras. Buenas tardes.*"

Hallie turned.

A small, wiry man hurried toward them, a smile wreathing his elfin face.

She couldn't help but return his engaging smile. "*Buenas tardes.*"

His dark eyes twinkled. He turned to Max. "Ah, *señorita*, you return. This is the friend you were expecting?"

Max's mouth tightened, but she nodded.

"Welcome to Los Caribuenos, *señorita*. I am Francisco Parador."

Hallie shook his hand. "*Gracias, señor.*"

"I am honoured to have you as a guest in my hotel. We do not have many visitors in our small village." He shrugged. "Too far out of the way." His bright eyes studied her. "What brings you here?"

Max cut in. "The room key, *Señor* Parador?"

He looked taken aback by Max's curt demand, but he bustled behind a polished, wood counter, and retrieved a small, brass key. Smiling at Hallie, he said, "If you need anything, please do not hesitate to ask, *señorita*."

She smiled her thanks and followed Max along a tiled corridor to narrow stairs leading to the upper floor.

Their room was small, but clean. The two single beds and a narrow chest of drawers filled the space. A small window was open allowing a breeze to filter into the room. She crossed to the window and inspected the

257

deserted market below. A variety of thatch-covered stalls containing stacked boxes of colorful fruits and vegetables were scattered around the small square. Chickens clucked in wire cages.

She leaned out the window and looked toward the wharf. She couldn't see Ryan, but the *Wind Song,* tied at the dock, was visible. Why hadn't he wanted to stay at the hotel with Max? Was he being chivalrous and letting her have a shower and a comfortable bed for the night, or was something more involved?

"I think it's time we had a little talk," Max said.

Turning away from the window, Hallie met the other woman's hard-eyed gaze.

Max removed a slim, gold case and extracted a cigarette. Lighting it with a matching gold lighter, she placed the cigarette between her red lips and inhaled. "What do you think you're doing?"

"What do you mean?" Hallie asked. "I'm doing the same thing you're doing. I'm waiting to catch a plane back to the United States."

"Not that, you fool." Max squinted against a cloud of smoke. "What happened between you and Ryan on the boat?"

Hallie's face heated, and she turned her back on Max and stared at the sleeping village. A few, colorfully dressed men and women bustled about the square, setting up their wares, preparing for business. Siesta was over.

"Hallie, I asked you a question."

She gulped. What could she say? If she told Max the truth, she'd be furious. Taking a deep breath, keeping her back to Max and her gaze fixed on the scene below, she said, "Nothing happened, Max, nothing important anyway." She bit her lip, uncomfortable with the lie and the grain of bitter truth wrapped within it. Nothing important *had* happened, at least as far as Ryan was concerned.

"I didn't think so."

Hallie turned.

Max's gaze swept over her, her derision clear. "You're hardly Ryan's type."

The urge to strike back was strong, but Hallie bit her lip and stopped before she blurted out exactly what had happened between her and Ryan on the boat.

Max lounged on one of the beds, smoking her cigarette, tendrils of smoke curling around her. "Ryan loves me. He always has."

A sharp pain stabbed Hallie in the gut.

"Ryan and Geordie's relationship is complicated," Max continued. "Geordie's always been jealous of his older brother." She shrugged, a smile playing on her full lips. "Geordie's not Ryan, I'll grant you, but he can charm a nun out of her habit." She chuckled.

Hallie had had enough. "So you dumped your fiancé and ran off with his brother because his brother had a *magnetic personality*?"

Max shrugged again. "What can I say? A momentary weakness. Our affair didn't mean anything. Not really. Ryan understands."

The callousness of Max's comment shocked Hallie. She couldn't imagine Ryan's anguish when the woman he loved ran off with his brother. The betrayal must have devastated him. Not only had his fiancée deceived him, but his own brother had as well. "You were engaged to Ryan at the time. If you'd loved him, you would have stayed with him."

259

Max's eyes narrowed. "So I was right. You are falling in love with Ryan."

Hallie shook her head, regretting her outburst.

"It's pointless to deny your feelings. They're written all over your face." Max stubbed out her cigarette on the dresser, uncaring how the burning embers scorched the old wood. "Be careful," she warned. "He may have been nice to you, shown you a bit of consideration, but you're a fool if you think his attention means anything. Ryan wants revenge on his brother. He'll do anything to get back at Geordie, even use you if he has to."

Hallie stared at her, each word the redhead uttered, dripping like acid into her soul.

"Ryan will do anything to get back at his brother," Max repeated. "Even if doing so means pretending to have feelings for his brother's girlfriend. After all, it's only sex, right? You know what men are like, any girl willing to spread her legs for them is fair game."

Hallie sat stunned. *Geordie's girlfriend?* "But, I'm not—"

Max cut her off. "Ryan wants Geordie to feel the same pain he did when Geordie and I had our affair."

"No—"

"You're a fool." Max stood, smoothing her tight shorts. She walked to the door, and paused, her hand on the doorknob. "The only reason he wants you is because he thinks Geordie loves you." She stepped outside, slamming the door behind her.

Hallie collapsed on the bed, Max's words echoing through the small room. *He only wants you because he thinks Geordie loves you.* But Geordie didn't love her. Ryan knew she and Geordie were just friends. She'd told him. A headache blossomed, and she rubbed her aching eyes.

Was Max telling the truth? Was Ryan using her to get back at his brother? Had he made love to her because of his thirst for revenge? A vision of Ryan touching her, teasing another moan from her, flashed before her. She hunched in pain as bitter realization sank in. He'd used her. Her gut lurched, and nausea welled.

She leaped from the bed and ran to the adjoining bathroom, spewing acrid bile into the stained toilet. Tears filled her eyes and streamed down her cheeks. *He'd used her.* The words ran like a condemning chorus through her mind, etching deeper and deeper into her soul.

A rising anger slowly replaced her hurt. She wiped her damp hair off her forehead. If Ryan wanted to use her to get back at Geordie, the last laugh would be on him when he realized Geordie and her were platonic friends, nothing more. He'd wasted all his charms on her for nothing.

She took a steadying breath. A shower first, and then she'd show Max and Ryan how little she cared.

Chapter 21

Hallie stepped out of the shower and reached for a towel. The shower had cleansed her body, but not her mind. An image of Ryan's heated gaze roaming over her nakedness rose before her. "*You are so beautiful,*" he'd said. She snorted. To think she'd believed him. What a fool.

She wiped the condensation off the small bathroom mirror and examined her reflection. Her face was pale, her cheekbones too prominent and her eyes too big for her thin face. Running her fingers through her wet, tangled hair, she sighed. In no way could she compete with Max's lush beauty. No wonder Ryan loved her. What man wouldn't?

Taking a deep breath, she straightened her shoulders. *Okay. He used you to get back at his brother. Accept his heartless deceit and move on.* She couldn't avoid seeing him. The village was too small, and she needed his help to leave Mexico. She'd better get used to seeing him and Max together.

Casting a final glance in the mirror, she pasted a smile on her face. She'd do this. She'd get dressed in her dirty, rumpled clothes, go downstairs, and meet Ryan and Max at the cantina. She'd show them she didn't care what happened between them. Like the clown from the old song, she might be crying on the inside, but on the outside, she'd be laughing and smiling.

A knock sounded on the outer door.

Max must have forgotten her key. She wrapped the towel around her damp body and opened the door. She gasped.

The man from the front desk stood in the hall.

"*Señor* Parador." Hallie tugged the damp towel higher, wishing she'd taken the time to dress before answering the door.

Two patches of red flamed across the swarthy skin on his face as he kept his eyes fixed on hers.

Heat rose on her own cheeks.

"I am sorry to disturb you, *señorita*, but I was asked to give you this." He held out a large plastic bag.

"For me?"

He nodded. "*Sí, señorita*." He shoved the bag into her hands and turned to leave.

She opened the bag, peeked inside and saw a skirt and a white blouse, as well as a pair of lacy, white, cotton underwear. She pushed the clothes aside. A pair of sandals, a comb, and a toothbrush lay at the bottom of the bag. "*Señor*, please wait."

He turned back. "*Sí, señorita?*"

She held up the bag. "Who gave you this?"

"A gentleman, *señorita*. A visitor like yourself."

A gentleman? Ryan? Ryan had sent her these clothes? Who else? Warmth surged through her, easing the vise-like band around her forehead.

"Is there a problem, *señorita?*"

"No, nothing's wrong. Not a thing."

She retreated into the room, closing the door behind her and hurried over to the bed. She removed the clothes from the bag with shaking fingers and laid them on the bed. Judging by the bright colors and simple style, Ryan must have bought the clothing at one of the market stalls in the village. Her heart soared. He'd known she wouldn't want to put on the same filthy clothes she'd worn for the past week. She laughed and danced across the floor, holding the full, red, wool skirt in front of her.

The blouse was soft, white cotton embroidered with multicolored threads in an intricate design along the rounded neckline. Handmade, flat, leather sandals completed the outfit.

She tried the clothes on admiring the way the blouse draped over her breasts and how the full swing of the skirt complimented her legs. Suddenly, the world was a lot brighter. *He cared.* The words sang through her mind. Why else would he have done this? *Because he's still playing you.* She flinched, but ignored the sly whisper with its bitter ring of truth.

Strains of music and the buzz of conversation filtered into the room through the open window. She looked at the street below, and her eyes widened. The small square had undergone a transformation. People of all ages jostled against one another as they bargained loudly for fruits, vegetables, chickens and goats at the many stalls set up throughout the market. Local crafts, clothing, shoes, straw hats, shawls and jewelry were offered for sale.

A trio of musicians stood in the middle of the square strumming Spanish guitars, the lilting music rising above the noisy throng. Tables had been set up, and platters heaped with food were being placed on each table.

She caught sight of Max and Ryan, and her heart

stilled. The tall, handsome couple stood out among the crowd of shorter Mexicans. Ryan's dark hair gleamed in the setting sun. Max's rich, red mane shone like a vibrant sunset. She clung to Ryan, her arm wrapped around his, her lush body pressed against his side.

He turned toward her and spoke.

The redhead's mouth opened in a giggle.

Hallie swore she heard the grating sound over the loud music and voices raised in conversation in the square.

Max leaned toward Ryan and kissed him on the mouth.

Hallie turned away, blinking against the sting of tears. If she'd had any doubts Ryan still loved Max, they'd been quashed. In spite of everything Max had told her, she'd foolishly harbored the hope the other woman was mistaken, and Ryan cared for her. After all, he'd sent her the clothes.

Ryan and Max were together. She'd just witnessed how together they were. What further proof did she need? Unable to stop them, tears streamed from her eyes and dripped onto her new blouse.

****

Ryan wasn't listening to Max's chatter as they strolled across the square toward the cantina. His mind was on other things, or, more correctly, another woman.

He'd messed up. Big time. He should have said something to Hallie when they were on the boat. Instead, he'd given her time and space to sort out her emotions. He exhaled a huff of air. Look what that had achieved? With each passing moment, she'd drawn further away from him until the divide between them was so wide he hadn't a clue how to approach her.

He should have forced a confrontation and made her admit making love together had meant something— to both of them. But every time he'd attempted to talk to her, she'd looked at him with those big, wounded eyes, and the words had died on his lips.

After all, what could he say? Tell her he was sorry? He'd screwed up? He hadn't meant to make love to the woman his brother loved? Yeah. And if you believed those lies, he had some oceanfront property in Arizona to sell.

Max's soft, full breast rubbed against his arm. He tried to edge away, but she held him tight. "Look, Max, I don't know what you're up to, but this isn't going to happen."

Her eyes widened with pretended innocence. "Really?"

"Any relationship between us is over, has been for a very long time."

"I don't believe you." She pressed her ample breasts against him again, her thighs molding with his as her lips met his.

He backed up, but she clung to him and deepened the kiss. For a second, a very short second, he forgot everything and enjoyed her luscious body and the teasing of her tongue as she toyed with his. But then he remembered this was Max, and he shoved her away, forcing her to let go. He cast a quick look at the hotel and caught a flash of gold in a second floor window. His heart sank. Damn. Hallie was watching.

Max ran a teasing hand over his chest, circling lower and lower.

"Stop this," he bit off, removing her roaming hand.

She batted her heavily mascaraed eyelashes. "Oh,

come on, Ryan. You know you want me." Her voice was husky, filled with promise. "Surely, you haven't forgotten what things were like between us." Her full red lips curved in a sensuous smile.

"I sure as hell haven't. I remember exactly how you treated me. You were engaged to me, yet, at the first opportunity, you ran off with another man. My own brother, for God's sake."

"I told you. Running off with Geordie was a mistake. I never wanted him. I wanted to make you jealous."

He snorted. "You're some piece of work, lady. And I use the term *lady* loosely." He turned and began to walk away.

Max grabbed his arm halting him.

"Let go," he growled.

She paled but kept her hand on him. "Ryan, give us a chance. We were good together once. Remember? We can be the same way again. I still love you."

He shook his head. "I don't think so." He glanced up at the hotel again, hoping Hallie wasn't watching.

"You can't want *her*." Her voice was shrill.

"Hallie is none of your concern."

Max's gaze turned calculating. "Not even if I tell you she's in love with Geordie?"

The words slid like splinters of ice down his spine. He shoved her hand off his arm and stomped away. He no longer headed toward the cantina. The last person he should see right now was Hallie. He'd betrayed his brother once with her. He wouldn't deceive him again. Some place in this damn village had to sell alcohol. He needed a drink…a dozen, stiff drinks.

And drink he did. He poured one shot of tequila

267

after another down his burning throat. But no matter how much he drank, he couldn't rid himself of the sour taste in his mouth, or his guilt. What sort of man sleeps with his brother's girlfriend? He lifted the half-empty bottle and poured another shot into his glass, downing the drink in one swallow. Grimacing at the roughness of the cheap liquor, he refilled his empty glass and drank again.

The little bar was almost deserted. The earlier crowd of boisterous drinkers had left, and only one other man lingered in the dingy bar.

Catching Ryan's gaze, the man called, "Hey, *amigo*," and grinned drunkenly, raising his glass in a sloppy toast.

Ryan ignored him, as he'd ignored the bartender's earlier attempts at friendliness. He didn't want to talk to anyone. Self-loathing filled him. He'd made love to Hallie and in the process betrayed his brother. Geordie had done the same to him, but his brother's treachery didn't excuse his own actions. To make matters worse, making love to the woman his brother loved wasn't the full extent of his betrayal. He hadn't just made love to Hallie. He'd *fallen* in love with her. He cursed under his breath.

He loved Hallie.

The bitter truth ate at his gut. He loved her, but he had no right to her love. Geordie loved her. And she loved Geordie. He refilled his glass, determined to drown his guilt even if doing so killed him. He grimaced at the rough taste of the liquor. Drinking this rotgut probably would be the end of him.

"Hey, *compadre*, buy me a drink?"

Ryan froze, the glass midway to his mouth. His

hand jerked, slopping liquor onto his pants. He turned, blinking in disbelief. "Geordie?"

His brother grinned, his familiar brown eyes twinkling. "None other, bro."

"What the hell?" Ryan fought to clear his booze-fogged brain. "What are you doing here?"

Geordie chuckled. "Talking to you." He sat in the chair beside Ryan and picked up the tequila and drank directly from the bottle. Coughing and gasping, he wiped his mouth with his sleeve and studied Ryan. "You look like hell."

Ryan's mouth twisted. "Thanks." He examined his brother. "You've changed." He grimaced at the understatement. He hardly recognized his brother.

Geordie's face was leaner, his cheek bones more prominent. He'd cut his dark blond curls and now wore his hair short in almost a military style. A mustache lined his top lip and lent his face a rugged look. But the greatest change was in his eyes. Gone was the perennial glint of mischief, replaced by dark, haunted shadows.

Geordie ran his hand over his cropped hair. "Yeah, I guess I have changed a bit."

Ryan noted the dark circles under his eyes and his gaunt, almost skeletal face. He'd lost weight, too much weight. "What the hell happened to you?"

Geordie shrugged. "You wouldn't believe me if I told you."

Ryan furrowed his brow. "How did you find me? How did you know I was here?"

"I have my sources. I heard Hallie's here too." He scanned the bar. "Where is she?"

"Who told you we were in Los Caribuenos? Montevedi?" Ryan grabbed the collar of Geordie's shirt and pulled his off his stool, yanking him closer. "You bastard, are you working with scum like him?"

Geordie paled, but he didn't look away. "Christ, is that what you think of me?"

Ryan didn't say anything, but he released his grip on his shirt.

"I guess I deserve your distrust," Geordie said. He sat back and sighed, taking another long drink from the bottle. "I don't work for Montevedi. I never did." His eyes pleaded. "You have to believe me."

Ryan searched his face for signs of subterfuge. The silence lengthened. Finally, he nodded. "Okay. What's going on then?"

"Before I explain, I have to know. How's Hallie? Is she all right? I know Montevedi had her in his clutches. Did the bastard hurt her?"

The questions, one after the other tumbled out, and with each one, the knot in Ryan's gut grew. If he was in any doubt Geordie loved Hallie, his brother's overriding concern for her showed he'd been a fool. "She's fine."

Geordie's face lit up. "She is? Oh, man, I was so worried. I'd never forgive myself if something happened to her." He hung his head. "It's my fault she's involved in this mess." He gripped Ryan's hand and shook. "Thanks for looking after her, bro." He blinked back tears. "I knew I could count on you. That's why I called you. I don't know how I'll ever repay you."

Ryan's hand trembled as he poured another drink. He swallowed the bitter liquor down, trying to tune out his brother's gratitude.

"Ryan?"

He forced himself to meet Geordie's gaze.

"Don't you think you've had enough to drink?"

"I haven't had nearly enough booze, little brother. Not nearly enough."

Geordie scowled. "Don't you want to know where I've been these past months? Why I'm here now?"

"Nope." He drained another glass. The room started to sway.

Geordie sighed and shook his head. "Where's Hallie?"

Ryan shrugged. "Try the hotel."

"I can't wait to see her." He rose from his seat. "Don't get too wasted, bro. We have a lot to discuss."

Ryan kept his gaze fixed on the drink in his hand until he heard Geordie leave. At last, he was alone, alone with his bitter, guilt-ridden thoughts. He lifted his drink for another swallow but tossed the glass against the wall, watching the glass shatter into a thousand pieces.

Like his heart.

****

Hallie splashed cold water on her face. She was through hiding in her room. It was time she faced Ryan and Max. What was she afraid of? She'd survived seeing them kissing each other. She'd survive anything else. With this rallying thought, she headed out of her room and down the stairs.

The square was crowded. Music and laughter filled the warm night air. Her stomach rumbled at the smell of chickens roasting on an open, charcoal grill, and she was reminded she hadn't eaten since early this morning.

She found Max sitting alone at a large wooden table. "Where's Ryan?" she asked, joining the redhead.

Max shrugged. "Getting drunk somewhere."

"Drunk? Why is he getting drunk?"

Instead of answering, Max studied her, beginning with the new sandals, moving up the colorful skirt and embroidered blouse, finally settling on her face. "The peasant look suits you. Where'd you get those clothes?"

Before she could explain, Hallie glanced up, and her breath caught in her throat.

A man, a wide grin on his face, approached their table.

She gaped, unable to believe her eyes. He'd changed. He didn't look much like the person she remembered, but, incredibly, unbelievably, the man striding toward her was the man for whom she'd spent these past days searching. "Geordie?" Tears of joy filled her eyes. She ran toward him and threw herself into his arms.

He hugged her, squeezing hard. "I'm so glad to see you, Hallie." He held her away from him, his gaze searching. "Are you all right? Montevedi didn't hurt you, did he? Please tell me you're okay."

"I'm fine, especially now you're here." She wiped her tears. "What about you? Where have you been? How come you didn't meet me in Antler Springs like you promised you would? Do you know how worried I've been? I thought…I thought you were dead."

"Hey, slow down. One question at a time." He chuckled, but in spite of his laughter, shadows dimmed his eyes.

"You look…different," she said.

He smiled wryly. "So I've been told."

"How…how did you find us?"

"I'll explain everything later."

"Well, well, well, if it isn't the prodigal brother,"

said Max. "I didn't think you'd show up here."

Geordie turned and grinned at the tall redhead. "You know me, Max. I never want to miss out on the fun." He leaned over and kissed her lightly on the mouth. "You look as sexy as ever."

Max smiled. "I see you haven't lost your charm."

Geordie chuckled, setting the dimples in his cheeks dancing. "So, what are you two beautiful ladies doing?" He placed an arm around each of their waists and hugged them to his side.

Hallie studied him and then Max. A ping of suspicion struck her. Why wasn't Max more surprised to see him? "Geordie," she said, "how did you know we were in Los Caribuenos?"

He shot a look at Max.

She shrugged. "You might as well tell her."

"Geordie," Hallie asked, "what's going on?"

"What a touching reunion."

Hallie stiffened at the slurred voice. She turned.

Ryan staggered as he walked toward them, a bottle dangling from one hand. "Isn't it great Geordie's here?" he asked, his words thick. "Now, this party can get started." He waved the bottle at them. "I've brought some tequila." He did a staggering spin, almost falling. "*Olé*."

"Hey, bro," said Geordie, "looks like you've had enough. Why don't you put the bottle down and come and join us?"

Ryan's face darkened. "Since when have you been the one to give me advice?" He shoved the bottle at Hallie and grabbed Max by the hand. "Come on. Let's dance." He dragged her to where other couples were shuffling to the festive music.

Hallie stared after them, unable to take her eyes off Ryan, even when he wrapped his arms around Max and drew her body to his.

Their hips swayed in time to the music.

Tears stung her eyes.

"What's gotten into him?" asked Geordie. "I've never seen him like this."

She shook her head. "I...I have a headache. I'm going to bed."

Geordie's brow furrowed. "Already? I just got here. I haven't seen you in a long time. I thought we'd talk, and you could tell me where you've been all these months. I worried about you, Hallie...everyday."

"I can't do this now. Let's talk in the morning."

"You're the second person tonight who's told me the same thing."

Ryan nuzzled Max's long neck as they swayed to the beat of the music, locked in an intimate embrace.

Hallie's gut wrenched. "Look, I have to go." She turned and fled, shouldering her way through the crowd, desperate to escape to the solitude of her room.

Chapter 22

Ryan pried his eyes open, only to squeeze them shut against the blinding glare. He counted to ten, took a deep breath, and opened them again. The room was still painfully bright, but if he squinted, he could bear the brain-piercing light. He sat up and grabbed onto the bed as the room spun. Sweat broke out on his forehead. A wave of nausea rolled over him, and he groaned.

He rubbed his face, wincing at the loud rasp of beard. His mouth tasted like something had died in it. His gaze lit on the empty bottle of tequila lying on the bed beside him. Disgust welled within as shadowed memories of the previous evening rushed back.

How could he have been so stupid? Did he really think getting drunk was going to make him feel any less guilty he'd slept with his brother's girlfriend? If booze was the answer then, he hadn't drank nearly enough. Not by a long shot.

He studied his surroundings and breathed a sigh of relief. He was in his own bunk on the boat. He shook his head, wincing when once again the room spun. Swallowing back bile, he closed his eyes. Visions of last night's fiasco filled his mind.

Trust his little brother to show up just when everything had gone to hell. He'd been okay until Geordie had appeared. He snorted. Well, maybe not okay, but he'd been dealing with his guilt, if getting mindlessly drunk was a way of dealing. But then Geordie had shown up and made his feelings about Hallie more than clear. He still loved her. Ryan gritted his teeth as he recalled how grateful Geordie had been, how he'd thanked him for looking after her.

If only he knew.

He'd looked after her all right. The second he was alone with her, he was all over her, touching her, tasting her, and loving her. Geordie would never forgive him. How could he when he couldn't forgive himself?

In his drunken wisdom, he'd accepted Max's offer of companionship. If he were wrapped in her arms, he wouldn't go near Hallie. Hell, Max wouldn't let him out of her sight. He was using Max, but she was a big girl. She could handle herself.

He scrubbed his face hard as a fresh wave of guilt assailed him. He'd drunk too much last night. *Shit, that was the understatement of the year.* The last thing he remembered was taking Max onto the dance floor.

He grimaced at the sour taste in his mouth. His tongue was thick and coated with fuzz. He needed coffee. A long day lay ahead. He had to secure the boat and then meet the rest of the group. He had a lot of questions to ask his brother, and he was determined to get some answers. Peering at his watch, he squinted until the numbers stopped moving. He'd better get a move on. They were to meet the plane which would take them out of this hellhole in less than two hours.

He stood, keeping a hand on the wall for support as the room swirled around him. He closed his eyes and willed the nausea away. Taking a deep breath, he opened them again. The room had stopped dipping and swaying. He took one tentative step toward the galley, and then another.

He'd shuffled another two steps when he froze and stared at a scrap of black fabric lying on the floor. A pair of white shorts lay beside the bra, and beside the bra, a lacy black thong. Nausea washed over him. Swaying, he forced himself to take two more steps and peered around the partition to the other berth.

Max lay on the narrow bunk, her body covered by a thin sheet, which did nothing to hide her ample curves.

He grabbed onto the wall. His head pounded with new intensity as he stared at the sleeping woman. Had they…? He couldn't finish the thought. He studied the discarded clothing and regarded Max's obviously nude form. He glanced at his own body and gulped. He wore his striped boxers. He'd be naked if something had happened. Wouldn't he?

Bits and pieces of last night returned as he racked his addled brain trying to remember: the pain of seeing Geordie's obvious love for Hallie reflected on his brother's expressive face, downing more drinks, dancing with Max, drinking even more. The rest of the night was a blur.

Max was here. Naked. He must have taken her back to the boat. Had they had sex? He groaned and rubbed his temples. He was batting a thousand. What sort of man was he?

Max's eyes opened, and she smiled. "Good morning, handsome." Her voice was husky with sleep.

He eyed her warily.

She pouted her full lips and patted the bed beside her. "Why don't you join me?" The sheet covering her full curves slipped lower, exposing one plump breast.

He swallowed.

"You don't have to look so terrified. Nothing happened last night."

"Nothing?"

"Nothing." A sad light dulled her green eyes. "Not that I didn't try my best, but you weren't exactly...interested." Her mouth twisted. "I must be losing my touch."

Relief washed over him. He tottered to the bed and sank onto the soft surface. "I guess I was pretty drunk."

"You were more than drunk, my friend. You were totally wasted."

He rubbed his aching temples. "What happened?"

"You don't remember?"

He shook his head and grimaced at the fresh upsurge of pain. "After we hit the dance floor, everything's pretty much a blur."

"You didn't last much longer. We'd danced only a few songs before you nearly passed out on me."

"I'm sorry."

"I've seen worse."

"How come..." He gulped. "How come you're...?"

"How come I'm here?"

He nodded. He was going to say "naked," but her words would do.

"Someone had to see you made your way home safe. Geordie and Hallie had disappeared. I was the only one left."

Her words hit him like a knife in the gut, and he winced with this new pain. Hallie and Geordie were together last night?

"You like her, don't you?"

He met her knowing gaze but turned away before

she could read the truth in his eyes. Too late.

"My God. I don't believe it. You're in love with her."

He opened his mouth to protest, but then stopped, knowing hiding his feelings from Max was pointless. She knew him too well. "I am," he said simply.

"Damn, I guess I should have seen it coming." Max sat up, covering her luscious body with the sheet. "Does she know? Have you told her?"

He shook his head. "My feelings for Hallie are irrelevant. She's in love with Geordie."

"I know how you feel," she said. "It's not easy loving someone who doesn't return your love, is it?" Her eyes were sad, her expression resigned.

He didn't answer her question. What could he say? She still loved him. Hell, she didn't hide the fact, but he didn't love her. Not anymore. He loved Hallie. A woman he could never have.

Hallie and Geordie were in love. The fact he loved her didn't change a damn thing. He took a steadying breath. "I'll make some coffee. You'd better get dressed." He turned toward the small galley, calling over his shoulder, "The plane will be waiting for us."

****

Hallie stirred and sat up, rubbing her aching eyes. She'd hardly slept last night. Once she'd escaped to her room, she'd lain awake listening for hours to the noise of the fiesta, trying to block out the image of Max and Ryan locked in each other's arms as they danced to the music, their bodies welded together.

A wasted effort.

Eventually, the music had died away, and the sound of the celebration faded. As the hours passed and

Max didn't return, her agitation grew. She regarded the other bed with its smooth cover and tidy bed sheets. Max had stayed out all night. With Ryan. What had she expected? The way he'd been all over the tall redhead when they were dancing told her everything she needed to know.

She smoothed a strand of hair off her forehead and took a deep breath. To survive the ensuing hours with any dignity at all, she had to be strong. She wouldn't let Ryan know how much his actions hurt. She wouldn't let Max see her pain. The redhead had made her desire for Ryan clear. Well, she could have him. The two of them could bloody well have each other.

Geordie was safe. She'd accomplished what she'd set out to do. Time to return to her life in Seattle. The others could settle the situation with Montevedi. Once she was back in the States, she'd never have to see Ryan again.

A short time later, she left the hotel and walked to the cantina. The small square was quiet in the early morning sunshine. A few villagers were shuffling about, cleaning up the remnants of last evening's festivities. One man, his face covered by his ragged straw hat, lay passed out on the ground amidst a flock of chickens clucking and pecking in the dirt. Two raw-boned, yellow-haired dogs hunkered under a table snarling and fighting over an old chicken carcass.

The restaurant shutters were open. Geordie sat at a large table, a heaping plate of food before him. He beamed when he saw her, leaped to his feet, and kissed her on the cheek. He drew her into a hug. "Good morning, gorgeous."

In spite of her misery, she smiled. His appearance

may have changed, but he was still the Geordie she remembered. He could charm a smile out of even the sourest person. "At least, one thing hasn't changed." She nodded at his steaming plate heaped with scrambled eggs and refried beans. "You always did have a good appetite."

He grinned, patting his flat stomach. "It's been a while since I've had a chance to eat a full meal."

She frowned as she took in his haggard appearance. He'd always been stocky, his face soft and padded. Not anymore. The man standing before her was thin, his cheekbones jutting out on his gaunt face, his body leanly muscled. "Where have you been all this time? What have you been doing? You've lost so much weight. What the hell happened to you?"

His eyes clouded, but he resumed his seat at the table, gesturing for her to join him. "I'll tell you everything once Ryan gets here." He glanced behind her. "Speak of the devil."

She followed the direction of his gaze, and her knees wobbled.

Ryan and Max stepped off the dock and headed in their direction.

Max's hand rested on Ryan's arm in a proprietary manner.

The implications of where the couple had come from hit her like a knife to the heart. She staggered.

"Hey, what's the matter?" asked Geordie, grabbing her arm to steady her.

She blinked back tears, biting her lip to stop any fresh ones appearing.

"Hallie?"

She turned away, refusing to look at him.

"Nothing. Nothing's wrong."

"Look, we've been friends a long time. I know when something's bothering you. Why won't you tell me what's wrong? Are you mad at me? Is that what this is about? I said I was sorry. I meant it. I never wanted you to be involved."

She kept her face averted from his probing gaze, but she couldn't help casting another glance at the approaching couple.

A satisfied smile wreathed Max's striking face. She resembled the cat, who had eaten the proverbial cream.

Geordie grasped her chin, forcing her to look at him. "Hallie, what is it?"

"Good morning, you two," sang out Max from half way across the square. "Sleep well?"

Hallie winced at the other woman's cheerfulness.

Geordie's sharp-eyed gaze swung from her to Max, and back again. A look of dawning understanding blossomed on his face.

She sank onto the seat beside him.

"Hallie, what's going on?" he asked.

She shook her head. Even if she could force a word past the painful lump in her throat, what would she tell him? She'd slept with Ryan even though she knew he still loved Max? What good would a confession do? It would only make him pity her.

Max and Ryan arrived and sat on the opposite side of the table, beside each other. They ordered coffee from the hovering waiter.

Hallie's hand shook when she picked up her cup, and hot coffee slopped onto her lap. She yelped and jumped up. A large wet patch stained the red wool of her skirt. Tears stung her eyes. *So much for not making a scene.*

"Here. Use this." Ryan stood beside her, holding out a paper napkin.

Face burning, she grabbed the napkin and furiously rubbed the stain.

"Are you okay?" he asked. The power of his gaze penetrated the veil of hair hiding her face from him.

She nodded, fighting to hold back tears. "I...I'm fine." Straightening her shoulders, she brushed back her hair and pasted a smile on her face. She laughed a hard, brittle laugh. "I guess I'll have to dry clean this skirt when I get home. I'll need it next Halloween."

Max and Geordie chuckled.

Ryan didn't, but he walked back to his seat and sat down.

Hallie blew out a breath. As long as she didn't look at him, she'd be okay. Not looking wasn't easy. Every cell in her body demanded she look.

Geordie, a teasing glint in his eye asked, "How are you feeling this morning, Ryan? A little headache, some nausea perhaps?"

Ryan scowled.

Max smirked. "He drank enough tequila to cause a national shortage."

"Well, at least he survived. I've heard some of the local hooch will kill a man," Geordie said.

Giving into her unrelenting urge, Hallie peeked at Ryan.

Dark circles underscored his bloodshot, startling-blue eyes. He hadn't shaved this morning, and the dark stubble combined with the harsh slash of his mouth, made him look more intimidating than usual.

He turned and their eyes met.

283

A frisson of awareness arced between them.

After an interminable second, he glanced away, and she breathed again. "When…when are we supposed to meet the plane?" she asked.

Max checked her watch. "In a little over an hour. A small, secluded airfield is a few miles from here. If everything goes as planned, the pilot should be waiting there for us."

"You're not getting on the plane," said Geordie.

"What?" asked Max. "Why not?"

Ryan glared at his brother. "Yeah, why not, *bro*?"

Geordie cast a quick look around the square and leaned forward. "It's a setup. The only thing waiting for you at the airfield is Montevedi's thugs."

"Come on," Max said. "I arranged the whole thing myself. I used a secure network. Montevedi doesn't know what we're planning. Only three people know our plans, the pilot, Chet, and the man who arranged the flight. I trust them implicitly."

"How do you know Montevedi's men will be waiting for us at the airfield?" Ryan pinned Geordie with a hard look.

Geordie's face paled beneath his tan. "Because I overheard his plans."

Silence descended over the table.

Hallie blinked. How could Geordie have heard anything Montevedi said? Unless—

Ryan grabbed Geordie's wrist and twisted. "What the hell's going on? Last night you told me you weren't working for Montevedi." Ryan bit off the words as if each syllable were a shard of ice.

"I'm not." Geordie winced as Ryan tightened his grip, but he didn't try and pull his arm away. "Not really."

Ryan released his arm with a final, sharp twist. "You'd better explain, *brother.* Everything."

Hallie shuddered at the menace in Ryan's voice.

"When this whole thing blew up," Geordie said, rubbing the red welt on his wrist, "when I couldn't pay those men back, I knew I was in trouble." He turned to Hallie, his gaze pleading. "I didn't mean for you to get involved. The whole mess went south so damn quick. I thought I could handle the situation before Montevedi's goons came after me." He grimaced. "I was wrong."

Hallie bit her lip remembering Geordie's condition the night he'd showed up at her townhouse, terrified and beaten half to death.

"At first," Geordie continued, "I did the only thing I could think of. I ran. But then I realized running wasn't going to solve anything. No matter how well I hid, eventually Montevedi would find me. I couldn't let him get to Hallie." He ran his fingers over his blond moustache. "I had to do something to settle things one way or another."

"Why didn't you come to me when this fuck up all started?" Ryan's voice was harsh. "Why didn't you ask me for help before it was too late?"

Geordie smiled, but his eyes were sad. "It's what I do, isn't it? I always expect you to help me. Every time I get in trouble, I run to my big brother, and you save me." He clasped Ryan's arm. "It was time I solved my own problems. Besides, you were busy keeping an eye on Hallie. She needed you."

Ryan shook his head. "And in the process you nearly got her killed."

Geordie's face lost what little color it had left. "I

didn't think they'd go after her, not once she disappeared. I thought when they couldn't find her and she was in hiding, they'd leave her alone. They wanted me, not her." He turned to Hallie, his gaze beseeching. "I'm sorry, Hallie, I…" Pain shadowed his eyes.

"It's okay," she breathed, swallowing back tears.

"Okay?" Ryan exploded. "What the hell are you talking about? Those men tried to kill you. Several times. They killed Buzz, for Christ's sake."

Hallie reeled from the intensity of his anger, but he was right. Montevedi's men had murdered Buzz and nearly killed Ryan and Vince as well. Geordie's thoughtless actions had caused a great deal of harm.

"I'll never forgive myself for what happened." Geordie's voice was rough with emotion. "Buzz was a good man."

A strained silence descended, thickening the air.

Hallie's gaze settled on one brother, and then the other. For the first time, the resemblance between them was unmistakable. Both men wore identical expressions of loss and desolation.

Ryan cleared his throat. "Tell us about Montevedi."

"Six weeks ago, I came out of hiding and met with your old friends at the DEA. I told them everything. Montevedi's responsible for smuggling millions of dollars worth of illegal drugs from Peru and Bolivia, through Mexico to the United States. As you probably know better than anyone, the US Drug Enforcement Agency is desperate to take him down." He shrugged. "They agreed to set me up."

"Set you up? What the hell do you mean?" demanded Ryan.

"They arranged all the details with the Mexican

Federales and negotiated with some resources on the inside, so I could infiltrate Montevedi's organization."

"But Montevedi knows you. He knows you took his money. Why would he trust you enough to accept you into his organization? Why didn't he just kill you?"

"Someone vouched for me."

"Who the hell would do that?"

Geordie's gaze slid to Max.

"What the hell?" Ryan scowled at Max. "What's he saying? Are you the contact in Montevedi's cartel?"

Max's face paled. She nodded.

Ryan ran his fingers through his hair. "I don't fucking believe this. *You* were the one." His eyes burned with fire. "All those years ago, when we flew our team here to take down Montevedi, you were the one who told him we were coming. You gave us away."

"You don't understand, Ryan. I didn't have a choice. I had to do what I did. Playing both sides was my job. I had my orders." Max grabbed his hand, but he shook her off. "Look, Ryan," she said, "I—"

Ryan cut her off. "Two men were killed in our attack. Two good men."

Max's green eyes were red and swollen, and tears streaked her cheeks, smearing her eye makeup.

Hallie couldn't believe what she was hearing. Max had been involved with Montevedi from the beginning?

"Don't be so hard on her, Ryan," said Geordie.

Ryan leaped to his feet and glared down at his brother. "What the hell do you know? What did you do?"

"After I left Seattle, I contacted Max. She set up the meeting with the DEA, and then arranged for me to finagle my way to the inside of Montevedi's cartel."

"You little shit! You never think of anyone but yourself. Did you even consider what would happen to Hallie while you were playing out this foolish charade? People always get hurt around you. Look what happened to Buzz. He was trying to help you. He didn't deserve to die."

Geordie scrubbed a hand across his face. "Don't you think I know what I've done? I'm going to have to live with my culpability every second of every day for the rest of my life." He turned to Hallie, his eyes pleading. "You have to believe me. I didn't think any of this would happen. The DEA told me they'd look after you and you'd be safe. I was just trying to make a difference. I didn't know anyone would be hurt." Anguish radiated across his face, carving deep grooves where no lines had been before.

Hallie blinked back tears and took his hand in hers. "You did what you had to." The events of these past months had taken a self-centered playboy and honed him into a man who looked like he'd been to hell and back. Whatever had happened, whatever he'd been through this past month, he'd paid for his mistakes.

"Ryan," Max pleaded, "you have to understand, I was only doing my job."

"You couldn't tell me you'd infiltrated Montevedi's network? You didn't trust me enough to tell me the truth? Your own fiancé?"

"Do you think being a double agent was easy for me?" she asked, her eyes fixed on Ryan. "For more than two years, I've lived a lie." She choked back a sob. "I was deep undercover. My job was to infiltrate Montevedi's cartel. He had to believe I was a traitor. The deception had to look real." Tears flowed down her cheeks. "I didn't want to lie to you."

"You're one hell of an actress, lady. You sure fooled me."

Hallie's mind whirled. Max was working undercover, trying to take down Montevedi? She'd been on the inside of Montevedi's organization the whole time, leaking information to the crime lord. Hallie shuddered. "You were the one," she said. "You told those men where we were staying in Montana. That's how they knew where to find us and were able to kill Buzz. How could you? He was your friend."

Max used a tissue to wipe her face. She looked at Hallie with reddened, swollen eyes. "I had my orders."

The bitter taste of disgust filled Hallie's mouth. "Orders?" she spat. "Did your *orders* tell you to leak the location of the airfield in Acapulco? Vince almost died there. And Montevedi's men kidnapped me. Montevedi is going after Ryan next. Is that what you wanted, Ryan to be another casualty of your precious DEA?" She was panting. Her heart pounded and nausea threatened to overwhelm her.

"Look, Hallie," Max said. "I'm sorry you were caught in the middle. I had my assignment, and Washington was determined to follow through with the mission. They still are. Too much is at stake to stop now. Just believe me when I say I wouldn't have let Montevedi harm you. I would have stopped the entire operation if I'd thought you were in any danger."

Hallie shook her head in disgust. What was she supposed to say? Was she supposed to tell her everything was fine? This woman had been the instrument of so much pain. A man was dead because of the DEA's devious plan. She shook her head again.

"I...I don't know what to think."

"How do we know we can trust you now?" Ryan asked. "How do we know you haven't told Montevedi where we are?"

"I'm through following orders. My actions have caused enough death and violence. My only concern right now is to get us safely out of Mexico." She faced Ryan. "I swear I'm telling you the truth, Ryan. I'll never betray you again."

He stared at her, his jaw tight, his gaze piercing. The seconds ticked by. He finally nodded. "All right," he said, "let's get on with this."

Max turned to Hallie. "Are we okay?" she asked.

All too clearly, Hallie remembered Montevedi's deadly lizards and his not-so-subtle threats. He was responsible for countless deaths and ruined lives. "Just promise me you'll get the bastard and shut down his drug cartel."

Max searched her face for a long minute. "I owe you an apology, Hallie. I think I've misjudged you."

Hallie nodded, realizing Max had declared a truce of sorts.

Ryan sat down again. "Okay, Geordie, let's say I believe you're not working with Montevedi. Why are you here? Why now?"

"You need my help."

Ryan snorted.

Geordie's face flamed.

"Where the hell were you when Buzz was killed or when Montevedi kidnapped Hallie?" asked Ryan.

"I told you, that wasn't supposed to happen. Hallie was supposed to be safe in the US. I didn't know she'd flown down here with you." He turned pleading eyes on

290

the group, his gaze seeking out each one of them in turn. "Once I heard Montevedi had Hallie, I did everything I could to get her out of there."

"Maria," Hallie blurted. "You're the reason she agreed to help me escape. You gave her the key to the window in my room."

"I wanted to do more, but convincing Maria to slip you the key was all I could do. Montevedi watched me like a hawk. I couldn't go near you without him knowing. I hoped if you had the key, you'd somehow get out of the mansion." His lips curved in a tight smile. "You didn't let me down."

Hallie's mind whirled. Geordie had been in Montevedi's mansion? He'd given Maria the key to the window? The entire time they'd been searching for him, he'd been in Montevedi's compound. Ryan's loud curse cut into her thoughts.

"Always thinking of yourself, aren't you?" said Ryan, glaring at Geordie.

"Look, I know you don't trust me. Hell, I've never given you any reason to, but you have to believe me. The moment I found out Montevedi had captured Hallie, I did everything I could to help her escape without blowing my cover."

"You still haven't answered my question." Ryan's eyes were hard, not giving him an inch. "Why are you here now?"

"After your attack on his compound and Hallie's escape, Montevedi was furious. He put a price on both your heads. Anyone who brought him information on your whereabouts would be rewarded. Every drug dealer and low life in Mexico is looking for you." He rubbed his temple as if easing a pain. "Someone ratted you out and gave away your escape route. I overheard Montevedi's plans to have his men ambush you at the pickup spot for your plane ride out of here. I had to act. I couldn't let him get to you."

"Okay, you've told us," said Ryan. "What are you going to do now?"

"I'm going back."

"Are you crazy? When we don't show up at the plane, Montevedi's going to know someone warned us of the ambush. He'll know you were the one."

"I'm in this too deep. I made promises. I can't back out of them." He stared hard at his brother. "I have to see this through to the end. I have to destroy Montevedi, to ensure he won't go after Hallie again. Or anyone else. Too many people have already died." He slid his chair back and stood. With a final smile at Hallie, he turned and walked away.

Hallie swallowed over the lump in her throat. The raw determination on his face made clear, this new Geordie would stop at nothing to get his revenge on the infamous drug lord. She glanced at Ryan, silently pleading with him to call back his brother.

He sat, his face closed, staring into his empty coffee cup.

How could he watch Geordie return to certain death? Hallie opened her mouth to protest but froze when Ryan stood, knocking his chair to the ground with a loud clatter.

"You're wrong," he called to Geordie's retreating back.

Geordie halted.

"You're not doing this on your own." Ryan's voice was loud in the nearly deserted square. "We'll take the bastard down together."

Geordie stood still.

"Together," Ryan repeated. "Like brothers."

Across the distance separating them, their gazes met.

Hallie held her breath as the seconds ticked on.

Okay," Geordie finally said. "But let's eat first. I'm starving."

Chapter 23

Hallie gripped the torn vinyl seat and hung on as the rust-encrusted, dented van bounced over yet another pothole on the sorry excuse for a road out of Los Caribuenos. After they left the cantina, they'd followed Geordie to where he'd parked his vehicle. He'd made several phone calls and was taking them to meet his contact with the United States Drug Enforcement Agency.

The van careened around a sharp corner, and Hallie was thrown against the hard body of the man seated beside her. She bit her lip, wishing for the hundredth time since this trip had begun Ryan had sat in the front beside Geordie. Instead he'd climbed into the back seat with her; the very cramped back seat, where every dip and sway of the car threw her against him.

The vehicle hit a pothole, and she fell across his lap. She tried to wriggle back to her side of the seat, but the tight confines and the rough road did not help.

Nor did Ryan. He sat there, watching, a sexy, lazy grin wreathing his all-too handsome face.

Butterflies fluttered in her stomach, and she gulped. "You could at least help." She shoved against his muscular thighs.

"Now why should I help when you're doing such a good job of sitting up yourself?" He chuckled, flashing his dimples.

More butterflies. With a final push, she righted herself and scooted over until her shoulder was jammed against the door. She braced her feet on the floor and locked her thighs, fighting not to move, no matter how many tight corners lay ahead.

She peered through the dusty, cracked, front windshield. Low, rust-colored hills covered with mesquite and stands of saguaro cactus rose on either side of the single lane, dirt road. There weren't any buildings or signs of human habitation. Other than a trio of buzzards feasting on mangled road kill, they hadn't seen a living creature since they'd left Los Caribuenos.

The van lurched around yet another curve, and her leg brushed against Ryan's. Her thigh burned where their bodies touched. She slid her gaze toward him.

All traces of his earlier humor had vanished. His face was set in tight lines; his lips pressed together, a furrow etched between his dark brows.

He must be thinking about Max, she thought. He'd just learned his lover had been keeping a big secret from him. Max's revelation of being a double agent was a shock for everyone, but worse for him. She could only imagine his pain.

She wanted to reach out and offer a soothing touch, but she tightened her hand into a fist and kept it at her side. His relationship with Max wasn't her problem. Once they contacted the DEA agent they were supposed to meet, arrangements would be made to send her home. Bitterness settled over her as she recalled the expression on Ryan's face when he'd told her of his decision to send her back to the States.

He'd eyed her warily, waiting for her to put up a fight and refuse to leave. She'd shocked him by agreeing. The sooner she returned to Seattle, the sooner she could begin to forget him. She bit down on her bottom lip. Who was she kidding? She wasn't going to get over Ryan, not now, probably not ever.

The hard truth was she loved him. The even harder truth: he didn't love her. He'd made his preference more than clear. He loved Max. Even after everything the redhead had done, he still loved her. Hallie swallowed over the thick lump blocking her throat.

"Hey, you guys," said Geordie, slowing the vehicle to a stop and opening the driver's door. "We're here."

Hallie blinked back her tears, relief washing over her.

Ryan opened his door and climbed out. The old vehicle rocked when he slammed the door shut.

Hallie inhaled several steadying breaths. *This will be over soon.* The phrase repeated through her mind like a mantra. *This will be over soon.*

"Are you okay, Hallie?"

She glanced up.

Geordie had opened her door and was watching her, a worried frown on his haggard face. He took her arm and helped her out of the vehicle.

She blinked in the bright sunlight. Ryan and Max were nowhere in sight. A small, metal-roofed hut stood in a clearing a few feet away, surrounded by stunted shrubs, piles of rocks, sun-bleached newspapers, and a heap of empty, plastic water bottles. "Where are the others?" she asked.

He pointed toward the ramshackle building. "Inside."

She brushed past him, but he placed a hand on her arm, stopping her.

"Hallie, I think I know what's troubling you."

She yanked her arm free. She had a pretty good idea what he was going to say, and she didn't want his pity. "We should go inside with the others."

He watched her for a long, tense minute, but then he sighed and nodded. "Okay, but this isn't over."

She hurried toward the entrance to the building feeling as if she'd been given a reprieve. In a way, she had. She didn't know what to say to Geordie. How could she explain she'd been foolish enough to fall in love with his brother? She stepped into the small building and paused, allowing her eyes time to adjust to the gloom.

Ryan and Max were talking to a tall, lean, gray-haired man.

Geordie stepped into the building behind her. "Mike, glad you made it," he said. "Here's someone you should meet."

The grizzled man stepped forward, smiling, his hand extended toward her. "You must be Hallie. I've heard a lot about you. It's great to finally meet you. I'm Special Agent Mike Loomis with the DEA."

She shook his hand, trying not to wince at his tight grip, all too aware of his probing gaze.

"You've had quite the adventure these past months, I understand." His eyes appraised her. "Geordie told me what happened in Seattle. Ryan and Max filled me in on the rest. I'm sorry for the difficulties you've been through."

She peeked at Ryan and flinched under his piercing gaze. Tearing her eyes away, she turned to Special Agent Loomis. "How soon can I return home?"

"I don't blame you for wanting out of Mexico. Not

many people kidnapped by El Lagarto live to tell of their experiences. You're one lucky lady."

"I had help."

"So I heard. Ryan was one of our best agents. I don't have to tell you his decision to quit the business was a real disappointment to the Department." His mouth tightened. "We never expected him and Max to team up again, but these are difficult times." His gaze lit on Max. "Special Agent Benoit has been a real asset. If not for her, we wouldn't have been able to embed Geordie in Montevedi's cartel."

"Mike's arranged for a helicopter to pick you up here and take you to Douglas, Arizona," Max said. "Once there, they'll fly you to Seattle."

Mike glanced at his watch. "The bird should be here any minute now."

Relief washed over Hallie. In a few minutes she'd be away from Ryan's disturbing gaze and her constant fear of exposing how much she cared for him. She wandered over to an old, rusted, metal chair and sank onto the hard surface as the others discussed Montevedi. Her mind was only half on their conversation, her emotions too wired, too raw to concentrate on what they were saying. But then, Mike's words caught her attention, and she sat up. "What did you say?"

All eyes turned to her.

"I…I know you're the experts, but…" Her voice trailed off.

"What's your point?" asked Max, her foot tapping a rapid tattoo on the dirt floor.

Hallie's face heated. "You said…you said something—"

"For God's sake," said Max. "We don't have time for this." She turned toward the others. "Hallie doesn't know anything. How could she? She's a civilian."

Hallie's anger flared.

"Let her talk," Ryan said, his gaze fixed on her. "Tell us what you heard, Hallie."

"You said something about Nuevo Laredo?"

Mike nodded. "Nuevo Laredo is a small town on the US-Mexican border, right at the start of Interstate 35. The highway runs through Texas and Oklahoma, all the way to the Canadian border. The road's a major drug route for Montevedi's convoys."

"What about Nuevo Laredo?" asked Ryan.

"I was with Montevedi," she said. "We were in his office and he was…" She swallowed. Images of Montevedi caressing the large, poisonous lizard rose before her. She shuddered.

"He was what?" Ryan asked.

"I told you he…he was making all sorts of threats."

Ryan nodded.

She took another deep breath. "Anyway, the phone rang. I left before he finished his call, but I heard part of his conversation. He was angry, and he was speaking in a loud voice with whoever was on the other end of the line. He mentioned Nuevo Laredo. I'm sure he did. He repeated the name a few times."

Agent Loomis stared at her, his lean body tense.

Max's irritation vanished, replaced by growing interest. "What else did he say?"

Hallie closed her eyes and replayed the one-sided conversation in her mind. Montevedi had spoken in Spanish, but she'd been able to make out a few words. "A date, I think."

"A date? What sort of date?" asked Geordie.

She struggled to recall every word she'd overheard. "My Spanish isn't strong, but I did take three years of conversational Spanish in high school." Her mouth twisted. "The only thing I remember from Spanish class is numbers, the days of the week, and the months of the year. Our teacher in senior year was a real stickler for memorizing dates."

Max's foot resumed the impatient tapping. "And?"

"I'm pretty sure Montevedi said something sounding like *decimo de Mayo*. *Decimo de Mayo* must be a date because I've heard of the Mexican celebrations on *Cinco de Mayo*. That's May 5th, right? There's a big parade every year in downtown Seattle for *Cinco de Mayo*." She stopped, realizing in her efforts to explain herself, she was rambling.

"*Decimo de Mayo*? Are you sure?" Mike asked.

"I think so."

"*Decimo de Mayo* is May 10th, the day after tomorrow." Mike glanced at the others. "Could Montevedi be planning a shipment then?"

"It's possible," Max said.

Mike's brow furrowed. "Nuevo Laredo has been on our radar for months. The town is fast becoming a favorite place for Mexican drug cartels to ship their drugs across the border." He looked thoughtful. "We've increased our patrols in the area, but the drugs are still getting through." His mouth tightened. "The last DEA agent sent into Nuevo Laredo disappeared. They haven't found his body. If we go into the town, we're going to have to be extremely careful. Nuevo Laredo is full of heavily armed militia controlled by the cartels. These drug gangs think nothing of killing anyone who gets in their way, especially DEA agents."

"Do you remember anything else?" Ryan asked Hallie. "Anything at all?"

She bit her bottom lip. She wanted to help, desperately, but she hadn't understood much of Montevedi's conversation before the guard led her away. She shook her head. "I'm sorry."

"Don't be. You've given us a great lead."

Their eyes met, and heat assailed her like a blast from a furnace. She struggled to breathe.

Max called his name, and after a heartbeat, Ryan turned away.

Hallie reeled back a step, catching her breath and slowing her racing heart. The same uncontrolled reaction struck her every time she looked at Ryan.

The throb of an approaching helicopter filled the air. Time to leave.

****

The rotors whirled, and with an increasing roar, the powerful, black helicopter lifted off the ground. Ryan narrowed his eyes against the glare of sunlight reflecting off the aircraft's rounded windshield.

Hallie sat in the front beside the pilot, headphones on.

Their gazes met.

His gut clenched, a stab of pain radiating through him. She was leaving. Going home. He'd probably never see her again. He rubbed the ache in his gut as the helicopter rose through the hot, dry air and kept his gaze fixed on Hallie, determined to imprint this last image of her on his mind. He grimaced. As if she weren't already tattooed on his heart and soul.

Squinting into the sun, he followed the helicopter's

path, hoping to catch a last glimpse of golden hair gleaming in the sunlight.

The aircraft banked and turned toward the distant hills, quickly becoming a speck on the horizon.

He inhaled a deep breath. *What a coward.* He hadn't told her how he felt. Hell, he hadn't even said good-bye. How could he when he'd wanted nothing more than to beg her to stay? But he couldn't. The mission they were embarking on was dangerous; too dangerous for an inexperienced civilian. The best place, the safest place for her, was back in the US. Knowing he'd done the right thing didn't ease the hollow ache in his gut.

He cast a final look at the empty sky. She was gone. Now he'd better focus on taking down Montevedi.

"Ryan?"

He turned toward his brother.

Geordie stood a few feet away, his gaze searching. "Are you ready?"

Ryan examined him, taking in the drastic changes. He looked different, and he acted different. Sometime over the past months, his little brother had grown up. He'd become a man. A rush of emotion overwhelmed Ryan, and he blinked back the sting of tears. He never thought he'd feel this way again about his brother, but he loved him. No matter what Geordie had done in the past, he was his brother, and Ryan loved him.

"I'm glad we're doing this together," Geordie said. A sheen of tears glistened in his brown eyes.

"Me too, bro, me too." Ryan coughed and glanced away.

"There's something I want to talk to you about,"

Geordie said.

"What is it?"

"We need to discuss Hallie."

Ryan winced. Even though he'd known it was coming, he'd dreaded this conversation. Geordie was going to tell him he loved Hallie, and they were going to get married and be together forever. He gritted his teeth. No way in hell was he going to listen to a confession of undying love. "Not now, Geordie." Not when the pain of losing her was so fresh.

Geordie looked as if he wanted to argue, but he nodded. "Okay. But as soon as this mission is over, we're going to have a long talk."

"Sure," Ryan said, willing to agree to anything if doing so meant putting off having to listen to Geordie expounding on his love for Hallie.

"Hey, you guys, Mike's ready to go," Max called from the door of the hut.

Ryan headed for the hut but halted when Geordie grabbed his arm.

"I mean it. We're going to have a talk about Hallie and like the conversation or not, you're going to listen."

Ryan ripped his arm from his grasp and strode toward Max.

"What's up?" she asked. "You look like someone stole your best friend."

He ignored her.

"Maybe you should listen to Geordie. Maybe he has something important to say to you, something you need to hear."

He snorted. "I doubt it." He brushed past her into the gloom of the hut. Grabbing a box of supplies, he hefted the heavy box on his shoulder and packed it outside to Mike's dusty, armor-plated, military vehicle.

He ignored the scowl on Geordie's face. He didn't want to discuss Hallie with him. He wanted to forget her and get on with his life. *You're lying. You'll never forget her. No matter how long you live, or what happens in the course of the rest of your life, you'll never forget Hallie Harkins.*

He had to focus on obliterating Montevedi. The vicious drug lord had committed too many crimes against Ryan's friends and family. He was going down. He'd destroy him if it were the last thing he ever did. And if Ryan had any say in the matter, Montevedi's demise wasn't going to be pretty.

He heaved the last box of supplies into Mike's vehicle and wiped the sweat off his brow.

Mike loped toward him. "All set?" he asked.

Ryan nodded. "This is the final box. Did you contact the Federales?"

"They're expecting us." Mike chuckled. "You wouldn't believe how happy they were to hear we know exactly where and when Montevedi's next drug shipment is taking place. They've been waiting for this opportunity for a long time."

Max and Geordie approached. Both wore guns strapped across their chests in shoulder holsters.

Ryan patted his own gun, cleaned, loaded and ready for action. He wanted to use the deadly weapon. He wanted to shoot something, or someone, real bad.

"What do you think Montevedi will do when he finds out he's lost his shipment?" asked Max.

Geordie laughed sourly. "He won't be happy, I guarantee you. I wouldn't want to be near him when he hears the news. He's one mean son of a bitch."

Ryan narrowed his eyes at Mike. "You're going to take him in, aren't you? I mean, the man's going to jail, right? He's not going to buy his way out of this."

"I sure as hell hope not. He wouldn't stay in prison for more than the blink of an eye. A man like Montevedi has connections. He'd be out before the ink dried on his arrest warrant."

"So what's the plan? We let him walk?" Ryan asked, dreading the answer. He wanted Montevedi to pay for what he'd done. The thought of the man who'd caused so much grief walking free made him sick.

"Montevedi won't be a problem. Once his cohorts in Peru and Bolivia hear what's happened, they'll be looking for him. They won't take kindly to the fact he's lost millions of dollars worth of their merchandise."

"What will they do to him?" asked Max.

Mike shrugged. "Don't know, don't want to know. All I can tell you is I doubt we'll ever find the body."

"Couldn't happen to a nicer guy," muttered Geordie, his voice bitter. Deep lines grooved along the sides of his mouth and furrowed across his brow.

Again Ryan wondered what his brother had endured at the hands of Montevedi. Seeing the anguish on his haggard face, he hoped he never found out. He doubted he could live with the knowledge.

"Let's move out. Montevedi's destruction awaits," Max said.

And the rest of my long, lonely life, thought Ryan. A life watching the woman he loved with his brother. He shook off the painful image.

He had a job to do. He closed his mind to everything but exacting revenge on El Lagarto.

Chapter 24

Hallie rolled over in bed, fighting free of the cloying weight of disturbing dreams. She opened her eyes and breathed a sigh of relief at the familiar surroundings. She was home. No poisonous lizards lurked in the shadows, their black tongues flicking the air, sharp teeth bared, ready to attack.

She sat up and leaned against the headboard. White lace curtains fluttered in the cool, lilac-scented breeze drifting through the open window. Springtime in Seattle couldn't be more different from the humidity and heat of Mexico, with the ever-present clouds of dust permeating the air, mingling with the lush odors of vegetation and decay.

Stop. Stop thinking of Mexico. What happened in Mexico was in the past. To get over Ryan, she had to look ahead to the future.

She'd been back three days, and she still struggled. Every creak or groan of the small townhouse set her on edge. She shouldn't be so nervous. She was safe. The DEA agent who'd met her plane and escorted her home, told her she wasn't in any danger.

Montevedi had no idea where she was, and the DEA intelligence reports gave no indication any of his henchmen were lurking in her neighborhood. Just to be safe, the Agency had requested the Seattle Police Department assign an officer to watch her townhouse.

They'd keep an eye on her until Montevedi was behind bars.

She yawned and rubbed her aching eyes. She'd hardly slept since she'd returned from Mexico. On the rare occasions when she did manage to sleep, dreams of danger and violent death tormented her. If the nights were bad, daytime was worse. At every turn, thoughts of Ryan assailed her, leaving her staggered, awash in bittersweet memories. Every pore of her body ached from his absence.

An image of Ryan and Max emerging from the boat after their night of passion in Los Caribuenos flashed before her, followed by a stab of pain. Tears welled in her eyes, but she wiped them away. Enough crying. Tears didn't ease the anguish of knowing the man she loved didn't return her love.

She tossed back the covers and stood. Walking toward the kitchen, she blinked against the bright sunshine filling the cheerful room. She frowned at the sound of childish laughter and peered out the window.

Two children, little more than toddlers, screamed as they ran through a sprinkler set up on the neighbor's lush, green lawn. Their faces shone with excitement. Their parents sat on the front porch of their house watching the children play.

They were new to the neighborhood and had moved in while Hallie had been in hiding from Montevedi's thugs. Since she'd been back, she hadn't ventured out and so she hadn't met them.

The man wrapped his arms around his wife, drawing her close.

Hallie stared, unable to look away as the couple embraced.

A red-haired toddler ran up and splashed a pail of water over the kissing couple.

The man howled with mock outrage and broke away from his wife and chased after the giggling child, catching him and wrapping his squirming body in a tight hug.

Hallie sagged against the counter, tears burning her eyes. She'd never experience such happiness and love. She'd always long for Ryan, a man she couldn't have. She pulled the cord and closed the blinds with a decisive snap, erasing her view of the all-too-happy scene.

Wiping at her tears, she switched on the television set on the kitchen counter, relieved when the sound of the TV filled the room, drowning out the squeals of laughter. She measured coffee grounds and placed them in the coffee maker. Filling the glass pot with water from the tap, she carried the pot to the counter.

The newscaster's voice filled the room. "…tragedy in Nuevo Laredo, Mexico. And now on to other, breaking news…"

The glass pot fell from her numb fingers, shattering on the floor and splashing water across the room. Her heart pounded so hard she barely made out the announcer's next words.

He was describing a house fire in downtown Seattle.

Rushing across the room, she grabbed the remote and switched channels, searching for another news report. She couldn't find any mention of a big media event happening in Mexico. Had she imagined the announcer's words? Her breath rasped in and out in a fierce cadence.

Nuevo Laredo had been in her thoughts ever since she'd boarded the helicopter and flown out of Mexico. Ryan, Max and Geordie were part of the group of law enforcement officers planning to stop Montevedi's next drug shipment. Their mission was dangerous, but they weren't undertaking the deployment alone. Mexican federal agents were assisting with the operation.

She'd fought to forget yesterday was May 10th, the day of Montevedi's planned shipment, but Nuevo Laredo and the planned DEA assault were all she had on her mind.

The news announcer had mentioned Nuevo Laredo. She was sure of it. Running out of the kitchen and into her small office, she settled on a chair before the computer. She chewed on her bottom lip, waiting for the machine to boot up. The computer seemed to take forever to download the international news website. The second the page flashed on the screen, her heart stopped. The words jumped out at her: "*Undercover DEA Agent Killed in Deadly Mexican Shoot Out.*"

With shaking fingers, she scrolled through the article. Her dread increased with each word. Mexican drug gang members had attacked a joint task force of DEA Federal agents and Mexican Federal Police, killing one DEA agent and injuring others. The attack had taken place in Nuevo Laredo, Mexico.

One agent dead.

The deceased DEA agent couldn't be Ryan. She'd know if he were dead; she'd feel his loss in her very soul. But what if he were one of the injured agents? She picked up the phone, dialed information and requested the number for the Drug Enforcement Administration office in Seattle.

An hour later, she slammed down the phone and rubbed her throbbing temples. She still didn't know anything. She'd been put on hold, and transferred from one department to another and back again. She'd talked to countless computers and even a few humans, but hadn't learned any useful information. No one admitted to knowing what had happened in Nuevo Laredo. They'd all referred her to their national press office.

She didn't want to talk to their damn press office. She wanted answers, and she wanted them now. There had to be a way to find out what had happened in Mexico. Once again, she turned to the computer and typed in Max's name. Her next move was a Hail Mary, but she was fresh out of ideas, and she had to do something. The screen flickered, and she sighed at the number of hits her search retrieved.

A half-hour later, she was still searching through Web sites without any success. How many Maxine Benoits existed in the world? She rolled her neck, stretched her aching shoulders and clicked on yet another link. She leaned forward. The grainy photograph was blurry and had been taken several years earlier, but this was the woman she sought. She'd never forget the curvaceous, redheaded beauty.

She scanned the site. The story was old, a review of an article Max had written while attending NYU in the Criminal Justice Master's program. Hallie's tired eyes strained to read the tiny print on the screen, but with each passing minute, her hopes dimmed. A six-year-old article wasn't going to help her locate Max.

Her gaze lit on a line near the end of the article. Eureka! The author of the article mentioned the name of Max's hometown. With a pounding heart, Hallie picked up the phone and called information. Max no longer lived in Maine, but maybe her family still resided in the state. Her hunch was a wild card, but if she found Max's family, they'd know where she was and how to contact her.

Hardly able to believe she'd found what she wanted, she blew out a gust of air. Max's mother still lived in Maine. After a great deal of fast talking, she'd convinced the woman she was an old college friend of her daughter's and wanted to reconnect with her for an upcoming college reunion.

She punched in the number for Max's cell phone and held her breath as the connection went through. The phone rang and rang, again and again. Her hopes sank.

The ringing stopped, and the call was answered. "What is it?"

"Max?"

"Who's this?"

Tears clogged Hallie's throat, filling her eyes and streaming down her face.

"Who is this?" Max demanded. "What do you want?"

Swallowing back the crush of tears, Hallie managed to blurt, "Don't hang up, please."

A long silence ensued. "Hallie, is it you?"

She nodded, and then realized Max couldn't see her. "Max....tell me...I have to know. Ryan? Is he...?"

Another silence ensued.

Her heart thundered in her chest. "Max, please," she begged. "Tell me. I have to know if he's all right."

"Where are you?"

The harshness in Max's voice struck like a sledgehammer, knocking the air out of her. She couldn't speak.

"Hallie, where are you? I'm coming to get you."

Hallie's mouth opened and closed but no sound emerged.

"Hallie?"

The command in Max's voice broke through her stupor, and she whispered her address into the phone.

"Okay. I'm at the airport. I'll be at your house in fifteen minutes."

Before Hallie could ask her again if Ryan was okay, the connection was severed. A dial tone filled her ear. She fell back on her chair. Why hadn't Max told her Ryan was safe? Pain rocketed through her. Max was at the Seattle airport. There was only one reason Hallie could think of for Max to be in town: Ryan was dead. She was coming to tell Hallie Ryan was the DEA agent killed in Mexico.

For the first time in three days, Hallie's eyes were dry. She wished she could cry. Maybe then she'd know she was still alive, not locked in this nightmare where she waited for Max to tell her the man she loved was dead.

****

"He's alive, Hallie. Ryan's alive."

Hallie searched Max's face. She'd prepared for the worst. When she'd opened the door and seen Max's pale face, she'd known her fears were a reality. "He's alive? Are you sure? You're not lying to me, are you?"

"I wouldn't joke about something like this."

Hallie closed her eyes, allowing the rush of relief to wash over her.

"There is something you should know though."

Hallie tensed and opened her eyes. "Wha…what is

it?"

Max prowled about the room, peering out the window and looking into the adjoining kitchen and bathroom. "You have a nice place here. The neighborhood looks quiet."

"Max?" Hallie pressed. "What's wrong? Tell me, please."

Max picked up a wooden, aboriginal mask and turned the finely carved object over and over in her hands. "I didn't just happen to be in Seattle when you called. I was on my way to see you."

Hallie swallowed over the lump in her throat.

Max set the mask down and faced her. "Ryan was wounded in the attack."

The room spun. Hallie staggered and clutched the back of the couch for support. "But you said—"

"I said he was alive. He has a bullet hole in his chest."

Hallie's knees wobbled. She clung to the couch. "Is he…?" she gulped. "Is he going to be all right?"

"The doctors are hopeful. When I left the hospital, they were taking him into surgery."

Hallie blinked back tears. "I have to see him." She hurried out of the room; her desperate need to be by Ryan's side when he came out of surgery overriding everything else. Opening a dresser drawer, she grabbed a shirt, yanked it over her head, and then tugged on a pair of jeans. One knee was ripped, and the T-shirt had a large paint streak across the front. She didn't care. She had to see Ryan. Making sure he was safe and well was what mattered. Running her fingers through her tangled hair, she turned toward Max who stood in the bedroom doorway watching her. "Where is he?"

Max remained silent.

"Look," Hallie said. "I don't have to explain my actions to you, but I want to be there when he wakes up." Tears stung her eyes, but she blinked them back. "I know he loves you, but I…" She stopped, not knowing what else she could say to convince Max to tell her where Ryan was hospitalized.

Max's eyebrows rose. "Even though you think he loves me, you still want to go to him?"

"I…I know you love him, and I won't interfere with your relationship, but I have to see him." She inhaled a shaky breath. "I just have to."

"Look," Max began and heaved a sigh, her green eyes dark hollows in her pale face. "There's no easy way to tell you this. Geordie's dead."

Hallie collapsed on the bed, all the breath knocked out of her. "Geordie?"

"He was caught in the cross fire. We couldn't save him. We had a medic with us, and he tried everything he could, but he couldn't help him. Geordie was too badly injured."

"No." Hallie shook her head. "Geordie's not dead. He can't be."

"I'm sorry, Hallie."

"No," she wailed, a long, drawn-out cry of anguish. *Geordie was dead.* Tears streamed down her cheeks. *Geordie was dead.* A dozen images flashed through her mind, all of Geordie: vibrant and full of life, charming everyone he met with his easy smile and quick wit, impossible to resist. *Geordie was dead.*

They were friends. And as a friend, she'd seen through his charisma to the real person he kept hidden from everyone, the Geordie searching to find himself, the boy who had yet to grow into a man. And then he'd become involved with Montevedi's drug cartel and everything had changed.

She'd never forget how different he looked the last time she'd seen him at the small, metal-roofed hut outside of Los Caribuenos. His physical transformation wasn't what had struck her; the real change was in his eyes. The eyes of the new Geordie had observed the world with cynicism and suspicion. His youthful face was lean and haggard, deep lines carved across his forehead. Who knew what hell he'd faced while he'd been with Montevedi?

He'd made mistakes, big ones, but no matter what he'd done, he was still her friend.

He'd risked his life to rectify his lapse in judgment. His bravery counted for something.

Geordie was dead. The words repeated through her mind, each time she heard them making his loss more real. She wiped her eyes and glanced at Max. "Does Ryan know? I mean, did...did Geordie...did he pass away before Ryan was shot?"

Max nodded. "He wanted me to tell you. He didn't want you to hear about Geordie on the news."

"So that's why you're here. Ryan asked you to come."

Max nodded, lines of strain marring her beautiful face.

"Thank you for coming," Hallie said. "This can't be easy for you." The man Max loved was in the hospital undergoing surgery. Another man she'd once loved was dead. "It's kind of you. I know you must be anxious to return to the hospital."

Max nodded. "I'd like to be in Ryan's room when

he gets out of surgery."

Of course, Max would want to be with Ryan, and he'd want her with him. Being close to the one you loved made all the difference in recovery from a risky surgery. A fresh wave of sadness washed over Hallie, but she swallowed back the tears. "Thank you for coming," she said again. "You should get back to the hospital. Ryan needs you."

Max studied her. "You're not coming with me?"

Hallie shook her head. She wanted to be with Ryan more than life itself but keeping vigil by his bedside wasn't her place. That place belonged to Max.

"Are you sure?"

She nodded, not trusting herself to speak.

Max shrugged. "Suit yourself, but if you change your mind, he's in Francis McQuarry Trauma Center in Houston."

Again Hallie nodded.

Max's gaze was piercing. "I don't get you, Hallie. One minute you're desperate to be at Ryan's bedside and the next you're not going. You're more of a fool than I thought you were." She turned and walked out of the room.

Hallie sat on the bed, listening to the sharp rap of Max's high heels as she crossed the living room and the slam of the door as she left the house.

She was alone. All alone. With only her memories for comfort. She fell back onto the bed and gave into a deluge of tears.

Chapter 25

Ryan swam through a thick ocean of fog toward the light. He fought to open his eyes but failed. A soft hand brushed his arm, spreading warmth and comfort, and he stilled his thrashing under the gentle pressure.

A voice penetrated through the mist. "Rest now. I'll be here when you wake up."

The woman's voice, achingly familiar, loosened the pain wrapped like a steel band around his chest. "Hallie…" He breathed her name on a sigh and gave in to the numbing blackness, her name on his lips. "Hallie…"

The fog wasn't as dense the next time he surfaced, but his eyelids were weighted with lead and refused to open. The steady, loud beeping of a machine nearby and the strong medicinal odor indicated he was in a hospital. *Why was he in the hospital? Was he sick? Injured?*

The pain hit him then, throbbing with each beat of his heart, rising to bone-jarring agony at the slightest twitch. With the pain came remembrance and numbing sadness.

Mexico. The shoot out. A sniper hidden on the roof of an old cantina, a place supposed to have been checked and cleared by his team. The shock of the bullet as the hot metal sliced into his flesh, and then falling, hitting the ground with breathtaking force.

Lying on his back, staring up into the bright ball of sun, blood pouring out of the gaping wound in his chest. Gunfire blasting, shaking the ground, the clamor deafening.

He was lying in the open, a sitting duck for the armed, drug cartel, sharp shooters. Bullets pinged around him, chipping the pavement. He had to find cover. *Move!* His muscles refused to obey his frantic command. It was as if he were encased in concrete. Any second now, another bullet would hit its mark, and his life would be over.

He faced his fate with a curious sense of detachment. His one regret: he hadn't told Hallie he loved her. Now she'd never know.

Then Geordie was there, leaning over him, saying something lost in the din.

Ryan opened his mouth to tell him he was in danger and to go back, but no sound escaped.

A hail of bullets punched holes in a nearby, parked car and riddled the walls of the building behind him.

Geordie lifted him in his arms and sprinted across the open expanse of the small intersection toward cover.

They almost made it. Mere feet separated them from safety when a bullet found its mark, and the nightmare worsened.

Geordie grunted and sagged, but he tightened his grip on Ryan and staggered forward, collapsing behind the armor-plated SUV.

Ryan lay on the hard-packed dirt, pain pulsing in waves through his open wound, helpless, as he watched first Max, and then Mike fight to stem the blood streaming from a ragged, open gash in Geordie's neck.

A medic rushed over. Frantic motions followed, shouting, bullets striking nearby.

The world began to fade, but Ryan held on, watching the flurry of activity, willing his brother to live.

Geordie turned his head toward him, his face pale and waxen, sunken eyes. His mouth opened, and a trickle of dark red blood leaked out, dripping on the ground. He coughed, and more blood spurted from the gaping, neck wound. His lips moved, and with an agonizing effort, he spoke.

A mortar round whistled overhead and landed with a low-pitched whump in the street. Clods of dirt and chunks of pavement rained down.

Ryan couldn't hear what Geordie was saying, but he read his lips and saw the desperate pleading in his eyes. His brother was begging his forgiveness.

Tears filmed Ryan's eyes and a sob tore at his throat, but he focused on meeting Geordie's desperate gaze. He nodded.

Geordie's smile illuminated his ravaged face, but in the next breath, his body stiffened, and then went limp, his eyes turning flat and blank as life seeped out of him.

"No," Ryan cried. "No." A fresh wave of pain overtook him. He welcomed the darkness and slipped into blissful unconsciousness.

Then the nightmare once again reared before him, bringing with it the fresh agony of loss.

Gentle hands wiped the tears seeping from the corners of his eyes, dampening his pillow.

Hallie. She'd come back. Just knowing she was here, beside him, eased the sharp edges of his grief. *His* grief? A wave of guilt washed over him. Hallie was grieving as well. He'd lost his brother, but she'd lost the man she loved.

Forcing his eyes open, he blinked, trying to focus through the sheen of tears. Sunlight streamed through a window, blinding him. He closed his eyes, but even that was painful. He forced open his eyes again and managed to focus on the cloudy world around him. He was lying on his back, pinned down by tightly tucked, white sheets. A tube dangled on his left, running down to his hand, and then disappearing somewhere behind him.

He blinked again. Max stood over him, her green-eyed gaze locked on his. He frowned. "Hallie?"

Max leaned closer. "What did you say?" Her lips trembled. "No, don't answer. You need to rest." She caressed his forehead, brushing back his hair with soothing strokes. "You gave us quite a scare. For a while, we weren't sure you were going to make it. But, I told the doctor you were too damn stubborn to die."

Where was Hallie? He'd heard her voice and sensed her gentle touch. He licked his dry lips. "Hallie?" Her name was a desperate croak.

"Easy, Ryan, don't try and talk," Max said. "The doctor said you need plenty of rest."

Understanding hit him like a splash of cold water and he moaned. Hallie wasn't here. She'd never been. He eyed the plastic lines snaking out of his arm to bags hanging from a monitor beside his bed. They were pumping all kinds of drugs into him. In his drugged state, he'd mistaken Max's touch for Hallie's.

He closed his eyes against the onslaught of fresh, burning tears. He'd never see Hallie again. She'd lost the man she loved, and he was responsible. He could only imagine how much she hated him.

An odd sense of relief eased his tears. If she wasn't here, he wouldn't be tempted to tell her of his pain. Not his physical aching. He could handle pain. The pain threatening to eviscerate him was the ache in the heart. She'd never know how much he loved her, how he couldn't live without her.

Weariness stole over him, but he wouldn't sleep. Not yet. He had to know she was all right. "How…?" he said, straining over the words. He shifted his body, and hot bolts of agony hit his chest. He groaned but tried again. "How…is…she?"

Somehow Max understood. "Hallie's fine. I told her about Geordie, like you asked me to. She's upset, but she'll get over it."

"Does she…she…?" Each word raised an agony of fresh pain. The room dimmed, but he fought against the approaching oblivion. He had to know.

"What is it, Ryan? What are you trying to say?"

"Forgive…?"

This time Max misunderstood his question. "It's okay, Ryan. I forgive you. It wasn't your fault Geordie didn't make it. No one blames you."

He shook his head and opened his mouth to try again, but the effort was too much. Darkness engulfed him before he could ask Max if Hallie forgave him.

"Ryan?"

Hallie called his name again, her soft voice drawing him out of his drugged slumber.

He'd been fooled once. He wouldn't be fooled again. She was in Seattle grieving Geordie's loss. He sank back into the dark.

The familiar scent of lilacs and vanilla swirled around him, and he breathed deeply.

"Ryan?"

Afraid what he'd see, afraid this was yet another cruel, drug-induced joke, he opened his eyes. A flood of warmth rushed through him. "Hallie."

She smiled, and it was as if the sun rose in a blast of light.

"Is it...really you?" he asked, terrified she'd vanish.

"How are you, Ryan?"

Ignoring the pain the slightest movement caused, needing to touch her, to make sure she was real he grasped her hand. Her skin was warm and soft against his callused palm. "You're here." Waves of agony washed over him, but he held on, clinging, hanging on as if his life depended on her very presence.

"I...I couldn't stay away. Not when Max told me you'd been injured."

He wanted to tell her he was glad she was here, more than glad, but the lump thickened in his throat, and he couldn't speak. He clung to her hand, reveling in the contact. For the moment, touching her was enough. Sleep stole over him. He fought its power but resisting was futile. He was too tired. *Hallie was here. Hallie was here...* The joyful refrain eased him to rest like a soothing lullaby.

****

Hallie watched Ryan sleep.

Beads of perspiration glistened on his brow. Even while he slept, he moaned and his face paled with each shallow breath.

She studied their joined hands through a film of

tears. His hand was large, the palm and fingers callused from working on the ranch. She tightened her grip gaining comfort from the contact, so glad she'd come.

After Max had left her townhouse in Seattle, Hallie had given in to her sorrow. Geordie was dead, and Ryan lay in hospital, grievously injured. Her worst nightmare had come true.

Hours passed, but then her tears ended, and she lay staring, dry-eyed at the ceiling. Geordie was gone, but Ryan was alive, and he was suffering. How could she stay away from his side when he needed her? Jumping to her feet, she grabbed her purse and ran out the door of her townhouse.

Max had glanced up in surprise when she'd spotted Hallie walking toward her down the corridor outside Ryan's hospital room. Her lips had quirked in a wry grin. "I wondered if you'd come to your senses."

"How is he?" Hallie asked. "How was the operation?"

"See for yourself." Max pointed toward the closed, hospital room door. "I'm going for coffee."

Hallie took a deep breath and opened the door to Ryan's room. She reeled at her first sight of him. Lying on the narrow bed, connected to a tangle of tubes, he was bare to the waist. The thick swath of bandages covering his chest provided a shocking contrast to his tanned skin.

Swallowing back tears, she sank into a chair beside the bed. The reality of seeing the man she loved lying in a hospital bed, hooked up to machines stole her breath.

The muscles in his arms and legs twitched and flexed as if he were trying to escape the torment of his injury.

She brushed a lock of dark hair from his forehead with a shaky hand. He stilled at her touch, and she continued her gentle caressing. The tears she'd been fighting streamed down her cheeks.

He'd been shot in the side at Buzz's house in the mountains, but that wound had hardly slowed him down. This injury was different. The numerous bags of fluid dripping into his veins and the constantly beeping machines hinted at the severity of his wound.

Her heart lurched. *He could have died.*

Instead, Geordie had paid the ultimate price for his foolish actions and the hell he'd put so many others through these past months. She hiccupped a sob. Ryan's ashen face was a testament to his suffering. He'd lost his only brother.

In spite of their differences, the two men had loved each other. Ryan's refusal to allow Geordie to take on Montevedi and his gang of thugs alone, and his insistence on helping Geordie had been the turning point where the rift between the two brothers began to heal.

Ryan moaned and stirred. His eyelids fluttered, and his eyes opened. "You're crying," he said, his voice a thin croak.

"How…" She swallowed tears. "How are you feeling?"

"I've been better." The corners of his mouth rose. He eyed their joined hands.

She released her grip.

"Don't, please. Holding you helps…helps the pain." He sighed when she grasped his hand and held it between hers. He struggled to sit up but fell back with a groan.

"Are you all right? Should I call the doctor?"

He shook his head. "I'm okay."

She almost laughed at the absurdity of his lie. His face had lost what little color his pale cheeks had. He clenched his jaw as he fought the pain. He was anything but okay. She hurried to the adjoining bathroom, grabbed a small towel, wet it under the tap, and returned to his side, dabbing the damp cloth against his forehead.

His breathing eased. "Thank you." His eyes searched hers. "How are you?"

"Me? I'm not the one who was shot."

"I'm sorry about Geordie. I know his passing is hard on you," Ryan said.

She sniffed and wiped her damp eyes. Geordie had been her friend, but he'd been Ryan's brother. His grief was so much greater than hers. "I'm sorry too. His death is a terrible loss. He…he had his faults, but he was a good man." She sobbed, barely able to get out the words. "In the end, he did what he had to do to make things right."

Tears leaked from the corners of Ryan's eyes.

With a gentle hand, she wiped them away using the edge of the towel. "We shouldn't talk about this now. You need to rest. Geordie would want you to get better."

Ryan searched her face. "Aren't you going to ask me what happened?"

"Max told me he was fatally wounded in the raid."

Dark shadows flickered in his blue eyes. "Geordie's death was my fault."

"How could his dying be your fault? He wanted to be involved in the mission. He was determined to strike back at Montevedi for everything he'd done to him and those he loved. You were only helping Geordie. No one could have known he'd be killed in the gunfight."

"His death is on me and me alone." He shook his head, wincing. "We let him down. Our team didn't double check all the nearby buildings for enemy snipers." He scowled. "A rookie mistake." He sucked in a ragged breath. "We thought we'd secured the perimeter, but one of Montevedi's men got by us. I was running across the street. My guys covered me, but…" He broke off and squeezed his eyes shut.

When he opened them again, they were red and damp. "The bastard shot me, and I fell down. I was an easy target lying in the open. It was only a matter of time before the sniper delivered the kill shot."

Hallie shuddered at the horrific image.

Sweat beaded on his forehead and upper lip.

"Shhhh," she soothed. "You don't have to tell me this now. You need your rest."

"No." His mouth tightened to a thin line. "No," he repeated. "I have to tell you everything so you'll understand."

His distress made her weak. "I'm listening."

His tortured gaze met hers. "I was a dead man. Geordie crawled across the open square and dragged me out of the firefight." He blinked back tears. "We almost made it, but then he got hit."

Tears streamed from Hallie's eyes as she listened to his all-too-vivid description of Geordie's last minutes.

"If he hadn't risked his life to save me, I'd be dead." He choked back a sob. "Why the hell did he have to pick that moment to be a hero?"

"He wanted to save you. He loved you. You can't blame yourself. He was your brother. You'd have done the same for him. I know you would."

"There's something I need to tell you."

She shivered at the intensity of his gaze. "What is it?"

He took a deep breath. "I have no right to say this, especially now, but I want you to know I—"

The door burst open, and Max strode into the room carrying two steaming cups. "It took forever to get this damn coffee."

Hallie snatched her hands from Ryan's.

"Oh, great, you're awake. I was beginning to think you were down for the count." Max appeared unaware of the tension in the room as she prattled on. "The doctors told me the bullet struck damn close to your heart, but I know how tough you are, and I knew you'd pull through." She handed one of the steaming cups to Hallie. "Here, I figured you could use some coffee."

Hallie didn't want any coffee, but Max gave her no choice, and so she took the cup. She wanted to beg her to leave so Ryan could finish saying what he'd been about to tell her.

Max set her cup on the bedside table and leaned over Ryan. "You don't look so hot. You're sweating. Do you need more pain meds?"

He shook his head.

"You're sure?"

Again he shook his head.

"You always were the macho male, but I love you for it." She pressed her mouth to his and kissed him.

Hallie's stomach churned.

Max lifted her head, chuckling. "You're really

something, Marshall. Even with a bullet wound in your chest, you're one hell of a kisser." She kissed him again. Her hand caressed the smooth, tanned skin of his uninjured side, slipping beneath the sheet.

Face flaming, Hallie leaped up sending the chair skidding across the tile floor where it landed against the wall with a crash. She had to get away. She couldn't bear watching the man she loved kissing another woman.

Tears burned her eyes, blinding her, as she ran for the door. She flung it open and escaped.

Chapter 26

"What the hell do you think you're doing?" Ryan jerked his head away from Max's warm mouth and searching tongue. A shard of agony hit his chest. He bit hard on his bottom lip, fighting to stay conscious and glared at Max.

She lifted her head, a sensuous smile on her full lips. "What does it look like I'm doing?" she asked, her hand gliding over his stomach. "Those drugs they're giving you must be pretty powerful if you've forgotten what this is all about."

With pain riding his every movement, he reached under the sheet and grabbed her hand and lifted it off his skin. "Stop this. Now."

She tugged her hand free, a furrow forming between her perfectly tweezed brows. "You're not still mad at me, are you? I thought we'd worked it all out. You know I was just following orders." She blew out a breath. "It's what we do. We follow orders. It's how the DEA gets things done. You know that. You haven't been out of the business long enough to forget loyalty to the company supersedes everything, even family, friends and lovers."

Ryan hardly heard her excuses. An image of Hallie's stricken face rose before him. He hadn't expected Max to kiss him, but before he could push her away, Hallie had fled. And then it was too late. The damage was done.

Max ran her fingers along his arm, tracing the ridges of his biceps. "Come on, Ryan. What's this all about?" She pursed her lips in a sexy pout and batted her eyelashes. "We were good together once. We can be again. You know we can."

"Take your hands off me."

Her hand froze, but she didn't remove it.

"Max, this isn't going to happen."

She forced a chuckle. "I know you're too injured right now, and you're upset about Geordie, but later, after you've healed, we can try again. Can't we?"

"Take...your...hand...off...me." He bit off each word.

"Come on, Ryan. You don't mean it. That's the drugs talking. We're meant to be together. We always have been." She removed her shaking hand and sat back, clasping her hands together on her lap. Tears brightened her green eyes. "If this is about what happened between Geordie and me—"

He cut her off. "This has nothing to do with my brother. What happened years ago, is in the past. I don't care anymore. I forgive you. I forgave Geordie before he died, though I should have forgiven him sooner."

She blinked back tears. "It's Hallie, isn't it? She's what this is all about."

He nodded. "I love her."

Max inhaled a sharp breath. "You love her?"

A smile tugged at his lips. "I love her." His smile grew each time he said the words aloud. "I love her!"

"Okay, okay, I get it. You think you're in love with Hallie. Are you sure it's not just the drugs talking?"

He shook his head. "I've loved her for a long

time."

Max rubbed her temples as if she had a headache. "This isn't a jealous thing where you want to get back at Geordie for what he did to you? You know he loved her."

A sharp jab of pain struck him deep in his gut as he thought of his brother. "My feelings for Hallie have nothing to do with Geordie. I love her. It's simple."

Silence descended, broken only by the beep, beep, beep of the machines by his bed and the distant sound of people in the hallway outside his room.

"Does she know?" Max asked. "Have you told her?"

He grimaced. "What do you think?"

Max heaved a sigh. "So she doesn't know."

He shook his head. A vision of Hallie running from his bedside as if pursued by the very devil himself, rose before him, and with it a crushing disappointment. Too late. He'd waited too long to tell her, and now it was too late.

"You have to tell her."

Max's urgent words broke through his turmoil. A bitter smile tugged at his lips. "Don't you think I want to? But how can I? She's suffering from Geordie's loss. She's been through enough."

Max laughed. "My God. I don't believe you. You almost died, you idiot. Do you realize that? You...almost...died. But you didn't. You're alive. Stop trying to bury yourself with Geordie in his coffin. There's already one too many Marshall in there."

He stared at her, letting her words wash over him. She was right. He had survived. He'd been given another chance. He couldn't waste it. He had to tell

Hallie how he felt. He grabbed the tubes hanging out of his arm and yanked, pulling them free. He winced but pushed the sharp pain aside.

"Ryan, what are you doing?"

He ignored Max's urgent cry, gritted his teeth and grabbed onto the bed rail and pulled himself to a sitting position. Sweat dripped into his eyes as wave after wave of agony washed over him. Black spots appeared at the edge of his vision. His chest heaving, shards of white-hot agony stabbing, he swung one leg over the edge of the bed.

"Ryan." Max gripped his arm, stopping him. "What the hell are you doing?"

He shoved her away, his body weaving, the room spinning. "I…have to find her. I have to tell her…"

"Okay, okay," Max said, her voice low and soothing, as if talking to a mad man. "Take it easy. You won't do her any good if you kill yourself."

He looked at her through a haze of pain. "I have to tell her I love her."

Max searched his face, and then she nodded. "I don't know why the hell I'm agreeing to this, but I'll help you." She brushed a strand of red hair off her smooth forehead. "Promise me you'll lie back down, and I'll find her and bring her back."

He studied her face. Did he trust her? Would she find Hallie, or was this another one of her deceptions? He'd crawl on his hands and knees through the fires of Hell to find Hallie and confess his love for her, but he couldn't do it. He couldn't even get out of this damn bed.

He blew out a breath. He didn't have a choice. He had to trust her. "Do it then," he said. "Find Hallie." He collapsed on the bed, his head swimming, pain throbbing with every heartbeat. "Find Hallie."

****

"I'm a fool," Hallie said. "A bloody fool." The words echoed in the empty stairwell, increasing the ache in her heart with each damning repetition. Anyone could see how much Max cared for Ryan. Even though he was half-dead from a bullet wound in his chest, his actions made his love for the redhead more than clear.

Max had kissed him.

He'd kissed her back.

Squeezing her eyes shut, she fought to block the image of Max's elegant, red-tipped fingers slipping beneath the starched, white sheet, caressing Ryan with an intimacy shared by lovers. She sank onto a dirty step. Only a fool would love a man who was so clearly in love with someone else.

For a few, blissful moments while she'd held his hand in the hospital room, she'd allowed herself to believe he loved her. She rubbed her chest, trying to ease the throbbing. Shoulders drooping, she stood and opened the door in the stairwell leading to the hospital's main lobby. Hanging around the hospital would only result in more pain and disappointment. She'd seen what she'd come to see. Ryan was going to recover from his wound. She should go home. Time to get on with her life.

"So this is where you've been hiding," Max said. She stood in front of Hallie, her arms braced on her hips, blocking any hope of escape. "I've been looking all over for you."

Hallie tried to step around her.

Max's hand shot out, and she gripped her arm,

333

holding her still. "I want to talk to you."

"Why? Do you want to gloat?" Hallie straightened her shoulders. "Look, you win, okay? I get it. Ryan loves you. Congratulations. I hope the two of you…" Her voice faltered. "I hope you have a great life together." She yanked her arm free and bolted for the exit.

She was hurrying through the glass doors of the hospital main entrance when Max caught up with her.

"Hallie."

"Leave me alone, Max. I'm going back to Seattle." She raised her hand to hail a cab.

"If you do, you're a fool."

Hallie blew out a breath. At last, something she and Max agreed on. She peered up and down the empty road. Where were all the taxis when you needed one?

"I can't stop you from leaving, but I can tell you, you're making a big mistake," Max said.

"The mistake would be in staying."

Silence ensued, and then Max touched Hallie's shoulder. "Look, I know you love him," Max said. "Anybody who has eyes can see how much you care. The kiss…in the hospital room…I was teasing. Do you hear me? The kiss was simply affection between two friends, nothing more."

A taxi turned the corner and headed toward her.

Hallie waved her arm.

The cab drew up to the curb and stopped.

Opening the rear door, she threw herself onto the seat.

Max held the door open.

"Please?" Hallie pleaded, tears streaming down her cheeks. "Let me go."

"I always suspected you were a fool. Your actions now prove I was right. Believe me, I don't see what the hell Ryan sees in you, but he loves you." She studied Hallie for a long minute and heaved a sigh. Releasing her grip on the cab door, she stepped back. "Go ahead. Leave. Get out of here. You don't deserve him." She turned and strolled back to the hospital.

Hallie stared after her.

"Where to, ma'am?" the cab driver asked.

Hallie ignored him.

"Ma'am?"

A wave of dizziness washed over her. She took a steadying breath and reached into her purse and threw some bills at the driver. "Nowhere. I'm right where I should be." She leaped out of the taxi and ran toward the hospital entrance.

Hallie was out of breath by the time she opened the third floor, stairwell door leading onto Ryan's floor. She hurried down the corridor. Her steps slowed the closer she drew to his room until she halted, staring at the closed door.

What if this was some kind of cruel joke? What if Max was lying? She wouldn't survive another rejection. With a sinking heart, she turned to leave. But then she stopped. What was she doing? Could she live with herself if she didn't at least try? What if Ryan really did love her? If she didn't confront him, she'd never know. She'd always wonder. Could she live with her coward's choice for the rest of her life?

She took a deep breath and retraced her steps. Swinging open the door to his room, she squared her shoulders and stepped inside.

He wasn't alone. Special Agent Mike Loomis was

with him.

The door closed behind her, and both men turned.

"Hallie," Ryan said, his face splitting in a wide grin. "You came back."

This is a mistake. The words screamed through her. She backed toward the door. "I…I see you have company. I'll come back later." She turned to leave, but Agent Loomis's voice stopped her.

"Stay, Hallie. You'll want to hear this."

She kept her hand on the door handle, her gaze fixed on the DEA agent. If she looked at Ryan, she wouldn't be able to focus on anything else.

"I was just updating Ryan on Montevedi," Mike said. "The raid in Nuevo Laredo netted us Montevedi's drug shipment." He grinned. "The load of drugs destined for the US was a big one, one of the largest shipments we've ever captured."

"You got the bastard?" Ryan's asked, his voice little more than a croak but stronger than earlier.

"We couldn't prove the shipment was his," Mike said. But then he grinned. "From what we hear, his suppliers aren't happy with him, not happy at all." His smile grew. "I doubt we'll be hearing from El Lagarto again."

"He's dead?" Hallie asked. Relief washed over her. She hadn't realized how much this meant, but after all the pain Montevedi had caused, he deserved to die.

"I sure as hell hope so," Mike said.

"You're not certain?" she asked.

"I wouldn't worry. These guys play for keeps. They'll deal with Montevedi better than a stint in a cushy, federal prison ever would."

Hallie risked a glance at Ryan.

He was watching her, his gaze searching.

Her breath caught in her throat.

Mike coughed, breaking the spell, and she turned from Ryan.

"I have to go," Mike said. "The press is all over this. And the Director wants answers. It's not often we lose a man in the field." He grasped Ryan's hand. "I'm sorry this operation turned out the way it did. Geordie was a brave man. You should be proud of him. He worked undercover with Montevedi's gang for weeks, and he passed us critical information on Montevedi's drug network. This shipment would have gone through, and the drugs would have ended up on the streets if Geordie hadn't done his part. Countless lives would have been destroyed."

Ryan nodded. "My little brother grew up fast these past months. He became a man I'm proud to have called my brother."

"Being a hero runs in your family." Mike held out his hand to Ryan. "Anytime you want to come back, the door's open. We can always use another good agent."

"Thanks," Ryan said. "But I think I'll pass. A DEA agent's life's not for me anymore."

Mike shrugged. "Okay, then." He turned to Hallie. "You've had a rough ride, but I have to ask you something. On the off chance Montevedi shows up alive, we may need you to provide evidence and describe what he did to you. Are you okay with testifying in court?"

Hallie shivered. Facing the Mexican drug lord again would be terrifying, but she nodded. Geordie had given his life to destroy Montevedi; the least she could do was tell her story and ensure he spent the rest of his life behind bars.

"Thanks," Mike said. "I know how much Geordie meant to you. This can't be easy."

"He was a good friend. I'm going to miss him."

Mike's brow furrowed. "Friend?" He glanced at Ryan. "But I thought you and him…" His voice trailed off as his gaze swung between Hallie and Ryan. Two patches of red settled on his cheeks. "Well, okay, then. I'm off. Goodbye, you two." He strode out of the room. The door swished closed behind him.

A palpable tension filled the small hospital room.

"You came back," Ryan said. "I'm glad you did."

"You are?"

He nodded and grimaced.

She flew across the room. "You're hurting." Grabbing the cloth she'd used earlier, she hurried into the bathroom to dampen the towel with cool water. Returning to his side, she laid the cloth on his forehead.

He smiled. "Thank you."

Their eyes met.

"Hallie…I…I…" he began.

"It's okay," Hallie said. He was in so much pain. He shouldn't be trying to talk. "You don't have to say anything. Not now. I'm not going anywhere."

"No, let me finish."

She recognized the stubborn set of his mouth. Nothing she said or did would stop him from saying what he was determined to say.

"I…I know you and Geordie…" His voice broke, and his eyes shone with unshed tears. "I know you loved him," he continued. "But I need to know if there's a chance."

"Chance?"

"For us. You and me."

Her heart thudded.

"I know I'm not Geordie, but…but I love you. I think I've loved you since the first night when I watched you fight off drunken cowboys in the Rusty Nail Bar 'n Grill in Antler Springs."

"You…you love me?" She rubbed a hand over her eyes, wiping away tears. "You mean it?"

He smiled. "I do."

"What about Max?"

"What about her?"

"You're in love with her."

He pinned her with a sharp gaze. "Who told you I was in love with her?"

"I…I saw you two. In Los Caribuenos. You were coming from the *Wind Song*. You and Max spent the night together."

His brow furrowed. "I didn't sleep with her if that's what you're thinking."

Hallie desperately wanted to believe him, but she was afraid.

"I got drunk," he said. "Too drunk. Max helped me to the boat and put me to bed. Alone. Nothing else happened." He took her hand in his. "Max and I were over a long time ago."

She examined their joined hands: his large and square, the back tanned dark, hers small and pale. A wave of warmth washed over her. He loved her. "After we…after we made love on the boat…" She halted, struggling to find the words to continue.

His vivid blue eyes watched her.

"I…I thought you regretted making love. I mean, you ignored me afterwards."

His mouth twisted. "What was I supposed to do? I'd just made love to the woman my brother trusted me to protect, the woman he loved." His eyes filled with shadows. "What sort of man betrays his own brother?"

"But why would Geordie care?"

"Come on, I know you loved him. And he loved you."

"You thought I was in love with your brother?"

"It was pretty obvious, at least to me. Geordie was so worried about you. He begged me to keep you safe. No question he loved you."

"I did love Geordie, but as a friend, nothing more. He loved me the same way."

Ryan shook his head. "He was *in* love with you. I could tell."

Memories of all the times Geordie had been by her side, lending her his strength, supporting her, overwhelmed her. An ache rose in her heart. If Geordie had thought their friendship was something more, why hadn't he said anything? She pursed her lips. She knew the answer. He hadn't told her he loved her because his declaration would have ended their friendship. She wiped her eyes. "I never knew."

"Would it have made a difference if he'd told you?"

Geordie's quick sense of humor, his endless enthusiasm and joy of life, the fun they'd had together had sealed their friendship. If she'd known he loved her, would her feelings toward him have grown deeper? Would she have fallen in love with him?

"Hallie?"

Tears streamed down her face as the full impact of her friend's death hit her like a fist.

"So you did love him," Ryan said, his voice flat.

She grabbed a tissue and wiped her face. "Geordie may have been in love with me, but I didn't care for him the same way." She took a deep breath and said the bravest words she'd ever said, "Not the way I love you."

Ryan's gaze was shuttered.

"Did you hear me?" she asked, her voice a mere whisper. "I said I love you."

"I heard you."

"And?" She held her breath.

"I was wondering if you'd be willing to marry a simple rancher and live in the boonies."

Her face heated. Would he never forget her stupid insult?

He chuckled.

The teasing glint in his eyes made her heart leap. "Even if you had four hundred pigs and lived in a tar paper shack, I'd marry you."

He drew her closer until her face was a mere breath from his. "Did I tell you I already ordered those hogs? They arrive at the ranch next month." The dimples in his cheeks danced. "How are you with a slop bucket?"

In answer, she pressed her mouth to his.

The kiss began as an affirmation of love, but he deepened the contact as passion flared to life, and Hallie gave herself up to sweeping joy.

His lips slackened and stilled, no longer teasing her with sensual promise.

She drew away.

His eyes were closed, his face relaxed, his mouth curled in a satisfied smile.

Even asleep, he was the most attractive man she'd

ever met. She brushed a lock of dark hair off his forehead. "Sleep well, my love." They had the rest of their lives to spend together. For now, he needed to heal.

But once he was better, look out. She fully intended to make him pay for falling asleep while kissing her. She settled into the chair beside his bed and took his hand in hers. She'd be here when he woke up, as she would be by his side every morning for the rest of their lives.

A word about the author...

C. B. Clark has always loved reading, especially romances, but it wasn't until she lost her voice for a year that she considered writing her own romantic suspense stories.

She grew up in Canada's Northwest Territories and Yukon. Graduating with a degree in Anthropology and Archaeology, she has worked as an archaeologist and an educator, teaching students from the primary grades through the first year of college.

She enjoys hiking, canoeing, and snowshoeing with her husband and dog near her home in the wilderness of central British Columbia.

CPSIA information can be obtained
at www.ICGtesting.com
Printed in the USA
LVOW01s0452010216
473108LV00005B/11/P